Advance Praise for

"You will find yourself comp[...] transported to a war zone [...] Ramadi and Fallujah. From the very preface—so gripping and extraordinary is this captivating narrative from a bona fide American hero who clearly writes from experience."

—George Wayne,
Vanity Fair and R.O.M.E.

"A gripping inside look at the psychological challenges of modern war. The riveting dialogue, brutal honesty, and keen insight into the nature and history of warfare make this a must read."

—Rita Cosby,
Emmy-Winning Journalist
& Bestselling Author

"Unexpected, powerful, and compelling... *War Story* is a portrait of the American warrior that you have never seen before. A witness to the existential tension, adrenaline, and camaraderie of warfare, as well as the pursuit of art as a mirror to the battlefield, Richardson's novel is a journey of blood, sweat, and paint."

—Ari Post, The Georgetowner

WAR STORY

A NOVEL

DAVID RICHARDSON

PERMUTED
PRESS

A PERMUTED PRESS BOOK

ISBN: 978-1-68261-871-4
ISBN (eBook): 978-1-68261-872-1

War Story
© 2019 by David Richardson
All Rights Reserved

Cover photo and author photo by Pepper Ailor

PERMUTED PRESS

Permuted Press, LLC
New York • Nashville
permutedpress.com

Published in the United States of America

To those who persevered…in Art and War

FOREWORD
BY DOUGLAS DECHERT

> "A hero ventures forth from the world of
> common day into a region of supernatural
> wonder: fabulous forces are there encountered
> and a decisive victory is won. The hero comes
> back from this mysterious adventure with the
> power to bestow boons on his fellow man."

> —Joseph Campbell,
> *The Hero with a Thousand Faces*

The hero myth is crucial for understanding the unique attributes and virtues of the American warrior. What differentiates the soldier from the common man? Why does one man hear a call to arms while his fellow countrymen are drawn to science, politics, music, or sport? Ordinary men seek fulfillment in the indulgence of their culture, within the safety and structure of their society and their homes; the hero seeks fulfillment by tearing himself away.

In *War Story*, David Richardson grounds the hero myth in the 21st century—not the "hero" of modern fiction or newspaper headlines, but the journeyman warrior rooted in ancient Greek mythology. This is a story of boots on the ground, of a soldier's singular odyssey. *War Story* shows us that a soldier is a soldier, regardless of the war into which he is born. In this novel, Richardson explores the universal nature the hero's journey through the story's protagonist, Major Clay Steerforth, USMC, and his Iraqi counterpart, Colonel Abdul Mujeed, Iraqi Army. The web of circumstances that propel these men forward land them together in the hottest spot of the war, their fates intertwined.

What sets this novel apart from the litany of generic, American war stories is the thread of Steerforth as an artist, which weaves its way throughout the book. While seemingly anomalous, this connects the hero with a deeper history beyond the Western tradition. In ancient and medieval India, the quintessential hero—the warrior king—was required to be not only triumphant in battle, but also a great poet, philosopher, lover, and painter. He was expected to be a connoisseur, a *rasika*. He had to be intellectually as well as physically formidable. What distinguished a leader from the rest of the fold was not just his military prowess, but his unparalleled ability to balance art and war, which together shape history and culture.

This is not a novel that engages with Middle Eastern geo-politics or the morality of U.S. military strategy. Nevertheless, some historical background would prove useful for the general reader, pertaining to the U.S. effort to restore a semblance of order in Iraq following its military invasion in March of 2003 and the near-immediate deposition of Saddam Hussein.

There are differing opinions regarding the necessity of removing Saddam from power. In the years leading up to the invasion, many on both the left and right of the American political spectrum believed he needed to be eliminated. It may have been more efficient to kill Saddam with a hellfire missile, but the Bush administration and the Pentagon decided an invasion was the right course of action. The ground assault was a success in that regime change was affected, but the follow-up was a flawed attempt at nation building which overoptimistically employed an insufficient number of troops.

In the aftermath of the invasion, U.S. military and civilian planners deployed a relatively small number of troops as advisors to assist a reconstituted, indigenous Iraqi army. The U.S. military hoped that this new Iraqi army, in its infancy, would be able to pacify a country tumbling towards civil war—a war that eventually broke out in a vacuum of order which Saddam's government had relatively maintained, albeit through severe brutality.

War Story unfolds in the midst of this scene. Our protagonist Steerforth requests a tour of duty in Iraq and gets put in charge of a handful of men attached to an under-equipped, poorly trained Iraqi army battalion. Steerforth must navigate his men through this unforgiving landscape as history chaotically unfolds around them.

Generally speaking, modern Iraq was primarily the construct of British politicians, diplomats, and petroleum engineers who carved out an oil-rich province of the former Ottoman Empire during the Treaty of Versailles after WWI. Iraq is a mixture of Shia, Sunni, and Kurdish Moslems, combined into a nation-state. This "Frankenstate" entailed a minority Sunni Moslem ruling class dominating a majority Shiite Moslem populace, creating a permanent tension. Our country supported Iraq's Baathist government for the fifty years prior to Desert Shield and Desert Storm in 1990–91 for compelling reasons: the Baathist party was secular in an ocean of fanatical Moslem fundamentalists, and Saddam and his Baathists started a bloody war with their Iranian neighbors in the 1980s. That war kept both Iraq and Iran occupied, rather than menacing U.S. interests in Saudi Arabia. However, when Saddam invaded Kuwait in 1990, it was determined by the Bush Administration as destabilizing to the region. Saddam and his Baathists went from being our clients to a long-term problem. *War Story* makes reference to Baathists being barred by the American-led coalition from serving in the new Iraqi army after the Sadaam's entire armed force was disastrously dismantled. In the novel, Steerforth trains and fights alongside a fledgling Iraqi force struggling to battle a horde of highly motivated and well-armed (by neighboring Iran) guerillas and terrorists from numerous countries, all drawn into Iraq to fight the invading infidel.

To fully imagine the circumstances of the action in *War Story*, an engaged reader might take into account both the limitations of their fighting protocols—their rules of engagement—and the state of readiness of the U.S. military on 9/11. These restraints on how and when soldiers use firepower tend to increase U.S. casualty rates, and you can bet that our troops in Ramadi and Fallujah were keenly aware of this.

As far as the state of equipment during the time of *War Story*, in spite of the armaments buildup after 9/11, our forces were still trying to restore the quantities of armaments and personnel that existed before the eight years of continuous procurement, maintenance, and personnel degradation under the Clinton administration. The technology and need for better body armor, armored vehicles, and benefits for troops were well known in the '90s and recommended to lawmakers; it simply was not a priority for those in Washington, and it cost lives when war did come. But Steerforth never laments the makeshift armored vehicles he and his team use in operations. They are simply what are available for the mission at hand. What could have been is irrelevant.

Besides booze, women, art, and cigars, one of *War Story*'s major themes is faith, which quietly haunts the novel like a recurring dream. For Steerforth, prayer has seemingly nothing to do with religion. Rather, as with so much of America, it is tied to the bonds of family and tradition. Steerforth never prays. Instead, he relies on his mother to intercede with God on his behalf. Through their affectionate, politely strained telephone conversations, Steerforth's mother becomes a spiritual liaison, a conduit for his own unspoken fears, hopes, and longings. Through these brief encounters, it becomes clear that Steerforth sees his physical fate as something separate from God's will—chalking it mostly up to luck. What is fascinating, however, is so does the Iraqi battalion commander he serves beside. In the face of battle, the trials of faith and the reckoning of one's mortality transcend structures of religion.

A careful reader might also notice that Steerforth and his men accurately reflect the traditional ethnic demography of America's perennial war-time volunteers: The Scotch-Irish Protestants of Appalachia, the South, Southwest, and Midwest, who settled America going back 250 years. These are the same men whose forebears were the first to enlist and the largest demographic segment of every mobilization for every war in our nation's history. Denigrated as hillbillies, rednecks, or white trash, this demographic—an under-represented and often brutishly portrayed segment of the American cultural landscape—are the men who incur the brunt of combat in America's wars. Combat casualty lists sorted by demographics prove this. (*Born Fighting*, by Jim Webb, offers a fascinating analysis of this cultural history).

Finally, few war novels or first-hand accounts of war dwell much on the prelude to combat. Not so for *War Story*. Nearly half of this novel's content occurs before Steerforth begins his combat mission. This creates an unusual existential void, a cognitive dissonance, which slowly cranks the tension of the impending combat.

Why is man fascinated by war? Richardson places this question at the heart of *War Story*. In drawing his protagonist through the battlefield and toward the answer, he derives his ultimate meaning from an ancient and perhaps unlikely source. Indeed, it is art that carries Steerforth through and beyond the odyssey of war.

PROLOGUE

Lieutenant Colonel Abdul Mujeed snapped awake. He felt under the folded blanket he used for a pillow, placed his palm on the handgrip of his PPK pistol, and eased the safety off with his thumb. There, lying in the back of his command vehicle in the darkness, he kept still, listening to the quiet static on the radio, his heart thumping. He wondered what it was that woke him from deep sleep. He listened—nothing but white noise.

What changed in the rhythm of this night? Perhaps a transmission from headquarters?

Unlikely, he knew. Concentrating, he waited for a break in the unending fuzz.

Nothing.

Turning his head slightly, he trained his ears towards the outside encampment, listening for his men moving about.

Nothing. No metal-on-metal sound of vehicle repairs underway; no thrum of engines or trucks moving equipment. No footsteps or voices. Unusual, even during the small hours of the morning.

Pushing back the blankets, he sat up, sleep gone for the moment. He reached for his battle jacket and pulled a pack of cigarettes and matches from the pocket.

Leaning his shoulder against the cold metal door, he lit a smoke and peered out the open window. Under the ambient light lay the patchwork of trenches, dugouts, and bunkers. He watched for movement.

Still nothing; his men were exhausted.

The empty static from the radio rose into the night, in tandem with the curling cigarette smoke. The day before, Mujeed considered giving his battalion the order to abandon their positions and pull back, but without guidance from headquarters, it was difficult to formulate a course of action or do much of anything except wait.

In the past few days, orders—any at all—came infrequently. Rational ones that identified even simple objectives were nonexistent. As he sat and smoked, he weighed his options, the empty static nearly forgotten as his mind ventured elsewhere.

The Americans moved fast. With each passing hour, he risked losing more of his men. At the same time, he realized he had few options, and the senseless noise of the radio gave no answers. He sighed and resolved to decide the next day.

Taking one last drag from his cigarette, he flicked the butt towards the rear of the vehicle, past the dropped tailgate. It turned somersaults and struck the ground; embers scattered into the darkness. The sight reminded him of ricocheting tracer bullets. He lay back, pulled the blankets over him, clicked his weapon back on safe, and closed his eyes.

After a few hours of shallow sleep, he woke again. He checked his watch—0520.

Recalling his resolution, he tossed back the blankets and rose to his knees. Strapping on his pistol belt, he tucked his weapon in place, reached for his jacket, and pulled it over the clothes he hadn't changed in eleven—no, twelve days. He felt around in the dark, found his flashlight, crawled out of the back of the vehicle, and took a deep breath of cool desert air. He walked to the front of the truck where his driver, covered with a blanket and canvas tarp, lay across the hood.

He reached out and shook the man. "Sergeant Achmed."

"Sir?" The man hadn't been sleeping.

"I'm going to the command post. Keep an ear to the radio."

"Nothing yet, sir?"

"No, Akram."

Mujeed strode through the darkness towards his bunker. Inside, he shined the flashlight on a small propane burner sitting on top of an ammo crate. He set the flashlight down and fished inside his pocket for matches. After lighting one, he turned the fuel regulator on the side of the burner until he heard the whoosh of butane. Touching the match to the stove, the gas lit into a stiff circle of hissing blue flames. He lifted the kettle, shook it, felt water swirl, and placed it on the burner.

He picked up the flashlight and turned it towards the map spread across a portable table. Neatly drawn in black and red grease pencil were unit symbols and arrows indicating avenues of advance and defensive positions. Clear enough, except the situation depicted was outdated by forty-eight hours or more. He put the flashlight down, ran his hands through his hair, and glanced at the stove. The flame was out so he touched the kettle—it wasn't hot.

"Shit," he muttered.

He pushed back the blanket covering the exit of the bunker and lifted his gaze to the sky. It had rained hard the day before; it was clear now, stars visible in the fading darkness. He stepped into the mud at the bottom of the trench that connected the nascent complex of bunkers and machine gun positions and peered over the parapet.

It was shortly after dawn, the 31st day of March, 2003.

Gently rubbing the stubble on his face, Mujeed spotted a cluster of his soldiers standing around a small fire. In the pale light, the flames glowed warmly. The men talked to one another in hushed tones, laughing from time to time. Normally he would be irate; even in the daylight the fire was a beacon for the enemy, the smoke visible for ten kilometers.

Discipline was breaking down.

He peered past the men. In the distance, on a slight rise just outside the perimeter, seven oblong piles of stones covered the graves of his men killed two days earlier. Seated in a circle, eating their issue of half-rations when a 155mm enemy artillery round landed among them, six died instantly. Conscious and writhing in pain from the shrapnel wound in his stomach, it took the seventh more than eight hours to expire.

Mujeed looked away from the graves and shut the echo of the man's agony from his thoughts.

Time to pull out, he decided.

Keeping his gaze on the men and the fire, he thought about the implications of his decision; court martial was not out of the question. An early morning gust of wind swept past him and crept beneath his jacket. He shivered and pulled his zipper up to his chin.

The idea of facing a trial was loathsome. This was his twenty-sixth year in the army, and soldiering was all he'd known since he was seventeen. As a lieutenant fighting the Iranians, he'd been wounded twice and decorated for bravery. Then there was this fight with the Americans; again he was decorated for bravery. After that, the long struggle during the embargo, and now this. Instant death fighting the enemy was preferable to being punished and disgraced.

Battling the cold, he swung his arms back and forth before bringing them to rest, folded across his chest. He exhaled, looked past his breath condensing in the cool air, and stared at his men. They hadn't seen him. Recalling the static on the radio and the silence from his superiors, he lit a cigarette and kept staring.

"Zuhair," he chuckled to himself.

He tossed the barely smoked cigarette into the bottom of the trench, churned it into the mud with his boot, and started towards the machine gun dugout where he'd seen his executive officer positioning vehicles the evening before. Finding the place, Mujeed stepped in and found a soldier knelt down, pouring sugar into a steaming teakettle. Surprised by his commander's sudden appearance, the man shot to his feet and, along with two other soldiers, came to attention.

"Good morning, sir. Peace be with you," they replied in unison.

Mujeed returned the greeting and looked around. The men had filled sandbags, scavenged lumber and corrugated tin, and fortified their positions—overhead protection included. He noticed a fourth soldier in the corner covered with a blanket.

"Major Zuhair? Have you seen him?" asked Mujeed.

"Yes, sir," one of the soldiers replied. Mujeed knew the man well. It was Corporal Awad.

He was a tall soldier with a mustache that arched over the corners of his mouth. With a thick neck, matching chest, and hands that could palm a watermelon, Awad could have intimidated the other soldiers with brute force. Instead, he chose to employ a gentle but firm demeanor the men responded better to. This made him one of Mujeed's best non-commissioned officers. His cousin, a man with a similar physique and disposition, was one of the soldiers buried outside the perimeter.

"He said he was going to check on First Company," said Awad.

Mujeed looked towards a PKM 7.62 machine gun pointed out the opening of the bunker.

The weapon was clean and oiled with plenty of ammunition stacked beside it. Next to the machine gun, placed side-by-side on top of a piece of canvas, were four RPG-7s.

Fires to start the day? Maybe. Dirty weapons, absolutely not.

Satisfied, Mujeed looked up from the weapons and out of the bunker. Just on the other side of the razor wire that encircled the camp, he saw a pack of seven or eight dogs.

"Damn dogs," he muttered.

He had read that Westerners loved dogs and that they actually let the creatures sleep in bed with them. Even for Franks, that was hard to believe. Soldiers from the next dugout threw pieces of ammo crate at the animals. Struck broadside, one black beast with half of a tail yelped and leapt backwards.

The soldiers pestering the dogs laughed.

"Ha! You see him jump? I hit the dirty bastard square in the ribs!"

The dog tucked its tail the best it could, crouched on its hind legs, and peered around. Another piece of crate landed nearby. The animal flinched and slunk into the morning shadows.

More laughter.

Mujeed looked towards the horizon emerging between sand and sky, half expecting to hear the thumping of enemy helicopters skimming above the desert floor, ready to strike. He glanced at his watch, then back at the soldiers. Their eyes were fixed on him.

"I'm off to find Major Zuhair. I'll see you men later. If he comes this way, tell him I'm looking for him," Mujeed said, stepping to leave the bunker.

Awad, who was crouched and pouring tea into tin cups, lifted a cup to him. It steamed heavily in the morning air. "Sir, would you care for tea?"

"Thank you, Corporal. Thank you very much. I tried to make tea earlier but didn't manage."

Awad reached for a shelf and pulled back newspaper, uncovering two large, roasted carp.

Mujeed saw flatbread, as well. After pulling a roll of newspaper from his trouser pocket, Awad peeled off several pages, carefully laid out a piece of bread, tore chunks from the whole fish, and placed them on top of the bread. "Where's the salt?" he asked.

One solider quickly opened a rucksack and rummaged a moment before withdrawing a plastic bowl with a resealable top. Pulling back the lid, he extended the bowl to Awad. The corporal pinched out a generous amount, sprinkled it over the fish, and neatly wrapped the newspaper around the food before handing it to his commanding officer.

Mujeed hadn't eaten in twenty-four hours. He sipped at his piping hot tea and smiled. Against his orders, the soldiers had likely left their positions to find the food. He held up the package in one hand. "Where did you get this?"

The men remained silent. Keeping the package aloft, he sipped and waited for an answer.

The tea exhilarated his senses.

After a moment, Awad replied, "I left the wire last night and got the bread in that town over there." He pointed out the bunker at a small rise of buildings a kilometer away. "The fish comes from the Euphrates."

Mujeed nodded.

"We cooked it this morning over there," Awad said, gesturing towards the fire Mujeed had noticed earlier.

Mujeed took a last swallow of tea, savoring it, and set the cup near the machine gun. From his pocket he pulled out an unopened pack of Miami cigarettes and handed them to the corporal. "Don't risk your life again. We're leaving today."

The two other soldiers gawked at the pack of cigarettes.

"Thank you, sir," said Awad, "I'll split them with my crew." He nodded at the man in the corner. "I went partly because of *jundi* Kasim's wounds. He's weak."

The blanket covering the wounded man had fallen back, exposing a bandaged head and arm. Mujeed knelt and looked closely at the soldier. Dried blood matted the man's hair and crusted on his face. A dressing made from strips of undershirt, wet with fresh blood, covered the side of his head. Mujeed asked, "What happened?"

"Sir, he lost most of his ear two days ago when mortars hit. It should have taken his head off. He's hit in the arm too."

"Luck," said Mujeed. He placed his hand on the wounded man's shoulder. *Thank God for luck,* he thought to himself.

Kasim opened his eyes. He was a soldier from Kirkuk; Mujeed had punished him once for stealing fuel. He leaned in closer, touched the man's cheek, and said, "*Jundi* Kasim, we're going home."

Kasim stared a moment and smiled faintly.

Mujeed stood and waved his hand toward his vehicle. "Go to my truck. Under the seat there is a medical kit marked in German." He paused. The men wouldn't be able to read it, German or otherwise. "It's not written in Arabic. It's a green box with a red cross on it. Tell Sergeant Achmed I said to give it to you. There's also a brown bottle, bandages, and a tube of grease-like medicine inside. You'll find a bottle of white pills inside the box as well."

Awad addressed the soldier who'd found the salt. "Yusuf." He pointed in the direction of Mujeed's vehicle.

The man clambered for his helmet and weapon and scrambled down the shallow trench.

"Clean the wound with the liquid from the brown bottle," Mujeed instructed. "It will fizz. That's normal—then put some of the greasy medicine on it and cover it with bandages. Give him four of the pills," he tapped his watch with his finger, "every four hours. Do you understand?"

"Yes, sir, I understand," said Awad.

The soldiers waited, half at attention. "Thank you, men." Clutching the package, Mujeed said, "I'll give half to Major Zuhair."

Tucking the food into his cargo pocket, he crouched low, left the machine gun dugout, and moved along the turns of the trench. Before he reached the next machine gun crew, he felt high-explosive shells splintering the earth. He plunged face first into the mud, smashing his palms against his ears to muffle the deafening sound.

The explosions were close, perhaps two-hundred meters away. He rose to his knees, peeked out of the trench, and searched for damage caused by the shells. With a roar, more rounds plowed the earth. He dove back down. Why the enemy wasn't using cluster bombs, called "steel rain" by his troops, he didn't know.

More impacts—within fifty meters. The ground shook violently. "Colonel! Get out of here!"

It was Zuhair calling from behind.

The earth trembled; Mujeed felt a tug on his jacket. "Colonel, let's go!" yelled Zuhair, yanking at Mujeed.

Shrapnel whirred over his head.

He forced himself to rise. Turning around, he moved along the trench, trailing his executive officer.

More explosions.

Dirt and mud showered him as he lunged for the ground. Looking up, he saw the soles of Zuhair's boots.

Zuhair didn't move. Mujeed closed his eyes.

The shelling continued; he waited. When he opened his eyes again, Zuhair had his head twisted towards him, a broad grin stretched across his face.

Amidst the clamor, Zuhair rose off his chest and scampered further down the trench. Mujeed followed.

High explosive shells continued to impact, but now farther away. Zuhair stopped and crouched down.

In the distance, more explosions.

Mujeed reached Zuhair, rested on his knees, and leaned sideways, his shoulder pressed against the trench wall.

Seeing his second-in-command stretch his neck and peek his head above ground, he reached up and slapped Zuhair on the back of the helmet and yelled, "Three Fingers, old friend, stop that. You'll get your fool head ripped off and I need you. We're leaving."

Zuhair dropped back into the crater, rolled sideways to face Mujeed, and shouted, "Abdul! I told you that last night!"

Zuhair only used Mujeed's given name when Mujeed called him Three Fingers. "When did you decide, Abdul?"

The name rang out as the shelling abruptly ceased.

Bemused, Mujeed looked at Zuhair. "It's stopped."

Mujeed poked his head from the hole, witnessing fresh shell craters and smoking vehicle hulks. After a second, he sank to the bottom of the trench, stretched his legs out in front of him, and leaned back against the dirt. Pulling the package from his pocket, he carefully folded the newspaper back, tore the fish and bread in two, gave Zuhair half, and bit hungrily into his portion.

They enjoyed a long moment of quiet as they shared the food.

"I'm glad you came to your senses," said Zuhair, chewing his last mouthful.

Mujeed scooted closer to Zuhair. "How long will it take to get the vehicles in convoy formation?"

Zuhair looked down, processing Mujeed's question, his ruddy face expressionless as he peered between his legs into mud.

Mujeed finished the remains of his bread, waiting for Zuhair's answer. "A convoy?"

"Yes. A convoy to get us all to Baghdad."

"We'll never get out in a convoy," said Zuhair. "The Americans will kill us all. Remember ninety-one? The Highway of Death?"

Mujeed had witnessed for himself the kilometers of destroyed tanks, torched buses, and charred bodies. "Then we'll break down into separate companies."

Zuhair shook his head. "Still too big. What will we do if we get to Baghdad, anyways? The Americans will be there.

Let the men split up by towns and regions, take single vehicles, and go home."

Although Mujeed knew Zuhair was right, he still found it difficult to concede. It challenged all he held true. "We wouldn't be a unit then. We wouldn't be able to fight," he said.

"We can't fight now. The war, this part of it, is over. If we don't split up, we'll be dead or captured. We'll fight the Americans another day."

"I could be put in prison or hanged for that."

"Colonel, who's going to hang you? Me?" Zuhair removed his steel helmet. "There's no government to do it anymore. The Baathists may as well never have existed. Saddam is likely dead already. If he's not, the Americans and the British will catch him."

Mujeed sat still, listening.

"Even headquarters is silent—if they're still alive. The Franks will stay this time, for a while, and they'll put their own cronies in charge. My brother, let your soldiers go."

From the bottom of the trench, Mujeed watched the sun climbing above the horizon and listened to his soldiers, their voices carrying to him as they searched for wounded and killed.

Zuhair pointed at the crumpled newspaper lying in the mud at Mujeed's feet. "Where'd you get the food?"

Mujeed bent his head in the direction of Corporal Awad's position. "From the men. They got it in town last night."

"They left their positions?" Zuhair was barely able to conceal his indignation.

"They're hungry. I would have too."

"They shouldn't have."

Mujeed waved his hand. "It doesn't matter now, Zuhair."

Zuhair nodded. "Colonel, we have nothing left but our vehicles and our personal weapons."

"I know, my friend," Mujeed said, "but I need time to think."

"I understand, sir, but we're running out of time. The Americans are coming. Two, three, maybe five hours away. They are close enough to hit us with artillery."

"What about you?"

Zuhair reached into his breast pocket with his left hand and pulled out two cigarettes. Sticking one between his lips, he said, "I'll be fine," and held the other out to Mujeed.

Mujeed stared at the smoke Zuhair was offering him, a Marlboro.

Zuhair used his three-fingered hand to pull a pack of matches from his pocket; he lit one without fumbling.

"You want it?" Zuhair asked before touching the flame to his own cigarette. Mujeed reached out and plucked the cigarette away.

Zuhair laughed and handed Mujeed the matches.

Holding out the Marlboro and marveling at it, Mujeed asked, "Where did you get this?" Zuhair laughed again. "Where did Moses get manna?"

"You old bastard," said Mujeed as he lit the cigarette. He shared Zuhair's laughter a moment before it evaporated. The choice sank in. "I'm giving up my command. What will we do?"

"Colonel, we'll go to Baghdad. Farah and your children need you." Zuhair pointed down the trench. "More than your men do right now. If Saddam's Fedayeen catch us, we'll stand a better chance together—just you and me. We'll take a UAZ. The soldiers can take the trucks and the officers the other vehicles."

Mujeed looked at his friend, the man's cigarette poised between his thumb and first good finger. "This is good," he said, dragging on his own cigarette.

"I've got more. We'll smoke them on the ride home."

"You're bribing me." Mujeed smiled. He turned away and craned his neck at the sun. "What will we do in Baghdad?"

"God willing, there will be an army again. The Franks won't stay forever. The Americans are fickle and soft—so soft that they send their daughters to war while their sons stay home and do women's work."

Mujeed rolled the Marlboro between his fingers and nodded.

"They'll stay long enough to help us build another army. When the time comes, explain to the Americans what you did. They won't hold it against you. God willing, you'll get another command."

God willing. Zuhair made it sound so simple. But right now, Mujeed enjoyed hearing this from his friend. He looked at his watch. It read 0710.

Mujeed stood up and looked around. A soldier was moving amongst the wreckage and, in the distance, he spotted the pack of dogs. After a second, Zuhair joined him. He heard laughter—somebody celebrating survival.

Laughter, thought Mujeed, *in the face of disaster—the best quality of a soldier.* He gave in. "You're right, old friend. It's too dangerous to move in convoy or even collect the battalion for a farewell. Get the officers to the command post. I'll meet you there at zero-eight and tell them myself."

Bending over and brushing mud from his trousers, Zuhair said, "Yes, sir," and climbed out of the trench. Mujeed climbed after him.

Mujeed watched his friend walk a few meters and begin to trot. A thin-framed man, nimbly traversing shell holes with an agile gait—a nondescript figure to most, but one Mujeed could recognize at a glance from a kilometer away. A hundred meters away, he saw what remained of the machine gun bunker he'd left fifteen minutes earlier. A shell had ripped away the sandbags, lumber, and corrugated roofing. Torn burlap and twisted metal lay in violent disarray. There was no sign of the soldiers who gave Mujeed the tea and food.

He headed for the wreckage. As he neared, he stepped on a piece of the corrugated tin; it groaned and buckled under his weight. Mujeed flinched and looked down. A soldier, crouched on both knees, looked up from the cavity in the earth, sobbing. It was the man Corporal Awad had sent to fetch the first-aid kit. Around him lay the corpses of Corporal Awad, Kasim, and the third crewman.

Mujeed stepped into the hole, eased his hand onto the top of the soldier's head, and let the man's sorrow shiver into his own limbs.

When the man's grief subsided into a whimper, Mujeed helped him to his feet and out of the crater. Stepping back down, he pulled pieces of tin over the three dead soldiers, climbed out again, and led the man to a group of soldiers. A senior sergeant took the man's hand, wrapped a blanket around him, and eased him into the back of a truck.

⌘

A minute before eight, Mujeed pushed aside the blanket that covered the entrance to his command bunker and stepped inside. All talk stopped as he let the blanket fall back into place. Two flashlights hung from the ceiling. Through the dim illumination and cigarette smoke, Mujeed studied what was left of his staff and company officers. Zuhair was there, standing in the back, behind the men. There were seventeen of the battalion's original thirty-six officers left. He knew them well. Fighters, all of them.

"Peace be with you," he began.

"Peace be with you," the officers replied.

Mujeed breathed deeply. "My brothers, we've had a tough time since the Americans invaded, I won't deny. They've overpowered us with technology, not bravery. We have fought well, but many of our brothers have fallen and it cannot continue. I'm disbanding our unit and sending you home."

Mujeed looked around at the faces and found no dissent amongst them. Perhaps he had solely been the one who held onto the belief they should remain together as a unit.

"I've attempted to contact the division for the past three days. I've heard nothing. I think they've gone home."

Mujeed paused again. He looked for doubt, but saw none.

"As you know by now, I've ordered the men to divide into groups by regions and towns. There are twenty-three trucks, and thirteen UAZ vehicles left. Major Zuhair has designated rally points here in the compound, arranged by provinces and towns."

Mujeed looked at his watch. "It's now just past 0800, and I want you to begin departing by 0900. Are there any questions?"

"Where are you going, sir?" one of the captains asked.

"Zuhair and I are going to Baghdad."

Another officer asked, "Colonel, what about the Republican Guard?"

"Tell them your unit was destroyed by American planes and artillery. Give them my name. Say I disbanded the unit when it fell below fifty-percent strength. They should be too busy trying to get away from the Americans to bother you."

Mujeed scanned the faces in front of him. Nobody spoke or broke his gaze. With the exception of the youngest lieutenant displaying a thin mustache, like him, all of his officers had grown beards. "Any more questions?"

There were none.

He held out his arms. "Well then, my brothers, it's goodbye for now. God willing, we'll see each other again."

The officers began filing past, embracing him and kissing him on his cheek. Mujeed looked around for Zuhair and saw him standing alone in the corner of the bunker. "Come now, brothers, say goodbye to Major Zuhair."

Somebody coughed but nobody moved.

"Come, brothers. Three Fingers loves you very much," said Mujeed. This caused the officers to laugh and relent; one by one, they approached Zuhair and bade him farewell.

Not long after, only Mujeed and Zuhair remained inside the bunker. He instructed Zuhair to find Sergeant Achmed, have him park the UAZ next to the command post, and load the generator into the back. In the meantime, he planned to say goodbye to his troops. "We'll be the last to leave."

"Yes, Colonel. Is anyone coming with us?"

"Just Achmed. He can fix the vehicle if it breaks down."

Outside the sun was bright and warm. Mujeed hurried along the trench, surveying the preparations for departure, already in full swing. The few remaining pieces of operational heavy equipment sat abandoned. Only the trucks and the Russian-made UAZ jeeps were of any use now.

A group of soldiers was piling into an idling truck. The driver, revving the engine and pumping white plumes of smoke out of the exhaust, was clearly impatient to move.

Mujeed climbed out of the trench and approached the soldiers. Those still waiting to climb in butted their muddy boot heels together.

"Sir," said a sergeant, bringing the back of his hand to his forehead, his palm facing Mujeed.

"Peace be with you, my brothers," said Mujeed, accepting the salute. "Don't linger. The Americans aren't far off. Sergeant, do they have their weapons with them?"

"Of course, sir." The sergeant ordered the remaining men into the truck. "Do you know what to do if you run into a Republican Guard?"

"Yes, sir. We will tell them our unit was destroyed," the soldier answered.

"Good."

"Colonel, was it this bad the last time?"

Mujeed contemplated the question for a moment, and answered, "No, Sergeant, we proved our point in Kuwait. The Americans and the British didn't enter Iraq. They were too afraid. We've fought well. You should be proud of yourself."

The sergeant nodded, bowed his head, and stepped forward to exchange a kiss with Mujeed. "As God wills it, Colonel."

After bidding the man farewell, Mujeed said, "Get in the truck, and take care of the soldiers for me."

The sergeant climbed into the passenger seat of the cab. Mujeed closed the door, stepped away, and raised an open palm toward the vehicle. The truck shifted loudly, coughed more smoke, and stalled. After two or three attempts, the engine turned over and the truck lurched forward. As it rolled away, the soldiers raised their AK-47s and shouted goodbye to Mujeed.

He waited until the truck was out of sight, then sought out other rally points, spending the next hour personally sending off his soldiers. By the end, his voice was hoarse, as much from emotion as exertion.

When no soldiers remained, Mujeed returned to his bunker.

Zuhair and Sergeant Achmed had packed his UAZ with a generator, weapons, ammunition, and fuel.

"We should depart now, sir," said Zuhair. "They're close."

Mujeed could hear faint gunfire to the south. "Hand me a canteen."

Sergeant Achmed pulled his own from his gear and handed it to Mujeed. Mujeed filled it from a jerry can in the back of the UAZ. "You've got plenty for the drive home, right?"

Achmed pointed to four jerry cans next to the generator and one strapped to the front. "All full, almost eighty liters."

"I'll be back in five minutes," Mujeed said. He climbed into the trench, stood in front of the entrance, and tore the blanket free. Sunlight flooded the dugout, dancing off the dust floating in the musty air.

Inside, Mujeed set the canteen down and stomped an empty ammo crate apart. He found a stack of loose papers, piled them in the middle of the bunker, and placed the pieces of crate on top. Reaching into his cargo pocket, he pulled out a set of operations orders labeled "Secret" and laid them on the pile. Then he pushed the map from the table to the floor, smashed the table apart with his boot, and placed the broken pieces on the stack. He picked up the map and tore it, adding the shreds to the stack. Finally, he poured fuel from the canteen onto the pyre, pulled matches from his pocket, lit the entire pack, and threw it at the heap.

Stepping back, he watched the flames lick the ceiling of the bunker, the white paper turning silver and curling into cinder.

Suddenly the space was full of smoke. His eyes stung. He coughed, bent the crook of his elbow over his mouth and nose, left the bunker, and climbed out of the trench, hacking.

Sergeant Achmed sat at the wheel of the idling vehicle while Zuhair waited in the back seat. Mujeed climbed in the passenger side.

Zuhair handed Mujeed a lit Marlboro. Sergeant Achmed ground the transmission into first gear and pulled away. Mujeed dragged on the cigarette and took one final look at the deserted position: destroyed vehicles, discarded equipment, smashed trenches, scattered trash, tangled wire, empty bunkers, stifling mud, drifting smoke, and—his eyes settled on a small hill overlooking it all—the graves of his men.

FIGHTING PURGATORY

CHAPTER 1

I rode my bike through Foggy Bottom in the direction of Georgetown, pedaling past the long lines of commuters stuck in rush-hour traffic. The balmy Washington, D.C., spring air felt good on my face and down the back of my sweaty shirt.

The exercise was welcome. Even though I'd napped in my office that day, I still felt the effects of a late night out boozing.

I was hung over a lot back then.

Thirty minutes ahead of a scheduled appointment with John Dunne, I stopped by Georgetown Tobacco, leaned my bike near the doorway, and stepped inside to the humidor. Relishing the aroma of cedar cigar boxes and rolling a few oily maduros through my fingers, I settled on a Gurkha Maduro and approached the kid behind the counter.

"How are you today?" I asked, glancing over at my bike.

"Doing great, Clay." As usual, he set his inventory papers aside so we could chat. I handed him the cigar. "It's nice out there. Glad to see the last of winter go."

He nodded. "Is this all you need today?"

"That's it."

The young man, a recent George Washington University graduate, pulled out his ledger and looked up the price. His tousled hair and relaxed manner reminded me of my own carefree post-college days.

"No cut, right?" he asked, working the seventies-era cash register with one hand and holding the cigar out to me with the other.

"No, I'll take care of that." I took the smoke and removed the cellophane wrapper.

"That'll be six dollars and thirty cents with the uniform discount."

I handed him a wrinkled ten-dollar bill.

After wetting the end of the cigar with my tongue, I bit a small piece of tobacco off the crest—a clean bite, no fraying. I'd spent a lot of Marine Corps time perfecting the technique, a perk of the job.

The young man reached for the lighter on the counter and pressed the igniter with his thumb. With a snap, butane escaped, passed the flint, and ignited. I leaned over and he pushed the pointed flame towards me. With an orange flare, the end of the cigar caught fire, then smoked out. I drew on it until smoke billowed and the entire end was a red ember. I licked my lips and drew again. Slightly sour, the cigar tasted good. "Thanks," I said.

"You hanging around?"

"Sorry, I can't. I'm meeting a friend. You pick up any of the books I recommended?"

"I did, actually…*Storm of Steel*."

"Ernst Jünger. The best firsthand account ever. Stripped of all the frills and agendas you normally get with many war biographies."

"Yeah. It's gripping. I'm halfway through. Thanks for the recommendation."

"Next pick up Robert Leckie's book, *Helmet for My Pillow*. It's the Marine Corps version of Jünger." I stepped back. "Take care."

With one hand on the handlebar and one hand holding my cigar, I coasted a few blocks on my bike to the corner of 31st and M. I parked and sat on a cement window ledge off the main drag, smoking and watching the streets of Georgetown.

The traffic—taxicabs, Mercedes-Benzes, and SUVs—horns honking, blinkers flashing, and bumpers nearly touching—barely moved. A line of vehicles stretched from downtown, waiting to turn onto the Key Bridge.

On the sidewalks, businessfolk at the end of the workday made their way to the Metro and parking garage. Some of these people were my patrons. Amongst them, Ivy League students, dressed sloppily to feign working class, window-shopped and took in the first inkling of spring.

I watched the smoke of my cigar crawl its way up through the still, heavy air. Dark clouds rolled from the west, promising to bring rain later in the evening. A plane approaching Reagan National rounded the cluster of buildings in Rosslyn on the other side of the Potomac River and descended towards Arlington.

Pulling on the cigar, I waited for John and thought about the war raging in Iraq.

John turned the corner from M Street, his limp more pronounced than the last time I saw him. I stood and waved. "John!"

He looked my way. "Oh, Clay. I didn't see you tucked away back there." He limped over to me, closing the twenty or so yards between us.

I shook his hand. "Hope I didn't startle you."

"No, I'm fine. How have you been?" His eyes wandered to my cigar. "I'm working on getting my money from Meyerstone."

"She should have paid you long ago." Dressed in the cosmopolitan uniform of gray turtleneck, blue jeans, and black leather walking boots, John rubbed his neatly trimmed gray beard. "I've forgotten. How much does she owe you?" he asked, his eyes fixed on the art gallery on the other side of the street.

"Just shy of sixty-five thousand."

He smiled crookedly. "That's absurd."

John, the only real artist I'd met in the city and the one who introduced me to the D.C. art scene, seemed pleased with himself right now, knowing the money my paintings commanded was in large part due to him.

"I need to run in and speak to the director about next month's show," he said. "It'll only take a minute. Do you want to come with me?"

I shook my head and raised the cigar to my lips.

John pointed at me. "You should quit that," he said before turning and walking away.

⌘

I pushed my bike and smoked my cigar while we hiked down M Street with John setting our pace. We arrived outside of Martin's Tavern, and I leaned my bike against the front window.

"Your bike will be okay?" John asked.

"Sure. If anybody tries to take it, I'll chase them down and take it back." John lifted an eyebrow. "You relish that sort of thing, don't you?"

I chuckled and dragged on the nearly smoked cigar. "It's not a question of liking it or not. It's just that what's mine is mine, and when somebody tries to take it from me, I am going to stop them."

"That's not very artistic," John replied, glancing sideways at me. "But yes, I can see you are a real capitalist."

I dropped the cigar butt on the sidewalk and squashed it with the heel of my cowboy boot. "It's the principle. Isn't that what this Meyerstone issue is all about?"

We walked inside and sat at a booth by a window where I could watch my Raleigh single- speed on the other side of the glass.

Settling in, I told John, "I saw her naked once."

"I'm sorry?"

"I saw her naked," I repeated.

John scanned my face, confused. "What?"

"Meyerstone. I helped her lay the brick walkway to her front door last summer. When I finished, I called to say I was leaving, and she hollered for me to come out back. I walked around the side of the house, and there she was, sitting in her hot tub, tits and oak leaves floating on the surface as if it was any old Tuesday." I tapped my forehead. "Drinking removes some stuff, but not that."

John shook his head, keeping his focus on the menu. "You should quit drinking."

I glanced around the room. Except for a couple of beat-looking men in suits leaning over the bar, the place was empty.

The waiter came, and John ordered a glass of Malbec. I ordered beer. I leaned back and asked, "Who is it?"

John kept scanning the menu while he spoke. "It's eating at you, isn't it?"

I cocked my head and palmed the table. "Of course it is. Even though my work is going nowhere with her, I've sold a lot through Meyerstone."

John chuckled. "You know I did most of the selling. Meyerstone never paid much attention to your paintings. She's enamored by the Marine thing."

"To hell with her," I growled. "I'm not the bearded lady at the circus."

John shrugged. "That's just her style; she knows artists need a backstory to make their work stand out to buyers. And you have a good one. Clay Steerforth—artist and soldier, creator and destroyer."

"I'm a Marine, not a soldier," I corrected him, my irritation with Meyerstone testing my patience.

I thumbed the corner of the menu and glanced at my bike.

"Anyhow, it's the Hutchinson Collection," he said.

It wasn't what I expected. "She's a has-been."

"She shows Rauschenberg and Stella; I'd hardly call her a *has-been.*"

"Okay, but they were already Rauschenberg and Stella when she started showing them." John sipped his wine. "You want to stay with Meyerstone?"

"No—that's a clown show." I shook my head. "I need a better dealer. How'd you swing it?"

"Through my job at the paper."

Our drinks came, and I took a long swig of my beer. "And Hutchinson wants my work?"

"I've talked you up. Worry about getting your paintings back from Meyerstone." John set the menu aside. "If you don't get them before you go after the money, you'll never see them again."

"Meyerstone doesn't suspect I'm closing our business relationship."

"Oh?"

"No, I can keep a poker face. It's habit."

"Yes, I'm sure you have it in hand. She certainly can't get you further along than you already are." With the sense of a veteran's insight, he added, "Really, there's little left she can do for you."

"Except pay me," I said.

"I've warned you, that's how dealers can be."

"I'm learning."

I finished my beer, waved the waiter over, and asked for another. He brought it straight away, and we ordered our entrees—fish for both of us. When I asked for mine cooked whole, head on, the waiter looked a bit taken aback and explained that all of the fish in the house was filleted.

John sipped his wine while I worked on my second beer. I reflected on Meyerstone, the money, and my paintings. "The book," I eventually said.

"What book?"

"Well, not a book, more of a catalog. When I have my next exhibit, I'm going to have a catalog of my paintings on hand. I'll tell Meyerstone that I need all of the work back so I can shoot photos of the paintings."

"Who's doing the catalog?"

"Sam Knox."

"Knox? He's one of your cadets, isn't he?"

"Midshipman—cadets come from the Army or Air Force. The Navy and Marine Corps have midshipmen."

John rolled his eyes.

"He finished school," I said.

"You're sure he knows what he's doing with an art catalog?"

"He'll design it on his computer, and I'll make the edits. It's hard to imagine that we used to have professionals for these things."

When our dishes arrived, I ordered a third beer, and we busied ourselves with eating.

It was nearly dark outside; the traffic had moved from slow to full stop.

"What about the lawyer?" asked John.

"I meet with him in two days."

"Lawyers are expensive, you know."

"It's not an issue. He wants a painting in exchange. His wife was one of the first people who bought my work when I came to D.C."

"When you were showing in restaurants and furniture stores?"

"Right, right. I sold a lot of paintings, and I met people like Nicholson—my lawyer."

"Selling paintings is great, but it's not everything."

"Thanks, Captain Obvious," I jabbed.

He ignored me. "Painting is about feeling—about a sense of things beyond what we typically experience. Don't force your work just to make sales. The *touch* you have is rare."

I sat back in the seat and nodded.

"Most artists can't understand abstraction. They see the surface and mimic other painters but never get beyond that. You started from scratch. People respond to your work because they can see you searching. That's the point—it's a search, not a solution."

That's how John talked; he meant well, but as I listened, my thoughts drifted from painting to the war in Iraq, something I intended to speak to John about.

"Have you been painting?" John asked, breaking into my thoughts.

"Sure. I spend many a late night fighting the beast—"

I noticed a man outside, a panhandler who hung around Georgetown. He stood next to my bike on the sidewalk—studying it. I rapped my knuckles on the window, startling him. He looked through the glass at me and I mouthed, "That's my bike," and pointed at it with the business end of my fork. He gave a small wave with both hands and meandered away.

"I know that guy," I said.

Somewhat bemused, John asked, "You do?"

I took a bite of fish. Lacking bones and skin to give it flavor, it was tasteless. "I made him do pushups once when he asked me for money. He wanted a dollar. I said I'd give him five bucks if he could do twenty pushups. It took him ten minutes and they weren't very good, but he got his five dollars plus two wrinkled one-dollar bills I pulled out with the fin."

John frowned. "That's awful."

The man walked a block and stopped again, attempting to grab the attention of bystanders.

"That was five years ago. Now I just give him money when he asks. It's cheaper, and I don't have time to waste anymore."

"I asked about your painting," John said.

I sat up straight. The thought of solitary sessions in my studio excited me. Hours of work that carried into the wee hours of the morning, the wonderful feeling of waking up on the studio floor, beer cans and cigar butts scattered about, and seeing a nearly finished painting. "Right," I said. "The series keeps going. I can't explain it, it just does. It's good."

"That's more than good. It means you've hit a vein, like striking gold. Stick with it." The waiter came to the table, cleared the plates. "Another beer, sir?"

I declined this time.

"Dessert?" the waiter offered. "No, thank you."

"Actually, I'll see the dessert menu," said John.

John ordered crème brûlée. When he did, I ordered two shots of rum and hot tea.

I looked out the window. The clouds had reached the city, and it was misting rain. The streetlamps and vehicle headlights reflected against wet pavement.

"What about a show?" I asked.

"Let me arrange a meeting with Hutchinson first. We'll see how it all plays out," John explained, dismissing my enthusiasm.

"Okay, we'll keep preparing the catalog, regardless."

"That's fine. You may want to mention that to Hutchinson. Perhaps she will share the cost with you."

"I don't want her to share the cost. I don't want anybody else to have a say," I said.

John sighed. "She'd get a say anyhow, it's her gallery."

"True, but I'd have eighty-percent control."

"Have it your way." John shook his head.

The waiter brought the desserts.

John struck into the crème brûlée, ending the discussion. I let the tea steep, splashed in rum, two packs of sugar, poured the toddy into the cup, and took a quick sip. It was steaming hot, and I winced. I held the cup in both hands, rested my elbows on the table, and gently sipped the tea as

I studied the people now filling Martin's. Two fashionably dressed women came in and sat at the bar. Both were attractive and around my age. Like me, they likely had a divorce or a few failed relationships under their belts and perhaps were resolved to a more practical arrangement—something built on common interest and shared experience, and had come to Martin's in search of it.

I decided it was time to break the news to John and end the evening. "One final thing," I said, setting my cup down. "I'm leaving D.C. in June or July."

He focused on his dessert and asked offhandedly, "Not routine travel, I take it?"

"I'm headed to North Carolina, Camp Lejeune, and then likely to the war." He looked up from the crème brûlée.

I stared back.

"Can you get out of it?" he asked, not understanding that I wasn't discussing options.

"My intent is to go to the war."

Scorn spread across John's face. He couldn't process this. "The war is ghastly right now," he scoffed.

I suppressed a grin. "That's war for you." I snapped my fingers and pointed at him. "It's not professional football—it's not a game."

John glanced at my extended digit and shook his head incredulously.

"I didn't join the Marine Corps to sit a war out. I'm going if they let me," I said.

"How long?"

"Two years, maybe. A year in theater and then back to Lejeune. Hard to tell."

John picked at the last bit of his dessert. I understood his disappointment. He'd spent a lot of time and effort developing my painting prospects. I was grateful for that, no doubt, but the war was something else entirely. John was an artist, and a good one at that. Painting and hobnobbing with the tastemakers in the New York City art community was how he spent his formative years. He'd never revealed to me what brought him to a relative backwater of the art world—Washington, D.C.; I guessed it wasn't good. He was near sixty, and I was likely the only Marine he'd ever spoken more than a few words to. Chance—me wandering into a Georgetown gallery where he was showing one Halloween evening—had brought us together. In general, people like me were anathema to him. The fact that I was a fellow painter made me palatable, and our friendship blossomed. Only now, six years after we first met, was he seeing the real Clay Steerforth, the one who'd dreamed of the adventure of war since childhood.

I motioned to the waiter to bring the bill. "I'll get the deployment out of the way first thing. I can paint out of my house in Wilmington."

John pushed his empty plate away. "What about painting when you're in Iraq?"

"Too weird for the other Marines. I'll take a sketch book."

The waiter brought the check. I pulled a wad of fives and tens from my pocket, tossed it on the table, and slid out of the booth.

Staring out the window John said, "Someday you will have to decide between fighting wars and painting."

I looked down and thought, *War fighting*. I knew little of the actual thing but fancied peacetime service not to my liking; the prospect of war and the financial freedom that allowed me to paint had lured me to stay in the service. The nineties and early noughties stretched heavy behind me—a long series of field operations, girlfriends, and attempts to conceptualize a vague vision of painting. When an actual war started and progressed, I found great pain being left out. Most of my Marine friends had already fought in Iraq or Afghanistan.

I hadn't figured it all out entirely, but when he looked up, I threw words at it to make the conversation end. "I reckon so, but for now, I can't live with myself…removed from the war."

⌘

It was dark and raining outside. I rode my bike the six miles home to Arlington, thinking far more about going to the war than the money Meyerstone owed me.

CHAPTER 2

I arrived outside the address of my attorney's office and looked for a parking spot. Parking in D.C. is risky business. Administering parking tickets is one of the few things the municipal government does efficiently, and since so few folks who work in the city live there, the elected officials have little to fear in repercussion.

I was early and it was raining, so I sat in the car listening to the news and smoking a cigar. Ten minutes before the appointment, I tucked a folder containing printed email exchanges and a timeline of my dealings with Meyerstone under my arm, then went inside the building and took the stairs to the third floor. When I pulled open the heavy glass door to the law firm's suite, an attractive young brunette sitting behind a desk greeted me with a smile.

"Please have a seat," she said. "Would you like some coffee."

"Coffee would be nice, thank you," I said.

Standing there in the clean, ventilated office, it dawned on me that I reeked of cigar smoke.

The pretty receptionist brought me a ceramic cup filled with coffee and returned to her position behind the front desk.

I set my folder on a white leather armchair, sipped the coffee, and waited, while the receptionist typed away at her computer. Finally, glancing up at a clock on the wall, she stopped, pressed a button on the phone, picked up the receiver, and informed Mr. O. P. Nicholson, Esq., that I had arrived. She listened for a moment before putting the receiver down.

"Mr. Nicholson will see you now, Mr. Steerforth," she said, standing and motioning me to follow her.

I picked up the folder and followed her down the hallway. Mr. Nicholson's office door was open; the receptionist stepped aside to let me pass.

A squarely built man with silver hair, Mr. Nicholson—from his hand-stitched navy blue suit to his baritone voice—exuded a professional demeanor others only pretend to possess. In his pressed white shirt, presidential cuff links, red paisley tie, and jauntily placed white pocket square, he seemed to me a man who could stare down a judge and deliver the punchline of a joke to a tough crowd with equal deftness.

The office was an accurate reflection of the man. His desk was made of unveneered maple and, though it was worn, the lightly stuffed brown leather furniture retained its original tautness and luster. Two signed modernist prints—Richard Diebenkorn and H. C. Westermann—adorned the walls. Along with the prints, three small Braque etchings hung square. On an adjacent wall were black-and-white photos of Nicholson casually posing with his colleagues.

I recognized one person. President Ford.

Mr. Nicholson stood up and held out his hand. "Good morning, Clay."

"Good to see you, Mr. Nicholson."

"Have a seat. And please, call me Oliver."

I sat down and glanced again at the photos on the wall. "Ford was the last man my father voted for."

Mr. Nicholson straightened his chair and glanced at the photo. "Many fine men would have folded under the enormous pressure thrust on Ford, but he played the hand he was dealt, never disparaging others or blaming previous administrations. I look at his photo every time I have a tough case placed in front of me."

"That's how I've come to see him," I said. "I recall reading he was awarded a Silver Star in World War Two. Back then, I guess even the Navy recognized talent."

We both laughed.

As quality folk tend to do, Mr. Nicholson began the visit by exchanging pleasantries. He asked me about my work at the university and told me about his early years in Washington. We discussed the city's rapidly growing real-estate market; he commended me for buying property and not renting. By the time we got down to business, my coffee cup was empty.

"So, this art business," he said as soon as I placed the mug on his desk. "Who owns the money?"

"It's mine," I said. I'd prepared for the meeting, but I could see by his affable grin that he'd stumped me with his first question.

Mr. Nicholson sat back and nodded. He rested his hands on his chest, folding them so that his thumbs and index fingers touched. "I'm afraid that has nothing to do with it. The money is *hers* until it's," he rolled his thumbs towards the ceiling and pointed the steeple formed by his index fingers at me, "*yours*—in your hands—in the security of your bank account. And, if your dealer doesn't have any money, then there's a good chance you won't get a dime."

"So we can't just call her, tell her you're my lawyer, and have her fork over the money?"

"It's not that easy," he said, grinning again. He pressed a button on his phone. A few seconds later, the brunette swooped in and removed my empty coffee cup from his desk.

"Did you sign an agreement with her?" Mr. Nicholson asked.

"No. The only proof I have is an email she sent me admitting she owed me money." I placed the folder on the table. "It's all in here."

"Well, that's a start." Mr. Nicholson picked up the envelope, unwound the string from the canvas button on the back flap, put on his reading glasses, and sifted through the pages. After a few minutes, he placed the documents neatly on his desk. "Are the unsold paintings with Meyerstone now?"

I nodded. "I'm going there next week to get them back."

"How long has she owed you this money?"

I scratched the back of my ear. "Over a year."

"Do you know whether or not she's financially stable?"

"Couldn't tell you."

Nicholson rubbed his chin. "How long has Meyerstone been at this business?"

"About twenty-five years," I said. "She's also an artist. Back in the seventies, she caused a rage with her debut show—all wood carvings of cocks."

Mr. Nicholson bent his head to one side and folded his arms. "You mean *dicks,* I presume, not roosters."

"Yeah, dicks. Cock and balls...man horns...the Jack Russell...."

He leaned back in his chair and let out a short laugh. "Okay, you trusted a real character to represent your work."

"You grow where you're planted," I replied.

With a nod, Mr. Nicholson reached for his Montblanc pen and began making notes on the pages I'd given him. "How long has she been dealing your paintings?"

"Five years."

"Did she give you any explanation for not paying you?"

I shrugged. "She says sometimes the gallery carries artists and sometimes the artists carry the gallery."

Nicholson shook his head as he wrote. "Quite the business model."

I raised my hands, palms towards Nicholson. "Hell, I don't know. I've never told her how to run her business. That's her gig."

I fidgeted in my chair. Mr. Nicholson was asking questions that I had never thought to ask Meyerstone. "But I'm not the only one she owes money to. She owes my buddy John and another guy I know."

Nicholson looked up at me. "You know that for a fact?"

"With John, yeah. The other guy drinks a lot, but I think so."

After working in silence for a few minutes, Mr. Nicholson put his pen down and collapsed his hands on his desk. "How does she get compensated?"

"She gets a cut, fifty percent."

Nicholson removed his glasses, folded his hands behind his head, and stared at me. "Holy shit."

"The gallery brings in the buyers," I said. "Fifty percent is the industry standard, as far as I know."

"Sixty-five grand," he said, shaking his head. "Odds are that she's already spent it. And if I know people, she's in hock to a larger sum too." He remained leaned back in his chair, his hands behind his head. "What's the deal?"

"From her side, no telling," I replied. "But from an artist's point of view, it's simple—most of us have no place to sell our work, so getting gallery representation is a big deal. There are thousands of us competing for a handful of available spaces. Money's discussed, but downplayed until it's too late. At the end of the day, most artists can't do much about it and don't know anyone who can. I know you—that's what I've got going for me."

"That's too bad," said Mr. Nicholson. He freed his hands from behind his head and reached for his pen and glasses again. "How long has it been since she's paid you anything?"

"A little over a year."

"When was she supposed to pay you?"

"Thirty days—industry standard."

As if startled, Mr. Nicholson looked over his shoulder and swiveled in his chair to face the window. I looked past him, searching for the target.

Nothing but rain spattering against the glass.

He remained quiet and still for an uncomfortably long time. I began to wonder if he'd changed his mind about our swap.

Finally, he turned back to me, holding his pen as if it were a dagger. "Here's what we'll do. You get the rest of the paintings back. I'll draft a letter to Meyerstone saying that I represent you and that we've talked. I'll strongly recommend to her that she pay the balance."

We sat, both staring at the documents on his desk.

"Look," Nicholson said after a moment. "We don't want to take her to court. You never know what a judge might say, and two men like us going after an eccentric woman just doesn't look good. So, essentially, what we're going to do is threaten her. We'll only show our cards if we have to."

"Works for me," I said. I checked my watch again. We'd been talking for thirty minutes.

"I've worked thousands of cases over the past forty years," said Nicholson, pushing himself back, placing the sole of his shoe flat against the edge of his desk, and raising his hand, "and all of them fall into the categories of the seven deadly sins: lust, gluttony, laziness, greed, pride, jealousy," he counted them off on his fingers, "wait…I'm missing one."

Nicholson gazed at the ceiling for a few seconds as if searching his mind for the sin he couldn't recall and began again. "People like Meyerstone begin to view themselves as entitled. They start demanding that the little people of the world—doormen, waitresses, and such—stop making eye contact with them. My point is she will insist, and probably believe, that it's her money." He pointed at me. "The good news is, as you've mentioned, you have the resources and—it looks to me—proof to push back."

I nodded. "I'm leaving for Camp Lejeune this summer."

"And you want this resolved before then?"

"Best case, yes."

Mr. Nicholson straightened his glasses, put down his pen, and reached for my hand. "Well, cross your fingers, Major."

⌘

It was still raining outside, a steady downpour. I remained under the awning at the building's entrance, trying to remember where the closest teashop was.

My cell phone rang. *"Clay, it's Barbara."*

The timing was uncanny. "How are you, Barbara?"

"Well, last night was quite a night," she crooned in her hoarse singsong.

"Sounds like it," I said. "What did you do?"

"Well, it's not what I did. It's what the city did. The City Arts Council had their little awards gala last night at the Hamilton."

I tested the rain with my hand. "How was it?"

"The food was awful." She chuckled. *"And would you believe they sat me next to that bitch from the Stein Collection? She's always gushing about her fucking healing oils and that ratty-ass Pekingese she adopted. She looked horrible. Got fat. But guess who received an award for Distinguished Career in the Arts?"*

I laughed. "Congratulations, Barbara."

"Mayor White presented it to me personally," she gushed. *"I wanted to invite you, but it was invitation-only. Just one of those things."*

"Not an issue," I said. "I'll see you next week."

"I had to give a speech. Of course, I hadn't prepared a thing, but I spoke about the need for ethics and integrity in the arts. It's just not what it was in the eighties. Things were fun back then people were honest."

"Well, that's people," I said without thinking. "Barbara, about my paintings—"

"Right," she said. *"Sorry, dear. Do you really need all of them?"*

"Yes. I need to get them photographed for a catalog."

"That's fine. I assume I'll have some input, since I'm going to have my name in it."

"Of course," I said.

When we hung up, I decided to skip the tea and stepped into the rain.

CHAPTER 3

The rain hadn't stopped. I raised the window in my condominium to let in the evening chill. Leaning with my palms on the windowsill, I listened to the rain splashing on the pavement and watched my neighbor pull his truck into a parking lot below. My work machine was turned on, reference books spread out and open on the kitchen table. I had nearly finished half the twist- top bottle of wine I bought at 7-Eleven, and I'd smoked two Parodi cigars. The cigars were better than the wine.

It was 2130.

I was in my third year at George Washington University, my official position being Associate Professor of Naval Science. Every time I looked at the tinseled banner and embossed lettering on my university-issued business cards, I laughed. Without Marine Corps backing, I would never have qualified to teach at the university, even as an adjunct professor. In place of the requisite educational background—the customary credentials professors use to clock in—all I had was a biology degree, fifteen years of combat training, and a few thousand dollars' worth of well-read hardback editions of war theory, battle histories, and personal accounts of combat.

The class I taught—course number NSC 2160, Evolution of Warfare—was a survey of politics, culture, technology, economics, and military tactics, all in the context of warfare since 1000 B.C. I started the fall semester with a brief examination of Homeric warfare and ended it in the spring with a discussion about the Persian Gulf War. The class was split between civilian students and midshipmen—thirty or so in all.

With only six weeks left in the semester, I was preparing lectures on Vietnam—the only series of lectures I struggled with.

Pouring wine into a wide-mouthed, pint-sized Mason jar, I recalled the first image of war that I remembered— troops debarking a Huey helicopter somewhere in Vietnam or Laos and running with their weapons through chest-high rice grass. It was an evening news piece on our black-and-white television. My mother was there with me—painting.

Right then, it dawned on me that I hadn't spoken to my mom since Christmas. Putting off the lesson plan, I picked up the phone, sat down at the table with the Mason jar, and dialed her number. It rang several times before she picked up.

"Hello?" Her voice sounded a pitch lower than the last time I heard it.

"Ma, it's me, Clay."

"Oh, Clare," she said. *"I'm glad you called."*

"Is something wrong?" I asked.

"No, no. It's just nice to hear your voice. I've got a late winter cold."

"I thought your voice sounded a little rough," I said.

"It's old age." I heard her rustle in the bed and waited for her to start again. *"I've been thinking about you, Clare."*

"I'm sorry I didn't come home for Christmas, Ma." I wanted to get the apology out of the way as quickly as possible.

Letting me off easy, she said, *"All the kids and grandkids were here. But I know you were busy working and painting. You just keep doing what you're doing. You know how proud of you I am."*

It didn't make me feel any better.

"How's your painting class going?" I asked.

"My class?" She seemed to forget momentarily. *"Oh, it's going just fine. I have twelve students now."*

"I'm glad you finally started teaching," I said.

"I guess I was just waiting for the right time."

"Remember, Ma, no matter how poorly the students paint, you have to encourage them."

She laughed, likely recalling how critical she'd been of her own children's artistic efforts. In every other walk of life she was a gentle woman, but when it came to teaching her kids to paint and draw, she was just shy of tyrannical.

In grade school, I once spent all afternoon copying the photograph of a stoic Civil War soldier from a library book, complete with ornate chicken-gut embroidery on the collar of his uniform and the reflection of light on the bowie knife he held in his hand. I had proudly taken it to her when I was finished; she overlooked the details and lambasted me because the picture was too small for the page.

Recalling her critique of the piece, I joined her laughter. "Go easier on them than you did on me."

"I was always so busy with you kids and your dad, I didn't have time to take it easy on you."

"I know, Ma."

"I liked the photos you brought home of your paintings. When was that?"

"It's been a while. Three years," I said. "When I left Camp Lejeune."

"How is the painting going, Clare?"

"I'll be showing my work again soon."

"That's great to hear." I could almost hear her smiling.

I looked at the study material on the table. "Hey, Ma, I'm about to give a lecture on Vietnam."

Silence.

After a long moment she said, *"That was such a terrible time."*

"I know. In fact…" I hesitated again. "Ma, I wanted to ask you about Leonard."

"That was over thirty years ago." She sighed. *"What do you want to know?"*

"The last time I was at Aunt Shirley's house, I noticed Leonard was awarded a Silver Star with his Purple Heart."

"I don't know. Shirley never talks about it."

"They're in the display box over the fireplace at her cabin in Oklahoma. You can't miss them."

"I didn't notice."

"Ma, what happened when he got killed?"

"Nobody really knows. Somebody said he got shot."

She was struggling to talk about it, but I persisted. "Weren't we on vacation in Arkansas when it happened?"

"That's right. We drove the eight hundred miles down there, you six kids and a dog piled into a station wagon, to see your dad's mother and go camping. You must have been about four."

Nineteen sixty-nine, I thought. "How did we find out?"

"Uh. Let me see," she started. *"Shirley called Aunt Joan back here in Michigan, and she called your grandmother. We were at a campsite on the Black River. Grandma Steerforth drove out to us in the middle of the night and called your dad outside. I knew it was bad news. I stayed in the tent with you kids."*

"So we just packed up and drove to Oklahoma?"

"That's right. I told your dad that we needed to leave the next morning. That was one of the few times I ever demanded anything. Shirley needed me. I just knew she did."

She paused a while but I didn't push. When she resumed, she sounded tired. *"Your dad was real good about the whole thing."*

"He was a vet—he knew the deal." I took a breath. "How did Aunt Shirley take it?"

"Not well. She was in bad shape when we got there. Wouldn't even talk. I just can't imagine it."

I remained silent, fearing my voice may be an intrusion on her memory.

"Finally I got her to speak. She said her faith in the Lord was shaken. That upset me. We got saved together when I was twelve. I didn't think she could make it through the funeral, and the Army hadn't even flown the body back from Vietnam."

"It must have been good for her to have you there."

"I did my best. As soon as we arrived, I told her we needed to get away and pray, so we went down to the river near the house." She cleared her throat. *"We read from First John. The passage is marked in my old Bible."*

I recalled my mother leaving for the funeral, a young woman wearing a skirt, a flowered blouse, and carrying a white purse, walking out to our car, away from me.

"The day of the funeral is one of my earliest memories," I said.

"You remember that?"

"I remember wanting to go with you. I cried because you were leaving. You said I had to stay with Dad. He couldn't stop me from crying so he swatted me and sent me inside the house."

"You never cried much," she said.

"There was a teenage girl there, cooking or doing the dishes. She gave me a toy airplane to play with. It didn't help. I laid down on a big rag rug in the living room and sobbed myself to sleep."

"That girl was your cousin Rose."

"How did Aunt Shirley find out about Leonard?"

"Somebody from the Army came to Shirley's house. Gayle, Leonard's wife, was living there," she said softly. *"But they wouldn't talk to Shirley, only Gayle. They married just before he left. Shirley picked Gayle up at the shirt factory, drove her home, and the Army told Gayle. Shirley's still hurt over that."*

"What ever happened to Gayle?"

"Shirley's only seen her twice since then. She came to the house once, shortly after. Then years later, Shirley ran into her in the grocery store."

I tried to imagine the two women seeing each other after such a long time. I thought about the folks I grew up around.

"Clare?"

"I'm still here, Ma. What about Mrs. Adams's kid?"

"Wade? Let me see. He was killed shortly after Leonard, oh, I don't know…around 1970."

"And Uncle Hayward's kid?"

"Danny was in the Marines, like you. He made it home from the war but died in a car accident right after he got back." There was sadness in her voice.

"What about your friend Lou? The one that died right after Dad?"

"Louise Dawson? I met her at church. She was Irish, not Catholic, though I'm not sure why not. Anyways, she got married in England to an American soldier who got killed late in the war. Somehow, she ended up here and remarried. Her son was killed just before Leonard. I remember the funeral."

Choked up, she quit talking.

It took her a minute to regain her composure. *"Come to think of it, Clare, there were lots of boys from around here that went to Vietnam. There must have been at least eight or ten between family, church, and friends who didn't come back alive."*

"What about Uncle Tom's kids, Ma?"

"Well, your Uncle Tom did well flying for the airlines after World War Two. That's where he learned to fly. Pete and Jim went to college in New York. For some reason they didn't go to the war. I've never been sure how that worked..."

I thought back to an article I'd recently read about what a travesty the U.S. policy on draft deferments was during the Vietnam era.

"Clare?" she asked, assuring herself I was still there.

"I'm still here, Ma. I'm not sure how that all worked either," I replied.

"How much longer will you be in Washington?"

"I don't know. Until this summer, or maybe until next summer. When I find out, I'll call you first thing."

"What about the war?"

"Not sure, Ma. I'll let you know."

At least that was true. I intended to ask to deploy to Iraq as soon as I arrived at Camp Lejeune. If I felt bad before, this was at a deeper level.

"The war worries me, Clare. Call me."

Lost in thought, I remained silent.

She said suddenly, *"Keep painting and I love you. I'll be praying for you, Clare."*

"Okay, Ma. I will."

The phone went silent. I listened for a moment to the emptiness in the receiver before I placed the phone in its cradle.

While I stared at the books spread across the table and drank from the Mason jar, the blue screen of the computer scrolled towards infinity. I grabbed the near-empty bottle of wine and climbed the stairs to my studio. Squatting on an upturned bucket, I inhaled the aroma of stale cigar smoke and ash, spilled beer, turpentine, and oil paint. I lit the butt of a cigar and studied the painting I'd started a few days before. WAMU's classical station was playing a piece by Lou Harrison.

Certain canvases seem to paint themselves, simply licking the paint off the brush when it's held to the surface. This painting wasn't one of them. I struggled with the piece; nothing happened. Finally, I grew frustrated, scrubbed the image out with a rag and turpentine, and quit.

I finished drinking the bottle of wine and smoking the cigar butt. Around 0200, I fell asleep on the floor.

CHAPTER 4

A pril 1st broke warm and sunny. Around noon, I packed up at the office, rode home on my bike, and drove to the U-Haul rental place in Alexandria. I picked a vehicle large enough to hold twenty or so paintings and headed to Meyerstone's gallery, far up on Wisconsin Avenue in Chevy Chase, Maryland.

It occurred to me that it was April Fools' Day.

In her time as an art dealer, Meyerstone had leased a number of gallery spaces in the city, Seventh Street near the Navy Memorial, where I first met her, amongst them. That ended when the landlord doubled the rent after the lease ran out. To her credit, and against tough odds, she managed to have two or three exhibits in the works at all times—enough to keep her name and hat in the ring. Now my paintings hung inside a shopping mall. If principle was the primary reason I planned to pull my work and leave her, this gallery space was the second reason. I didn't fancy the idea of having my paintings peddled out of a space next to Crate & Barrel. Come the holiday season, customers were bound to wander over and ask what Black Friday deals could be had and, knowing Meyerstone, she'd produce something.

Mulling this over, the drive passed quickly.

I parked in the docking area and spent some effort convincing the Ethiopian garage attendant that I was there on business. He eventually let me back the truck up to the loading dock. I stepped foot into the gallery at 1400 on the dot.

Meyerstone wasn't there but one of her employees was. Her name was Elsa. She was on her hands and knees, wrapping my paintings in plastic sheeting when I walked in.

She looked up and said in a sharp Eastern European accent, "Hello, Clay, nice to see you."

Besides laboring for Meyerstone, the woman was a sculptor who sold her work—miniature watercraft made from sheets of burnished stainless steel—through the gallery. Gently touching her lip with her forefinger and blinking her eyes when she began a thought, she possessed a sincere demeanor. A year earlier, she confided in me that Barbara had sold her work and failed to pay her.

"How are you, Elsa?" I asked.

She smiled. "Things are pretty good for me."

I looked around the gallery, and there was nobody but us two. "Where's Barbara?"

"She just called and said she'll be in shortly."

"Oh…okay. I'll load the paintings." I reached for a piece already packaged. Without stopping, Elsa asked, "Do you need help?"

"No, I can handle it. Just keep wrapping."

"Have you heard about Barbara's award?"

I looked at Elsa, her black hair pulled back, sweat accumulating on the nape of her neck.

"She told me," I said.

I stared a moment, then started for the van, paintings in hand.

It took us forty-five minutes with her wrapping and me loading to nearly finish the job.

Meyerstone still hadn't arrived.

"I think that's it," I said.

Still on her knees, Elsa tore a final piece of packaging tape from the roll and carefully placed it on the last painting. Once finished, she wiped the sweat from her face and neck and looked up at me. "Do we have them all?"

"I've got twenty-three paintings. Do you have an invoice?"

She stood up, walked to the receptionist's desk, and shuffled through some loose papers.

Finding what she sought, she handed me two typed pages listing the titles, prices, sizes, and mediums of each painting. I counted the number of listings—all the paintings were accounted for.

"You will not be waiting long for Barbara. She called again and she said she'd be here in twenty minutes."

"I have to go."

Elsa smiled gently. "Well, you know how Barbara is. She's always late." She paused and touched her lip with her finger. "You will be leaving the gallery now, Clay, this is true?"

I hesitated. I held the last painting in my hand; I was nearly out the door without a fuss. "My poker face isn't so good, eh?"

She paused a second, piecing through my statement. "Well, I think your face is fine, but you're not usually so thorough."

"Yes, I'm leaving."

"Have you told Barbara this?"

"Not really."

"You will tell her though?"

"My lawyer will." Not wanting to sound so severe, I added. "She left me little choice." Elsa looked around the gallery space and then back at me. She leaned in and whispered, "How much money does she owe you?"

"Nearly sixty-five thousand dollars."

She nodded. "This money…I do not think she has it."

"Does she still owe you money?"

Elsa nodded.

"Have you spoken to her about it?"

She shrugged. "This job…I need it. And my work can be seen here with Barbara. What is the alternative?"

"She should have paid me…both of us."

"You have said this to her, yes?" She looked up at me, hopeful.

"Of course I did—three times."

"Barbara owes a lot of money to many people. I see the paper in the drawer. It grows and does not shrink *ever*." She shrugged once more, indicating that she didn't care to know the depth of her employer's business matters.

I took the opportunity to measure Meyerstone's fiscal depravity. "I've heard she doesn't even pay rent here."

"This is true. She meets with the City Arts Council and the owners of the property and makes deals."

"Well, I wish her the best. You too. Take care."

Elsa opened her arms, pushing past my outstretched hand, and hugged me. Both of us were sweating. "Take care, Clay, darling."

When she released me, I walked out the front—there was no back door.

⌘

I pulled onto Wisconsin Avenue and headed south, my paintings bouncing with each bump. On the right side of the road, just south of Chevy Chase, there was an Arab-owned cigar shop. I pulled over.

Standing outside smoking, I called Mr. Nicholson and informed him my part was done. Then I called John. He was surprised.

"You have all of them?"

A thin cloud of smoke climbed away from the end of the cigar and dissipated into the warm air. "I'm having a celebration smoke as we speak."

"You should quit smoking," he scolded.

Ignoring his comment, I said, "I told the lady working with Barbara what I was doing."

"Which woman?"

"Elsa. The woman with the accent. Kind of sexy. Polish maybe?"

"I know who you're talking about, and she's not Polish. She's Lithuanian. Why did you tell her?"

"She confided to me a while back that Meyerstone owed her money. Trust me, she won't say anything to Meyerstone."

"Barbara owes her money, too? Oh Lord," he gasped.

"Did I tell you about the award?"

"What award?"

I relayed the story of my phone call with Meyerstone, skipping directly to the parts I knew he'd get a kick out of.

"Now that she's *somebody,* she'll be more on guard for her reputation. She doesn't want to go to court and show the whole town her ass if she can help it. She'll come up with the money," I explained, then changed subjects. "What about the Hutchinson Collection?"

"Yes, that." John said. *"Pick out your best work—four or five pieces. I'll call and set up an appointment for next week."*

After we hung up, I realized it felt good to be free.

Driving back to the U-Haul store, I turned on the radio and tuned the station from pop to country. They weren't playing George Jones or Ronnie Milsap, so I turned it to a classical station. Ravel's *Boléro* was playing. I left it on.

CHAPTER 5

Mujeed stood on the roof of the Baghdad apartment, back from the edge but close enough to see the street below. From there he could see his house, roughly five hundred meters away. The lock he'd placed there six months earlier was still in place. He had been back in Baghdad just over a year.

Initially, the city was peaceful. The soldiers the Americans left behind stayed busy patrolling the streets in their vehicles.

He thought it was a shame that the Americans hadn't started out conducting foot patrols, rather than riding inside Humvees with mounted machine guns and behind bullet proof glass. Had they mingled with the Iraqi people, they would have found them welcoming and friendly.

Then the peace turned to violence. Mujeed anticipated this shift when two men loitering outside the local mosque approached him. They were strangers, likely Baathists, recruiting fighters and raising money for an insurgency against the Americans west of Baghdad in Al Anbar. Mujeed politely explained that he'd been an officer in the Iraqi army and hoped to return to his profession when the Iraqi people gained their freedom again. He told the men he admired their spirit of resistance, an Iraq tradition dating back to the British occupation, and before that the Turks.

Two weeks later, the same men returned to the mosque, this time demanding Mujeed provide money for their cause. They explained that they were not necessarily anti-American but planned to use force in negotiations to regain power in the Iraqi government. Mujeed sensed the men's boiling frustration; its source was the favoritism the Americans showed towards Shiites. He sympathized but felt their methods were counterproductive to his fragile country's future. So in a pointed exchange, Mujeed adamantly refused to support them in any way. Undeterred, the men vowed to visit Mujeed at his home and discuss the issue further.

Immediately afterwards, Mujeed went home and told Farah to pack enough belongings for an extended stay at her brother's house. After dark, he loaded the suitcases and blankets into the trunk of his old Mercedes. The trunk lid wouldn't shut, so he tied it closed.

He worked through the night, burying at the base of the courtyard wall that squared off his house the four AK-47s he'd brought home from the war. Then he collected his official military credentials, his war medals, and the deed to his house and put them in a plastic bag. He stuffed the plastic bag into a toolbox and buried it a meter deep under the refuse pile in the back corner of his property.

Near dawn, Mujeed gathered Farah and the children and drove them to her family's farm thirty kilometers east of the city. Her brother had recently received four hundred fig trees from the U.S. government. He needed help on the farm and welcomed Mujeed warmly. Although his brother-in-law insisted he remain, Mujeed stayed only three days, leaving the car and walking back to Baghdad to find Zuhair.

He found his former executive officer at home in the old part of the city.

"Colonel, you are safe here. Those people don't come here. It's too dangerous for them."

"I'll stay only until I can find a place near my house to live."

⌘

Zuhair spent the days waiting in line to speak to American and Iraqi officials regarding projects being contracted to Iraqi business and tradesmen.

Mujeed took apart Zuhair's generator, cleaned it with fuel, and replaced the worn gaskets with ones he cut from the sheets of rubber Zuhair purchased in the *souk*. In the evenings, they smoked cigarettes, drank tea, and talked about their last days together, fighting the Americans.

When he grew enough beard to disguise himself reasonably well, Mujeed took a taxi to the outskirts of his neighborhood and walked the rest of the way to his friend Salim's house. Salim, Mujeed's battalion commander during the first American war, kept a furnished apartment for his son. The young man had emigrated to Canada during the American embargo and rarely returned to Iraq.

He made his request and Salim was happy to offer assistance, asking no questions.

Mujeed promised him in return the second generator he used to supply electricity to his home.

Perched atop the main two-story building, the apartment was an addition to the original structure. Below it was a warehouse Salim rented out. Salim and his two wives lived on the first floor. He had two small children from his second, younger wife. Most nights, Mujeed slept outside on the roof of the warehouse. Sleeping under the stars reminded him of being on operations with his men.

During a nighttime brownout, Mujeed and Salim climbed over the three-meter-high wall of his property and retrieved his military credentials, medals, two AK-47s, and generator.

The violence got worse when the weather warmed. The Iraqi police and Americans came under repeated attacks by the groups opposed to the presence of American soldiers and being excluded from government.

Mujeed visited Farah and the children once a month, never staying more than a few days.

Farah's only complaint was being away from her archeology work at the university. Mujeed's father had warned him that women like Farah eventually took more interest in work than their husbands. He'd first met her at her cousin's wedding in Tikrit. On furlough from the Iranian front, Mujeed wore his dress uniform and his recently awarded combat medal. Only nineteen, and one of two women not wearing a headscarf, Farah had been bold enough to approach him without introduction. Casting her large gray eyes on the medal pinned to his left breast pocket and gently stroking it with her elegant forefinger, she'd asked him in a near whisper what he'd done to earn such a beautiful decoration. Stricken by her beauty and confidence, Mujeed barely managed to explain the medal was for sustained leadership in combat. The next day, escorted under the watchful eye of Farah's aunt, they spent two hours seated on a blanket in a park astride the Tigris River, chatting and eating dates garnished with powdered sugar and crushed walnuts. He left three days later, but not before proposing marriage to Farah's father and receiving a promise from her.

Two or three times a week, Mujeed visited Zuhair. More than anything, he enjoyed this time with his friend and fellow officer. Despite the state of affairs in Baghdad, Zuhair was uncharacteristically carefree; he thrived in the chaos.

Zuhair gave Mujeed the name of a man who helped him gain part-time employment reading wiring blueprints and supervising electrical power installation in reconstructed Iraqi government buildings. That was how Mujeed first met young American lieutenants and captains assigned to assisting with the rebuilding efforts.

From Zuhair, Mujeed learned the Americans planned to hand over control of the country to a new Iraqi government. With help from the Americans, the new government was rebuilding the army. This excited both men. Mujeed missed the sense of purpose serving in the army brought him—the brotherhood and, of course, the financial security.

Standing atop Salim's house, Mujeed watched his own home while he smoked a third cigarette. Over the drone of the generator in Salim's courtyard below, Mujeed heard Salim's voice and his young wife moan. He thought of Farah, imagining her as the young woman he'd married, encouraging and craving sex.

CHAPTER 6

I t's no secret that lecturing can be a soapbox for preaching a narrow version of a subject to impressionable youth. Students, adolescents who don't know all that much, tend to admire their professors. In the land of the blind, the one-eyed man is king. I generally tried to be dispassionate with my students, but when it came to lecturing on the Vietnam War, I found that difficult.

The first two sessions went smoothly. The discussion focused on the French involvement, the early days of the United States in an advisory role, and the American build-up after 1965.

Then, as I discussed the Tet Offensive, the specter of my own prejudice somewhat clouded my responses to my students' questions.

"Go ahead," I said, calling upon a midshipman with his hand raised.

"Sir, we're discussing Vietnam in another class. The professor claimed the military industrial complex was a leading cause for increased American involvement in the war. How much do you think our mission in Vietnam was influenced by that?"

"I don't know, really. I'd say going down that road is rather murky. How's that?"

The young man didn't reply, so I explained. "There may have been a loose correlation between the political influence of military industrial moguls and our leaders' decisions; however, I doubt it. I suspect the military industrial complex, as your professor terms it, had nothing to do with it. Little of what I've read indicates America's war readiness pushed us further into Vietnam."

I placed my laser pointer on the table next to the overhead projector, walked to the window, and stared outside. Because class was in session, the urban campus was quiet. "Although we dropped a lot of ordnance," I clarified, "we fought the Vietnam War on the cheap. Airplanes, rifles, artillery, volunteers, and some draftees—that wasn't where the big money was then, and it still isn't today. In fact, back then, the big money was in missile systems, ships, and aircraft, all designed to take on "The Bear"—the Soviet Union. Vietnam was a sideshow. And in my opinion, when one starts blaming things like the military industrial complex for the war, you're on the verge of conspiracy theories. Does that answer your question?"

"Yes, sir, it does," the midshipman replied, appearing to comprehend.

I couldn't help but wonder what sweeping grand theories the midshipmen were being fed in other classes.

"Let me add this, though. When one fails at something, as the U.S. did in Vietnam, there are thousands of folks standing by eager to hock their version of the causes, the whys, the explanations, and the inside stories. You see where I'm going with this?"

"No, not really, sir."

"Well, take the American Civil War—have you ever wondered why there is so much written about it?"

A few students nodded.

"There are volumes written on that war, and there are more to come. Drill down a little further, and you'll find Gettysburg is the most studied battle ever—of all wars. Go to the bookstore and look in the military history section, half of it is dedicated to the Civil War, and much of that to the Battle of Gettysburg. Has anybody done that?"

"Sir?" Another student raised his hand. I lifted my chin at him to go ahead.

"I was in the bookstore the other day, and I saw a minute-by-minute account of two units that faced off at Gettysburg, some place called Little Round Top. It amused me that somebody dug down that far."

"Part of that is simply because we can," I said. "What other war inspired thousands of detailed firsthand accounts, from both sides, and are written in the same language? Many of the accounts are conflicting, by the way. The volumes give academicians something to do—untangle the past."

"And the main players on each side all knew each other," another student commented.

"Right. But here's the point I'm driving at. There seems to be far more written about why the South lost the war, and specifically the Battle of Gettysburg, rather than why the North won. Most accounts are focused on Lee, and every Confederate with a star on his collar that made bad decisions, rather than the strengths of men like Meade, Reynolds, Buford, and other Union generals. In fact, those names are largely unknown unless you're a Civil War buff."

"Sir?" A senior student, Midshipman McCook, raised his hand. "Go, McCook."

"Perhaps it is simply human nature to dig for the root causes of failure rather than uncover the source of successes, at least in war."

"You may be onto something, McCook, which brings me back to our subject—Vietnam. It's something we lost. *That*, I think, is the fixation with it. As for the actual combat tactics, it's far from interesting. Some at home cheered and some were baffled by the loss." I sat on the radiator by the window. "Some say we could have won. More say it was not winnable because it was unjust, our strategy was bad, or we sided with Catholic elites. Believe it or not, some people used to argue that it was because communism was a superior political ideology. In the end, we simply didn't have the national will to keep fighting. My point is, the reasons for losing are legion, and that provides easy fodder for discussions and speculation. Any more questions?"

"Yes, sir, I have a question." It was a civilian student. "Go ahead," I allowed.

"Last semester, you mentioned the Just War Theory was one of the main reasons proposed for why America's involvement in Vietnam was ultimately destined to fail. Are there grounds to believe that?"

My silence stretched a moment as I wondered how to navigate this. I settled into place on the radiator and replied, "No, I don't think so. As you may recall, I'm not a believer in the Just War Theory. A *just* war is a war that a country can justify, and justice varies with time and place. Generally, if you win, you are able to justify whatever you did to achieve victory. Besides that, it's a Christian concept, and I don't care to mix my war and religion."

"But isn't it the case that the Civil War for the North is a more just war than the one the U.S. waged in Vietnam?" the student asked. "Not at all," I said.

A deafening silence followed; the students stared at me, astonished. I laughed. "By the way, I just realized why this half of the course is so much tougher to teach than last semester. Can anyone guess?"

A midshipman in the back of the class raised his hand.

"Willington," I called, pointing to the former Marine sergeant. Seasoned from time in the Fleet Marine Force, Willington typically kept his distance from the other midshipmen.

"Sir, it's because we've learned something about the history of war, so we're asking tougher questions. And sometimes there aren't any satisfactory answers."

"Willington, my man, you are correct. Perhaps I've done my job. You've discovered what I say is not gospel."

Somebody let out a short laugh.

I organized my next thoughts, examining my students' expressions. "Back to the question about the relative justness of the American Civil War and the Vietnam War. Think back to our past conversations and consider this: we rarely ask who was most just when we speak of the Spartan and Athenian camps engaged in the Peloponnesian War. Another case: there are those who side with the Carthaginians, not the Romans, in the Third Punic War. I contend it's easier to argue the Romans were simply acting out of self-interest when they sacked Carthage a final time. No good guys, no bad guys, just folks looking out for their own self-interests." I waved my hand. "Only when we get to the Crusades do we tend to disparage one side—Western Christians in that case—as unjust. In reality, the Crusades were the West's counter-offensive in a much broader conflict for control of Eastern

Europe, the Near East, and North Africa. Most folks hold the American Civil War as the pinnacle of a just war, only second to the Allies' fight against the Axis forces in World War II. Even then, some see dropping the bomb on Japan as unjust. But can we really frame each period of history, each war, that way? What am I getting at?"

Four or five students raised their hands.

I called on Willington again, a safe bet. "War is amoral," he said.

"I wouldn't go that far, because I do believe that there are moral and immoral facets of war, especially for the individual. But wars between tribes, roaming bands of armed men, empires and nations, they are neither just nor unjust. They're simply wars." I called on a civilian female with her hand raised. "Ma'am?"

"Is it that the victor defines what is moral and what is immoral, or what is just and what is unjust?"

"*To the victor belong the spoils*—both material and philosophical. You're ninety-percent correct. The other ten percent is unknowable. If I were giving out prizes, you'd get one."

The class laughed.

I spread my arms. "In the broad stroke of history, it's easier to see that groups of people engaged in war are acting out of self-interest, or at least what they think is self-interest. I say *at least* because sometimes one loses and then realizes their actions *didn't* actually promote self- interest. In other words, what may seem advantageous to one's self-interest at one point may change. It fluctuates with public sentiment and politics. My advice to leaders going to war is don't do it unless you absolutely have to, and then win no matter what. Losing is bad, very bad. The U.S. lost the war in Vietnam, and that was bad for our country. Many consider that war unjust, but I strongly suspect relative outcomes have influenced our perceptions of justness. In the end, folks fight for self-interest, and a just war is one you win."

I surveyed the faces. "Is everybody tracking?"

A few students nodded, so I proceeded.

"At the personal level—for the individual called to fight—justness and self-interest work a little differently. Some have a choice, but others don't. Take the Trojan War, for instance. We only know about it from Homer's epic, ancient commentary, and from relatively recent archaeology. So, we really don't know much. Have you ever wondered if there were men left behind, men who refused to go to that war?"

"Yes, I actually did," replied one of the students.

"What do you think?"

"Well, when you read the *Iliad,* you get the idea that none of the Greeks stayed home. In other words, they all fought."

"Right. And then you read the *Odyssey,* and you realize that some Greeks did in fact remain behind. If you believe the legend, Odysseus didn't want to go. The Trickster feigned insanity, was found out, and only then went on the expedition. When he returned to Ithaca twenty years later, he likely encountered men who'd stayed behind, even before he shot his wife's suitors down with his bow. What do you think these men who remained behind said to him?"

Nobody answered.

"Anybody?"

Still nobody.

"Perhaps some of these men said something to this effect to Odysseus: 'Oh, you poor old tricky-dick bastard, you went to that fiasco of a war? Had it been the wars of old, I would have gone. Your war was a bad war, fought only for the benefit of Menelaus and Agamemnon.'"

The class remained silent.

"Or, take Caesar's invasion of Britain in 50 B.C. or so. Imagine you are a legionary returning to your farm on the Italian peninsula after the war. You have walked a long way— through Belgium, Transalpine Gaul, et cetera. Then on your way home, you encounter another farmer, an extremely prosperous one since he's been tilling his land while you've been out campaigning with Caesar and his crew. The farmer says to you, 'Yeah, you went to fight that war? Old fellow, you've been duped. Me? I would have gone had it been the Punic Wars.'"

The radiator got hot, so I stood up, brushed off the seat of my trousers, and strolled to the front of the class. A three-foot wooden pointer lay in the cradle of the chalkboard. I picked it up and turned around.

"Or let's get closer to home," I said, slapping the pointer into the palm of my hand. "It's the summer of 1865 and you're a Union soldier. The victory parade that passed down Pennsylvania Avenue—only few hundred meters from where we are right now—is over, you've mustered out of Sherman's army, and you're walking back to Ohio." I paced in front of the blackboard. "It is hot and you're thirsty, so you stop by a tavern. While drinking a beer, you strike up a conversation with a man your own age, who says to you, 'Oh, you fell for that tomfoolery Old Abe tossed at you? That wasn't a war worth fighting. All it did was free the slave folk down South. Next thing ya know, we'll have to run 'em off from around here. It was a war for eastern industrialists—Yankees. Had it been the War of 1812 or the Revolution, I would've been the first to join the ranks.'"

I was getting wound up, so I sat on the table where my lecture material sat, crossed my legs, and tapped the leather sole of my shoe with the pointer. "Are you getting the idea?" I asked. "Anybody?"

"Sir?" Midshipman McCook responded.

"You get it, McCook?"

"I think so. You're saying that it's hard to judge something as just or unjust and that in retrospect, nine times out of ten, we realize people are simply acting out of self-interest."

"Exactly. And people justify their personal actions by pointing towards some past war they view through rose-colored glasses. I contend it's absurd for those who opt out of a current war to point to a past war and claim that they would have gladly served because it was a good, proper, or just war." I continued tapping my shoe with the pointer.

"One last thing. I believe what I'm telling you because of personal experience. I don't know how many baby boomers I've met in the bars and taverns of Michigan, Chicago, Oklahoma, California, Virginia, or Washington, D.C., that have spoken to me about not serving during the Vietnam War. But when they do, the conversation normally starts like this: 'Things were different back then. If it had been World War II or the Korean War, I would have gladly served. But it was the sixties, man, and things were different. That was an unjust war.'"

I stood up, gripped the pointer at each end, held it out in front of me parallel to the floor, and bent it. "Well, I can't know that. All I know is that wars come and go. Some men serve and some don't." I bowed the stick to the point of breaking and then eased off. "Some, like my cousin, get killed and leave behind folks who grieve. In general, those who serve and live are proud of it, and those who don't serve normally feel the need to justify their actions."

Surveying the polite faces, I decided to end there. I had lost them.

"And that is what I think of that!" I waved the pointer and laughed, breaking the spell.

"I'll see you next time, and we'll finish up on Vietnam." The class filed out. Willington and McCook stayed behind. "Gentlemen, what is it?" I asked.

"Sir, in my German philosophy class, we've been reading Kant, and he believed that someday war would become obsolete," Willington posed. "In other words, it would simply become too destructive."

Scratching my forehead, I walked to the window and said, "Wishful thinking. Man and war are intrinsically bound. Even with 'The Bomb,' war is still a major undertaking for mankind. In war, man recognizes something he fancies he's gotten beyond—we are in fact killers."

I put my hands in my pockets and watched crowds of students spilling into the streets and continued, "Despite the appalling waste of money and the shattered souls, few argue that man isn't fascinated by war and doesn't sense in it some grandeur, although I can't say what that grandeur is. If one doubts this, consider the movies, video games, news programs, books, reenactments, trade shows, clothes, toys, magazines, university classes, and TV shows that are war related. These types of things attract large audiences and garner huge sums of money. That said, I'm not about to challenge Kant on the details of this issue, or any issue for that matter."

"Yes, sir," said Willington. "He's dead now anyway. But Kant also asserted that until there is no war, a country should arm itself."

I raised my brow. "Out of self-interest?"

"After what you said today, yes, I'm assuming," replied the young man.

"Very interesting, Willington. I'll have to pick up Immanuel's work again—it's been a few years. What you are saying makes me think, though. Have you ever seen the Clint Eastwood film *Unforgiven?*"

"I have."

"I've watched it ten or twelve times. Remember when Eastwood's character enters the tavern at the end of the movie? His hat is pulled down over his eyes, and his spurs are jingling for the first time in the film…"

"Yes, sir, and he's looking for whoever killed his friend Ned, Morgan Freeman's character…"

"Not quite. He's actually looking for the guy who owns the saloon. The one who displayed Ned in the coffin on the porch."

McCook chimed in, "That's right!"

"So Eastwood's character shoots the saloon owner. Then Gene Hackman says, *'You just shot an unarmed man!'* He's indignant, and Eastwood breathes, *'Well, he should've armed himself if he's going to decorate his saloon with my friend.'*"

We chuckled.

"Well, that's what Kant is saying—out of self-interest, you better arm yourself or suffer the consequences. The justification and morality come later with the discussion of the historical events, and then, normally, only if one loses or needs a personal alibi. But I'm not a philosopher or an ethicist and, as you mentioned, Kant's not available."

Willington laughed. "I thought you'd like that, sir."

"I'd be interested in discussing this with somebody who is well-versed on such matters," I said.

"Sir, back to Vietnam," began Midshipman McCook.

"What about it?"

"So why do you think the Americans were so antiwar then and, it seems to me, not antiwar today? At least they're not marching in the streets protesting the war in Iraq."

I nodded towards the window, guiding the young men's attention to the crowds outside. "There was no more antiwar sentiment then than there is now. It was a *Don't-Send-Me* movement."

"Folks must feel the same today. Why aren't they as vocal?" asked Willington.

"Simple," I said. "The draft." I waited for one of them to respond. When they didn't, I continued. "War's a big subject, and most folks are too busy with daily issues to care about much else. They only care about war when it becomes fashionable or if it touches their lives. During Vietnam, the draft only caught those who couldn't or wouldn't avoid it. That's the difference. Today we have a volunteer force that we pay well. The war touches few lives, and those it does affect are volunteers—idealist types or the duty-bound, some say mercenary. To actually fire a weapon in combat, one has to double volunteer—volunteer for the service and then for combat arms, specifically. Only then does one stand a chance of being in harm's way. Back during the draft, it was possible for anyone to end up firing a rifle in combat. There are pros and cons to the draft. Some people don't do well in the military. Others do, and they return to civilian life with a great understanding of self and firsthand knowledge of the world. That's the World War II scenario."

"And the cons?"

"The draft is a long way from egalitarian. There's always a way out for those with means; people with money have options. They may riot to get out of it, as they did in the sixties. In the Civil War, one could pay three hundred dollars for somebody else to go. In the Vietnam War, you could get a college deferment and opt out. School ends eventually, though."

"So that was the deal?"

"Yes." I stepped to the window, opened it, and turned back to the two midshipmen. "Many in the Vietnam and the Civil Wars opted out. During the Vietnam era, just as today, you didn't have to be very intelligent to go to college, you just needed a way to pay for it. In general, those who could pay for college opted out of Vietnam, and those who couldn't got drafted. But once college was over, anyone was fair game. As the war dragged on, though, your chances of going increased."

"Ahhh," said Willington. "So if you had the resources to go to college, you got out of the war. Then as graduation loomed, so did the draft."

"Exactly." The chatter and laughter of students passed through the open window. "And *thus* the concentration of the antiwar movements on college campuses. The war and the draft ended about the same time. The writing was on the wall, though—the U.S. was going to drop the draft and adopt an all-volunteer force. That would have subverted the Don't-Send-Me protests regardless of how long the war went on. There's little reason to protest today since the war touches so few lives."

Willington and McCook picked up their backpacks.

"Now you know why I don't like talking about this subject," I said.

"It ruffles feathers?" asked McCook.

"Yeah. I step on toes." I shuffled my notes into a pile. "In fact, I end up stepping on toes of people I like, professors and preachers included. Some students have parents who took that route, and I have friends that took that route.

It's an uncomfortable topic." I grabbed my laser pointer and motioned Willington and McCook to the door.

As we walked out, I said, "Also, I must say, it's personal."

CHAPTER 7

A soft breeze slipped through the open window, rattling the wooden slats of the venetian blind, pushing in the moist air. The fragrant smell of damp soil filled the room; I thought of North Carolina—waking up in my bag on the hood of a Humvee after a night in the field.

Pulling myself out of the rack and going to the kitchen, I heated water in a teakettle, put four Lipton teabags in a pot, and poured water over them. I sat at my study table with my head in my hands.

A woman's voice, thick with Southern accent—an elixir to my ears—called from my bedroom. "Hey, what are you doing? Are we leaving?"

"No, sweetheart, I'm curing my hangover. I'll be there in a minute."

I glanced at my watch—1100. I was scheduled to meet John at 1400 at the National Gallery.

I poured a cup of tea, returned to the bathroom, and fumbled around for a bottle of U.S. Navy-issued ibuprofen, large white pills with five-digit lot numbers embossed on one side. The 800-milligram tablet slid down easy with the hot tea. I set the cup on the edge of the sink and crawled back into bed beside my Southern belle.

An hour later I woke up and left the room.

My headache easing, I called John and let him know I was thirty minutes behind schedule. I heated two cups of tea in the microwave and walked back to my bedroom. When I entered, the woman sat up in bed, covering her breasts with the sheet.

"Here you go, sweetheart," I said, handing her the cup of tea. "I'm meeting my pal at two." I bent over, kissed her forehead, and headed towards the bathroom.

I shaved in the shower, dressed, greased my hair with Vaseline, and left the bathroom.

Thirty minutes later we left.

Being Sunday, there were few cars on the road. We chatted about her work on Capitol Hill; I described to her my time as an armed service social aide in the White House. She was intrigued.

"I hated it," I said.

"Why?"

"I came to D.C. to train midshipmen and paint pictures, not escort folks trying to glad-hand the president for a favor. Besides that, I'm a Marine and there's a war going on—I feel stupid trotting around the White House in a dress uniform at a time like this."

We passed the George Washington Masonic Memorial near the King Street Metro station in Alexandria and drove to the colonial part of Old Town. When we parked, she waited inside while I got out and opened the passenger door.

"I like your paintings. That cigar smell makes me think of my paw-paw." She kissed my cheek. "Call me."

⌘

I strolled across the marble floor in the central atrium of the National Gallery and spotted John, braced against the cement stair railing. An immense aluminum mobile by Alexander Calder twisted from suspension cables above us, casting a faint shadow over him.

"Where have you been?" he asked.

"It's the Lord's Day," I said. "I slept a little late."

He gave me a jaded smile, pushed himself off the rail, and started walking, his limp as pronounced as the last time I'd seen him. We made our way to the lower-level cafeteria in silence.

I paid for tea and pastries, and we sat across from a window that retained the gallery's waterfall sculpture. Water cascaded from above a series of stone steps and splashed against the glass. I nursed my steaming cup of tea, cradling it between my hands and breathing into it.

"You look sick," John said.

"I was out late."

"So I gathered." John brushed his bald head with his index and middle fingers, an echo of his hairier days. When he put his hand to his beard, I noticed the ring on his finger, the stone and band weathered from years of wear. It was a gift from his father, a man who served in the OSS during World War II and then later in the CIA. John was born in India while his father was on post there. His paintings carried a lushness and mystery consistent with Indian influence.

"One of the midshipmen turned twenty-one," I said. "They're fun kids. After the bar closed, me and a guy named Willington went for pizza with a couple of Hill staffers—sisters they claimed—working for an Alabama congressman."

"You should—"

"Roger that," I said, taking a sip of my tea. "I'll run it off this afternoon."

"You can sweat out the hangover," John said, "but it's not going to help your painting."

"Yeah." I shrugged. "Maybe a little war will straighten me out."

"You're ridiculous." John surprised me with the quickness to anger. "You're going to die in an oil field on the other side of the world over nothing. I know I'm old and crippled, but you've riled me to the point of protesting this entire bloody fiasco."

I fought back the urge to smile. An unfamiliar combination of affection and indignation came over me.

"Have you ever considered that antiwar protestors may be violating my civil rights?" I asked cautiously.

He stared at me.

"How about this…. What if folks gathered outside this museum, held up picket signs, and started screaming about the government throwing away tax dollars on arts funding?" I made a sweeping gesture around the crowded room. "Imagine a throng of angry types chanting, 'End this art!'"

"Don't be flippant," said John. "I'm serious."

"It wouldn't be long before an army of painters, photographers, filmmakers, and poets got their panties in a wad over their right to create and the significance of their role in the social fabric."

"Art doesn't kill people."

"True, but war persists," I said. "It very likely always will. It's older and more prolific than organized religion. It's older than the revered cave paintings in France we fawn over. It's carved into four thousand-year-old stone walls. In tribal societies, it's essentially recreation, or was until very recently. I know you don't want to hear it, but war is integral to mankind."

I waited for him to reply. He ignored me.

"Nobody protesting war today is in any danger of being asked to fight, so I recommend people hang up their sanctimonious banners. Fighting is a calling, no different than painting or poetry." I shook my head. "What does the soldier archetype do without war?"

"That's unsavory." John was still irritated.

"John…" I took a breath, "perhaps some men find their purpose in war. My people do. That is all I am saying."

"I won't entertain it."

I stared past him to the window, listening to the water pound steadily against the glass. "I'm thinking out loud," I said, feeling like a bully. I gazed down and picked up my pastry. Holding it to my nose and sniffing it, I said, "I'm going to eat this. What *is* it?"

"It's an éclair," John said with a short laugh. "Don't tell me you've never eaten an éclair before."

"My mom loves stuff like this." I bit into the pastry, and flakes fell from my chin to my lap; its sweetness hurt my teeth.

"Have you talked to her lately?"

"My ma?" I sniffed powdered sugar up my nose, coughed, and swallowed hard. After washing down the bite of éclair with tea, I wiped my mouth with the back of my hand and said, "Yes, just the other day."

"How is she?"

"She's getting old."

"Did you tell her about Iraq?"

"No. We talked about Vietnam and painting."

"Rice paddies and Rauschenberg."

I laughed. "I needed material for my class. The war hit my family close, and she gave it to me firsthand."

I took another bite of the pastry and wished I'd cooked bacon and eggs for breakfast. John looked puzzled. "You talk to your students about your family history?"

"Not really. It's just part of a pile of thoughts that color my lectures," I said. "Anyway, my mom seems to be doing well. She's teaching a painting class." I drank more tea and asked, "How's your painting?"

"It's flowing," he said. "I'm happy with it."

"Sold anything?"

"Ha, no," he laughed. "I'm getting ready for a show in Brussels."

"Brussels?"

"Next spring. A collector friend of mine works in Russia and has contacts there. He introduced me to the gallery."

"Congratulations. It always feels good to have something to work towards."

As we sat drinking our teas, the throb of conversation in the cafeteria became sharp; my headache returned. I reached into my pocket, fingered an ibuprofen from between nickels and quarters and popped it into my mouth. Taking a last gulp of tea, I said, "Let's go look at the arts."

We abandoned our empty cups and rode the escalator to the main hall.

The central room of the National Gallery reminds me of the inside of an aircraft hangar—expansive and filled with light. Unlike a hanger, though, it's fractured and broken with sharp angles and wide corners that beckon one's eyes to move around the space. It doesn't need much in the way of paintings for decoration—the architecture is a masterpiece in itself. Still, a curator had sprinkled the space with a sparse arrangement of subtle works that most folks simply sauntered past without noticing.

There was a Giacometti bronze—a dejected-looking stick-thin figure in mid-stride that made me think of nineteenth-century illustrations from Charles Dickens's novels. Mr. Dick from *David Copperfield* came to mind. Behind it, dwarfed by the huge wall it hung on, was a small self-portrait by Arshile Gorky, a muted painting of browns and grays with red earth tones, perhaps an unfinished study. A cluster of David Smith's sculptures were placed on the other side of the room, twisted planes of brightly painted steel that looked to me like abandoned auto body parts I'd seen in the desert around Twenty-Nine Palms. In the center of everything was an Andy Goldsworthy installation—a collection of short dome huts built from stacked slabs of stone. I read somewhere that Goldsworthy claimed these stones were unaltered from the natural shape and condition in which they were found. I didn't believe it. Artists tend to make stuff up to embellish their own lackluster backstories.

"What did he say?" John asked suddenly.

Surprised, I looked around and made sure he was talking to me. "What?"

"Oh." He looked around, distracted. "The lawyer, I mean."

I laughed. "He sent Meyerstone the letter. Yes, and Babs squealed like a stuck pig."

"That's not nice. She's Jewish."

"After she replied, he turned it over to me for another try. He said she's acting like a jilted lover."

"What kind of lawyer is that?"

"A good one. He wants to keep it out of court. She emailed him a diatribe saying she was shocked, hurt, and deeply insulted. It was so pathetic, I started wondering if it was all worth it."

"Money is money," John replied, motioning down a wide hallway with a five-foot-by-five-foot Roy Lichtenstein painting hanging on the wall. The piece, done newspaper-comic strip style, featured a blonde woman speaking to a square-jawed man. In falsetto, I read the words in the speech balloon out loud, "Why, Brad Darling, this painting is a masterpiece! My, soon, you'll have all of New York clamoring for your work!"

John laughed. "I saw one of his first shows. Nobody realized then the glory days of print were over. That was his genius. He captured cartoon as art a decade or so before the newspaper began to die."

I looked at the piece again, seeing it differently after John's commentary. "I emailed Meyerstone a few days ago asking her to look at things from my side," I said to John. "I told her I hoped the landscaping I did for her still looked good."

"A fine touch," John said as he walked towards the elevator.

I pushed the elevator button. "She wrote back immediately, a screed of spelling errors and bad grammar, saying the only thing I knew how to do was give orders. She said I was an ingrate and that she had artists pounding down her door. She reminded me that she supported me, despite my lack of formal art training and pedigree."

"Did she actually say *pedigree?*" John scoffed.

"She did. What really irked her, though, was the fact that I got a lawyer."

"It didn't irk her—it terrified her. If an art dealer gets taken to court over such financial matters, it doesn't matter what the outcome is, it's ruinous. No one serious will have anything to do with a dealer who has a reputation for not paying their artists."

"Her claws were out." The elevator bell rang and the doors opened. "She mentioned charging me twelve thousand dollars for the show's overhead," I said, stepping inside. "She even had the nerve to say that this cost would come out of whatever money I claimed she owed me."

Dismayed, John lifted his eyebrows. "What?"

"It was a good counterattack," I chuckled.

"We never discussed anything like that with her."

"Of course not. I would never pay an upfront fee to a gallery."

"That's called a vanity gallery," John said. "It's for rich men's wives."

We rode to the top floor where the Rothkos hung in a small gallery with a ceiling that reached thirty feet to tinted skylights. It was the best space in the museum—beautiful, yet simple; it could make any painting look important. We stood in silence marveling at Rothko's towering, dark canvases. The hazy light from the ceiling revealed subtle variations of black, brown, and gray paint—nuances in color and a tonality undermined in darker light and easily washed out with too much light.

"He did these paintings near the end of his life," John tutored. "One of his last commissions was for a chapel in Texas. Houston, I think. His assistants helped him with them."

I scanned the area, taking them all in at once. "There's something about good abstraction that pulls you into the mystery immediately, and then you read the backstory and it's even better. Rothko is like that for me."

John remained silent, rubbing his chin and gazing around. "Rothko would not only call you a fool for reading the backstory, but also walk away smiling," he said, waving his hand towards the piece. "But that's so much of the beauty of Rothko. Critics called his work transcendental, a new mythology for the twentieth century. Rothko was given to rambling, endlessly and angrily, about the moral virtue of his work. He hated being compared to his contemporaries, and he insisted that no one understood art like he did. He rejected all representations—landscapes, figures, and symbols, even shapes. He was too good for *shapes*. Yet he refused the label of abstraction. He resented other painters, and he vilified his patrons. Did you know he even changed his name—Rothkowitz—in the 1940s because he didn't want people to know he was Jewish?"

Before I could interject, John continued.

"Then Abstract Expressionism died in the late fifties, along with a lot of his friends, and he became a living legend. He was distraught that people simply saw him as a financial investment and no longer thought about the spiritual aspect of his work. Then depression set in. He smoked and drank, and stayed holed up in his studio for days on end. But he certainly was committed to his work."

"Well, he got something right," I said. I gazed around at the pieces. "I've noticed everyone *likes* him. I brought some midshipmen here a few months ago, and we walked around the galleries. When we walked past to Barnett Newman's work, the midshipmen, bless their hearts, laughed out loud, but they liked the Rothko. They couldn't tell you why—hell, I can't tell you why, either."

"I'd hoped that you could," John said.

I shrugged. "Aaaah. I can tell you why Lee failed at Gettysburg, but I can't tell you why Rothko's work rings true. It might destroy it anyway." I took a few steps back to widen my vantage point. The large, dark canvas dwarfed John's figure as he stood staring into its gray depth. "What I like the most is that he hit on this thing and stuck with it. He didn't quit."

"He struggled with it," John replied, still facing the canvas. "He was always making variations. Some appear minor, but they weren't to him."

John moved his hand towards the canvas as if to touch it, then pulled it away and plunged it into his jacket pocket.

We were silent for a time. John stood looking at the painting while I meandered behind him, taking in the piece from different vantage points.

"So depression set in because Rothko couldn't cope with his own success," I commented. "Then what?"

John backed away from the painting. "When pop art, the whole ironic thing, became the rage in the sixties, Rothko got sidelined and never forgave the public for it."

"That particular irony, Warhol and the rest, bores the hell out of me." I said. "It's *Mad Magazine* art. Honest sentiment is mocked as sentimental foolery."

"Irony? Yes, that's tiring," John agreed. "Rothko's work isn't ironic—it's mythical."

"Was it selling?"

"Oh, God, yes. And at some point, it was all pre-ordered. He priced it so that he stayed under a certain tax bracket."

I laughed. "I like that. What year did he kill himself?"

"1970."

"That's the same year that the Kent State shootings happened."

John rubbed his forehead. "Yeah. I was in college and remember it well."

I nodded.

We moved around the upper gallery, viewing the pieces without speaking much more.

When John tired, he sat down. After memorizing enough from the paintings to recall later on, I sat beside him.

"Let's go look at Modigliani before we have lunch," I suggested.

"You never come here without visiting him, do you?"

"Nope. He's only second to Rembrandt as a portrait painter."

"Well, you've learned how to say his name properly, so there's that," John laughed. "When I first heard you refer to him, I thought you were mumbling about Italian food."

Supporting his leg with his left hand, John slowly managed to get himself upright.

"Your limp is bad today," I noted.

He smirked. "You worry about your drinking, and I'll worry about my limp."

We took the elevator down and found Modigliani's *Large Seated Nude*—a voluptuous nude woman, cream colored, on a red background.

Like most of his work, the painting caused me to think about the artist himself, dressed in his corduroy suit, smoking cigarettes, and sharing a bottle of wine with the model in his studio. The lush beauty of the figure captivated me. I thought of the girl from Alabama waking up in my bed and hiding her own nudity from me, and I wondered what the model may have actually been like. In my mind, I contrasted the brazen seductiveness of the woman in the painting, crafted sometime before Modi's death in 1920, with the cold, banal, sexless nudes Lucian Freud was still painting.

"Alright, you deviant. You've had your fill," John said after a few minutes. He started out of the gallery, motioning for me to follow.

On the way out we passed a Motherwell—*Reconciliation Elegy, 1978.* I stopped and stared.

"What was Motherwell up to?" I asked.

"Well, not necessarily beauty," he said without looking up or stopping. I remained a few moments, then caught up with him in three long strides. "It's a bit academic," he explained. "His most famous work is the *Elegy to the Spanish Republic* series. He claimed they were altars, memorializing the heroic effort of the Republicans during the Spanish Civil War, yet he also said that they were funeral lamentations. Perhaps he never decided."

"It's not Muzak. I like his work," I said. "It's much better than Picasso's take."

"I'm glad you sorted that one out so easily," John said with a laugh and shook his head. "I met him a couple of times—he was a nice man."

We left the National Gallery and walked across Constitution Avenue, past the bronze bas- reliefs at the Navy Memorial. Over lunch, John said he would arrange a meeting with Hutchinson later in the week.

It was nearly five o'clock when we parted.

When I got home I ran four miles, sweating out the previous night's booze. After that, I worked on a painting, thinking about Rothko, Modi—and Motherwell—then went to bed.

CHAPTER 8

H e hadn't introduced himself as Lieutenant Colonel Mujeed in over a year.

Occasionally, he ran into one of his men. The officers were discreet; the enlisted men were not necessarily. One young *jundi*, overjoyed to see his former commander in the *souk*, yelled out, "Colonel Mujeed!"

Mujeed approached the man, embraced him, and put his arm around his shoulder as they walked through the crowds of people buying everything from spices to auto parts to a new import—cellular phones. In a hushed voice, Mujeed explained, "In these times, I am simply known as Abu Mahmood."

Now, Mujeed sat at the Ministry of Defense near the old Saddam Hussein Airport, waiting to be interviewed for a new Iraqi Army position. He wore a Western-style jacket, a collared shirt, and trousers, and sat on a white plastic chair with his back against the wall. Ten other men sat beside him. Mujeed recognized some of them as former military officers. He'd been told to report to this location by American soldiers at the forward operating base in his city district.

He carried a folder with the certificates for each of his promotions. Also in the folder was a letter, bearing the official seal of the post-Saddam Hussein government. It was signed by the district governor and an American; it stated Mujeed had never been a member of the Baathist Party.

He'd waited nearly four hours already, but he didn't mind since the lobby was air conditioned. Smoking was banned in buildings occupied by the American government, so each thirty minutes or so, he stepped outside to smoke.

The corridor bustled with activity. Americans hurried back and forth, eyeing the men waiting. They all carried side arms and drank coffee from thick ceramic cups marked with unit symbols and rank insignia.

Every once in a while, a fat Iraqi man wearing a Western-style jacket over a *dishdasha* stepped out of an office near the end of a hallway, clipboard in hand, and called a name above the din. Sometimes one of the men answered; other times those waiting explained the man in question had stepped out for a cigarette. Mostly, though, nobody answered, and the man continued calling names from the list.

Finally, Mujeed heard his name, stood, and strode towards the man with the clipboard. Mujeed rested his right hand on his chest. "Peace be with you."

The man returned the greeting and asked, "Are you Abdul Mujeed from Al-Adel District, Baghdad, formerly Lieutenant Colonel Mujeed of the Iraqi Army, Engineer Branch?"

"I am," replied Mujeed.

"Welcome. I am Dawoud Hamoud, an assistant deputy for the Ministry of Defense, Recruiting."

Deputy Hamoud signaled for Mujeed to enter the central office.

Partitioned off from the waiting area and other offices with construction-grade lumber and plywood, the room was crowded by a large wooden desk pieced together from new

lumber, three empty chairs, and two men. An American soldier, wearing a standard-issue field gray uniform—a uniform
Mujeed had grown well acquainted with over the past year—
sat behind the desk. He bore the U.S. flag on the upper right
sleeve of his uniform, various badges indicating airborne
qualifications above his left breast pocket, and branch of service—artillery Mujeed guessed from the crossed cannons—
and rank stitched to his collar.

The other man, sitting cross-legged in a chair by the wall,
appeared to be Arabic but wore an unmarked U.S. Army uniform. He looked to be half Mujeed's age.

Squeezed around the edges of the room, boxes of files
sat, piled waist-high against each wall. On the desk was a
small, black briefcase-like machine with wires running from
the base of the device, across the desk a few centimeters, and
disappearing into a hole drilled in the plywood; the lid of the
contraption leaned away from the soldier. Mujeed guessed it
was a computer. An air conditioner, fitted snuggly in place
with cardboard and wide silver tape, stuck out from a small
window behind the American officer. Four large fluorescent
light fixtures lit the space sharply.

Followed by Hamoud, Mujeed entered the room
and waited for a cue, never quite sure what American
protocol entailed.

The soldier stood up from behind the desk, placed his
right hand gently on his chest, and said in practiced Arabic,
"*Salam Alaikum.*" When he extended his hand, Mujeed
reached out and shook it.

"This is Lieutenant Colonel John Ekvall." Hamoud
introduced the colonel in Arabic.

Mujeed was unable to recall enough English to greet the
man, so he replied in Arabic that it was a pleasure. The young

man spoke to the American in English and then Hamoud in Arabic. Mujeed guessed by his accent that he was Iraqi but he couldn't place the dialect.

Finally, the young man turned to Mujeed and introduced himself. "Sir, my name is Yakub. I'm an Iraqi-American, and I'm Lieutenant Colonel Ekvall's interpreter."

Ekvall waved his hand at the chair and spoke.

Yakub translated, "Sir, Colonel Ekvall would like for you to have a seat. Would you like coffee?"

"Please," answered Mujeed, taking a seat in a wooden chair opposite the American. He placed his folder on his lap and folded his hands on top. Nobody spoke while Yakub poured coffee from the pot resting on a stand beside the wall. "Milk and sugar?" he asked.

Mujeed nodded. "Please."

Yakub handed Mujeed a white Styrofoam cup full of coffee. "Sir, the colonel would like to ask you a few questions."

Mujeed sipped the coffee; the sugar and milk soothed the bitterness of the drink.

Colonel Ekvall exchanged words with Yakub in English and handed him a sand-colored file, which Yakub handed to Mujeed. "Please review the information inside and confirm whether or not it is correct."

Mujeed placed his cup on the plywood table, opened the folder, and began reading the Arabic. The two pages inside described his professional career, nearly exactly as he had reported it to the Americans and the district officials in Al-Adel.

Name: *Abdul Babukar Mujeed*
Rank: *Lieutenant Colonel, Iraqi army, Saddam Hussein era*
Age: *43*
Years of Service: *24*

Specialty: *Engineer*
Baathist Affiliation: *Not known*
Last Service: *Sixth Iraqi Division*
Education: *Graduate (Engineering), Iraqi Military
 Academy, Baghdad (1979?)*
Awards: *2 x for valor*
Foreign Travel: *None (Iran and Kuwait
 during Combat Operations)*
Language: *Arabic—No English*
Wife: *Yes (1)*
Children: *4*
Sect: *Sunni*
Recommendation for Future Service: *Class I*
Medical Status: *Claims to be in excellent physical health.
 Most recent physical—1999 (administered by a Unit
 Medical Officer).*
Notes: *Served in the Iraqi army for 24 years. Engineer
 Platoon Leader and Company Commander during
 Iran-Iraq War, 1982-86. Wounded (Gunshot Wounds
 to the Right Hand and Arm).*

*Promoted to Captain in 1988. Instructor, Engineer
 School, 1988–89. Commander, Engineer Company,
 in First Gulf War. Promoted to Major in 1998, and
 Lieutenant Colonel, 2001. Fought near Nasiriyah as
 Commanding Officer of the engineer battalion (Heavy
 Equipment), March–April 2003—until the unit was
 destroyed. Returned to home and family in Baghdad.
 Assisted Provisional District Government of Baghdad in
 reconstruction efforts (2004 to present).*

*Interviews as politically neutral. Desires to continue
 service in new Iraqi army.*

Mujeed read the two names at the end of the report. One was Iraqi. The other was a Western name with a corresponding signature. It may have been the young American captain who interviewed him two months earlier. The report sounded more official than he remembered the interview being.

Mujeed closed the folder and handed it back to Yakub, who gave it to Colonel Ekvall. "Sir," asked Yakub, "is the information correct?"

"Most of it is," said Mujeed, proceeding carefully. "However, I received a wound to my shoulder, not my hand and arm. I also received a wound to my left foot, from machine gun or rifle fire; I couldn't tell. Also, I've never been affiliated with Baathists. It says 'Not known,' but it should simply say *none*. I'm carrying a letter from American and Iraqi officials that says so. And I've been in the army twenty-six years, including my service as a cadet, not twenty-four."

"Sir, the Baathist comment is standard classification for former army officers."

Mujeed exhaled slowly. He'd spent three hours with American soldiers and Iraqi bureaucrats convincing them he had no political affiliations.

He forced a smile at the American. "After twenty-six years of service, seven years at war, and being wounded twice, don't you think I would be a full colonel, or even a general by now, if I associated with the Baathists? I'm Sunni, and I was an officer in the old Iraqi army, but isn't it obvious that I have no political affiliations?"

Yakub translated Mujeed's comments; the American listened and nodded before picking up his pen and making notes in a green cloth-covered notebook.

Mujeed picked up his cup and swallowed the remaining coffee, wishing he could understand more of what was transpiring. When the American finished writing, he spoke to Yakub.

Yakub translated, "The colonel apologizes for the mistakes. He says your record demonstrates that your past service is exemplary, and he promises to make the corrections."

Mujeed recalled enough English to reply, "Thank you."

Without looking at Yakub, Colonel Ekvall spoke to Mujeed in long sentences, pausing now and then.

"Sir, the colonel says the Americans are working with the Iraqi government to build a regular army. The Iraqi National Guard is being disbanded. Initially, the new army will be infantry battalions and brigades only. Eventually, it will expand to artillery, tanks, engineering corps, and other units. Colonel Ekvall asks if you are willing to report to Camp Taji for training with an infantry battalion."

"Of course," Mujeed said without hesitation and with great relief.

"He agrees," Hamoud sang out.

Mujeed hadn't dared let himself hope the Americans and the emerging post-Saddam-Hussein Iraqi government would let him resume his calling.

Yakub spoke with the American officer again, then to Mujeed said, "One last thing. The colonel asks if you are willing to work with the Shiite and Kurdish soldiers, all in the same unit."

Well aware the Americans were concerned about this issue, so much so that the new identification card issued to him by the district government identified him specifically as Sunni, Mujeed replied, "My last unit was half Shiite, the rest Sunni and Kurds. We were a family. I can work with Christians too."

The colonel spoke again, and Yakub said, "Colonel Ekvall thanks you for your time. He says that he and Hamoud will strongly recommend you for further service to the Iraqi and American military board and will correct your record before he submits it. Colonel Ekvall suggests you return home and make preparations to move to Taji. You will need to see the medical officers for a physical examination, today."

"Thank you," Mujeed repeated in English. Then in Arabic, "Is that all?"

"That's all," replied Yakub. "Please walk across the hall and register for a physical. An orderly will direct you to the clinic."

Mujeed picked up the folder resting in his lap, stood, and came to attention. As he did, the American officer rose from his seat and extended his hand to Mujeed. Mujeed gripped it tightly and looked the officer in the eye. When he let go, he glanced at the two other men, thanked them in Arabic, and turned to leave.

"Colonel," said Hamoud.

The word struck Mujeed; he restrained a smile and looked down at the man stuffed in the chair, his hands resting on top of the clipboard in his lap.

Hamoud said, "Please don't speak to anyone about this interview." Mujeed answered with a nod and left.

CHAPTER 9

I wrapped up my lectures on Vietnam. After class, I ran the midshipmen six miles in formation. Although regulation specified I was to run them no more than three miles at one time, I never paid attention to the rule, and the midshipmen never told anyone. They were proud of the stamina I drove into them.

That evening John called and informed me that Hutchinson had agreed to see my work.

"Thursday at 3:00 p.m. We can leave from my place," he said. *"Don't smell like cigar smoke."*

I shook my head.

As soon as I hung up, I dialed Sam Knox's number. He was still at work. "Anything new?" I asked.

"I'm working on a project for Wounded Warriors," he said. *"We're taking amputees on a fishing trip in Idaho."*

"We need more people like you."

"I do what I can."

"Sam, I need a favor—mosh skosh."

"What's going on?"

"My catalog. Can you gin up a draft by tomorrow evening?"

"Uhhh, yes, I think so."

"Sorry for the short notice."

"It's fine. I can do it. I'll find my one true love some other night. Send me the names of the pieces I photographed, and I'll get it done."

"I'll send them as soon as I get home."

We agreed to meet the following evening in Georgetown and have a smoke.

⌘

I arrived at the cigar shop at 1800, bought two Montecristos, and sank into a worn, leather-upholstered chair before lighting up. Artifacts—vintage pipes and old smoking gadgets—crowded the shelves. Period advertisements and cabaret posters by Toulouse-Lautrec, Alphonse Mucha, and Jules Chéret lined the walls; ancient husks of dried tobacco hung from the rafters.

When Sam arrived, I had the cigar waiting in my out-stretched hand. He plucked it from my fingers with a smile, replacing it with a thin, matte-finished paperback catalog, titled in sans serif, *Clay Steerforth: The Trojan War Years.*

I thumbed through the pages while Sam lit up. He pulled on the cigar, adding fresh clouds of smoke to the room. "I used that Marca-Relli book you gave me as a template," he said. "It made life a lot easier."

"The colors in these photos match my paintings almost perfectly."

"Take it home and see how accurate they really are. I can modify them, but I'd need to come by and take a look at all of the paintings first."

"Yeah, I figured as much. That's why I wanted to get started on this project early. I'll likely ship out before the dust settles on it."

"Are you deploying when you get to Lejeune?"

"Hard to know. Even if I knew now, it would change by the time I got to the unit."

"But you are definitely going overseas?" he asked with some excitement.

I nodded. "I hope."

"I'd like to be in your shoes," he said.

Sam was from the Shenandoah Valley; most of his kin had served in the military. He was diagnosed with asthma in his third year as a midshipman, preventing him from being commissioned and barring him from enlisting. When he finished college, he found another way to serve.

"Are all Marines going to Iraq right now?" he asked.

"Iraq's number one, but there is still some action going on in Afghanistan and the Horn of Africa. But yeah, Iraq's the main gig these days."

"Lots of wounded soldiers come back hit by IEDs," Sam remarked.

"It seems to have turned bad over there this past year. You see it in the news, but I've learned that you won't really know until you get there. Still, I can't help looking forward to it."

"You sound like the other people I meet—soldiers and Marines. A lot of them are missing legs or arms, but most say they miss their units and wish they could find a way to go back."

"That's understandable. A lot of veterans have trouble adapting to civilian life once the war is over for them—not because of any psychological crap, but because the regular world is dull and lonely compared to a life with your friends in the field." I thumbed through the catalog again. "What do you need me to do?"

"Make your notes—just write them down in the margins. Check the sizes and the titles. Then we will do it again until we get it right. Call me when you've finished going through it, and we'll get the next draft going."

We sat for a while longer, smoking and watching people come and go. He told me about the upcoming fishing trip, the Wounded Warriors organization, and the struggles some of the soldiers faced. They were familiar stories, but no less moving.

"You've done your damnedest, Sam," I said, putting the catalog down. "It's important that we have people back here taking care of the folks when they return from this war. The worst part of the Vietnam War wasn't fighting in the jungle, it was what happened when they got back here in the States."

Sam smiled. "You're right," he said, looking at his watch. "I've got work in the morning. Thanks for the smoke."

"I'll buy you a *box* when we pull this thing off," I joked. "Thanks again."

"No problem, sir. I'll make it so."

Sam—six-foot-four, lanky, and shaved bald—walked out, the cigar twixt his fingers and a thin trail of smoke following in his wake.

⌘

I looked around M Street, down towards the Potomac where my car was parked, then up Wisconsin Avenue. I had a fleeting thought of Meyerstone as I walked towards the river. On my way, I passed *Chi Chai Chang*—a teashop I often frequented—turned around, and went inside.

The teashop was no larger than a spacious living room, an open space with rosewood railings and high walls that ended at a large overhead skylight. It reminded me of the National Gallery on a very small scale. Countless clay teapots sat on display shelves that lined the walls, matched in number by the wide selection of teas stored in metals boxes, all labeled with black and red Chinese characters.

Floor cushions and low-rise traditional tables provided a comfortable place to sit, but the Chinese hostess seated me at one of the Western tables. From past experience, she knew I wouldn't take my boots off.

I ordered Lapsang tea. The hostess brought the teapot, placed it on a stand, and lit the small burner underneath it.

"Let it brew for three or four minutes." She smiled, bowed slightly, then fluttered away.

After the tea steeped, I poured a cup and took a sip, breathing in the smoky aroma. Leafing through the catalog, I scribbled notes. Halfway through my second cup of tea, the front door chimed and I looked up.

A stunning woman with a shock of thick, black, shiny hair and wearing a blue silk floral dress—the type with buttons all the way up to the chin—walked in. Wearing five-inch heels, she walked with knees that almost knocked, causing her sway at the waist. She was thin with nice hips and a round bottom.

She ordered from the counter and then walked in my direction: large round eyes, a small nose, and a rosebud of red lips—her pinkish skin stretched over high cheekbones, a pointed chin, and a flat forehead. She glanced at me as she passed, her eyes resting on my catalog.

As she sauntered by, I sniffed gently. She smelled good. I assumed she would remove her high heels and sit on a pillow, but she sat at a table near my own.

I focused on my catalog.

After a couple of minutes, I heard a chair scoot against the floor and the clack of her heels. I looked her way as she headed towards the sales counter. Again, she glanced at my catalog. I turned the page for her to see. On her way back to her table, I made eye contact, flashed a small grin, and looked down before I could gauge her reaction.

From the corner of my eye, I saw the Chinese woman serve her tea.

The woman just in view, I wrote in my catalog, waiting for an opportunity to engage her.

When I sensed she was looking my way, I snapped my head in her direction and caught her—her beautiful neck craned, big eyes opened wide, trying to steal a good look at the pages. Sensing victory, I leaned back in my chair. "Do you want to see?"

With a nod and an accent I took for Chinese, she said, "Yes, I do."

"Bring your tea here," I said. She started to move and I stood. "Excuse me. Let me help you."

I picked up her teapot and burner. She followed me to my table, and I pulled a chair up next to mine. When she sat down. I touched the book and explained, "It's a catalog of my paintings. We're still revising it."

She moved her body in my direction and looked up at me. "These are your paintings?"

"They are." I glanced at her dress. "Where are you from?"

She smiled, lighting up the whole room. "I'm Mongolian. I go by Kate."

"Kate?"

"My real name is Khulan." She said softly, "It means *wild donkey.*"

"I'll stick with Kate." I held my hand out; she gripped it firmly. "My name is Clay."

"Can I see?" She leaned towards the book and turned it back to the cover, reading, "*Clay Steerforth: The Trojan War Years.*" She rubbed the matte finish of the front cover with her finger. "How long have you been painting?"

"All my life. I learned from my mother."

She focused on the pictures for a moment. "What are they?"

"They're monuments to the characters in the *Iliad.*"

"I read that in high school."

"In Mongolia?"

"No. I finished high school here."

Kate flipped through the catalog a few times without speaking. I drank my tea, watching her.

"Your paintings are beautiful," she said after a while. "Do you sell them?"

"When I can," I said, sparing her the details. "What do you do?"

"I'm a student. And I work at The Hattery in the Georgetown Mall across the street. I make and sell hats."

"I've been there before, but I don't recall seeing a hat shop."

She sipped her tea. "You should come by. I work from three to eight."

"I will."

We sat for a while, talking about Kate's childhood in Mongolia, riding horses—bareback—herding cattle, and living with her family in a *yurt*. I told her I was a Marine.

We left when the Chinese hostess began stacking chairs on the tables. I put Kate in a taxicab and bid her goodnight.

CHAPTER 10

I borrowed my neighbor's Dodge pickup, piled five paintings in the back, and slid the draft catalog underneath the seat. After I picked up John, we drove to the Hutchinson Collection. A gallery assistant greeted us and told us the gallerist would be with us shortly. As we carried the last piece in, Hutchison came out from the back. Four or five years older than me, with blue eyes, and thick dirty-blonde hair falling to her shoulders, she was attractive. Her minimalist attire—red blouse with a black skirt and high heels, no jewelry—fit the image of an art dealer. Yet the sharp smell of perfume told me she'd freshened up before entering the room, and I decided I wouldn't need the catalog I'd forgotten in the truck.

Following introductions, she and John caught up. When she turned her attention to my paintings, arranging them to her liking against the wall, I left her and John alone and walked the gallery. Her current exhibit featured Frank Hurley's photographs of the 1914 Shackleton expedition to the South Pole. As I began my second survey of Hurley's black-and-white prints, Hutchinson looked up from her appraisal and agreed to handle my work. We shook hands, and I left the paintings behind.

We climbed into the cab of the truck. "That was easier than I thought," I said to John.

"She responded well to your work."

"Something dawned on me when we were in there," I said, turning the key in the ignition.

"What?"

"A photograph is far better at capturing reality than a painting." I paused, trying to gather the frayed threads of my thoughts. "There *is* something special going on in those photos she's showing of Shackleton and his men. It's beyond the simple portrayal of a ship frozen in the Antarctic and men in dire circumstances. I can't top it."

"You're not a photographer."

"No, I mean I can't do it better with paint. Like Alexander Gardner's or Matthew Brady's Civil War photos, they capture the gore of war better than any painting can. When artists try, it's usually by juxtaposing some dramatic version of war's tragedy against inept political or military leaders, as if we don't know this already." I backed down the drive onto the one-way street. "It's irony, some sort of statement I guess, but it falls flat because all it's doing is stating the obvious. It's simply funny—*ha-ha* funny, or it should be."

"You might have a point." John was only half-listening.

I straightened the wheel and pulled away from the gallery. "But now I know why I like Motherwell's version of the Spanish Civil War better than Picasso's."

"Keep going," replied John. I had his full attention now.

"Motherwell's work causes me to contemplate the undertones of the war, the mystery.

With the Spanish Civil War theme, he was on to something, I just don't know what it is. Picasso's *Guernica,* on the other hand, simply makes me think about Picasso and cubism—that's what it's about—not the war itself." I snapped my finger and pointed at John. "There are plenty of photos that tell the Spanish Civil War gore story better than Picasso. Besides, Picasso didn't feel too strongly for his fellow countrymen; he stayed in France, painting, while others fought the Fascists."

"You should tell Hutchinson that. It may help her sell your work," John said. "Leave the part about Picasso not fighting out—that's absolutely ridiculous."

The traffic was heavy. Even the Q Street route to John's house at New Jersey and 7th Street, N.W., was jammed.

Watching for cars, I said, "So, I met a girl last night."

"A girl or a woman?" John asked without missing a beat. "What are they going by nowadays?"

"I don't know. It changes every couple of years."

"We met at the teashop—you know the one next door to the sex shop in Georgetown—the one that has souvenir dildos of the Washington Monument in the window. Just around the corner from Georgetown Tobacco."

John stared out the window at the ancient trees and rows of houses lining the North Georgetown avenue. "Mmm…I know it, yes."

"Sexy and sweet."

"What does that mean?" he asked. "She had huge boobs and she showed them to you?"

Because of his puritanical prudishness, John was usually unfunny. That, combined with his gayness, made the comment highly entertaining and liberating for me. I laughed hard.

"Don't get me wrong," I said, "boobs are great. However—I'm a butt and face man. You have to think about what you want to wake up and look at the rest of your life. She claims she's a Mongol."

"You mean she's Mongolian?"

"Accent and all."

"You sound like you're describing something out of the thirteenth century. *The Mongol Hordes*."

"Let me tell you, a horde the likes of her could conquer any country. The men would quit fighting, and it would be up to the women to take up arms."

"Well, perhaps she will encourage you to stop carousing. That won't help you, regardless of what you read about other artists. Modigliani painted his best work when he was off alcohol and drugs, and so did Pollock."

"I'm not like them—I don't buy booze with pocket change."

"What are you talking about?"

"Folks say the best indicator of whether or not somebody drinks too much is if they buy booze with change. If you're scrounging around the house, shaking out your trousers and upending the couch pillows just to find a few quarters to buy a forty-ouncer, then you have a problem. Otherwise you're good."

"Who are these *folks* by the way?"

"Marines I know—friends of mine."

John laughed. "That's called *rationalization*—making excuses."

We left the quietude of Georgetown, passing over the Buffalo Bridge at Rock Creek. I weaved around the cars, buses, cyclists, and pedestrians converging in the chaos of DuPont Circle at rush hour.

"I'm going to see her tonight, and I'll likely have a drink, if it's alright with you."

"Don't let me stop you," he said. "Where are you meeting her?"

"She works at the Georgetown Mall—the Hat Factory."

"You're courting a milliner!" he squawked, then broke into full laughter. "Imagine that. I guess you'll have to start wearing a fedora."

"I'd wear a hat with flowers if she asked me to." I chuckled more at John's sudden enthusiasm than the imagery I'd conjured up. "You remember the kind that our grandmas wore to church?"

"Well, don't fall too far in love," he said. "It will ruin your painting."

"No it won't. I once asked my mom about that."

"You did?"

"I was in my late twenties, and I thought the Marine Corps had done my painting in. I got desperate and called her. She said, 'Quit worrying and keep working.' She never quit, and only God knows what that woman went through with seven awful kids, a dead husband, and a gypsy soul."

"Mothers are magical," John said.

We neared his house on New Jersey Avenue.

"Oh! I almost forgot." I reached under my seat while peering at the road between the spokes of the steering wheel. "The catalog. I need your opinion." I pulled it out and handed it to John.

I stopped in front of John's row house and waited for him to respond. He looked at the catalog for a minute. "Change the font. This one's awful. An art catalog isn't a military document, for Pete's sake. Use Arial."

"Okay, noted."

"I'll write the essay and perhaps Hutchinson will write an introduction." He turned the pages one by one and pointed to a shot of me in Georgetown, lighting a cigar while squinting at the sun. "It's good work. Get a better photo of yourself. You look pissed off in this one."

"Roger."

"Here." John handed me the catalog. "Good luck with the girl."

⌘

Instead of battling the traffic back to Arlington, I drove to the cigar shop on L Street, N.W. I burned an hour sitting near a window, smoking a ten-dollar cigar, listening to Frank Sinatra—the only music that cigar shop ever plays—and watching city folk wearing their city faces and making their way through the city streets at the end of the day.

I drove back to Georgetown, parked under the Whitehurst Freeway, and turned on WAMU. Reclined in my seat, I listened to the McNeil/Lehrer NewsHour and dozed off.

When the host announced the names of those killed in Iraq, I sat up. A few years earlier, on the same broadcast, I learned a Marine I'd played football with in high school had been killed in action. As I listened, I recalled a scene from my own Mideast experience: riding in the cab of a truck leading a convoy of Marines through the mountains in Jordan, the Arab driver smoking a hookah pipe and playing cassette-taped music at full volume the entire time. I felt a longing for those days, but I felt something stronger—the nagging fear I'd come to know in recent years. Not fear of going to the war and being wounded or killed—no—the fear of being left behind, of being omitted.

When the newscast ended, I got out of my car, inserted quarters in the meter, put on my jacket, and walked inside the

Georgetown Mall. I found the hat shop. Kate was straightening a row of driving caps on a shelf when I arrived.

"Kate."

She wore a floral dress and looked just as beautiful as I remembered. She smiled. "I was wondering if you were coming by."

I smiled back. "I said I would."

"I remember, but you never know."

I was shocked by the mess. Even by my standard, the small shop was a disaster. On flimsy shelves and racks were hats of every kind, Styrofoam mannequins with crudely drawn faces, old wooden hat blocks, an overcrowded display of neckties, a few knock-off Zippo lighters, and a mess of other accoutrements typically found at a gas station or in a hoarder's house. The state of disarray made me wonder why the building management hadn't closed it down.

"So this is it?"

"Yes. Welcome to the Hattery." She beamed. "The only hat shop in Washington that sells, makes, and cleans hats." She spun around, her dress flaring, and waved her hand as if the mess were a boutique on Connecticut Avenue. "Give me a minute to close the register."

I wandered to the back of the shop.

A television sat on a table next to a pile of twenty or thirty videocassettes, boxed sets of the *That Girl* TV series and *The Godfather* amongst them. The cardboard container of somebody's carryout spaghetti had been tossed, open, on top of the entertainment. Beneath the soles of my boots, the carpet was stained with grime and liquid spills. A tan, threadbare, velvet couch sat against the wall. With a pile of magazines substituting for a missing leg and stains to match the carpet, it was the type of thing I'd seen on many a country front porch, only lacking the dozing hound on top of it. Above the couch was a picture of Sinatra, no less, wearing a fedora. Near Frank was a headshot of Malcolm X, and next to it, a photo of the Black Panthers. Every picture was crooked.

"Ready?" she called.

I walked back to the front of the shop. Kate shut the door and locked it. "What do you want to do?"

"Let's go to the waterfront."

She handed me her coat. "Great. They have ice cream there."

I took the coat. "Okay. I'll smoke a cigar," I said, helping her into it.

As we walked away, she said, "I thought I smelled cigar on you last night."

I laughed. "Speaking of smells, I wanted to ask you— what type of perfume do you wear?"

"Oh, do you like it?"

"I do."

"Coco Chanel Mademoiselle. I've been wearing it for six years. I never wear anything else. I don't cheat on my perfume."

I laughed again and extended my arm for her to take.

I gave her money to get ice cream, sat on the steps overlooking the Potomac, and lit a cigar. The last orange glow of sunset glazed the river. I looked towards the Virginia side of the Potomac. Arlington Cemetery. I thought back to the list of names I'd heard on the radio, about my cousin Leonard and the kids from my hometown my mother had painfully recalled.

"It'll be summertime in a month," Kate said, sitting beside me, her ice cream cone in hand.

"This waterfront reminds me of summer…and painting."

"Why's that?" she asked, twisting her body towards me.

"The first summer I was in D.C., I came here a lot for a break from the heat in my studio. I'd sit right there," I pointed to the waterfront bar, "drinking gin and tonics, thinking about my paintings, and watching the summer swelter sink into the water."

"How do you think about painting?"

"That's a good question," I chuckled. "I was thinking about what to do with it." She wrinkled her forehead.

I pointed to the buildings beyond Roosevelt Island. "I lived in an apartment over there in Rosslyn. It was small, but I wanted to be near the city, so I could look for an opportunity to show my work. I painted in my living room with the air-conditioning off, the windows open to let the turpentine fumes out, filling up my house with paintings."

"How did you start showing your paintings?"

"I met a guy here in Georgetown. He made it happen. I'd painted seriously for fifteen years before that—all in a vacuum until then."

She slipped her arm through mine and leaned on my shoulder. "I'm feeling cold."

"Sorry about the smoke," I said.

She leaned in closer to me. "That's okay. I like it here with you."

"How long have you been working at the Hat Factory?"

She laughed. "The Hattery?"

I shook my head. "Right."

"Almost two years now. I love working there, even though the owner doesn't pay me on time."

"Ha!"

"What's so funny?"

"We have similar problems. Who's the owner?"

"His name's André Dumas, or Andy. He inherited The Hattery ten years ago when the original owner died. I've seen old photos; it was very nice back then."

"I did notice it was somewhat cluttered."

"I used to clean it every Saturday, but I gave up. Andy and his friends make a mess, hanging out in the back, eating carryout and smoking the pot. His friends call him Kompt."

"*Comte?*"

"That sounds right. I don't know what it means."

"Count, I think, except in French. How much does Andy owe you?"

Kate shrugged and licked her ice cream cone. "About five-hundred dollars. He tells me to take cash from the register but then leaves with it so I can't."

"Is he going to pay you?"

"When he gets around to it. I have to beg him for it."

"I'd like to meet him."

"Come by any time."

We sat on the stairs until well after dark, then I drove her across the river to a high-rise apartment full of immigrants.

After dropping her off, I stopped at the 7-Eleven, bought a bottle of wine, and drove home. Sitting in my studio listening to the news on the radio, I thought of the evening with Kate. I stared at a painting, drank four-fifths of the bottle from a teacup, and then went to bed.

⌘

The next day at work, via email, Headquarters Marine Corps sent me orders to report to Camp Lejeune no later than 15 June. I called the regiment immediately and asked the executive officer when I was going overseas; he didn't know. I didn't ask any more questions and simply assured him I would arrive on time.

CHAPTER 11

Barbara,

As I've communicated to you multiple times now, it comes down to this: Either you agree to pay me the balance you owe me, or tomorrow morning Mr. Nicholson will file a case against you in D.C. court. As you know, you admitted to me via email that you owe me a balance of $64.8K. Furthermore, I have witnesses who will testify that you owe them money as well. Instead of making this public, and out of good will, I am again offering a ten percent discount if we can resolve this by June 1st. You can pay me over a three or four-month period. Let me know your decision.

Clay

I hit the send button and went to the pull-up bars on the campus square, cranking out fifty dead-hang pull-ups in sets of ten, and then I went for a run.

Shirtless, I followed the footpath around Roosevelt Island. I breathed deeply, inhaling the fragrance of a new growth of tree leaves. Exhilarated by the thought of going to Camp Lejeune and possibly the war, I quickened my steps, finishing the third mile in under seven minutes and then resuming a slow, steady pace.

In the past month, I'd seen Kate nearly every evening. Looking forward to seeing her made the multitude of mundane tasks inherent to moving easier to execute. As I ran through Rosslyn, over the Key Bridge, and into Georgetown, I wondered how to tell her I was leaving.

⌘

When I got back to my office, Midshipman McCook was there, sitting in the mid-century oak office chair I'd rescued from the dumpster two years earlier. I'd discovered the midshipmen referred to it as "the hot seat," a place they sat if I had given them an important job in the battalion or just before coming to attention and receiving administrative punishment, which I doled out on rare occasions.

"McCook," I greeted the young man.

He stood and came to attention. "Sir, I came to speak to you about the commissioning ceremony."

I sat on top of my desk and motioned to the oak chair. "At ease, McCook. Sit back down.

Are we ready?"

"Almost, sir."

"What can I do for you?"

"Sir, can you recommend a gift for the captain?"

I stared at him.

McCook asked, "Any ideas, sir?"

"A box of cigars. I know where to buy them."

"Sir, the captain doesn't smoke."

"I know that. But he doesn't know what he's missing. You could buy him a card to go with it and write a sentence or two explaining the pleasure of smoking."

"Maybe, sir." McCook looked confused. "But none of the Navy midshipmen will agree to that. You taught the Marine midshipmen to smoke during our field evolutions—"

"Don't tell anybody that," I drawled.

"Sir, with all of the fuss about smok—"

I waved my hand. "I hope I'm never an NROTC commanding officer—can't even get cigars as a gift. Get him Shelby Foote's three-volume series on the Civil War then."

"What was that, sir?"

"The captain claims he's a reader."

"He doesn't seem like the type," McCook said doubtfully.

"He is," I assured him. "And he could use some further professional military education."

"Sir, pardon me?" McCook grinned.

"He tried to stump me one day on the war," I explained. "Last winter, as I strolled back from class, he stopped me. Apparently, he'd heard I was teaching you all that General Grant was a drunk. He tried to tell me Grant's drinking was simply a rumor inflicted by his political rivals here in D.C."

"That's what he told us, I remember."

"Well, I asked him if he knew who Grant's closest friend was. Of course, he didn't. I told him it was Sherman and asked him if he knew what Sherman said about Grant. Same thing—clueless."

McCook laughed.

"Sherman said that Grant stuck by him when he was crazy, and that's why he stuck by Grant when he was drunk. The captain left me alone after that. Get him Foote's trilogy.

Even if it just sits on the shelf like the rest of his books, he'll look sophisticated."

"I'll float that to the class."

"Let me know if they protest. If they do, I'll override them."

"Roger, sir."

"Okay. A week from Sunday. We're set to go, correct?"

"Yes, sir."

"How many seats?"

"One thousand."

I pointed out the window. "And they will all fit on the lawn in front of the Marine Corps War Memorial?"

"We measured it. Yes, sir."

"Guest speaker?"

"Three-star admiral from the Naval Academy."

"Band?"

"The Air Force is providing a brass quartet."

"Backup plan?"

"Souza Hall at the Marine Barracks."

"Last thing…"

"Sir?"

I pointed at McCook. "The program—no mistakes. Get it to me by tomorrow and I'll review it. No typos, wrong dates, or bad grammar."

"I'll have it to you in the morning."

I snapped my fingers and pointed at the young man. "Good job, McCook. I'm starting to like you."

"Thank you, sir. It's been three years." We both laughed.

"Let me know if I can do anything else for you, McCook."

"Aye, aye, sir. Permission to be dismissed," he requested, coming to attention.

I waved towards the door. "You're dismissed, McCook."

The young man executed a crisp about-face and began to leave.

"McCook," I interrupted, "don't tell anyone that story about the captain. He's a dignified man and a good officer. He means well."

"Roger, sir." McCook walked out.

I leaned over and tapped my keyboard; the screensaver disappeared. A new email was waiting:

Mr. Steerforth,

I recall the agreement. So that I can put this behind me, I will make the first payment on June 1st and complete the balance of $64,800.00 (minus ten percent) in four installments of roughly $14,600.00 each. I will send the checks to Mr. Nicholson's office, and he can forward them to you.

Barbara

I looked at the email for several seconds before I replied, trying to discern what would have motivated her to send the checks to my lawyer.

Barbara,

Thank you. Look forward to hearing from you.

Clay

I called Mr. Nicholson from my desk phone. "She agreed to pay."

"No caveats?"

"She took the ten-percent deal you recommended, in installments, with the first one starting June 1st."

"Good. I didn't want it to go to court. Judges peek under the blindfold occasionally."

"She's going to send the checks to you, by the way. Any idea why?"

"Right. I recommended that to her. You're leaving, and I don't want her to get the idea that distance would assuage your grievance and make it easier for her to justify not paying. People are greedy."

I chuckled. "She's called me just about everything she could in the past month or so."

"Wrath," he said.

"Say again?"

"She's wrathful. That was the seventh deadly sin that I couldn't recall when you were last in my office."

"Greed, wrath. Anything else?"

"Other than hubris, probably not. That's three of the seven, about par for the course."

⌘

Three days later, I took Kate to Alexandria for dinner. After eating, I picked up a cigar from the tobacco shop on the main drag. Folks dined at street-side cafes and strolled the cobblestone streets, window-shopping or relaxing on benches by the river. The dusty yellow streetlights flared against the sunset and reflected off the Potomac, the beautiful glow broken only by the scattered silhouettes of small skiffs and yachts bobbing gently on the water. A mile downriver, the construction workers and engineers building the new Wilson Bridge were still working, the rhythmic clang of the multi-ton pile driver pounding iron stanchions into the riverbed, casting a repetitious, metallic *ping!* across the river's smooth surface that echoed against the shore.

We caught the ferry and rode upriver to Georgetown; I bought Kate ice cream. Sitting on the steps and watching cranes dive at the surface of the water, we said little. Having performed a variation of this date a number of times now, she had taken to calling it "our tradition." In the distance, I spotted the rickety ferry that delivered us churning upriver, returning. That's when I told her I was leaving.

"Why didn't you tell me before?" she asked with tears welling in her eyes. "I didn't think I'd have to worry about it."

Blindsided and confused, she asked, "What do you mean?"

"Well, when we met, I thought we'd go out a few times and that would be it. How can you ever know such a thing?"

She began to sob.

"I'll come back as often as I can," I said, putting my arm around her and stroking her thick hair. "You can visit me." There was little else I could say.

She doubled over, her head in her arms, and began to make a sound between a low moan and a howl. Occasionally, her back would heave, she'd catch her breath, and I'd think she was through; then she'd start again.

Her profound sadness made my heart ache.

Folks passed, averting their eyes. I pulled her close. It took a while, but she came around. I decided not to mention Iraq.

Finally, she said, "I thought you were in love with me."

"I am. That doesn't—"

She started crying again, nearly as loud as before, and stayed that way until she was all cried out. When she pulled herself up, her makeup was smudged, her eyes red.

I hugged her tightly and kissed the top of her head.

We boarded the ferry and sat on the stern, holding hands and watching the monuments pass by as we coasted down the river.

I drove her back to my place and made tea for us. Drinking from small ceramic cups, we sat at my study table and talked. Afterwards, Kate lay on my bed and cried herself to sleep.

In the morning, I served her tea in bed. She wanted steak and eggs, so I left her there and went to Safeway. She was still in bed when I returned and only got up when she smelled the food cooking.

I dropped her off that afternoon and went inside to meet her mother, a woman a few years older than me. Kate's two sisters weren't there. The woman spoke little English but demonstrated her hostess skills by frying me Mongolian dumplings and serving me milk tea.

⌘

The next day, I dropped by The Hattery. Nobody seemed to be in.

The boom box, normally playing pop music, thumped and wheezed out an updated version of that old television tune about Tennessee hillbillies striking oil and moving to Beverly Hills, California.

I can't recall exactly, but this was the gist of the cover:

> *Hump dee ho!*
> *Hump dee ho!*
> *Whoop, whoop, whoop.*
> *Let me tell ya notha story 'bout a man named Jed.*
> *He wuz livin' in the city, barely*
> *kep his baby's mama fed.*

Then one day he wuz stealin' him some food,
and out from his pocket rolled a big fat doob.
Hump dee ho!
Hump dee ho!
Whoop, whoop, whoop.
Well the police saw him, and
dey threw him in the pen,
and there he sits, wid his hands on his chin.
He never went to California,
and I'm only here to tell ya,
all that stuff 'bout 'Merican dreams,
is only bullshit, or so it seems.
Hump dee ho!
Hump dee ho!
Whoop, whoop, whoop.

I walked to the back of the shop where I found a man about my age, forty or more pounds overweight, reclined on the ragged couch, sound asleep, his mouth agape, snoring. He was an eater. The remains of two or three carryout containers lay scattered on the table and floor.

As I turned to walk away, he sat up halfway and rubbed his eyes. "Can I help you?"

I turned back. "I'm looking for Kate. I'm Clay."

"Oh, hey." He struggled to raise himself from the sofa, bracing one fist against the cushions, scooting forward, and extending the other. "I'm André Dumas, Kate's boss. I've heard a lot about you."

I shook hands with the man, and he sank back into his seat. "Where's Kate?"

"She stepped out to go to the bank. Have a seat."

The only option was the sofa. I pushed aside a newspaper, a soda can, and a jacket, and sat on the edge, resting my elbows on my knees and positioning my hands so that the tips of my fingers touched together.

"Yeah, Kate's told me a lot about you," he said. "She says you're a Marine and that you're about to go to North Carolina."

"That's correct."

"Where you from?"

"A small southern enclave in Michigan called Waterford Township originally. You?"

"I grew up in New Orleans. I'm French-Creole."

"Dumas? Right. As in Alexandre Dumas, the French—"

"Oh, you know!" He lit up. "In fact, I am a direct descendent of Alexandre Dumas. My great-great-great-grandpappy, Dumas's child, relocated from Paris to New Orleans around 1850, so the story goes. My name is actually André Napoleon de la Dumas."

"Really? I thought—"

"Yeah, but I go by André. People call me Andy. My great-grandpops added the *de,* and my grandpops added the *la,* or that's the legend."

"*The Count of Monte Cristo* is one of my favorite books," I said.

"Yeah, I saw the movie. It was fantastic."

I looked at the videocassette boxes. "You've got quite a collection."

"I like movies. My talent is music, though. In fact, hear that?" He leaned an ear towards the boom box. "I produced that. Maybe I can leave the hat business one day. Here in the D.C. music world, my boys, they call me *Komte.* I spell it with a 'K'—you know, just a little modification of the original French." I nodded. "Hmm."

André motioned with his hand. "So, what do you think of The Hattery?"

I gazed at the mess around me. "Kate likes it here."

"Oh, I know she does. Man, she is a hard worker. The best I've got."

My gaze remained on the disorder. "I'm glad she has a job. She pays for school. She's got a family, too—it's four women loaded up in a one-bedroom apartment on the eighth floor of a high-rise. Her mother doesn't speak English, and her youngest sister is still in high school. That leaves Kate and her twin sister to make rent."

The Kount didn't reply.

He sat relaxed, legs sprawled, feet beneath the table, hands folded on his ample stomach, head leaned back onto the sofa, eyes fixed on the ceiling.

I watched and waited. Wearily, he glanced my way.

"She lives paycheck to paycheck. And the bills pile up," I said.

He sighed deeply. "I know what you mean."

I waited.

André shrugged. "She'll get paid...regardless of the vithissitudes of the business world. You don't have to worry."

"I won't. Tell Kate I waited but had to run."

⌘

·On the Sunday the midshipmen were to be commissioned, rain was forecast. Between 0800 and 1400 that day, Midshipman McCook called me five times, panicked. It was the same every time, no matter what I told him.

"Sir, are we going with Plan B?"

"Is it raining at the War Memorial?"

"It's not here in Foggy Bottom, but the forecast—"

133

"Then it's not raining at the memorial. Stick with Plan A. If it starts raining where you are, call me, and I'll call the captain and *he'll* make the call."

That day it rained in Bethesda, Alexandria, Shirlington, Anacostia, Springfield, and everywhere west of the Beltway, but it didn't rain in Rosslyn.

The commissioning was scheduled to start at 1700. I arrived at 1500 to review my master of ceremonies script and get the midshipmen, the color guard, and the brass quartet in place.

Kate wore an emerald-green dress she bought with the money Andy paid her. I wore dress blues.

All the seats were filled, the spillover standing in the trees fifty yards back from where I stood at the podium at the base of the memorial. I read my script and introduced the guest speaker. He spoke for thirty minutes. When he finished, the midshipmen's people clapped loudly. On my cue, the class stood and took the oath of office from the admiral. As I announced each midshipman's name, assignment, and home state, they came forward, shook hands with the admiral and the captain, and left with their commission inside a blue or scarlet folder. I made one mistake—I pronounced Illinois with a hard *s*.

After the band played the National Anthem, I grabbed my script and left the podium as fast as possible, trying to avoid any sticklers standing by to point out my error.

I moved through the crowd—family and friends congratulating the newly commissioned officers with hugs, kisses, and best wishes. The air was thick and sticky, my wool uniform damp with sweat. As I hurried towards the tree line, a woman hoisted a string of flowers around my neck, hugged me fiercely, and explained she'd come all the way from Hawaii to see her niece made a Navy officer. When I freed myself, I headed to the shade but didn't see Kate. I stopped and looked back, past the buzzing throng and up at the towering bronze figures raising the flag at Iwo Jima, and I wondered if I'd ever fight in a battle where the name would afterward be chiseled and gilded beside Belleau Wood, Guadalcanal, Inchon, Khe Sanh, Somalia, and all the other famous battles at the base of the memorial.

"Clay." Kate was walking through the trees towards me, Sam and John beside her. She hugged me, and Sam shook my hand. When I clasped John's hand, he said, "It's not *Illinois-ss*, it's *Illinois*—no 's.'"

"Thanks, John," I said. "I was hoping to sneak off without having my eye poked out over that, but I'm glad you're here to see me go blind in one eye."

"Where did you get those flowers?" asked Kate, tugging at the lei with unconcealed envy.

"Some kid's aunt," I said. I reached up, took the lei off, and placed it ceremoniously around Kate's neck.

We began walking away, and I looked back at the memorial again and saw Second Lieutenant McCook, flanked by Willington and four or five of the newly minted Marine officers headed for me. McCook carried a gift-wrapped package in his left hand, the shape and size familiar to me.

"Wait here," I said and walked towards the officers.

The lieutenants came to attention and saluted. "Sir, we want to thank you for taking care of us," said McCook.

I returned their salute. "It was my pleasure, Marine, but I'm glad it's over."

"It's not over yet, sir," said one of the lieutenants. "The Fleet Marine Force awaits us."

"You don't know the half of it," I laughed. Suddenly I was sad to be parting from them.

Lieutenant Willington nodded at the trees. "Sir, who's the girl?"

"That would be my girlfriend."

"She's hot. Where's she from?"

"Mongolia—a real live Mongol," I said. "When I first saw her, some bad people had her locked up in a cage making hats. I went there at night, broke her out. She's been following me around ever since."

They all laughed and then we fell silent in a long, awkward pause.

Except for Lieutenant Willington, who was twenty-three when he arrived at my doorstep at the university, they were all nineteen or so when I first met them. Back then, they still had pimples, only shaved every two or three days, couldn't do twenty pull-ups all at one time, and hadn't been through the rigor of Officer Candidates School in Quantico. They were different now—men—but still innocent of the responsibility about to be foisted onto them.

I knew, and I think they may have sensed, we would never all be together in one place again.

"Sir," started McCook again, holding out the gift to me. "We bought these for you."

I reached out and took it. "Thank you, gentlemen. I hope the captain likes his books as much as I will certainly enjoy these."

MIDDLE PASSAGE

CHAPTER 12

"**M**ajor Steerforth, how was Washington, D.C.?"

"I enjoyed it, sir. I didn't like the Navy much, but I liked teaching and training the midshipmen."

I glanced past the colonel and out the window at a flight of V-22 Ospreys flying low over the New River. Their twin rotors rattled the windows.

"Have a seat, Clay."

From prior fleet time, I knew Colonel Jack Haverty, the commanding officer of Tenth Marines, the artillery regiment I'd left three years earlier and was now returning to. It was home to me.

For the formality of checking in, I wore my olive-drab Service Alpha uniform. June in North Carolina. Sweat accumulated beneath my wool shirt and seeped through under my arm pits to the gabardine jacket.

The colonel sat back and looked me over. His eyes rested briefly on the ribbons above my left breast pocket, reminding me I had not yet deployed to the war. "Married yet?" he asked.

"No, but I've got a girlfriend," I replied. "A new one."

"What happened to the one who worked for the senator?"

"She went to the White House."

"And the new one?"

"She makes and sells hats," I laughed. "And she's in school."

"Young, I take it?"

"Yes, sir."

The colonel nodded and rubbed his chin. "Still holing up in your attic in a bathrobe, smoking cigars, and painting?"

"I've stuck with the habit, yes."

"Sell anything?"

"I have."

"How much does painting work out to by the hour?"

I chuckled. "That never crossed my mind, sir, but I'll crunch the numbers and let you know."

Colonel Haverty smiled, wove his fingers together, and leaned towards me. "What do you want to do, now that you're back?"

I didn't need to be asked twice. "When can I go to Iraq?"

He leaned back in his chair and shook his head. "I knew you would ask, but not soon, if at all. The division is there now. We're the rear party, and I'm the acting division chief of staff. I spend most of my time at the Division Headquarters— the XO runs the show here, where we need every swinging Richard we've got. You'll stay put for a while and help keep us afloat."

My heart sank. Somewhat bewildered, I asked the stock questions majors returning to the fleet ask. "Does one of the battalions need an executive officer?"

"Do you want to do that?"

I hesitated. "It would be good for my career."

"I want you to take Headquarters Battery Regiment, Clay."

"The commanding officer?"

"Yes. It's been a revolving door for a year. We've got a brand new captain in the slot right now—the kind still shitting lieutenant chow—and it's a major's job. There's a hand-ful of sections rotating in and out of theater every six months. Otherwise, it's all the sick, lame, and lazy that didn't go to the war. Morale is low. Maybe you can square it away."

"Aye, aye, sir. I'll take it," I said. "Commanding anything is better than being an executive officer."

"My sentiment as well." He grinned at me. "Still have the house in Wilmington?"

"I do."

"That old BMW?"

"All 250,000 miles worth of it. It's outside."

"It may be time to buy a new one, Steerforth. Get settled in your house and come back to work next week."

"Roger." I stood and came to attention. "Thank you, sir."

He extended his hand across the desk and I shook it. "Welcome back, Clay."

⌘

My house in Wilmington was near downtown. The rent-ers left without knocking holes in the walls, leaving piles of garbage in the bedrooms, or tearing down the picket fence. The movers dropped off my gear, and I set up my studio in the living room. I spent the next week stretching canvases and running the trail that circled the cypress-studded lake near my property.

In the afternoons, I took up residence in a cigar shop downtown and got acquainted with the patrons. All were curious about the war, but besides hearsay, I had little to tell them that they didn't know from the news. Near the cigar shop, a contemporary art gallery had opened. When I stopped in to look at the work, I didn't tell the owner I was a painter, deciding to finish a painting first and then bring it to him.

The next week, I went to the office and met the captain I was replacing. He gave me a rundown of the 450 Marines assigned to the unit—half were in Iraq.

"The division took the good stuff and sent us every broke-dick Marine and miscreant they had left over. The sections rotating in and out of theater are good. They keep to themselves," he explained.

"Punishments?"

"I spend half of my time holding office hours. DUIs, smoking pot, domestic violence, UAs, deserters, you name it, sir."

"Where's your first sergeant?"

"Don't have one, but one's inbound. She's due anytime."

"*She?* I've never worked with a female Marine before," I said.

"You will now. There're forty-seven females in the battery."

I made a sour face.

"Yeah. When the word came that the division was headed to Iraq, half of them got pregnant, nearly overnight. In other words, they shot themselves in the foot."

"Just as well," I said.

"It's either here or there. If it's in Iraq, we have to ship them home and find a replacement—a real pain in the ass."

"Anybody say anything about it?"

"Who would? You can't punish somebody for getting pregnant."

We did a quick turnover, reviewing the pending punishments and legal cases, discussing the status of the vehicles in the motor pool and training regimen. Finally, we practiced and executed a change of command.

Then I was in charge.

⌘

"First Sergeant!" I called into the next office a few days later.

First Sergeant Claire Angelique Fontaine walked into my office. Since meeting her, I'd learned she was a clarinet player from Louisiana, a Cajun—or *coonass* as she termed it—who joined the Marine Corps as a bandsman fourteen years earlier.

"Sir?"

I handed her a piece of paper with a list of training objectives.

Eating an apple, she chewed and read out loud. "'Enforce the Weight Control Program.' Good, sir. Fucking-A. I like that. We've got fat-bodies. 'Running and calisthenics only for PT' is always good. 'Go to the field once a month.' That's a tough one, and 'Motor Stables'—I don't know shit about vehicle maintenance. 'Marine Corps Martial Arts Program,' MCMAP? That shit's tough, and people get hurt, sir." She handed me back the list.

"Leave the field and vehicles to me. You can have the fat-bodies and the PT. I've got the MCMAP program too, but I need instructors." I waved the paper at her. "If we can do these five things, we'll be successful. The rest—rifle ranges, licensing drivers, and all that other stuff—is routine."

"Okay, sir. I'll start working on it."

At zero-seven a week later, I arrived at my office. Just as I sat down behind my desk, I heard shouting from the room next door.

"You cunts! You think shacking up in the barracks and getting your brains fucked out is going to get you anywhere? The only thing you'll get is nobody else that ever wants to fuck 'em back in. Half the bitches in this battery are non-deployable because they're knocked up. You cunt-whores! Get the fuck out of my office! And don't let me catch you getting fucked again!"

It was First Sergeant Fontaine.

The hatch of her office opened, and the light shuffle of females in combat boots scurried away. Fontaine appeared at my hatch, red-faced, her muscular hands on her ample hips, black hair pulled back in a doughnut-shaped knot tight enough to double as a face-lift. Her light brown eyes beamed.

"What was all that about?" I asked.

"Sir, I came at 0530 and walked through the barracks. No shit, I found those females in the NCO rooms getting fucked and put a stop to that shit, just like that!" She snapped her fingers in the air and grinned broadly, crow's feet forming in the corners of her eyes. "How'd ya like that, sir?"

I stared blankly, her choice words leaving me somewhat bewildered. There was something erotic in her demeanor, particularly the finger snapping and the sheer pleasure evident in her facial expression and body language. It was as if she'd consumed the pending sexual climax herself, seizing for her own body all the excitement and pleasure by simply bringing the act to an abrupt end: she had affirmed her power.

"Is there a regulation against that?" I asked.

"Well…not specifically, but two of them are lance corporals, and they were in the rack with corporals. *Fraternization* would be the specific charge, if we were going to charge them. The other one we can't do much about; she's a corporal, too—it's just bad for morale."

"What about the males?"

"They left before the females came in. Same treatment."

I took a sip out of a quart-sized Mason jar I'd pulled a sock over and filled with tea.

"Sir, what the fuck is that?" she asked.

"My thermos."

"You drink coffee out of that?"

I reached for the Mason jar and drank. "No. It's tea."

"Tea? What kind of shit is that, sir?"

"I'm a tea drinker."

She stared at my thermos a moment before continuing. "I found you some MCMAP instructors, even one who can *make* instructors. The kind with the black belt and red tab."

"An instructor trainer? Have him come see me."

"Aye, aye, sir. But the motor stables…."

"What about them?"

"Each section does motor stable on a different day."

"They don't now. You pick a day, any day, I don't care. All hands, including me will be in the motor pool on that day—every week. If we don't get the vehicles in shape, we can't go to the field."

"Roger, sir."

I sat thinking about First Sergeant Fontaine and drinking from the jar. My first impression was that she was more than I'd hoped for in a right-hand man.

⌘

In front of the barracks in a large pit ringed with sand-bags, we began our Marine Corps Martial Arts classes. The young Marines relished learning hand-to-hand combat; morale increased immediately.

Since I already had both a tan and a gray belt, I was able to test for my green belt a few weeks after training started.

Each Wednesday I attended a staff meeting at the Regimental Headquarters building, located a stone's throw from my office. A recurring topic was the casualty reports from Iraq; as the summer wore on, the pace at which Marines were killed and wounded in the Anbar Province accelerated.

I started training for my brown belt and instructor qualification the first week of August.

Even for a Marine, the MCMAP instructor trainer, a twenty-eight-year-old staff sergeant, stood out for his physical condition, the result of leading Marines in hundreds of calisthenics each day for months on end.

"Sir, how old are you?" he asked on the first day of class.

"Forty."

He grimaced. "Well, you have us all by ten years and some by twenty. Just don't have a heart attack on me."

There were ten of us in the course. Commencing at 1300 each day, we started with calisthenics, alternating sets of four-count jumping jacks and pushups, knee bends until our thighs burned, two-minute plank sessions, torso twists until we were dizzy, and leg lifts I quit counting at eighty. After thirty minutes of that, we split into two teams of five, hoisted five-hundred-pound sections of telephone pole on our shoulders and raced each other in a series of hundred-yard sprints. At the hour mark, we took a water break and switched to Marine Corps Martial Arts techniques—kicks, strikes, ground-fighting maneuvers, throws, and punches—repeated over and over until muscle memory set in. After another break, we learned new moves and practiced them on each other. Finally, worn down to half strength, we competed in ground fighting, boxing, pugil sticks, knife fighting, weapons retention, and using our rifles as cudgels. We knocked off about 1700, always exhausted.

The Marines beat me in nearly every ground fight I fought.

For the first week I was so sore I struggled up the two flights of stairs to my house. I couldn't even paint.

If the thermometer ever dropped below black-flag conditions, ninety-degrees Fahrenheit, I don't remember.

⌘

The instructor trainer blew the whistle and waved his hands, stopping the fight.

I stepped back, wiped the sweat from my face with my gloved hand, and spat my mouth guard into the other.

"Damn, sir, you nearly knocked him out, even after that beating he gave you." He looked at my opponent and asked, "Marine, you okay?"

"Yeah, I'm okay," he answered. "I saw stars."

I shrugged. "I got lucky."

I fought another Marine. This young man was quicker than me. He struck me repeatedly in the face. Even though I saw stars, the blows didn't have the intended effect. We kept fighting. I glanced a lead hand punch off the side of his head, causing him to drop his guard for an instant; a rear hand punch to the middle of his forehead drove him back. He stumbled and dropped to his knees.

The instructor trainer stopped the fight. The next day I sparred again.

My opponent pounded me hard until I hit his ribcage with a forward elbow strike, knocking him off balance. I followed with an uppercut that almost knocked his headgear off.

The instructor stopped the fight. "Shit, sir," he giggled while steadying the Marine. "You can't ground fight worth a damn, but you sure can take a beating and come through in a stand-up fight."

⌘

Near the end of the course, we skipped calisthenics and went straight to a ground-fighting exercise. Ten of us sat in a circle facing one Marine in the center. When the instructor barked "Go!" the Marine in the center fought each of the other Marines for two minutes until he'd fought all ten. After that, another Marine rotated to the center spot, and the drill started over again. I was the last Marine to take the center. Finishing my spell, I couldn't walk out—I crawled.

As I sat recovering, I spotted Major Jeff Scofield, the regimental logistics officer and the senior major in the regiment, standing near the headquarters building, watching us. Nearly the same age as me, Jeff could still run three miles in just over sixteen minutes and was humble about it. Those of us close to him called him "Skeeter" due to his sleek build, pointed nose, and bowed legs. He stood with his arms folded, waiting. After a few minutes, I excused myself and walked towards him.

"What's up, Skeeter?" I asked, leaning over, resting my palms on my knees, sweat dripping off my forehead.

"Clay, I found something for you," he said.

"Found something?" I looked up at him. "You mean like pussy? No thanks, I've got enough."

"That young stuff's beating you down, eh?" he laughed. "No. Second Recon needs a combat-arms lieutenant colonel. They're willing to take a major."

Taking a moment to process what he was offering, I stood erect, placed my hands behind my head, and arched my back. "Doing what?"

"Advising an Iraqi infantry battalion. You'll be the officer in charge of ten Marines on a MiTT—a Military Transition Team. You will train and fight alongside the Iraqis. And—"

"I'll take it."

There *it* was. I breathed deeply and looked around at the practice field. The other Marines were now gathering the martial arts gear into mesh laundry bags, the training over for the day. I wiped the sweat from my forehead and the back of my neck, contemplating the implications of Jeff's words. "What about Colonel Haverty? He gave me this job."

"He's in D.C. on a promotion board."

"The XO?"

"He's on leave. I'm running the regiment."

I nodded. "When does Recon need an answer?"

"I told them you were their man. I knew you'd say yes."

"Thanks," I said. "I was afraid I'd get stuck in a staff slot."

"I know. That's why you're out here trying to kill yourself. You're perfect for the job. It requires a combat-arms officer, and you've had two battery commands. Plus, you've been an instructor before."

"When do I leave?"

"Between January and March."

"When do I transfer over to Second Recon to start the work-up?"

Jeff shook his head. "Don't know. Likely September or October. Your team will need time to train for the mission."

I offered him my hand. "Sounds good. Can't thank you enough for watching out for me."

"Not a problem," he said, shaking my hand.

As he walked away I called, "Jeff, call Second Recon and tell them that I'm in. Don't let them give it to somebody else."

He faced me and grinned for an instant, then dropped any semblance of fraternal congeniality. "Don't worry, Clay. Nobody wants the MiTT job—it's dirty in a messy way—you'll probably get yourself killed or wounded. Good luck."

CHAPTER 13

I sat staring at the painting and sipping Wild Turkey.

Emptying the teacup with a gulp, I stood up, stepped back, and lit a cigar. Looking at the painting again, I pulled the stretched canvas from atop the cinderblocks, where it leaned against the wall, and tossed it to the floor. I splashed turpentine across it and rubbed away the image with a rag. Taking a tube of black paint in hand, I squeezed a thick strip onto the palette, smeared my seventy-nine-cent Home Depot brush in it, and began roughing in shapes.

I worked another half hour. Still not satisfied, I scrubbed out the lines and started again. Failing a third time to achieve a composition that fit the canvas, I stopped, left the room with the cigar and booze, and walked outside onto the porch.

It was nearly two in the morning and cool for September. A dense fog crawling up from the Cape Fear River hung in the air and dripped from the Spanish moss that clung to willow oaks lining the streets.

Smoking the cigar and sipping bourbon, I listened to the occasional horn of boat traffic on the river, less than a quarter mile south.

A breeze blew in, shifting the fog and carrying the coastal Carolina fragrance—the mild rot of swamp and saltwater estuary mud.

I let the frustration of failure wash away from me and went back into the studio. This time I started with red.

It didn't work. Failure number four.

If you can't make it good, make it red. If you still can't make it good, make it big and red.

It was the one thing I took away from the professor who taught the painting class in the Masters of Fine Arts program at the George Washington University. It's likely he stole it from Rothko. I failed the course because I quit bringing my paintings to the group critiques. In fact, I quit attending the critiques at all, simply because the jargon about intention and process made me laugh. It still does.

I sat in the studio staring at the canvas, smoking and sipping the whiskey, taking in the distant sounds from the river and letting my thoughts wander to other milestones in my life as an artist.

When I was a kid, I did a drawing of a log cabin with a bearskin stretched across the door. Near the cabin, I penciled in an axe buried in a tree stump and a stone water well. I carefully rendered wisps of smoke rising from the cabin's chimney. My teacher chose the drawing as the best in the class and hung it in the school hallway with the other classes' award winners. No other kid in the school didn't know I drew it. At the end of the year awards assembly in the gymnasium, the principal gave me a blue ribbon for best fifth-grade drawing.

After that, I told people I was an artist.

A series of drawings and paintings, done in the style of my mother, won me an art scholarship for college. I dropped art and chose biology after my first year. I didn't paint or

draw for four years but returned to it a few days after gradu-
ating magna cum laude.

Then, there was my first show—at Meyerstone's place.
The gallery crowd milled about the warmly lit downtown
space, drinking wine and sampling the hors d'oeuvres.
Few looked at my work or asked me questions. Somehow,
Meyerstone found it appropriate to introduce me to the
audience as one of her *bargain artists.* Since I had already
drunk a bottle of wine and was selling my work for fifty times
more than my mother had ever fetched, I didn't care. John,
however, was appalled, and the girl I'd brought along was
livid. I spent the rest of my time at the opening chatting with
John and charming the girl out of confronting Barbara.

I chuckled at the memories, picked up the cheap brush,
churned it into the green paint on one of the ceramic plates I
used for a pallet and then into the canvas.

Something happened around 0330 that morning.

The lines, the rhythm of the image, and the shape of the
canvas coalesced. I felt the lift and moved quickly to consolidate the gain. Rapidly squeezing paint from the tubes—
more green, orange, black, and two types of red—mixing
in the Japanese dryer, turpentine, and linseed oil to stretch
the pigment and ensure that it would be tacky dry the next
night, I filled the shapes on the canvas with color. The whole
production took less than an hour once I found the psychic
sweet spot.

I stood back when it was done and looked. I'd make small
adjustments in the morning—otherwise, it was finished.

After a minute I turned off the light and switched on
my Swiss-manufactured storm radio. Wilmington's National
Public Radio station was broadcasting the BBC. I lifted the

window and relit my cigar, the outline of the painting glowing dimly in the ambient light from outside.

A fresh breeze pushed in, mixing with turpentine fumes and smoke. I breathed in the aroma, dragged on my cigar, and felt euphoric.

The words of a British radio announcer grabbed my attention: *"We'll take you now to Iraq to hear the latest progress of the American effort in the Anbar Province. Robert, describe the environment for us...."*

I took the radio to the living room, lay on the sofa, and listened to the broadcast.

> *"Clive, I'm here at the Government Center in Ramadi, Provincial Capital of Anbar Province, with U.S. Marines from Twenty-Nine Palms, California. The U.S. military's plan to pacify Iraq has run into trouble right here in Anbar, where it urgently needs to succeed. This province, its vast desert badlands stretching west from here to the Syrian border, remains the center of the country's deadly insurgency.*
>
> *From all accounts, it's been like this right here in Ramadi since last year when U.S. forces captured Fallujah. Here in the heat and dust, Marines conduct patrols and battle daily with insurgents. A day doesn't go by without firefights, deadly IED explosions, and ambushes. The fighting, Clive, goes on day and night. I've been here three days—the entire time the sound of gunfire in the background. Yesterday, two young Marines were killed when their vehicle hit an IED not 200 meters from the building I'm in now.*

For these Marines, there seems to be no end in sight..."

When the reporter finished, I turned off the radio and lay in the dark, imagining the scene the reporter described and wondering what was in store for me.

Sometime around dawn, the foghorns on the river hummed me to sleep.

CHAPTER 14

I hadn't received orders to Second Recon yet, but I'd been assured I wasn't forgotten. At zero-seven on a Thursday in September, I tested for my brown-belt instructor qualification and passed. That afternoon, the regimental executive officer called me to the front of formation—rows of Marines standing at attention—shook my hand and handed me a red vinyl folder embossed in gold with the Eagle, Globe, and Anchor. Enclosed was a Marine Corps Martial Arts Instructor certificate.

The next day I got into my car and drove to Arlington. I didn't call Kate before leaving.

I made the drive in five hours flat and checked into the Key Bridge Marriott in Rosslyn. Standing in front of the window and looking over the city, I called Sam. He answered, but from Montana where he was fishing with wounded troops. We agreed to meet at Christmas.

Then I called John and arranged to meet him.

It was after 1800 when I called Kate. She didn't answer, so I left a message. "Sweetheart, it's Clay. I've got a surprise for you. Call me."

She called back twenty minutes later. I was in the bathtub. *"Clay?"*

"It's me."

"Where are you? You sound funny."

"I'm in the bathtub," I said, "at the Key Bridge Marriott. Can I come and get you?"

"Yes! When?!" She banged around in her mother's kitchen, clanging cookware together, cleaning up after dinner.

"It's not all good news."

Sounding concerned, she asked, *"Is something wrong?"*

"I came home to tell you that I'm going to Iraq."

For a minute there was only silence coming from her end. She whispered, *"When?"*

"After Christmas."

"Why?" she asked, her voice cracking.

Nothing I could say could be enough. "That's just part of the deal."

"I hate when you say that." The disappointment in her voice gave way to a bit of laughter.

After the bath, I put on a white hotel robe, pulled my boots on, and slid open the glass door leading to the balcony. I stepped outside, drew a deep breath, and gazed around. The late summer sunlight cast its golden rays on the city— Georgetown University to my left, Dixie Liquor at the end of Key Bridge, the Watergate to my right, upriver the Roosevelt Bridge, and the Washington Monument beyond that. The first tinge of yellow and orange was in the tree leaves on Roosevelt Island. I lit a cigar. Five months earlier, I'd run around the island, excited for a chance to go to the war. Something dampened my mood now—an uncertainty that robbed me of any romantic anticipation I'd had back then. What if I failed at my mission? Failed paintings were one thing; failing at the mission I accepted was another. Painting?

The stakes were small. War was another matter. Failure at that was a type of death I feared.

I pulled at the cigar, imagining what lay ahead. Watching the setting sun strike the granite monuments, I realized coming home in a body bag was better than failure.

When I arrived at Kate's, I called to let her know I was outside. It was still another fifteen minutes before she stepped out of the elevator and entered the well-lit space of the glass-enclosed apartment lobby, two suitcases in tow. I got out of my car while she passed through the building exit.

"What are those?" I asked, looking down at the pink canvas bags. "My stuffs," she said, struggling with the plural form of the noun. "Your stuffs? Where are you going?"

"To North Carolina."

I broke into a fit of laughter; she looked at me, glaring, feigning defiance. We hadn't even said hello. I walked to the other side of the car where she stood and put my arm around her.

"Get in—we'll talk about it."

"I'm going!" she said with renewed spunk I didn't have the heart to extinguish.

⌘

We slept late the next day and went to breakfast at Bob and Edith's on Columbia Pike.

It's an old-school diner with a burned-out "E" in the neon sign. The cooks put butter on everything, and the waitresses still serve Lipton tea rather than the newer varieties that have come into vogue. You could even still smoke with the party crowd there—from midnight to zero-five.

We placed our orders—an omelet and potatoes for me and blueberry pancakes for her.

To little avail, I tried convincing Kate it was better for her to remain at home and stay in school. She said she'd help her mom with rent by giving her the money she had saved for tuition. As a concession, she promised to return at Christmas and begin school again in January.

"What about your job with Dalai Lama?" I asked.

"Who?"

"André de la Dumas? Andy? The Count? *De la Dumas?* The Dalai Lama?"

"Oh! I forgot. Two days ago some people came and shutted down The Hattery."

I winced. "Shut it down?"

"Taxes. They had badges."

"Where was Dumas?"

"I haven't seen him in a week. I think he knew they were coming."

"The turd burglar left you holding the bag?"

"What?" she asked, confused.

I shook my head. "Never mind. What did you do?"

"They wanted to know where Andy was, and I didn't know. They asked me to leave and put a lock on the door. I called Andy, and he said it was all a misunderstanding."

"Has anyone ever shut the place down before?"

"No. The mall people come by demanding Andy pay the rent. Andy said he would talk to the mayor about the taxes."

"He knows the mayor?"

Kate shrugged. "He says he does."

"And?"

"I think he's open for business today." She looked down at her pancakes. "He owes me money."

The next day at noon, I took Kate to see Andy. I walked around the shop, surveying the disorder, while they talked out their business.

Andy gave her the money out of the cash register.

She hugged Dumas before leaving, genuinely sad to be quitting the Hat Factory.

⌘

I picked up John on Monday, and we drove to Adams Morgan for lunch.

He was distant on the way over, and nothing I said could get him talking. Even when I turned on the radio and sang along with The Eagles' *Take it to the Limit*, he didn't scold. After we sat down I asked what had his tongue.

"You're different when you come back," he said.

"Different?"

"Your speech, your demeanor—it's aggressive, crass. It was like that last time too."

"That's the environment of the Marine Corps. The strong eat the weak. If you don't fight back, you end up bloody and at the bottom of the pecking order. It's like that twenty-four-seven."

"Don't you have friends?"

"Sure, but I don't see them much. Most are deployed."

John tinkered with his teaspoon, tapping it on the edge of his water glass.

I'd never considered the effect that being amongst Marines all the time had on me and how it was perceived by civilians. "I know what you mean," I said.

He looked up. "So you know?"

"Sure. It's a cycle I go through. I'll be back to normal eventually. We keep telling ourselves that."

John laughed, put the spoon down, and picked up his menu.

I asked him about his spring show in Brussels. He was optimistic. Either way, he explained, he was happy with his painting. I could determine how John's painting was going from his mood on a given day.

Eventually I asked, "Have you heard anything from Hutchinson?"

"You haven't spoken to her?" he asked incredulously.

"I've been busy."

"She's putting your work in a group showing next spring."

I cocked my middle finger against my thumb and released it upside the menu. "Well, that's something," I said. "I'm having a show in November down in Wilmington."

John arched his eyebrows.

"Wilmington is a small town. I doubt my stuff will go over well there, but I met a guy who likes my work. I've worked fifteen pieces for him."

"That many?"

"What else do you think I do while I'm in North Carolina? I come home from work and paint."

"No late-night carousing?" he asked sarcastically.

"Mmmm, that's changed a bit."

He scowled. "It's about time."

"It's not my age," I replied with a head shake and a grin. "Don't get me wrong, I love driving home after an all-nighter in my ole ninety-one, as the stars fade and dawn cracks a smile. It's Kate."

"Well, good for her."

"No, good for *me*."

⌘

Sitting on an ammo crate next to my Humvee, I penned Mr. Nicholson a thank-you note. Above me, the coastal Carolina sun beat through pine trees that cover Camp Lejeune with a coniferous blanket. First Sergeant Fontaine called my name; she stomped towards me, her face flushed red with anger. I stifled an urge to grin and put down my pen and paper.

"What is it, First Sergeant?" I added teasingly, "It must be a hell of a sight."

"Corporal Harder told the Motor-T chief to kiss his ass. Son of a bitch. We should have sent him to the colonel the last time he did this."

"Bring him to me," I said, all humor drained from my voice.

"It's that fucking Lance Corporal Graves too. He was supposed to pick up chow an hour ago. I found him back at the Motor-T section playing spades with—"

"Bring them both to me."

She stared at me impatiently. "What are you going to do, sir?"

"Send them to Iraq," I fired back, catching her off guard.

"Sir, what the fuck? Those two? They'll pull the same shit there."

I raised my hand, motioning her to stop. "They act the way they do because they hate it here."

"Sir, are you sure that's their fucking problem?"

"Have you ever seen one of those Marines fall out when we run the battery?"

"No, sir."

"In martial arts class, Harder beat me in ground fighting—twice. He qualified with me as brown belt. The only reason he's not an instructor is because he's only a corporal. And Lance Corporal Graves—"

"Sir, he gets out of the Marine Corps in seven months."

"I bet he'll extend. They're young men—they didn't join the Marine Corps to stay in the rear with pregnant females, malingerers, and their handlers, while a war unfolds on the other side of the world. Go get them."

When she stormed away, I reached into my cargo pocket, pulled out my cell phone, and called back to the regiment for the division personnel officer's phone number.

It took the first sergeant fifteen minutes to corral both Marines and put them at attention in front of me.

I looked up at the corporal. "Harder, what's your problem?"

"Sir?"

"Do you want to go to Iraq?"

He was less prepared than First Sergeant Fontaine had been. "Sir. What? With all due respect, I been asking to go for—"

I cut him off. "Graves? Where's the chow?"

"Sir, I thought—"

"Yeah, and Andy thought shit was candy," I said.

Graves looked confused. "Sir?"

"Never mind. Do you want to go to Iraq?"

"Sir, yes, but—"

"You get out in seven months, correct?"

"Sir, I do."

"Would you extend to go?"

The Marine started to grin, revealing his gold front tooth. "In a heartbeat, sir."

"Hold on," I said, dialing in the phone number and waiting while it rang.

"Division Personnel Officer."

"Chief Warrant Officer, it's Major Steerforth."

I eyeballed the two Marines as I spoke. Both could barely contain their delight, but they kept their bearing. Punishment for petty infractions they knew how to deal with; they didn't care anymore. Being kept out of the war was different—*that* was demoralizing, emasculating to these Marines. Both men had come to my attention when I saw their names on the list of Marines who repeatedly volunteered to deploy. When I inquired about them, nobody could tell me why they'd never been chosen by their section chiefs to be released for combat duty. I suspected it would eventually come to this; we were kindred spirits.

"That's correct," I said into the phone, noticing the two Marines taking on a renewed sense of pride as I talked. "One is a motor transport mechanic, and the other one is a heavy equipment operator…. Yes, licensed to drive a tow truck…. Roger, both volunteered to go…. No, not a problem. They're packing their gear as we speak…. First Sergeant Fontaine will deliver them to you tomorrow by 1300."

I hung up, looked at the two Marines standing at attention, and commanded, "Pack your shit."

⌘

Kate loved the ocean. We spent Saturdays driving out to Carolina Beach, picnicking from a basket she bought in a secondhand shop in downtown Wilmington. Even though the air was cool, the Gulf Stream hugged close to shore, keeping the water warm. The first time I tried to teach Kate how to swim, the surf stripped her bikini clean off. She stayed in the water while I got a towel to cover her up.

We cooked at home, and I spent the evenings painting. A hurricane blew through, and we rode it out at the house.

There was still no word on when I should report to Second Recon.

I stopped by the unit and introduced myself to the commanding officer. He told me I had first choice of any gear available. He didn't know where I was going once I arrived in country.

November came.

One day I came back from a six-mile run and sat down in my office wearing my PT gear.

The phone rang. It was the regimental XO. "Sir?" I answered.

"Clay, report to Second Recon on 1 December."

I dropped my feet off the desk. "Any word on the other Marines on my team?"

"Nada."

"Did they mention when we would deploy?"

"Second Recon thinks mid-January."

"That's six weeks' prep time. Really, just four—can't get anything done at Christmas."

"Not much time," said the XO.

"Anything else?"

"Nope. Mentioned something about Ramadi. Your replacement is inbound. He checks aboard next week."

⌘

I helped the gallery in Wilmington hang the show. The owner promoted it in the local press. Opening night, I got drunk for the first time in nearly five months. I heard one woman comment to her husband, "I don't get it. It looks like pants to me. If it's about the Trojan War, why doesn't he just paint a picture of Helen seducing Mark Anthony?"

My replacement, a captain, came directly from Tbilisi where he'd been training Georgian forces. After I gave him a rundown of the situation, we executed a change of command; this time I was on the opposite end.

On the last day of November, I went to see Colonel Haverty in his office at the Second Division Headquarters and briefed him on the past six months.

"How did you like commanding Headquarters Battery, Clay?"

"I did what I set out to do."

"Good," he said. "You qualified as a brown-belt instructor?"

"I did."

"What was that like?"

I laughed. "The hardest thing I've ever done in the Marine Corps."

The same day, I stopped by the Headquarters Battery office. While I answered the new captain's questions about recent courts-martial cases, I heard, "You fat fuck! Look at you. Pull your T-shirt up! How can you stand yourself? You're twelve pounds over the standard. You miss the fat-body run again, and your fat ass will be seeing the captain for office hours. You fat fucking chowhound, I better not catch you eating anything but tuna fish—and no fucking mayonnaise. Get the fuck out of my office. You disgust me, you fat pig."

It was Fontaine.

"Is she always like that?" the captain asked me.

"You'll get used to it," I said. I reached out and shook his hand. "See you next September."

⌘

I met my team on the first day of December, five officers and five enlisted men. I made the eleventh. The same day, the Second Recon Battalion commanding officer confirmed for me we were going to Ramadi. We received our combat gear and spent the next three weeks at Camp Lejeune ranges, firing our weapons, driving Humvees, and practicing close-order battle drills at Combat Town, a small village built to practice urban combat.

I drove Kate back to Arlington two days before Christmas, checked into the Marriott, and had dinner with Sam and John. Sam handed me another draft of my catalog. John didn't like the finish on the cover. I winked at Sam. When John went to the head, I told Sam that if the matte finish was good enough for Marca-Relli, it was good enough for me.

On Christmas Day, Kate and I drove to the Alexandria waterfront, drank a jar of tea, and watched the cold Potomac flow by. She cried as I drove away to Wilmington.

I packed my gear the night before I left for Camp Pendleton, California, to link up with First Marine Division. The last item I put into my rucksack was my hard copy of the *Iliad*, Robert Fagles's translation. After that, I called my mother. We talked about her classes, and I told her about the Hutchinson Collection and the show in Wilmington.

When I told her I was going to Iraq, I lied and said I had a job on base—away from any fighting.

She was silent for a long while in phone time. I imagined her dressed in her nightgown, sitting on the edge of her bed with the lamp on and talking to me on the old, square, beige press- button desk phone she kept on the nightstand next to her worn note-laden Bible.

Finally she said, *"I was afraid you would go. I'll be praying for you, Clare."*

CHAPTER 15

The First Marine Division commander, a tall Marine with iron-gray hair and a physique that looked as if he had just climbed down from a recruiting poster, met and welcomed us when we got out of the vans that drove us from LAX to Camp Pendleton. Referring to his unit's symbol, he told us we were now part of the Blue Diamond family.

We received more gear, including an extra pair of boots, beefed-up first-aid kits, extra cold weather gear, and SAPI plates for our protective vests. I had never seen the body armor before and was surprised by its heaviness.

After four more days of briefs on Iraq, we went to a firing range and, along with our M4 carbines, fired AK-47s. I found it to be a good weapon with a sound distinctly different from its American counterpart.

Little of the final days in CONUS stuck in my mind afterwards. It was a haphazard affair, and no one, including me, had a real understanding of what it took to prepare for the mission we were about undertake. It was still the early years of what we'd eventually term "The Long War," and the Marine Corps was just grasping how much the battlefields of Iraq and Afghanistan would spread us thin and necessitate changes in tactics, techniques, and procedures not experienced since our days fighting the Banana Wars.

Finally, we were off again, this time in USMC white buses bound for Nellis Air Force Base, where eighty of us piled into an Air Force C-17 and flew to Iraq.

⌘

We touched down at Baghdad International—formerly the Saddam Hussein Airport—on a chilly overcast day. Across the tarmac, the eleven of us lugged our gear towards a bus hired to carry us to our staging area, Camp Victory. We were elated to have finally arrived in-country.

Our assigned residence was a Bedouin-type transient tent with coal-burning stoves, cots, and space for forty. We were the only occupants. The sun never shined while we were there, and nobody bothered us with more briefings.

Biding the time, most of the Marines on my team watched movies on their laptop computers—comedies mostly. I played chess with Captain Leo Essex, a Marine from my own regiment at Camp Lejeune, and now my operations officer. He smoked cigars. Like me, Leo was eager to get to the business of training and fighting alongside the Iraqis.

Even at Camp Victory it was difficult to get unfiltered news of the war; rumors abounded.

One afternoon I trudged through the mud and drizzle to get a haircut in a barbershop, a trailer packed with U.S. servicemen and a few Brits. I took a number and sat down beside a sergeant from the 101st Air Assault. He sat staring straight ahead, holding his scoped M14 between his legs, muzzle up.

Without turning to me, he said, "Sir, you headed in or out?"

"In," I answered.

"Where to?"

I stared at the man's profile. "Ramadi." Besides the six weeks' worth of uncut hair, sweat and grease had stained the soldier's collar black. Not a hair on his head was gray; razor stubble showed only above his lip and on his chin. He was, maybe, twenty-one.

Talking through the wad of tobacco stuffed in his cheek, he said, "Just came from there.

Hate to tell you this, but you're fucked."

"Yeah?"

"I was here in '03 during the drive to Baghdad—a cake walk compared to what Ramadi is right now. I've been there since last August."

"Doing what?"

"Killing people, mostly," he said and spat into a plastic water bottle wrapped with olive-drab duct tape. When he lifted the spittoon, I saw his fingernails were yellow, except where he had chewed or torn them back. There, blackness had settled into the crevices. "They're dug in like rats, especially around the train station. Every time we flatten the place, they come out and fight some more. They even blew up a fucking tank."

I knew from reports the insurgents were rigging 152mm Russian-manufactured artillery shells as IEDs.

"How'd they manage that?"

"Fifty-gallon acetylene tank buried in the road." He bent his head to the side and raised his shoulder to scratch his ear. "The crew escaped, but when the tank retriever came in, the shit really hit the fan. The fuckers killed two of us. When the quick reaction force showed up, they killed four of them."

"I'm relieving a MiTT team there."

"Then ya'll are really fucked. The Iraqis suck."

"That bad?"

"As soldiers? No. I've worked with them. They just don't have anything except rifles and helmets—no Humvees, no grenade launchers, no mortars. Nothing. Best thing I can say for them is they die well."

"What brings you here to Camp Victory?"

The soldier turned to face me. Because his hair and eyebrows were nearly black, the blueness of his eyes caught me off guard. "I'm escorting the body of one of our dudes."

"Sorry," I said, catching the man's eye.

"Number eighty-five!" announced a barber in a thick Pakistani accent.

Getting up to take his seat in the barber's chair, plastic spittoon and rifle in hand, the sergeant said, "Thanks, sir. Good luck."

With a fresh haircut, I walked back to the tent and poked my head inside. I didn't see Leo, but Master Sergeant Bruce, the senior enlisted soldier on my team, was sitting on a cot putting his combat gear together.

"Top, you seen Captain Essex?" I asked.

"He went to chow about forty-five minutes ago. Can I help you, sir?"

"No, I'll be out here having a smoke. If he comes through the back flap, tell him I'd like to speak to him."

I had just lit my cigar when Leo emerged from the tent. "Sir, are you looking for me?"

"You got a second?"

I walked away from the tent. Leo followed. When we were out of earshot, I asked, "How's everybody doing?"

"Fine, sir. Why?"

"Just wondering. Any word about Ramadi?"

"Nobody knows anything about it. You?"

"I spoke to a sergeant from the Hundred-'n'-First escorting a dead soldier home. He says the fight there is pretty stiff."

"Hmm," Leo pondered. "Staff Sergeant Craig told me the adjutant from one of the battalions in the regiment lost his legs in Ramadi back in December. Apparently, he was in a seven-ton on Route Michigan and got hit with a recoilless rifle—killed the driver instantly."

From Camp Victory, we flew to Camp Taji to receive five days of briefs and training for advising Iraqi soldiers. It was our last stop en route to Ramadi. Marines were waiting for us when the bird touched down. One of them was Major Pete Lucas, a Marine I had served with years earlier. He was part of the training cadre at Camp Taji. He escorted me and the Marines on my team to our temporary quarters and then invited me for coffee at the chow hall.

After dropping everything except my rifle and pistol and digging my soft cover out of my cargo pocket, I left with Pete, fitting the cover on as I walked out of the wood-framed barracks. On the way, we passed an Army colonel. I saluted him; he didn't return the gesture.

"This is a no-salute area," said Pete.

The chow hall was a heated tent large enough to fit two hundred troops. Ten or fifteen soldiers and Marines sat watching the televisions installed along the sides.

Pete pressed the spigot on a vat and drained coffee into a Styrofoam cup. "When did I last see you, Steerforth?"

Preparing tea for myself, I thought a second. "Quantico. The summer of '92, I think. We trained Naval Academy midshipmen together."

"Not since then?"

"Maybe at the Amphibious Warfare School in '99."

"Right. Yeah, that's it. You hung out in D.C. a lot." I shrugged. "Likely."

We stepped away from the beverage vats and stood in the middle of the tent under a set of fluorescent lights.

"How'd you draw this gig?" he asked.

"I dodged all the staff jobs and jumped on this when it came along."

"Where you headed?"

"Ramadi."

"You must be replacing the team working with Third Battalion, Second Brigade, First Division—Three-Two-One."

"Not sure."

Pete sipped his coffee. "Who you got on your team?"

"The senior Marine after me is Captain Leo Essex. He's an artilleryman like me.

Volunteered for the job to get away from staff work. My senior enlisted man is a master sergeant, Master Sergeant Bruce—"

"A little short guy with a big black mustache?"

"That's him," I laughed.

"He's a good Marine."

"I've got four lieutenants, two of them are second lieutenants." Pete winked at me. "Brand new?"

"One of them has combat experience—a month or so."

"Well, a month's a month. Any other combat vets?"

"My doc. Nobody else."

"Hmm," Pete mused.

"I've got a gunny, he's a logistics type. He's teamed with my logistics lieutenant, Lieutenant O'Shannihan, who's also an artilleryman."

"Lots of arty types on these teams."

"Yeah, the war's an infantry fight, which leaves us with not much else to do. Anyways, I've got a Sergeant Ski—he's my intelligence Marine. He works with Lieutenant Lott, a trained intel officer. I've got Doc Binder, one of the combat vets, and another lieutenant—Webb. Webb's an Amtracker. And then, I've got a staff sergeant; forward observer type. Kind of odd actually, our regiment simply dumped him—he's got a DUI."

"Oh shit. Really?"

"Yeah, he's a little odd. We had four weeks to get ready and—"

Pete shook his head. "Only four weeks? You're supposed to have four months."

"That's all the time we had."

"That's fucked up."

"Maybe, but this staff sergeant—Craig is his name—he's got the shakes."

"The shakes?" Pete asked.

I held out my hand, palm down, and wiggled it, fingers spread. "Yeah, I noticed it the first time I spoke to him, the same time I found out about the DUI. We were getting licensed to drive Humvees, and he said, 'Sir, I'm really sorry to tell you, but I can't drive a Humvee.' I asked him why not, and he told me he recently got a DUI. I told him that *I* wouldn't be pulling him over in Iraq asking for his license, and I didn't think anyone else would either, so who cares?"

Pete laughed. "Look, Steerforth, it's good you see things like that. Some wouldn't. It sounds like you've got a green crew, but you'll get past that. Most of the teams I see headed out to train the Iraqis are just sort of patchwork—Marines nobody else wanted."

"I think I'm about half and half. Some wanted to be here, some just ended up on the team." I sipped the tea. "They're my Marines though."

"Keep your team tight, Steerforth. Focus on training the Iraqis to take over the fight from us. Don't make the mistake of focusing on getting equipment for them. The Iraqi logistics chain is slow to nonexistent. In the meantime, they need basic infantry training."

"We'll focus on that," I said, listening intently.

"And remember, some Iraqis have combat experience, fighting us and the Iranians. What they need is to develop young soldiers. Right now, the officers are the only ones making decisions."

"The Arab model?" I had some idea that this would be the case. I had listened to a lieutenant colonel talk about it back at Pendleton and had seen it firsthand in Jordan.

"Speaking of that, the worst mistake I see are teams deciding their job is stopping Arab corruption. Don't let that consume you." Pete put his cup down on the table and rested an elbow in the palm of his hand, rubbing his chin. "Another thing—some of the teams want to make the Iraqis as good as Marines, and that ain't going to happen."

"It's probably like herding midshipmen?"

"That's a little demeaning to the Iraqis who are worth a shit. But yeah, except it's another culture, they're all armed, they speak Arabic, and you're in combat with them."

"What else?" I asked.

"Remember, you are here to get *them* to fight. Don't kick the door down yourself. Train them to do it, then watch them while they give it a shot."

"Anything else?"

He stretched his lips back and rubbed under his lower lip with his index finger. "Uhhh…. Oh, yeah! Don't get caught up in the trick-or-treat syndrome."

I had no idea what he was talking about, and he could tell.

Pete grinned. "Officially, the U.S. units are supposed to be *partnered*, working side-by- side with Iraqis, just to be in the battle space. Partnering can be a pain in the ass for U.S. units engaged in combat operations."

"Is that the term being used now? Partnering?"

"Yes, but some U.S. battalions simply don't want to bother with it, regardless of what they say. But just as going trick-or-treating on Halloween when you're sixteen is *nix-nix*," Pete said, making a cutting motion at his neck with his hand, "you can get around it if you take your little brother along with you."

"I had a niece I did that with," I laughed.

"So you know the deal. Most U.S. battalions don't give a damn about actually partnering with the Iraqis, but they will come and ask to *borrow* them—that's the term they actually use. It makes their operations technically fit with the partnering guidance."

He paused, seemingly searching his mind for further advice, then abruptly asked, "You still painting?"

I finished my tea with a single swig, set the Styrofoam cup on the table, and forced out a short laugh. "Pete, how the hell do you remember that?"

"How could I forget it? That's the main thing I remember about you." He pointed at my head. "That and your long hair."

"I never quit painting, and I still think that haircut you all get scares the hell out of civilians and hides receding hairlines. We should outlaw that—it makes us look like serial killers."

"That's great—that you stuck with painting."

"That's what I was doing in D.C. so much back in '99."

"Yeah, and that summer we trained middies, you stayed shut-up in that suite you had in O'Bannon Hall painting. I used to come down and check on you."

"I recall that."

"Once I busted in, and there you were, buck-ass naked with a paint brush in your hand, standing in front of a canvas."

I looked at Pete, his skin bathed in the cold blue hue of fluorescent light. "Funny how time goes by so quickly," I said. We hadn't seen each other for years, yet we'd picked up as if we had spoken to each other a month ago. It was comforting to me.

I heard gunfire in the distance.

Pete listened for a brief second. "Back then, who would have imagined us sitting here in the middle of a war and laughing about you painting naked?"

⌘

I met my boss, Lieutenant Colonel Steeples, a squarely built F/A-18 pilot who bore a perpetual grin. He had the incoming MiTT team that advised the Iraqi brigade. I also met his boss, the division advisor, Colonel Marr. Unlike my battalion MiTT team, slated to serve seven months in the country, both colonels had teams that were scheduled to remain in Iraq for a full year. Like me, they had a cadre of ten or fifteen Marines assigned to them.

Colonel Marr's operations officer was a lieutenant colonel I immediately recognized, although I couldn't recall from where. His name was Mike Dean.

One evening I lingered in the barracks, finishing a chapter in Paul Fussell's book, *The Great War,* while my crew went to chow. As I hurried to catch up with them, I passed Dean.

He stopped me. "Steerforth, don't we know each other?"

He stood with his hands on his hips studying me. I could do little else but stare back.

Shorter than me and nearly pudgy, he was slightly pigeon-toed. His demeanor made me uncomfortable. He struck me as part of the phony-tough rather than the crazy-brave.

"Maybe, sir. I thought I recognized you."

"You're headed to Ramadi, right?"

"Yes, sir."

"What's with the hair?"

"Well, sir, I like it like this," I said. "Zero-to-three inches. It's within regulations."

"Barely. I'll tell ya, when I'm not doing this," he pointed at the Eagle, Globe, and Anchor stitched to his left breast pocket, "I practice law, and I know bullshit when I hear it."

"I'll keep it within regs, sir."

"Do that, Major."

"Yes, sir." I saluted him out of habit. "No saluting here," he said crossly.

The men who briefed us at Taji were retired black-ops types contracted through the U.S. government. They never told us what organization they worked for previously. All they said if you asked was, "I worked for a government agency." Each had operated in Iraq, Afghanistan, or Africa in the years since September 2001. To a man, these fellows believed the solution to Muhammadeans willing to fight against NATO forces was a well-aimed bullet.

Taji was split in half. One side was a U.S. Army base. Our side was the MiTT indoctrination school and Iraqi boot camp. We visited the Iraqi training facilities. I found their living conditions Spartan. They slept on thin mattresses in open squad bays with concrete floors and heated with kerosene stoves. Despite the temperature in December and January hovering in the low forties, they possessed little cold weather gear. Rumor had it, the U.S. government had delivered coats, gloves, and long underwear to the Iraqi Ministry of Defense. If it did, the Iraqi soldiers never saw it.

For sustenance, they ate flatbread, bean gruel, and rice.

THE MISSION

CHAPTER 16

A mission never goes as one foresees it. You make a plan for one-hundred percent success; if you get eighty of that, you're lucky. If you achieve sixty percent and live, you declare victory and let history and your own memory be the judge. Less than that, you spend the rest of your life explaining the failure away—or simply suffering in silence.

We flew in blackout conditions.

Hunkered down, trying to avoid the cold air rushing through the door gunner's hatch, I peered past the Marine manning the 240G, seeing the occasional light on the desert floor sail past. I shivered, pulled my scarf over my face, and waited. After twenty minutes, I spotted a mass of lights on the ground in the distance; it grew larger as we approached.

The heavy-lift helicopter touched down in an expeditionary airfield, and we rushed off, one behind the other, lugging our gear and fighting against the downdraft of the bird's rotors. A ground crew herded us through the dark, away from the helicopters.

Our transport pulled back into the air. Helicopters always sound as if they are struggling to fly—lifting off is agony.

I heard shouting above the roar.

"Drop your gear!" yelled one of the ground crew.

I glanced up to see the black hulk climbing away. As it groaned and beat its way into the cold black night, I tried to imagine being the young pilot controlling the gangly machine.

By now there were fourteen or fifteen men milling amongst my team. Somebody shouted, "Major Steerforth!"

"Right here!" I shouted; to Leo, standing next to me, I said, "That must be the other team."

A voice very near to me asked, "Where's Major Steerforth?" I raised my rifle over my head. "Here!"

A Marine wearing wire-rimmed glasses stepped in front of me. "You Steerforth?" I gripped my rifle in one hand and extended the other. "That's me."

"Damn, I'm sure glad to see you, Marine. Lieutenant Colonel Tim Augen."

"Major Clay Steerforth, sir. Nice to meet you."

"How was the ride in?" he asked.

"Okay, sir. We were boots on the ground ten days ago. I didn't think it would take so long to get here."

"No worries, Marine. We're not scheduled to fly out for two weeks. Toss your gear in the back of one of the trucks."

"Roger, sir."

"Grab your gear, this way!" barked Leo, lifting his pack. Augen's Marines were already helping my crew carry their gear to the trucks.

"Give 'em a hand, Marines!" the colonel belatedly ordered.

The colonel lifted my seabag to his shoulder and moved out. I followed.

"It's been quiet here lately," he said as he walked. "We'll get you in the rack and start rolling in the morning. We live outside the main wire at Camp Phoenix, a mile from here, right next to the gray water pond, where all the porta-shitters from Camp Ramadi get dumped."

⌘

I wasn't the first out of the rack the next morning. One of the colonel's men was on radio watch. He heated water for me while I dug my shaving kit, towel, and Mason jar from my seabag. Most of the water I used to make tea, the rest I poured into a canteen cup, which I carried outside along with my gear. I found an ammo crate nearby, put my stuff down, and sat on it.

It was a calm, cold, clear morning, just after dawn, the moon still visible.

I slung the towel around my neck, cupped steaming hot water into my hands, wet my hair, lathered my face, and then stroked my tingling skin with the razor. After each, I cleaned the razor by dipping it in the water and tinking it against the rim of the tin cup. Any Marine since WWII could have guessed what I was doing simply from hearing the sound and knowing the time of day. When I was satisfied no stubble remained, I rinsed away the soap residue and toweled dry my face and hair. Refreshed, I pulled a comb from my kit and stood up. As I ran the teeth over my scalp, pulling my hair straight back, I gazed around. There was not a tree in sight.

To my left, a dirt road, paralleled by a ten-foot security fence on top of a six-foot berm, stretched eastward towards a lone guard tower fifteen-hundred meters away. Five or six kilometers farther east, a city-sized cluster of squat buildings rose above the flat desert floor, silhouetted by a dusky pink blaze of pending sunrise.

The single-story rectangular building where I slept was built with mud bricks and was scarred in places by ordnance impacts. It brandished on its roof the telltale sign of a command post—a series of radio antennas and two flags. One, red, white, and black—the Iraqi national flag; the other, tattered, red and gold—the United States Marine Corps ensign. They hung beside each other.

Two hundred meters away from the command post were three buildings similar in construction, only larger. Barracks, I presumed.

Parked in front of the command building were five thin-skinned military vehicles of foreign manufacture, the ones that had carried us from the airfield the night before. Parked beside them were four Humvees, the side of each stenciled with a yellow palm tree and underscored with six-inch white lettering, reading "3-2-1 MiTT." With half-inch steel bolted all around, they were modified versions of the original fiberglass-covered model.

I sat back down on the ammo crate, lit a cigar, sipped tea from my jug, and looked towards the east. The soft rim of the sun edged over the city, burning away the pink hue, replacing it with an orange blaze.

A faint breezed kicked up. The flags atop the command post fluttered and snapped. The stench of fresh sewer—a bouquet of chemicals, urine, and feces—entered my nostrils.

"Welcome to Camp Phoenix," said Colonel Augen from behind me.

He was standing just outside the command post, bespectacled and dressed in a T-shirt, an olive-drab towel draped around his neck and a black hygiene bag dangling from his hand. He removed his glasses and wiped his face with the towel. "Is that breakfast?"

"Yes, sir—an Okinawan breakfast," I replied. Setting my thermos at my feet and removing the cigar from between my front teeth, I lifted myself from the ammo crate and greeted the colonel. "Morning."

He nodded my way. "What the hell is that?"

"Okinawa for second lieutenants was slim," I said. "Ya fly in, check into the unit, and you're on your own. Back in '93 and '94, there was no place to eat breakfast, so I started smoking the butt of last night's cigar instead."

Laughing, he pointed towards my feet. "Not that," he said. "*That.* Is that a Mason jar?"

I looked down at my thermos and back up at him. "Yes, sir."

"You carried that all the way from the States?"

I dragged on my cigar and blew smoke. "Deep inside my pack, socks stuffed inside, and wrapped in a poncho liner."

He pointed again, this time at my cigar. "Mujeed's a smoker too. It drives me crazy, sitting in his office while he puffs away."

"Who's Mujeed?"

Behind his glasses, the colonel's left eyeball wandered off center; the right one remained pointed at me. "He's the commanding officer of the Iraqi battalion. Been in command since they stood up at Taji."

Hearing gunfire some ways off, I turned towards the horizon at the silhouette of the town I'd noticed minutes earlier. The gunfire came from that direction.

"They're at it today," Colonel Augen said. "That's Ramadi—Third Battalion, Seventh Marines and an Army National Guard unit own it. Well, they don't really own it—they share it with the Mooj. It ebbs and flows. From the sound of it, it's flowing right now."

"The Mooj?"

"Short for mujahedeen. It doesn't make much sense; that's just what we call 'em."

"I saw the city last night as I flew in," I said. "How long has it been going on?"

"Since late '03. It shifted east for a while, but it came back here after we took Fallujah."

"Long time."

"This is ground zero for the fight in Anbar. 'Course I don't know what's going on in the rest of the country." Making a tube shape with his hand and holding it to his good eye, he said, "I see the world through a soda straw."

"Ya'll been here the whole time, sir?"

He shook his head. "We came here in October. Moved from the farmland where the fight was wide open. Here, it's a street fight, right in your face, and I'll tell you what, I've never experienced anything quite like it."

"The nightmare we've been told about since we were at The Basic School," I conjectured.

"This is it." He waved his hand towards the skyline of Ramadi. "We'll get you all out to the Government Center and go on patrol in the next few days. We operate with a company from Three-Seven that holds the government complex and the area around it. The remainder of Three-Seven, the National Guard, the Hundred-'n'-First, and a handful of other types have the rest of the town. There's SEALs out there too. The Iraqis don't have battle space of their own. The objective is to train them so they can take it from us, then we can go home for good."

"They can't handle it by themselves?" I asked.

"Oh, hell no," he replied. "Mujeed could manage; he's no bullshit, but he needs help getting his battalion ready. They only learned to fire their rifles at Taji."

"How long has Three-Seven been here?"

"Since August or September. A unit from Camp Lejeune will replace them next month."

Looking towards Ramadi, I was forced to squint at the sun now burning above the buildings. "I ran into a soldier from the Hundred-'n'-First at Camp Victory who didn't have much good to say about this place."

"Probably not."

We stood, squinting at the city and listening to the gunfire.

"It looked pretty big from the air," I said. "How many people live in Ramadi?"

"Four or five hundred thousand. It's bigger than Fallujah. That's part of the issue."

I glanced at Augen. He kept his gaze fixed to the east.

"Fallujah is contained," he explained. "It was easy to control access to it when we took it.

Ramadi's different, there's more places for the Mooj to come in from, and the Syrian border is not that far away. More places to hide too." He looked southward and pointed at a cluster of brown buildings about eight-hundred meters away. "That's a bedroom community of Ramadi. Some of the Mooj commute from there, but we never go. There's not enough of us."

"So it's bigger?"

"It's certainly bigger. And the big plan coming out of Baghdad is to have a *political* solution for Ramadi, not a kinetic one."

"I've been hearing that term. Is that the new catchword for shooting back at the enemy when he shoots at you?"

"Yeah. That's what we call it, and believe me, it's kinetic out there. I don't know what the political solution could be."

"No. Can't tell what the Trojan horse would be in this case, either," I said, pondering out loud the magnitude of my pending task. "Maybe we'll see."

Augen folded his arms across his chest and shook his head. "You may or you may not.

The plan is to move Mujeed and the battalion to Fallujah and reunite them with their brigade. We don't hear much from higher headquarters here. But if Mujeed and his dudes go—you go."

"When?"

"Don't know. We were supposed to move in November."

I took one last drag from my cigar and flicked the butt towards the Port-a-John that stood ten meters away. It hit the ground, bounced forward a few times, collided with the shitter, and came to rest—still smoldering.

The colonel laughed. "Mujeed does the same thing with his cigarette butts."

"Is he inside now?"

Augen shook his head. "He's in Baghdad. He'll be back at the end of the week. A third of the battalion is always on leave, a pain in the ass for us. The day before Thanksgiving, we lost twenty-three *jundi* when the leave convoy hit an IED not far from here." All expression vanished from his face. "We helped recover the bodies, and we moved the wrecks—body parts fucking everywhere."

The colonel stared blankly at the horizon. He reached his right hand behind his head and scratched his left ear, then dropped the arm to his side. "Let me get a shave, and then we'll go meet Zuhair, the battalion executive officer. After that, we'll take one of those Russian jeeps, and I'll show you Camp Ramadi." Pointing down the road towards the guard shack, he said, "It's over there. Houses about three-thousand soldiers." A grin stretched across his face. "Damn, Marine, I'm sure as shit glad you're here."

⌘

"Nick!" the colonel yelled when we entered the command post.

We walked down a dirt-floored hallway crowded with Marines from the two teams and flanked on each side by five or six rooms used by the colonel's team as sleeping quarters and office spaces. My own men stood around chatting idly while the colonel's crew moved with the purposed cadence of routine business.

"Nicky Boy!" he laughed. "Nick's your interpreter. He hates when I call him Nicky.

When we got here, we called him "Nick the New Guy" because he was so young—right out of the package. Pretty soon it became Nicky. Then one day he found out that Nicky could refer to a woman, so he refused to answer to it. So now it's just Nick. Nick!"

A thin young man, a boy really, about my height stepped out from one of the rooms. His pristine face, bronze and likely never touched by a razor, was bisected by a long, narrow nose. He was equipped the same as everybody else with Marine Corps digital desert-patterned trousers, a standard-issue green T-shirt, and standard-issue tan suede boots. Topping it all off was a 9mm U.S. military Beretta pistol stuffed down the front of his trousers, the handgrip visible above his belt.

He stretched his arms back, yawned, and replied, "Suh?"

"Sleep well, Nick?" the colonel asked.

"Suh, I did," he said, walking towards us.

The colonel placed his hand on the young man's shoulder. "Nick, this is Major Steerforth. Clay, this is Nick, the best interpreter in Anbar Province."

The young man smiled, and we shook hands. "Nice to meet you, suh. I'm Nick—*Nick*," he repeated, still grinning. His teeth beamed like a toothpaste advertisement.

"I'm Major Steerforth. Nice to meet you, Nick."

The colonel gripped Nick's shoulder, shook the man slightly. "Not only is he doing great things here, someday Nick's going to be a dentist just like his dad. We're just a stop along the way."

Nick grinned again.

"Nick, go see if Major Zuhair is in," commanded Colonel Augen.

After the young man walked away, Leo approached me. "Sir, the Marines need to shave and square their gear away. Do you need them this morning?"

"Yeah." I looked at my watch. "It's zero-eight now. How about ten-hundred out front by the Humvees?"

"Suh." Nick appeared at the end of the passageway. "Major Zuhair is in."

⌘

Colonel Augen and I sat in white plastic deck chairs across a dusty plywood desk from a clean-shaven Iraqi officer. His face was marred with acne scars, his black hair combed neatly back, accentuating a receding hairline. On each shoulder board of his neatly pressed, U.S.-issued, desert leaf-pattern camouflage utilities was a single royal crown insignia indicating his rank. A miniature Iraqi flag was sewn on his upper right shoulder. When he raised his hand to drag on a cigarette, backwards—holding the filter between his thumb and ring finger, the ash pointed away from his hand so that when he took a drag, his palm nearly touched his chin—I noticed he was missing the index and middle finger on his right hand.

A large fan in the corner churned the smoke around the room.

Nick introduced us and explained to me that tea was being prepared.

"You'll have to get used to drinking tea," Colonel Augen commented quietly without looking my way.

"I'm a tea drinker," I said. "That's what was in that jar."

"Tea with lots of sugar in it."

"Of course. I worked with Jordanians back in '95."

A pot-bellied man around sixty years old and wearing a filthy white T-shirt and a pair of nineties-era, U.S.-issue, chocolate-chip-patterned trousers entered the room. Instead of combat boots, he was wearing plastic sandals. In one hand he carried a teakettle, in the other a stack of Styrofoam cups. He set both on the desk that separated us from Major Zuhair.

A younger man, dressed in solid green Castro fatigues, an AK-47 slung over his shoulder, followed with a bowl of sugar and plastic spoons. He placed them next to the teapot and cups and walked out. The older man poured four cups of tea, mixed in five or six spoonfuls of sugar, and exchanged a few words with Zuhair. Before leaving, he flashed a semi-toothless grin our way, tossed a small wave, and said, "Hello."

Zuhair took two of the cups, handing one to Nick and keeping one for himself. He waved his hand at the remaining two. "Chai?"

The colonel took a cup from the desk. I followed his lead. I tasted the tea. It was hot, very sweet, and high quality.

"Thank you," I said to Zuhair.

Zuhair lit another cigarette and leaned forward towards the colonel. While he spoke, Nick translated.

"Suh, Major Zuhair says he welcomes your team and is looking forward to working with you. He says he's grateful for all Lieutenant Colonel Augen has done for the battalion and knows you will do your best to help the unit. He apologizes that Colonel Mujeed is not here to make first introductions."

Nick spoke English exceptionally well; except for the *suhs*, his accent was slight.

Zuhair spoke again, and Nick translated. "He says the battalion is improving in their tactical abilities, and he knows Lieutenant Colonel Augen will brief you on what the unit is capable of. He says their biggest need is armored vehicles and rocket-propelled grenades. He also says that because of Lieutenant Colonel Augen and his Marines, the battalion was able to get the materials needed to fix this command post and barracks."

The two Iraqis briefly exchanged words again.

"He wants to know if you have any questions for him," said Nick.

I sat for a few seconds thinking, then I addressed Zuhair. "I don't have any questions right now, but I will soon. My men and I are glad to be here, and we're looking forward to working with the battalion."

After Nick relayed my words, Zuhair nodded. "*Shukran*, Major Steer…"

"Steer-forth, *Sati*," Nick said slowly.

Zuhair nodded. "*Shukran*, Major Steer-forth."

Colonel Augen and Zuhair spoke through Nick for a while, discussing tasks the colonel wanted to complete before departing.

We drank another cup of tea. When the conversation trailed off, we left.

"Zuhair runs a tight ship," Augen said once we were out of ear-shot. "The *jundi* are terrified of him—they claim he shot some soldiers for desertion in Mujeed's old unit, just before it broke apart during the '03 fight with us. Mujeed teases him a lot, but they're thick as thieves."

I was curious. "He and Mujeed were together in the old army?"

"Yeah. They worked a deal in Taji to stay together. I don't know the details."

"Not too different from the way we do things," I noted.

"Yeah, but don't kid yourself. They do a lot of very odd things here, you'll find out."

"Who was the old guy that brought in the tea?"

"That's Hussein," he said with a quick laugh. "He's Mujeed's cook and his nurse. That's all he does—no combat. Wherever Mujeed is, as long as it's here in garrison, Hussein's not far away."

"What about that other guy? The one who brought the sugar."

"That's Sergeant Achmed. He runs Mujeed's personal security dudes."

I thanked Colonel Augen and walked outside, looking for Leo and my men.

⌘

"Sir, you want them in formation?" asked Leo.

"A school circle's good."

At Leo's direction, the men from my team gathered around me, and I gave them a breakdown of our immediate future. Each needed to get with their counterpart from Colonel Augen's team and find out what had been done so far to train the Iraqi battalion.

"We'll build on what they did. Develop five or six training objectives from what you learn. Hand them over to Captain Essex, and he'll consolidate them into a training plan we can execute over the next few months. That will be our roadmap. Nothing sexy. Any questions?"

Doc Binder was the first to speak up. "Sir, I've already spoken to the doc from the other team, and he says that the Iraqis ain't got shit for medical."

"No medics at all?" I asked.

"They got medics, but they're barely trained, and they don't even have basic medical kits. I'm talking no bandages, no aspirin—no nothin'."

"Shit," said Leo. The men laughed.

I shook my head. "Well, there's your first objective—build first-aid kits. Ask the National Guard for help. If you can do that, we've progressed."

Second Lieutenant Randolph spoke up. Randolph hailed from Charleston, South Carolina, but spoke without a drawl. "Will all of us be conducting operations with the Iraqis, sir?"

"Yeah," I replied. "Five or six of us at a time, at first. Then twos and threes once we get the hang of it." I scanned the faces of the men on my team. "At Taji, there was talk from the other teams that only combat-arms types would go on patrol. I don't care if you're intel, artillery, infantry, or logistics, we'll all tote the same load out here. All of us are trained riflemen and know enough tactics and techniques to teach the Iraqis the fundamentals of combat and then show them how it's done."

I looked around at the Marines, inviting more questions. "Sir?"

"Sergeant Ski?" I made eye contact with the short, balding man.

He tossed his cigarette to the ground and crushed it with his boot. "I keep hearing that we're leaving here and going to Fallujah soon."

"Who told you that, Marine?"

"Marines from Colonel Augen's team. Heard it at Taji too."

"Rumors are rumors until the last minute when they come true. Put it out of your mind until we get firm word."

The six-foot-three University of Michigan grad from California, First Lieutenant O'Shannihan, raised his hand. "Sir, we've been here eight hours, and five of that was sleep, but I've already seen four variations of Iraqi uniforms."

We all laughed again.

"I saw one guy in a white T-shirt, plastic sandals, and no shave. He must have been near seventy. He said hello. I guess it's all funny, but they don't seem to have much of anything. It's going to be an uphill battle."

"Yep. For you and Gunny, it is going to be tough," I said. "Your job is not to get them gear—work with the Iraqi logistics section and teach *them* to get gear through *their* system. Like Doc, you may get some windfalls from the Army or Marine battalions, but I don't expect you to get them equipped. Teach them."

I waited for more questions. When none were asked, I said, "You're dismissed. Thanks."

Leo hung around after the other Marines left. We discussed how to track Iraqi progress and capture the lessons learned of day-to-day operations. I told him to begin a logbook, a record of our operations.

When we were done talking business, Leo asked, "Sir, did you know Lieutenant Mahone?"

"Mahone? That sounds familiar."

"He was the adjutant that got hit and lost his legs here in Ramadi, the one I told you about at Camp Victory."

Mahone. I knew the name and recalled the previous summer when a young lieutenant stopped me on my way to a regimental staff meeting. He said he knew me from a Mess Night that I attended at The Basic School in Quantico, Virginia, two years earlier. Assigned as an adjutant to one of the battalions, he was on his way to Iraq, and excited. I matched the name and circumstances. "I do know him."

"One of the Marines on Colonel Augen's team said that Mahone volunteered to run building supplies between Fallujah and here, some of it for this position, dodging IEDs, RPGs, and small arms fire every day. That route is black, has been for a long time."

"I only met him twice. He was motivated."

"Right, sir. The shitty part is that his boss is fighting a battle back home with the division just to get a valor device for his Navy/Marine Corps Commendation Medal."

I shook my head. "That's shameful."

CHAPTER 17

Two days later, Marines from Hotel Company Three-Seven arrived at Camp Phoenix in armored seven-tons. Their company commander, a man named Dixon, asked if he could join us on patrol. A square-jawed Marine with a fresh shrapnel scar running from the outside corner of his eye to the base of his ear, Captain Dixon spoke with an Elizabethan accent characteristic of the Northern Neck of the Rappahannock River. We smoked a cigar together and chatted about his time in Ramadi. He'd lost twenty-five pounds and thirty-three Marines—twenty-one wounded and twelve killed.

"I won't miss this place, sir. I've lived three lifetimes in six months. The worst part is writing the letters home to wives and parents," he told me while we smoked.

Dixon's men transported a half a dozen of us, plus Nick and a platoon of Iraqis, to the Government Center, a city-block-sized fortress of sandbags, Hesco barriers, bulletproof glass, observation towers, radio antennas, and concertina wire. From there we set out on foot for our first patrol. Captain Dixon and five of his Marines handled rear security.

My first memory of leaving the wire at the Government Center is stepping into a street flooded with rank, ankle-deep raw sewage and looking up over the entrance of a blown-out building to see a brightly colored, bullet-ridden, eight-by-four-foot commercial sign graced with a hand-painted figure of a musclebound man sporting a wife-beater and gym shorts. Over his head and bowed under the strain of two large black globes of iron at each end, the man heaved a barbell.

We moved in a loose pair of files. Top Bruce and I stuck together while Lieutenants Randolph and O'Shannihan accompanied the Iraqi officers leading the patrol.

We stopped five or six times, allowing the Iraqi soldiers to question locals.

I saw no buildings untouched by bullets or explosive ordnance. Window glass and household debris littered the streets; above our heads and stretched in every direction ran a jumbled maze of black and white utility wires.

There was no garbage collection in the city—the Iraqis dumped their trash in empty lots and burned it. The acrid fumes of burning plastic, paper, and rubber tasted like scorched popcorn and irritated our throats and nasal passages. We wore wet bandannas over our faces to stifle the stench; they did little to help. When we approached two-lane roads or open areas, the lead element gave hand signals and tossed smoke grenades to screen our movement. The smoldering piles of garbage smoked so much that the grenades were often unnecessary.

In the streets, we encountered mostly old men and teenagers loitering outside of the damaged buildings smoking, drinking tea, and chatting with one another. Some of the kids pushed around carts and arranged shop wares. Occasionally we caught glimpses of women—usually in pairs and with children in tow, and always clad in black burkas—flittering from one place to another. They never looked our way.

Goats and feral dogs roamed freely. I wondered how the Iraqis knew who owned which goat and doubted anyone claimed the dogs.

As we passed through the *souk*, a place where vendors displayed dry goods, clothing, old tools, secondhand auto parts, and 1980s-era electronics, we halted. Top Bruce and I squatted together next to a building.

Top covered our rear while I faced forward.

A gunnery sergeant from Colonel Augen's team crouched near me. "Sir, six months ago, we couldn't do this."

"You mean patrol here?" I asked.

"Not so much that. We can do it easily now because it's winter. Warm weather will bring the Mooj out with a vengeance." He glanced up and down the street at the Iraqi troops. "I mean move in a formation like this."

"They were that untrained when you got here?"

"Roger, sir. On patrol they simply wandered off. There were negligent discharges all the time. They argued with each other and even stole from the locals."

"Really?"

"Yeah. Most of the *jundi* can't read, so everything they learn, they learn hands-on. After a while, we figured out who was who. There are a handful of literate ones we can talk to—they teach the others and keep order."

He pointed towards the lead trace of the patrol thirty meters away. "See that soldier with your lieutenants and the Iraqi officer?" Randolph and O'Shannihan were standing with two Iraqis.

"The one talking to Randolph?" I asked.

"Yeah. His name is Sergeant Muhammed. He's a Kurd and speaks English he learned watching old Westerns. He's the best *jundi* in the battalion and has helped us out a lot. Some of the officers do okay with English too."

I nodded.

"You'll figure it out, sir."

I caught O'Shannihan's eye. He raised an eyebrow and signaled for me to hold position. "I'd better," I said to the gunnery sergeant.

"Sergeant Muhammed and ten or twelve others trained with the SEALs right after we got here. The SEALs came to Camp Phoenix and said that they wanted to help train the Iraqis. They liked Sergeant Muhammed and took him along one night to hit some high-value targets. Word has it Muhammed shot them in their beds with his pistol, making it easy for the SEALs. But then two of the SEAL-trained Iraqis got burned up in a vehicle while we were working with the National Guard. Colonel Augen said they looked like roasted pigs when they pulled them out of the burned hulks."

"Any of our guys killed or wounded?"

"No Marines, but four or five of the National Guard soldiers got killed. Somehow, the Iraqis blamed the SEALs, even though the SEALs weren't around. Mujeed refused to let his men work with them after that."

I noticed two Iraqi civilians staring at us from across the *souk*. I stared back. One of them manned a donkey cart covered with a tarp. They turned away and moved on.

"You get used to that," said the gunny. "The Arabs got their own way of living and thinking. Crazy stuff. I've seen them howl and rip their clothes when one of their own gets killed. They tore all the electrical wire out of their barracks, burned the insulation off, and sold the copper in Baghdad for a buck. I've heard weirder things. I ain't figured them out."

O'Shannihan motioned that we were moving, and I stood. "Thanks for the gouge, Gunny. Let's go, we're moving."

We finished the patrol, ending up back at the Government Center. We hung around the courtyard of the complex, making ourselves familiar with the compound until the Three-Seven Marines were ready to drive us back to Camp Phoenix.

From the back of the seven-ton, I studied the city as we rode past. Entire walls and sections of buildings were sheared off, revealing wrecked rooms and stairwells to nowhere—abandoned bed clothes, furniture, and appliances strewn in the midst—the naked remnants of domestic living.

⌘

I stuck close to Colonel Augen. He introduced me to the commanding officer of the Pennsylvania National Guard brigade operating adjacent to the Marine battalion. Framed photos of nearly a hundred of his soldiers killed since the unit arrived in Ramadi hung in the main hallway of his headquarters building.

I also met the commanding officer of Three-Seven—the type of man who makes one proud to serve in the Marine Corps. He had a good grasp of the Iraqis' plight, and he was sympathetically frank when addressing the difficulty of my task.

"Mujeed's got a full mission to carry out with half-trained soldiers and no gear," he explained. "They're not there yet. Captain Dixon and I will help you any way we can, but we're leaving soon. Three-Eight will take our place in early March."

Colonel Augen and I discussed my idea of building on what he and his Marines had accomplished. He said I was on the right track.

⌘

Ten days after we had arrived at Camp Phoenix, Colonel Augen walked out of the command post with his towel and hygiene kit. When he saw me standing outside smoking breakfast, he raised his hand to shade his eyes, squinted into the rising sun, and said, "Mujeed's back."

"Came in last night?"

"About zero-three. He's a full colonel now."

"Is that a good thing?"

"Not if they pull him out and reassign him. Otherwise, I don't care. Good for him."

"He's kind of late, isn't he? The day we got here, you said that he'd be here in three or four days."

"Don't sweat the small shit, bro," said the colonel, walking off to the hygiene area. "You're on Iraqi time now."

⌘

Mujeed smoked his cigarette the same way Zuhair did—backwards. Also, like Zuhair, his uniform was impeccable.

Zuhair was present, sitting in a chair behind Mujeed's left shoulder.

Hussein served tea, this time with a dish of mixed nuts—an unsalted, wider variety than served in the States. They were delicious.

Mujeed sat forward in his seat. "Major Steerforth, I want to welcome you to the battalion."

I nodded.

"Colonel Augen tells me that you…you and your Marines understand some of the…difficulties my battalion has with equipment. I look forward to working with you."

When he was finished speaking, he took a hard hit of his cigarette, sat back in his chair, and blew smoke at the ceiling.

Not a tall man, Mujeed was powerfully built, barrel-chested, and thick-legged. His complexion was smoother than Zuhair's, and he had more hair. He appeared to be in his mid-to-late forties. He kept his right hand rested on his cellphone when he was not drinking tea or smoking his cigarette. His kept his left arm to his side, rarely moving it. I noticed a paperback book, half the cover torn off, lying on his desk. It was printed in English, but I couldn't make out the title.

"*Sati*," I said, "we've been patrolling with your men. They're well trained."

Nick translated, and Mujeed leaned towards me, nodding.

"I look forward to working with you as well," I said.

Mujeed nodded again.

"Congratulations on your promotion."

After Nick translated, Mujeed grinned, sat back, stretched his right arm over his head, and said something in Arabic. Zuhair chuckled and shook his head. I hadn't seen him smile before.

"Suh," Nick translated, "Colonel Mujeed says thank you, and it is true that miracles happen but only one at a time. He is a colonel, but the Ministry of Defense won't get around to paying him for it until Zuhair gets promoted to lieutenant colonel. A very long time from now, says Colonel Mujeed, since Zuhair is like an angry camel—his personality."

Everyone laughed.

Mujeed spoke again, and Nick followed up. "The Colonel asks that you and your men work as closely with him as Colonel Augen's team did. He invites you to dinner tomorrow night. It will be a goodbye dinner for Colonel Augen and his men and a welcome dinner for you and your men."

I pulled two cigars from my pocket and offered one to Mujeed. He took it and placed it next to the paperback.

I bit a small piece off the end of mine; Mujeed offered me his lighter. I accepted and lit the smoke.

We spoke through Nick for a few minutes, and I told Mujeed about our first patrol. He laughed when I mentioned the burning garbage.

"Suh," Nick said, "the colonel says that you will see that life in our country is much different than in America."

Colonel Augen and I left Mujeed's office. "Be careful what you eat tomorrow," he warned. "The food's dodgy. While it's far better than what the *jundi* eat, it's still risky." He waved his hand in front of him. "Don't insult them, but get a sniff of whatever you put in your mouth. Parts of the chow are recycled, and sour—*rotten* sour. If you're lucky, you won't get the shits."

I wasn't lucky.

⌘

Just before midnight a few days later, my crew and I drove Colonel Augen's team to the dirt-patch airfield at Camp Ramadi. Exactly two weeks had passed since we'd arrived. While we stood in the dark waiting for the helicopter, Colonel Augen said, "Good luck, Clay. Stick with your plan, stay tight with Mujeed, but don't ever forget that he's an Arab. Focus on training his men and getting him his own battle space. Don't try to figure them out."

"Aye, aye, sir, will do. Thanks for the good turnover."

"You'll need it. Be careful out in town. Don't be a hero."

"I won't, sir."

I heard their bird coming in the distance. It got loud fast. The downdraft from the blades churned loose sand into a storm. I took the colonel's rifle, and he heaved his pack onto his back. After handing him back his rifle, I hoisted his sea bag onto his shoulder.

When I turned my face away from the dust and pebbles, the colonel slapped me on the back and shouted, "Good luck, Marine! I'd tell you to get a decent haircut, but I know you won't!"

⌘

Alone, I sat by the small fire we kept near the command post, smoking a bedtime cigar and reading a passage from the *Iliad* with my flashlight. The other team had been gone less than an hour.

"Sir, it's getting warmer out."

It was Leo, approaching from the building behind me.

"Hate to see them go," I said.

"They were good people."

"It's just us eleven and the Iraqis now."

"Yes, sir. Speaking of the Iraqis," he said, "I've been talking to the operations officer, Major Thalmer."

"He's a former school teacher, isn't he?"

"Speaks English too."

"I've heard him. What's up?"

"He thinks some folks at the *souk* know more about the Mooj than they're letting on, and he wants us to go back."

I thought about staring down the two men at the *souk*. "Why does he think that?"

"On patrol last week, Sergeant Muhammed identified some people—men he's never seen before. He says they don't fit."

"What does Hotel Company think about that?"

"They know Sergeant Muhammed and think it's worth checking out. They can come tomorrow, talk it over, and do a patrol with us the day after next."

"Okay," I said, standing up. "Tell O'Shannihan and Randolph to get with the Iraqi platoon that went last time, and we'll plan to go. I'll tell Mujeed."

"You going again, sir?"

"Yeah, I'm going."

"I'd like to go too."

"Four or five of us will go with the platoon. I'm sure Hotel will send half a dozen Marines. Make it so, Grasshopper."

"Roger, sir."

"And Leo, make sure the logbook gets updated when we get back."

"Got it. Have a nice evening, sir." He walked away.

I stood smoking, book in hand, looking towards Ramadi. The sound of an explosion and a burst of machine-gun fire reached me from the city. Something there caught fire. Watching the pulsing glow of fresh flames burn brightly and tracer bullets transit an arc and disappear, I imagined Odysseus standing on the beach at Troy staring at the citadel he faced three thousand years earlier.

CHAPTER 18

At midmorning, the sun already above our heads and burning away the morning chill, we left the Government Center and headed for the *souk*, nearly thirty of us in patrol formation.

Lieutenant Randolph and Staff Sergeant Craig traveled up front with an Iraqi lieutenant and Sergeant Muhammed. Leo and I moved in the middle with *jundi* stretched out in front and back. As before, Marines from Hotel Company brought up the rear.

Going on patrol gave me a chance to see how the Iraqi officers and *jundi* operated. The more I knew about their capability and tactical acumen, the better I could advise Mujeed. Each time we stopped to give the Iraqi lieutenant and Sergeant Muhammed a chance to speak to locals, I took my map from my cargo pocket and tracked our checkpoints.

At a stop near the turnaround point, I knelt down near Leo. Lieutenant Randolph turned from the head of the patrol and began walking towards us.

"Randolph wants something," I said. "He's not lost. We're only two klicks from the Government Center."

Randolph knelt down. "Sir, the Iraqis want to keep going. One of the locals says there's some kind of Mooj staging area about a klick north of here—up near the hospital."

A Marine from Hotel Company walked up. "Sir, the hospital is a hot spot," he said.

"How hot?" I asked the Marine, a lieutenant.

"It's sort of a sanctuary and off limits to us." He nodded northward. "It's up near Racetrack."

"Racetrack?"

"The main road up that way. We get hit by a lot of IEDs there."

I thought a second and asked the lieutenant, "What do you think?"

"It's hard to tell." He took a knee. "Those Iraqis you got, they speak the language and see nuance. All we see are people standing in the street."

"Sir," interjected Randolph, "the Iraqi men said they heard racket up that way early this morning."

"Could have been anything," I said. I glanced at Leo. He arched his eyebrows.

"Okay. Have the Iraqi lieutenant call back to Phoenix and tell Mujeed. We'll check it out."

"Roger, sir," said Randolph, standing and walking back to the front of the patrol.

"Keep a close watch out back there," I instructed the Hotel Company lieutenant. "It's doubtful, but it could be some type of trap. You've done this a lot; you know the deal."

"Roger, sir." He stood and walked off.

Leo shrugged. "It's worth a try."

We moved out, leaving the *souk* behind. After ten minutes, we entered a residential area and stopped.

The Iraqi lieutenant and Sergeant Muhammed walked up a short flight of stairs, knocked on a door, and spoke to the occupants of a townhouse.

Five minutes later we were on the move again, this time through a section of the city with cars propped up on cinder blocks, auto parts—doors, fenders, and hoods—stacked in piles, and a single six-cylinder diesel motor suspended by a chain from a railroad tie braced diagonally across the corner of a cinderblock wall. There were plenty of men standing around idly, following our movement with blank stares, but others moved with purpose, handling equipment, wielding tools, and giving instructions. We kept moving, winding up in another residential area where we stopped again. I could see a hundred meters up and down the street. The formation closed up, stretching about fifty meters from end to end. Randolph, the Iraqi lieutenant, and Muhammed scaled stairs to a house and stepped inside.

Kneeling down, I faced the rear trace of the patrol and listened to Leo, behind me and facing the other direction, tell me the racket the men heard in the *souk* was likely locals repairing autos. That's when I saw a blue four-door Mercedes come around the corner, approaching the rear of our formation.

"Leo!"

"Shit," he muttered.

The lieutenant from the Hotel Company motioned for the vehicle to stop. I raised my rifle, cheek against plastic buttstock. I heard a single shot, then the roar of machine-gun fire; I sensed falling snow and saw the vehicle's radiator grill over my front sight post. More gunfire; the fractured air hurt my ears. I squeezed the trigger of my rifle eight or ten times. With each bark of the gun, the spring in the stock buzzed against my jaw and punched my shoulder. The sedan lurched to a halt. I sniffed the sour smell of smokeless powder. Silence. Leo shook his head. All around us lay spent shell casings and ribbons of white utility wire, sliced from above by the hail of bullets.

"Stay put, Leo," I said.

The *jundi* around us chattered excitedly. I strode up and down the street, motioning them to stay in place. Moving to the rear of the patrol where two *jundi*, the Hotel Company lieutenant, and one of his Marines were crouched together on the side of the street, I took a knee.

Randolph's voice rang out from the radio strapped to my protective vest. *"Sir, what happened?"*

I pressed the go-button and spoke. "Stay put and watch your end. I don't know yet."

"Roger. Out."

I looked at the Marine, a staff sergeant.

"Sir, the vehicle whipped around the corner. We signaled the fucker to stop, but he kept moving. I fired a warning shot at the ground in front of it and then somebody opened up," he said, never taking his eyes off the blue sedan.

The lieutenant glanced around the area. "These people know not to get near our patrols in vehicles. We've been announcing that for months—ever since we had four Marines killed by a car bomb."

The vehicle was riddled with bullet holes, the windshield shattered. Fluid dripped from the engine, forming a shiny puddle on the asphalt. All else was still.

"I'll go take a look, sir," said the staff sergeant. "Keep an eye out."

"Roger." I nodded him on.

"I'll call back to the rear and inform them of what happened," said the lieutenant.

The staff sergeant crouched low and moved towards the vehicle, his rifle at the ready.

I aimed my rifle to cover him, the *jundi* near me following my lead. The lieutenant talked on his radio, giving a situation report to his headquarters.

Approaching the Mercedes, the staff sergeant scanned the area with his rifle, inspecting beyond the flanks of the vehicle. Then he jumped up, stole a look through the shattered glass, and dropped back to a crouch. Taking his rifle in one hand, the staff sergeant opened the driver-side door, reached inside, and yanked a body halfway out. In the Marine's grip, the body remained there a moment, suspended at a forty-five-degree angle. When he yanked again and let go, the body fell to the ground.

"Jones!" the staff sergeant yelled in our direction.

A Marine behind me jumped up and darted to his side. He and the staff sergeant spoke briefly, inspected the vehicle, then circled the area to the end of the street. When they returned to the Mercedes, the staff sergeant waved his hand in the air and shouted, "Clear!"

I walked over to the car, the lieutenant from Hotel Company by my side.

As we neared the vehicle, the lieutenant said to the staff sergeant, "I just spoke to Captain Dixon—ten minutes and they'll be here. We can't leave it here."

I glanced down at the dead man. "No, we can't leave this."

I stepped closer. The corpse lay at my feet. Urine, sweat-sodden wool, and grease—it reeked. The body lay on its side, filthy hands sticking out of a coarse, worn, viridian man-dress. The neck was broken and twisted so that the face was upturned, a pool of crimson blood accumulating on the black tarmac. Minutes earlier, a full head of black hair covered the man's head—now half of it was gone, along with the flesh and bone it had clung to. The mess that remained was matted with coagulating blood. I noticed the rough dirt-crusted feet and the grimy plastic sandals hanging from them. Flies lighted on the flesh and mutilated skull—brains and pieces of bare white bone. There was something familiar in the color and contrast of hues—crimson and white on a black background—the paintings of Francis Bacon.

It was revolting. I turned away.

"Find anything?" I asked the staff sergeant.

"Nothing, sir."

"The trunk?"

He shook his head. "Nothing."

"Sir, what happened?" asked Randolph, now standing next to me, staring at the corpse.

"Where's the Iraqi lieutenant?" I asked him.

"Talking to the *jundi*. They claim the Marines shot first."

"It doesn't matter," I said. "He should've stopped. Problem is, we didn't find anything."

"Nothing?"

"Nothing," answered the staff sergeant.

Randolph kept staring at the corpse. "Did you swipe him?"

"Swipe him?" I snorted. "You think I've got a kit?"

Letting his rifle hang free from the sling looped through his protective vest, Randolph reached across his chest to the pocket on his upper left sleeve and began undoing the button. "I've got one."

"You've got to be shitting me, Lieutenant," laughed the staff sergeant.

Randolph knelt next to the body. "I kept it from my last tour." He tore open the package containing cellophane gloves and squares of chemically treated gauze. Pulling the gloves on, he carefully wiped the dead man's hands and arms with the pieces of cloth. When he finished, he tucked the squares back into the packaging and returned them to his pocket.

Humvees from Hotel Company arrived and Captain Dixon got out of one. He inspected the Mercedes while his Marines stuffed the body into a black body bag. Surveying the scene, he shook his head and looked at me. "Shit happens, sir. You won't get used to it. Sorry."

With the body strapped to the hood of a Humvee, Dixon and his men sped away. We left in a hurry, trotting through the streets towards the Government Center two miles away. Each Marine lugged fifty pounds of body armor, ammo, weapons, and radios. The *jundi*, carrying half that weight, struggled to maintain pace. Shuffling along, I thought about the dead man and wondered what he was doing approaching our patrol. I couldn't help but think he had simply made a wrong turn, onto the wrong road, on the wrong day. An image of a family waiting for their father to return home and then tragically finding out he was dead came to mind; I pushed the thought away.

When we got back to Camp Phoenix, I dropped my gear in the can Leo and I shared, sank into my rack, and fell immediately to sleep.

Sometime during the night I roused, my limbs and torso heavy, my breath shallow and uneven. Leo shifted in his bed and mumbled in his sleep. Recalling the previous day's patrol, I remembered the dead man.

⌘

The sun hadn't risen, but I was already outside sitting next to the fire, staring at the flames, my quilted poncho liner draped around my shoulders. The image of the corpse came to me again, and I pulled the nylon fabric tighter. When I inhaled the crisp air, my breath skipped, as if I'd been crying. I tried to recall a previous time when I'd experienced such feeling of residual doom.

Leo joined me, a steaming cup of coffee in hand.

"Morning, Leo." My breath condensed in the air. "We sure killed that guy yesterday."

He handed me a cigar; I rolled it between my fingers.

"Sure did, sir."

I stared into the fire. "I'm exhausted."

"Didn't sleep well?"

"I woke up in the middle of the night with an odd feeling." Letting my poncho drop back, I stuck the cigar between my teeth and held the palms of my hands at the fire, trying to pinpoint how I felt. "It's like when you're a kid, and you cry yourself to sleep and wake up still whimpering about whatever it was that caused the grief."

Leo dug into his pocket searching for matches. I handed him mine.

"But, I can't think—"

"He had explosives residue all over him," said Leo. He lit his cigar. "Captain Dixon called last night and told Randolph. You were sleeping." He handed me back the matchbox. "The swabs turned up positive. Civil Affairs did the forensics."

"That's good."

"It's likely he was casing us out. If we hadn't killed him, he may have come back loaded with a bomb."

"Did you see the body?"

"No. You told me to stay put."

"That staff sergeant from the Hotel Company yanked it out of the vehicle like it was a sack of feed." I rolled my palm upwards and thrust my hand towards the ground. "And *thud*."

I struck a match and lit my cigar. "Thanks."

"Wife sent them."

"Thank her for me."

Leo nodded. "Sir, have you called home?"

"Home?"

"Your mom or your girl?"

"I will." A breeze blew smoke into my face. I coughed and leaned away from its trajectory. "I don't want them to get in the habit of hearing from me. I'll call them at the month mark."

"That's two days from now."

"Remind me," I said.

I moved the ammo crate out of the way of the smoke and sat back down. "Leo?"

"Sir?"

"When I looked at that guy and saw the blood, crimson colored, white pieces of bone, and pinkish brains on the tarmac, oddly, I thought of Francis Bacon."

Leo sucked on his cigar.

"Not the scientist," I said. "The British painter."

"I know who he is."

"Ever seen his work?"

"In books, yeah."

"It's a little different in the flesh, but you get the idea." I stoked the fire again. "But it's not just the colors. It's the way Bacon scraped and scrubbed the paint onto the canvas, creating the appearance of smeared, bruised flesh."

"It sounds like you looked pretty close. At the paintings, I mean," Leo said.

We sat for a while in silence, smoking. Only the occasional distant gunfire interfered with the sound of the wood burning. I stared off at the flat horizon and remembered.

"Oklahoma."

"Pardon me?"

"Oklahoma. The best I can recall, I was a small boy the last time I had this feeling."

Leo waited.

"My cousin from Oklahoma got killed in Vietnam," I explained. "I cried when my ma left me with my dad and went to the funeral. I fell asleep crying and woke up still upset."

Leo started to speak, then fell silent.

"The real strange thing about killing that guy was not his brains on the tarmac and thinking of Francis Bacon, but it's that for a second, I wondered when the police were showing up." I held my cigar between my fingers and pointed it at the fire. "Think about it, Leo. We accused that guy, tried him, and executed him all in the span of fifteen seconds. The entire legal system condensed into a few gestures, a warning shot, and a hail of bullets."

Leo shook his head and looked off towards the distant city, purple against the rising sun.

I threw more wood on the fire, waited until it caught flame, then said, "Leo, *we're* the law out here."

CHAPTER 19

We learned from Captain Dixon that his company's replacement, Kilo Company, had arrived in Ramadi with the rest of Third Battalion, Eighth Marines to take his unit's place at the Government Center.

I lounged in the radio room at the command post, browsing through a two-week-old copy of *Stars and Stripes,* while Sergeant Ski eavesdropped on the Hotel Company's command net, listening to Captain Dixon patiently give advice to Kilo Company as they conducted their first turnover patrol.

"Hello."

It was Hussein.

"Hello," he repeated, flashing gaps of missing teeth on the left side of his jaw. Sporting a week's worth of gray stubble and dressed the same as when I first saw him, he held out three pieces of flatbread and something wrapped in newspaper. "Feesh, Major?"

I took the food and thanked him, *"Shukran,* Hussein, *shukran."*

"Afwan. Hello." He disappeared.

"You going to eat that, sir?" asked Ski.

I unwrapped the package and sniffed the fish—*fresh.* "Any salt around here?"

"Yes, sir, on the fridge." He nodded in the direction of the appliance. "You don't know where that's been."

"In the water, at least until this morning." I reached for the salt packets.

"Yeah, in the Euphrates with the dead bodies and the sewage."

"It's carp. They're natural filters. I've been eating it for two weeks—no problems yet. Better than whatever we ate that night at Colonel Mujeed's welcome-aboard dinner."

"You ate that?"

"You didn't?"

Ski shook his head. "I pushed it around on my plate and spilled some on the deck, but I didn't put that shit in my mouth."

"You don't know what you're missing, Marine."

"Wait until your balls turn orange, sir."

"Cadmium Orange or Naples Yellow with crimson mixed in?" I asked.

"Pardon me, sir?"

"Nothing." I peeled away a charred sheet of silver scales and pulled a warm piece of oily flesh off a section of thick bone, sprinkled salt on it, wrapped it in a piece of the unleavened bread, and stuffed it in my mouth. Around a mouthful I asked Ski, "Want some?"

"No thanks, sir. Knock yourself out. I'll have some bread, though."

I handed him a piece of the flatbread. From behind me, Leo said, "Sir, you've got mail."

I turned around. Leo had his neck stretched so that only his head stuck through the doorway.

"Who's it from?" I asked.

He stepped inside the radio room with a package and stack of envelopes in his hands. Reading the label on the package, he said, "This is from John Dunne," and handed it to me. He held up a bundle of colored envelopes bound with a rubber band. "These fancy letters are from Kate." He flipped them around, revealing a single white envelope on the other side. "And that one is from a...Mrs. Norma Steerforth."

I pulled the single letter from the packet. "That would be my ma," I said and slid it under my thigh. "Set the rest there on the fridge."

I pulled a hunk of flaky white flesh from the bone and held it out to him. "Fish?"

"No thanks, sir. That shit will kill you." Leo smiled down at me.

"Leo, what's got you so happy? Somebody tickling your nuts?"

"Package."

"Smokes?"

"Maybe—maybe other goodies too."

"Books?" I bit into the bread and fish.

He cocked his brow. "That and other things."

I nodded and swallowed. "Let me know."

"Will do, sir. Don't forget to call home. It's been two days." Leo disappeared from the doorway.

I turned my attention back to the food. "What's going on, Sergeant Ski?"

"Nothing, sir. I think the patrol is coming back in."

When I finished eating, I pulled my mother's letter from under my leg and my jackknife from my cargo pocket. I carefully cut open the envelope, leaned back on two legs of the folding chair, put my feet up on the radio table, and pulled out the letter.

Dear Clare,

Other than my father, twenty-five years dead, she was the only person who ever addressed me as such. I glanced down the page admiring her cursive penmanship—legible, firm, and graceful, with a hint of flair—there were no words scratched out or scored through.

> *I hope you are doing well. We missed you at Christmas. It's been a long winter. The thermometer reads 14 degrees, and there is two feet of snow on the ground. The squirrels have been hogging the bird feed from the poor little sparrows, and the cat sits in the window watching them for hours with hungry eyes. I started painting classes right after the holidays. I have fifteen students now, and I really enjoy them. Your cousin Donna has been painting with us. You may not remember her, but she is one of Uncle Keith's girls. She is very talented. She's a real Sherburn. That's where you get your talent. Thank you for calling before you left. It was good to hear your voice, and you always seem to find a reason to laugh.*

> *Each day I pass by the piano and see your picture. You look so handsome in your green uniform. This morning I thought how much you look like my father. I pray for you each day, and so does my church group. If there is anything you need, write to me, and I'll see what I can do. Please be careful and get home safe.*

> *Hugs and kisses from your old mom. Love,*

> *Mom*

In the space left at the bottom of the second page, drawn in ballpoint pen, was a snowy scene of a bird perched on a bird feeder hanging from a tree limb.

I stuck the letter back inside the envelope, folded it in half, and slid it into my left breast pocket. "I'm going to step outside for a smoke."

"Roger, sir," said Sergeant Ski.

The bundle from Kate contained six letters. I put them in my cargo pocket, saving them to read by flashlight after I hit the rack.

In the package John sent were two books: Clement Greenberg's *Late Writings* and H. D.'s *Helen in Egypt*. Included were a dozen postcards printed by the Museum of Modern Art featuring Motherwell's *Elegies to the Spanish Republic* series. On the back of one was written,

> *Bought these in New York. Remembered the time you spoke fondly of Motherwell. Hope you like them. On my way to Brussels. Wish me luck. Stay out of trouble.*
>
> *John*

Admiring the stark black-and-white images on the postcards and remembering the day at the National Gallery when I asked John what Motherwell's paintings were about, I thought of my own art, and what I was trying to achieve with the Trojan War paintings. Motherwell was the only branded modernist painter I knew who had tackled the topic of war in such a direct manner. For somebody like me there is a plausible explanation for choosing such subject matter. I tried to imagine what Motherwell's reason might have been.

At dusk, I lit a fire. Thirty minutes later, I saw headlights coming down the road. It was Leo and the other Marines returning from supper. Two of the Russian vehicles pulled up and parked. Leo got out of one and walked in my direction.

"Nice night, sir."

"How was chow?" I asked.

"I ran into a captain, a guy who was in Alpha Battery with me when we were lieutenants."

"Interesting the way we run into folks we know out here." I tucked the books and postcards back into the packaging. "Remember the operations officer from the Division MiTT?"

Leo stared at the fire and shook his head. "Don't think so, sir."

"A little shorter than me, a fat face? He shaves his head."

"Oh, yeah. A lieutenant colonel."

I nodded. "I know him from somewhere, but I can't remember where."

Leo took a seat on an ammo crate. "Give it time—you'll recall."

"I irritate him."

"Why do you say that?"

"He stopped me one day at Taji." I laughed.

"What's so funny, sir?"

Lifting my cover off my head, I said, "He told me to get a haircut."

Leo chuckled. "Was he joking?"

"Nope. Dead-ass serious. Yankee accent and all." I peered into the fire and tried to remember where I knew Dean from. "Did you ever notice when you were at The Basic School that the people with the screaming high-and-tight haircuts were the first ones to fall out of long hikes?"

"Not really, but you may be right."

"The Basic School is not where I know him from, though."

"Maybe a drink will help you remember."

"That's what she sent you?"

He flashed a fiendish grin.

Lifting my cover again and waving it in the air, I shouted, "Son of a bitch!" and then sang, *"Amazing Grace, how sweet the sound that saved a wretch like me. Hell yeah!"*

Leo threw his head back and laughed. "Indeed, sir, I thought that's how you'd feel. She sent six Listerine bottles—full—says it's Auchentoshan."

"Baby, it's been a long month."

"I'll be right back," he said, trotting off to the command post.

I pulled my leather cigar case from my pocket and shook out two smokes, lighting one for myself and keeping the other in my hand for Leo. He returned five minutes later with two canteen cups and eased a Listerine bottle out of his cargo pocket. Gingerly twisting the cap off with his thumb and forefinger, he poured a generous shot into each cup and handed one to me. After twisting the top back on the bottle, he slid it back into his pocket.

I took a sip of the earthy Lowland Scotch and coughed. "What a treat, Marine," I said and handed him the cigar.

"Here's to high crimes and misdemeanors," Leo toasted.

I touched my cup to his. "Sorry. I got excited. Tell your wife I said 'much obliged.' We won't be getting any of this from Kate."

Leo stared into his cup as if it held secrets, then asked, "She's not a drinker?"

"She's not good at it." I took a small sip and smacked my lips. "She's a convert. Grew up Buddhist. Came over to our side when she was sixteen or so. She's Episcopalian, I think."

"A high Christian!"

"Yeah, like Robert E. Lee. He wasn't Catholic or Baptist. Low-grade Christians like us."

"I'm agnostic," said Leo, "but I didn't know that about Lee."

I sipped again and felt the whiskey burn in my chest. "That's why Longstreet was the outsider. Lee and Jackson didn't drink or smoke, but Longstreet, he sure as hell did." I held up my cup in one hand and the cigar in the other. "He played cards with his staff at night, too. Lee and Jackson, on the other hand, hosted tent revivals in the camps. I don't think we'll be having those here."

Leo laughed. "That's good, sir. It's probably best not to get these Muslims all hopped up on the Lord…at least not out here while we're alone with them."

"That may be bad diplomacy." I drank again and looked over my shoulder at the command post. "Speaking of bad, our nuts will get pounded flat with a hammer if somebody finds out about this."

"Sir, the lieutenants have had it for two weeks."

"What?" I whispered loudly. "Little bastards. Why didn't they share?"

"They offered. I told them we'd find our own."

"Nice and vague." I smiled. "Good thinking."

We sat watching the fire, sipping the whiskey, and smoking. Leo broke the silence. "Sir, how's it going with Mujeed?"

"We mostly just smoke, drink tea, and talk. I think we talk more than he and Augen did."

"Why's that?"

"Augen hated the smoke and didn't hang around for small talk." I dragged on the cigar. "Mujeed told me about the end of the old Iraqi army. Said he and Zuhair abandoned the fight and let his men sneak home to save what was left of them."

"How did they get back together?"

"At Taji. They arrived there at the same time and, apparently, Mujeed swapped him for the executive officer from his own battalion."

Leo cocked his head. "That simple?"

"It's Iraq, Grasshopper," I said. "Nick told me Mujeed got hit leaving Taji, heading home to visit his family in Baghdad. Hussein nursed him back to full duty."

"Yeah, you seen Mujeed's left arm? It's stiff as a board—Hussein is essentially his cook and nurse."

"Hussein's got his own story too." I stretched open my mouth and pointed at my bottom left row of teeth. "Those teeth?"

"I've seen them," he said. "Well, I've seen where they aren't."

"He got them shot out in the Iran-Iraq War. He told me through Nick that he was firing a machine gun and had his mouth open—you know, to keep his teeth from clacking to pieces—and a bullet went in one side and out the other, taking a few fangs on the way. He laughs about it."

"Luck."

"Close call, yes. Anyways, Mujeed seems to me a good soldier. I think he's more capable than just tagging along in someone else's battle space. The gear for his men is his main concern."

"That's obvious. They're supposed to get armored Humvees soon—Thalmer heard it from the brigade."

"Do O'Shannihan and Gunny know?" I asked.

"They do."

"Good. I suspect when they do arrive, brigade will want to keep them for themselves.

Mujeed's like a whore in church about the brigade commander."

"Any idea why?" Leo questioned.

"Can't tell. They've got their own politics, or *people skills*, as folks say, depending if you're on the inside or outside. Mujeed says they served together—"

Before I could finish my sentence, we heard footsteps. I looked towards the command post and saw Lieutenant Lott approaching.

"Evening, gentlemen."

"Marine, how are you?" I asked.

"Fine, sir. Nice evening for a fire."

"Lieutenant Lott," said Leo, "give the major and me a few minutes. We're talking business."

"Oh, sorry, gentlemen," he said, turning and walking away.

Once he was out of earshot, I asked, "How's he doing?"

"The other lieutenants don't like Lott much."

"No?"

"He runs his mouth a lot."

"About what?"

"Stuff about whacking off and how stupid the Iraqis are. Immature kid shit."

I stared into the fire. "Immature or not, we need Lott. We need every swinging dick we've got. Keep an eye out, and don't let the others gang up on him. We can't afford an odd man out."

I checked to see if anyone was around before continuing. "What about Craig? His hands shake all the time. What's wrong with him?"

"No telling, sir, but he's solid. Let me tell you, that day we killed that guy in the car—"

"I remember."

"Staff Sergeant Craig kept the *jundi* calm."

"He spoke to them?"

"No, he went up and down the road, just being present and calming them down."

"The *jundi* told Mujeed we shot first." I sipped whiskey and recalled the dead Mercedes and the corpse in the road.

"That's bullshit."

"Of course it is. The *jundi* fired as many rounds as the rest of us. Bullets were snapping over my head, clipping that mess of utility wires. The only Marine behind me that fired was Craig—he had his M-4 and that twelve-gauge he totes along."

"That's what I remember too," said Leo.

"That's what I told Mujeed. I also told him about the forensic kit. He seemed to understand and said he'd pass it to his men."

"Another drink?" Leo reached in his cargo pocket.

"Christmas in February, sure."

Leo poured us each another two fingers.

I sipped. "Mujeed's battalion is capable of more than patrolling. They stay in formation; they don't shoot in *every* direction when they do shoot—"

"The blossom of death, you mean?"

"Yeah. Colonel Augen said that was common when he first arrived. But let's move on. The Marine battalions are changing over, so now's our chance. Getting the Iraqis up and running is our ticket out of here in the long run." I laughed. "That's why MiTT teams are the *main effort* for U.S. forces in Iraq."

"What are you thinking?"

"Company-sized operations—cordons and searches, multiple patrols at once, maybe even some ambushes."

"I'll speak to Major Thalmer," said Leo.

"And I'll speak to Mujeed." I paused, pondering a strategy. "With the new Marine battalion and company commander, we'll just act as if the larger operations are normal for us. I'm sure Captain Dixon and his boss will speak highly of Mujeed and his crew. I hope Kilo Company and Three-Eight are as good as Hotel Company and the rest of Three-Seven."

"They were solid."

"They were. Ol' Captain Dixon, he was the real thing. He even took the time to go on the first patrol with us."

We finished our drinks; when I stood up, I was dizzy.

CHAPTER 20

"The Health Compound?" I asked, looking at Leo and Staff Sergeant Craig.

Craig curled his thumb and middle finger tightly around a squat cardboard can. After shaking it with a repeated thump of his forefinger against the lid, packing the fine granular tobacco into the crest of the container, he twisted the lid off, pinched out a half teaspoon, and placed it between his lower lip and gum. He wiped his mouth clean of the residue and nodded. "Yes, sir."

I caught a whiff of the Copenhagen's sweet fragrance.

Leo folded his arms and parroted, "Yes, sir."

"Clarify it for me. You aren't talking about the hospital?" I asked.

"No, sir," explained Craig. "The hospital's north and east of the Government Center; the Health Compound is a few blocks south."

"What's there?"

"Not sure, sir," said Leo. "Kilo Company wants to check it out, and so do the Iraqis. To see what the workers there know about the Mooj."

"Okay. What size patrol?"

Craig spat tobacco juice into the dirt. "One company. Irregardless of how many *jundi* are there that day—we never know until the last minute—plus a squad from Kilo. They'll come over for a sand-table brief with the Iraqis."

"Okay, it's a go. I'm sure Mujeed will buy in," I said, ending the discussion.

⌘

When the weather warmed, I started drawing. Each evening I could, I escaped the bustle of the command post in one of the Russian jeeps, drove aboard Camp Ramadi, and scribbled away with a felt-tipped pen and a Moleskine sketchbook. I licked my thumb and smeared the pen marks where I needed halftones to create perspective or mass. In this manner, I recorded the scenery of the four-mile-square base: a patchwork of Hesco barriers; endless loops of concertina wire; old, brick, one-story Iraqi army buildings that U.S. forces now occupied; water and guard towers; M1 Abrams tanks; motor pools full of Humvees; and a single mound of man-made hill adorned with camouflage netting and sprouting antennas—all connected by shin-deep muddy roads and duckboard footpaths. This was my link to painting.

⌘

Mujeed sat behind his desk smoking a cigarette. Hussein, having already served a first round of tea, returned to deliver the second. Through Nick, Mujeed told me he had four children and a wife who taught at a university. When he asked about my family, I told him how my mom had driven newly manufactured, Korean-War-bound U.S. Army trucks in convoys from Michigan to New Jersey during the early fifties.

I hadn't seen Zuhair for ten days. "*Sati*, where is Zuhair?"

"He's on leave, Major," Mujeed answered rather seriously, but without help from Nick. "Your English gets better each time we talk," I said.

He grinned, reached behind to a small table, and picked up a dog-eared paperback book—the one I had noticed the day I met him—and held it up for me to see: *The Da Vinci Code*. "Major," Mujeed said, "I want to ask you something."

"Yes, sir?"

He placed the book in front of him and, without looking at Nick, began speaking excitedly at me in Arabic.

"Suh," said Nick, "Colonel Mujeed wants to tell you that he likes the women's freedom thing that you have in America."

"Women's freedom?"

"No, uhhhh…woman lib…." Mujeed corrected Nick.

Stumped, I pondered a moment. "Women's liberation?"

Mujeed nodded.

"What about it?"

He spoke to Nick, who translated, "Colonel Mujeed says he thinks it's a good thing and wishes Iraq had this."

"That's hard to believe," I said, but waved Nick off from translating. Mujeed began talking at me again, his excitement unabated.

Nick translated. "He says he loves his wife but wants another. It's not that his wife is bad; she is the mother of his children. It's just that she has this job at the university and…." Nick appeared confused. He quit translating and spoke to Mujeed.

Mujeed answered quickly, and Nick began again. "Well, she's getting old."

"How old?"

"His age, maybe a little younger, he didn't say exactly," answered Nick.

"Okay, I got it. Go ahead."

"She's getting old, and he wants a young woman. He says that he could divorce his wife like people do in America, but he can't...or he won't."

"Why not?"

Nick translated my question to Mujeed, and they spoke their language for a while.

"Okay, sir, I think I've got it. Colonel Mujeed says he wants to keep his wife. He doesn't want to divorce because he has to consider her family, but he wants another wife—a younger one. Two wives."

I glanced at Mujeed; he nodded at me, not smiling.

"The problem is he can't afford two. If he had two wives and couldn't support them, his standing with the people would go down. It would be the same if he divorced his wife and married a younger woman. His community wouldn't talk to him, and it could cause him to lose his job because his wife would be poor and have nowhere to go. He says he would lose all of his...I don't know how you say it in English, but we call it *wasta*."

"Sounds like you mean credibility—*gravitas* maybe?"

"Probably, suh. I don't know that word, but maybe," answered Nick.

Mujeed leaned forward on his desk, his right hand tapping his cell phone as he looked back and forth at Nick to me.

I gestured for Nick to continue.

"But if he *could* divorce his wife without all the people punishing him, he could have a young wife, and that's why he likes women's freedom."

"Liberation," I corrected. "Hmmm." I thought hard, struggling for a way to untangle all of this; no great cultural equalizer came to mind. "You get the idea, but in America, women's liberation is actually the name of a concept—a social movement."

"Yes, suh, women's liberation, like you have in America," said Nick, clearly out of his comfort zone.

"I see," I said. "So he's got a wife, the mother of his children…" I spoke slowly for Mujeed's sake. "He wants to keep her, but he wants a young wife too, and he needs a lot of money to keep two wives. Since he doesn't have the money for both, his best alternative is to divorce, which he doesn't want to do."

Mujeed nodded. "*Na'am*, Major."

"And he can't do that because his community will reject him for putting his wife out on the street. But, if he were in America, it would not be a problem—nobody there would say anything because a divorced woman can take care of herself."

"*Na'am*." Mujeed pulled a pack of Miamis from his pocket, plucked one out, and grinned.

"Stuck between a rock and a hard place," I mumbled as I ran my fingers through my hair. "Well, sir, it's not quite that simple. Even in America some families still frown on divorce, especially when kids are involved."

Nick translated and Mujeed nodded.

"Secondly, divorce costs money in America. I think in Iraq, a man can simply go home, tell his wife it's over, and that's it—not so in America. A man has to pay a lawyer to handle the divorce, and a judge does the deed in court. And, on top of that, depending on the circumstances, the man has to pay his wife something like half, or more if there are children and property involved. In other words, it's harder than it looks."

Nick translated. Mujeed smoked, deep in thought. After a minute he spoke in English. "Yes, Major, but still, this women's liberation is good. It gives the man freedom to have a new life with young woman and not be punished."

⌘

The next day, a lieutenant from Kilo Company arrived at Camp Phoenix with ten Marines to brief and rehearse the Health Compound mission. These were the first Marines we met from the Three-Eight. In preparation, the Iraqis built a ten-by-ten-meter terrain model with rocks, sticks, and string depicting roads, buildings, and major terrain features we'd find at the Health Compound. Wood blocks represented the three-story, dormitory-style health facility. Like the Government Center complex, the Health Compound encompassed nearly a city block of variously sized buildings, all surrounded by a ten-foot high cinderblock wall. An Iraqi lieutenant from the company Mujeed designated to execute the operation briefed the Iraqi portion of the mission plan to his men and the Marines.

After the Iraqi lieutenant finished, the lieutenant from Kilo Company took his turn. He briefed his part of the mission, including the primary and secondary routes he intended to take to the Health Compound.

When the briefs were over, we rehearsed the patrol formation and conducted a practice cordon and search in an abandoned building near Camp Phoenix.

On the day of the operation, Mujeed rode with us to the Government Center. We debarked, coordinated with the squad of Kilo Company Marines, and prepared to set off. Mujeed remained at the command post with the Kilo

Company commander, Captain DeMarco. There, he could monitor his men's movement on the radio. As planned, we took a separate route from the Marine squad. Staff Sergeant Craig and Lieutenant Webb moved up front with the Iraqi officers, while Lieutenant O'Shannihan and I traveled together near the rear of the patrol.

Our route took us through a graveyard, the first I'd seen in the country. It appeared the locals buried their dead in shallow graves and then simply piled rocks on top. In the full sunlight and heat of the day, the scenery was as bleak and surreal as a de Chirico painting. I looked at every other forked stick and twisted piece of debris twice, thinking I may see a lifeless limb or skull sticking out, getting a jump on the Second Coming.

The Iraqis and my Marines arrived at the Health Compound first. Not seeing anyone from Kilo Company, I switched to their frequency on one of two radios I carried. For some reason, they traveled an entirely separate route than briefed the day before and arrived at the compound from the south. A dangerous move since, essentially, it took the rest of us by surprise. I found it odd but chalked it up to miscommunication.

The Health Compound was deserted. The metal double doors in front were secured with a heavy lock, which the Iraqi lieutenant decided they couldn't break and didn't want to shoot off.

Empty handed, we returned to the Government Center and then Camp Phoenix.

A few days later, Staff Sergeant Craig, Lieutenants Randolph and Lott, and an Iraqi squad spent a night in ambush near the Health Compound. With his M4 and a night-vision scope, Staff Sergeant Craig killed a man placing an IED in the road. It was the first such operation we performed in which no Marines other than my own went along.

Anxious to see my men, I waited outside for them to arrive back at Camp Phoenix, Leo and Sergeant Ski standing by my side. At zero-six they came, walking. I drank morning tea and smoked while they gave me an after-action report.

"It sounds funny, sir, but this *is* Iraq," reasoned Craig.

"I'm not saying you're wrong," I said. "But who knows? They may just keep pigeons as pets."

"Sergeant Muhammed saw them with me. About zero-four, two men in man-dresses unloaded the cages. Can't be sure, but I think that's what it was. Sergeant Muhammed said he's seen them use pigeons before."

"Signal pigeons." I mulled over Craig's assertion and tried to remember if I had seen such a thing in past patrols or reports. "What does Sergeant Muhammed have to say about working with the SEALs?" I asked, changing the subject and buying myself time to think. Just as Colonel Augen's team had, I'd come to trust Sergeant Muhammed. When he was a part of the mission, things tended to go smoothly.

"He said he loved it."

"Why did Muhammed and the others quit working with them?"

"I don't know."

"Sir," Leo interjected, "Major Thalmer said the training was good, but one of the SEALs pinned a *jundi* down with his boot one day during sniper training."

"Well, shit. The old bottom-of-the-foot Arab insult thing," I said.

"That's all it took?" asked Sergeant Ski. "I'm not sure what the big deal is. My wife sticks her boot up my ass every morning before I leave for work, and I still go home to get some."

"You dirty bastard," Lieutenant Lott cracked.

Ski retorted, "Sir, with your mouth?"

"Okay, okay," I said irritably. They were doing well as the intelligence section of my team but were as chatty as two virgins planning a honeymoon. "Leo, how did we get from a boot on a neck to all of them quitting the training?"

Lieutenant Randolph yawned before responding. "It was when they got burned up in the vehicle, sir. In fact, it wasn't actually the deaths, it was what happened to the bodies afterward. Apparently the bodies were so badly charred that nobody could tell which body was which, so no one knows which one got sent back to which family. The *jundi* suspect the bodies were switched. That *bad luck*, they say, was caused by the boot sole of a SEAL."

"I heard the same story," said Leo.

"I'll have to ask Mujeed. That's far out." I lifted my cover and scratched my head.

Craig wiped his mouth and spat. "Anyways, sir, I think the pigeons are a real thing."

"I'm not saying you're wrong, Marine, it's just not the type of thing you expect. I mean it's hard for me to believe— this is the twenty-first century."

"Sir, come on," said Sergeant Ski. "None of us expected a fat Iraqi in flip-flops to show up feeding you fish either."

"Okay. Keep an eye out for pigeons during missions. Signal pigeons, huh?" I turned to Leo. "What's next?"

"Kilo wants to go down near the railroad tracks to check out a mosque. They got word weapons and bomb-making stuff are inside."

"How far from the train station?"

"About three klicks."

"Okay, let's stay away from there. We infidels can't go in the mosque, can we?"

"We can't, but the Iraqis can."

"Do the Marines from the Kilo Company know that?"

"I think so," replied Leo.

Randolph yawned again.

"Leo, pick a day and we'll go," I said. "How far is this mosque?"

Craig bent his head, eased in a fresh dip, and shifted his eyes towards the city. "About fifteen-hundred meters—a klick and a half—south of the Government Center."

⌘

On the appointed day, we set out for the mosque. A half klick outside the Government Center I heard rifle shots—M-16s and AK-47s. The j*undi* began yelling so loudly on the Iraqi net, I turned the volume nearly to zero and pressed the go-button on my other radio. "Drifter-Four, what's that? Over."

"No contact here, Drifter-Six," Randolph answered. "Roger…break…Drifter-Three, is that you?"

"Drifter-Six," replied Staff Sergeant Craig. *"Roger. Somebody fired at us from the southeast. We engaged."*

"Roger. I'll be there in three mikes. Out." I looked at Top Bruce, my battle partner for the day. "Let's go take a look."

I knew from the mission brief where Craig was located; two hundred meters away, he, Lieutenant Webb, and Sergeant Muhammed were providing overwatch for the operation.

When I got near, I called Craig on the radio, and he guided me to his exact position on the second story of a townhouse. Top Bruce stayed on the ground floor watching the street while I scaled the stairs.

Careful not to expose myself to the window in the room, I entered and found the three men. From the vantage point, they had a clear view overlooking a series of vacant lots full of smoking garbage and a row of two-story buildings a few hundred meters beyond.

I knelt and asked, "What happened?"

"Two dudes in man-dresses fired at us from over there." Webb pointed in the direction of the buildings beyond the lots.

I looked around. On top of a small bed with bare mattress springs, the single piece of furniture in the room, an AK-47 variant and a Dragunov sniper rifle lay on a burlap bag. "Where'd you get those?"

Webb nodded towards the window. "In the garbage, right outside."

I peeked out at piles of debris heaped against a low brick wall. "How'd you see them?"

Craig lifted his scoped rifle. "We've been here two hours. That bag didn't look right."

Webb was grinning ear-to-ear.

"Somebody tickling you, son?" I asked.

He wiped his mouth with his sleeve. "No, sir."

"Then what's got you so happy?"

"He went and got the weapons," said Craig.

"I told him I would go, sir," Sergeant Muhammed said, letting me know he'd been watching out for the young man.

"Sir, I was scared shitless, until they started shooting at me," said Webb. "When I heard the rounds hitting around me, I grabbed the bag and ran like hell. First time I ever been shot at."

"How do you feel about that, Leather Nuts?"

"Sir, actually, it feels good—*real* good. I'm still shaking." He glanced at Craig. "Not Staff-Sergeant-Craig-like shaking, though."

We all laughed.

Staff Sergeant Craig said, "Kiss my ass, sir."

"You're lucky you're shaking, Marine, and not going stiff inside a black rubber bag on your way to Graves Registration in the back of a Humvee," I said to the young officer. "Be careful. I don't want to have to say goodbye to you inside the fridge aboard Camp Ramadi."

"Sir?" asked Muhammed. "What's taking so long? We've been up here two hours."

I was wondering the same; we should have covered more ground by now. "Maybe Randolph and his Iraqi are working something out," I answered the Kurd.

"I thought that's why we did the rehearsal," said Craig. "The longer we sit here, the more time Mr. Mooj has to figure out how to ambush us."

I pushed the go-button on my radio. "Drifter-Four, what's the holdup? Over."

Randolph answered, *"We're Oscar-Mike."*

"Roger. Out." I said to the three men, "Okay, they're on the move. I'm headed back to the street."

As I descended the stairs, I heard Craig's voice above me and then the echo on my radio. *"Fucking birds! I see the pigeons. Stand—"*

The remainder of the transmission was drowned out by bursts of machine-gun and rifle fire from two or three different directions.

I moved towards the door where Top Bruce was crouched. Despite the reduced volume, I could hear the Iraqis yelling on the radio. The firing grew heavier. Tracer bullets shot from the direction of the mosque flashed past the open door.

"We're stuck here, sir," said Top Bruce.

"Stay put, Top." I ran back upstairs.

Craig and Muhammed had their weapons trained out the window.

"Two guys just fired from those buildings over there." Webb gestured at the structures beyond the garbage lots.

Craig kept his eye trained through his scope. "Thanks to the pigeons, we got shots at both of them. I hit a third one. He fell. They're shooting at our patrol."

Outside, the firing increased. Some of it came from the buildings my men were watching. Craig and Muhammed began firing. My ears rang. When Muhammed stopped to change out his magazine, I stepped up and began shooting in the direction of the buildings. A flash of man-dress darted from one building to another. A second later, over the open sights of my rifle, another followed and I squeezed the trigger; the man dropped.

"You got him, sir!" yelled Craig.

I kept firing, as if I expected the man to stand back up.

Lieutenant Randolph's voice rang out on the radio.

"Drifter-Six, this is Drifter-Four. Over."

My rifle empty, I stepped back. Sergeant Muhammed took my place.

"Drifter-Six, this is Drifter-Four. Over."

I looked past Muhammed towards where I'd shot the man; the body was gone.

"Drifter-Six, this is Drifter-Four. Over."

A faint trail of smoke drifted out of the muzzle of my weapon.

"Drifter-Six, this is Drifter-Four. Over."

I fingered my radio and pushed the go-button. "Go, Drifter-Four."

"Sir, we've got a jundi *down hard. I need a hand."*

"I'll be there in two mikes. Out." Eyes wide, Webb stared at me.

"He's right up the road," I said, "maybe a hundred meters. Keep shooting. Kill anything that's not Marine or *jundi*."

I leaped down the stairs, crouched next to Top Bruce and peered at an angle out the doorway, looking for Randolph; a white blaze of snapping bullets flashed past. I reeled back.

Top Bruce shook his head. "Sir, we ain't going out there."

I held my weapon in one hand, sniffed, and wiped my nose with the other. "Something's wrong." I pushed the release button and caught the empty magazine as it dropped from the well. "Randolph's got a guy down, and he says he needs help." I pulled a full magazine from my vest, tapped the back corner on my helmet, pushed it in place, and slapped it home with my palm. I racked the charging handle back, and let it go; a round slammed into the chamber. For assurance, I pushed the forward assist with my palm. "Stay here," I said. "I'll call you."

I couldn't imagine having to justify to myself why I didn't come when asked. It wasn't a hard choice.

Top Bruce shook his head and moved to cover me.

I sucked in air, bent low, and crept into the street.

CHAPTER 21

We never made it to the mosque. All chance of surprise gone, we walked back to the Government Center where I climbed the stairs to the second deck of the main building to Kilo Company's command post. I found Captain DeMarco and Mujeed talking through an interpreter.

Mujeed stood and began putting his gear on when I arrived. DeMarco sat near the radio, legs crossed, eating MRE pound cake and drinking a Red Bull.

"How's the war?" I asked.

"Not bad, sir," replied DeMarco. "Just talking to your boy here."

"You mean Colonel Mujeed?"

"Yes, sir. Trying to get you people out here in town."

I rested my eyes on his cake. "Where are they supposed to sleep? On top of your Marines? This place is packed."

He cocked his thumb at the window. "The buildings in the compound."

There were five abandoned buildings inside the compound of the Government Center, at one time occupied by a fledgling Iraqi police force. Shattered glass lay in shards everywhere inside, and there was no plumbing or any place for the Iraqis to cook. Any police had long since left the city or been killed.

"Not an option. Besides, Mujeed's already got a company living down at Observation Post Hyrea with one of your platoons," I said, referring to a post a klick east on Route Michigan and manned by both Marines and Mujeed's *jundi*.

DeMarco pulled out his Ka-Bar, grabbed an MRE from a case of twelve, and sliced through the heavy plastic bag. "Suit yourself, sir. As you know, I own all the ground around here. Just trying to get them in the fight." He pulled out a vacuum packed brownie from the bag, tossed the rest of the MRE aside, and tore the wrapper open with his teeth.

"They're in the fight, Captain. Been in it since before last year at this time, long before you got here. See you later."

As I walked away with Mujeed, I heard DeMarco yell, "Hey, Company Gunny! Move the smoking area farther from the building. That fucking smoke is killing me!"

We rode in trucks back to Camp Phoenix.

In full battle gear, we stood in a circle outside the command post conducting an after-action review.

"I was surprised to see you running up the street full of machine-gun fire," Nick said.

I laughed. "I kept my head down. Otherwise, I would have lost my nerve. Randolph, what was the holdup?"

Randolph removed his helmet. "Kilo decided they wanted to go first, surround the mosque, and have the Iraqis follow and go inside. Lieutenant Mustafa insisted that his men go first, just as we planned during rehearsal." He shook his head. "The whole thing was childish, except more hand waving and posturing. The Kilo lieutenant insisted, so Mustafa went inside the house and sat down. He wouldn't budge after that."

"Yeah, I saw him sitting on the couch looking at the lunch some Iraqi family abandoned and pouting like someone pissed in his oatmeal, or whatever they eat for breakfast."

Holding his helmet in one hand, Randolph raised the other in the air. "Arguing took twenty minutes. By the time the Iraqi lieutenant stormed off, the Kilo platoon commander was ready to call it quits. It took another twenty minutes to get it back on track. We were about to step off with the Iraqi sergeant in the lead when the *jundi* got hit."

"Good on the sergeant," I said, spinning the incident in a positive light. "An NCO in the lead, that's progress. I'll speak to Mujeed about his lieutenant." I could see Randolph was frustrated with our Marine counterparts. "Who in the hell knows about the Kilo lieutenant." I took my helmet off and ran my fingers through my hair. "Kilo's getting on my nerves."

"Give 'em time, sir," said Leo.

"Time? They've been here a month. How much more time do they need? How come Captain Dixon and his boss understood all this and DeMarco can't?" I asked, impatiently. "I've heard them refer to us—our team, us Marines, and the Iraqis collectively—as *you people*. DeMarco thinks the Iraqis are glorified pets."

Leo crossed his arms.

I stood for a moment, contemplating the Kilo Company commander's ignorance. It mystified me.

The Marines waited.

"How'd you know about the other wound, Randolph?" I asked.

He shrugged. "While I cut off his trousers and began dressing the wound, I told Nick to strip him. The leg wound was bleeding badly, and the bone was sticking out."

"The *jundi* kept saying his stomach hurt, suh," interjected Nick.

"Right," Randolph recalled. "And there it was, right across the gut, through the adipose tissue, gushing blood. Nick slapped gauze on it and bandaged him up."

"Good work, both of you," I said. "He would have bled out right there without you two."

Lieutenant Webb had his trophy—the Dragunov sniper rifle—slung over his shoulder. Staff Sergeant Craig was carrying the AK-47, tucked in beside his M-4 and twelve-gauge. "You too," I said to them. We got the jump on them when you saw those birds. Were they really pigeons?"

"I don't know, sir. Probably," began Craig. "I told—"

"I know, I know, you told me so." I glanced at Leo. "Get it in the logbook. No one- paragraph summary. I want three pages at a minimum, and don't forget to mention the birds."

"Okay, sir," said Leo. "And I'll talk to DeMarco about being patient with the Iraqis, captain to captain."

"Thanks. By the way, Randolph. Did the *jundi* medic try to treat the wounded man?"

"Sir, I've got to hand it to the medic. He was shaking all over, but he had his kit out. He gave Nick bandages while we worked. To him, it was probably as if we were doing brain surgery. He stuck by us, though."

CHAPTER 22

Mujeed went on leave, his second since I'd been his advisor. I made sure to pay a visit to Zuhair each night. We only talked business.

One evening, I was in back of the command post doing pushups when Leo and Sergeant Ski approached me.

I sat up, hunching oriental style, feet flat on the ground, calves touching the backs of my thighs, arms crossed and rested on my knees.

Leo massaged his chin. "Sir, there is no easy way to tell you this."

"You're not going to believe this one," Ski chimed in.

Leo slid his hand around the back of his head and scratched his scalp above his ear. "Two of the older *jundi* raped one of the younger ones, sir."

I leaned back on my heels, grimacing. "Raped? You mean, like, fucked him in the ass—*forcible sodomy* raped?"

"I didn't ask for details," said Leo.

"Hmm. That can't be good. You sure?"

Sergeant Ski took a quick drag of his cigarette and blew out smoke. "Pretty sure, sir. I heard it from Sergeant Muhammed yesterday, and I was standing right there when Major Thalmer told Captain Essex."

I rocked on the balls of my feet. "Then it's likely not simple rumor." I took a deep breath. "I don't think Zuhair will mention it. Mujeed may not say anything either." I tried to imagine discussing the issue with Mujeed and then asked, "Do the lieutenants—Randolph and the rest—know?"

Leo shook his head. "Don't think so."

"No need to tell them. It's one thing to be young and risking your life every day, it's another to know it is on behalf of animals."

"I've never heard of an animal doing that," quipped Sergeant Ski. "Roger, sir," said Leo. "Sorry to bother you."

"You're my men. There's no such thing as you bothering me."

⌘

For the next week all was quiet. We conducted five or six patrols, an ambush, and a cordon and search. The patrols were routine excursions through the ruined city. Only time and date and *NSTR*—nothing significant to report—went into the logbook. The quiet was odd. No snipers, no wild-shot rocket-propelled grenades, nothing but nauseous trash fires, bombed-out buildings, goats, and dogs.

Then we went back to the Health Compound.

Staff Sergeant Craig, Lieutenant Lott, Sergeant Muhammed, and a handful of *jundi* stepped off from the Government Center forty minutes before the rest of us, bound for an over- watch position in a vacant house on the adjacent block. When it was our turn, Lieutenant O'Shannihan traveled up front, coaching an Iraqi lieutenant and twenty *jundi*. I traveled in the rear with Top Bruce and Sergeant Ski.

A squad of Kilo Marines joined us at the objective, and this time they arrived as briefed. The lock was still on the door. We cut it off with a pair of industrial bolt cutters lugged along for that purpose. Except for a handful of us, everybody went inside the three-story building looking for evidence of Mooj.

There were two entrances to the compound—one to the north and one to the south. Top Bruce, Sergeant Ski, and I remained in the courtyard crouched amongst the rubble and trash, twenty meters or so apart, guarding the northern approach. Three *jundi* with a PKM took up position near the southern entrance.

I was in the midst of telling Top that the place looked like California, if one only looked at the tops of the palm trees and the blue sky and nothing else, when we heard machine guns and explosions a kilometer in the distance. I gripped my M4 and looked across the rubble at Top. His lips puckered under his black mustache, and he nodded. I searched for Ski but didn't see him. Ten seconds later, more gunfire and explosions rang out from the same direction, closer this time.

I squatted low in the crumbled masonry and debris. Over the radio, Craig's voice boomed, *"All Drifter Elements, this is Drifter-Three. There's a kid over here releasing pigeons. Out."*

Almost on cue, two rocket-propelled grenades streaked over our heads, leaving behind their distinct subsonic warble and exploding into the side of the main building with a crash. Loud bursts of machine-gun fire followed, ripping into the structure's masonry, sending cement fragments and dust in all directions. The Marines and *jundi* inside began returning fire from the windows on the second floor, all in our direction.

At the south gate of the compound, the *jundi* fired their PKM non-stop, pouring an entire three-hundred-round belt of ammo through the gun at one time. For an instant, I hoped we trained them well enough not to melt the barrel.

I had bigger concerns, though.

Top, Ski, and I were in a bad spot. With the Mooj firing over our heads from outside the compound, and our own people firing at the Mooj from inside the building, we were caught in a crossfire. I called out, "Top, we gotta go!"

"Waiting on you, sir!" he yelled back.

"Stand by!" I shouted and scrambled to my right.

Fifteen paces away, I found Ski, curled like an upright centipede; chin tucked against his SAPI plate, weapon clutched in his hands and pointed skyward, forearm muscles corded tight as rope. Poor bastard had stalled out.

"Sergeant Ski!" I hollered. Deafening explosions and small arms fire drowned my voice out. His head jerked to the left when I slapped the side of his helmet. He looked up, eyes wide, mouth agape, face sheet-white.

I grabbed him by the protective vest and hauled him to his feet. "Let's go, Marine!"

Pulling Ski behind me, I shouted for Top. Bullets snapped over my head, more RPGs crashed against the building. Bits of rubble rained down on top of my helmet and dusted my protective vest. I pulled Ski down close beside me, keeping a tight hold on his vest, and motioned for Top to come closer. The three of us huddled near an abandoned fuel freighter parked in the compound and fenced off with concertina wire.

The possibility of the freighter being hit and exploding crossed my mind.

Top and I tucked our heads together, and I pulled Sergeant Ski in. "When I say go, make for the front hatch."

I shifted my feet under me. "*Go!*"

Top lit out for the door, bent low, his rifle clasped in one hand—parallel to and almost touching the ground—his other hand clapped on the top of his helmet.

I tightened my grip on Sergeant Ski and leapt to follow—but I dragged to a stop. My protective vest and trousers were caught in the tangle of concertina wire surrounding the tanker.

Top was halfway to the door. Sergeant Ski remained motionless. I pulled him close, put my face next to his earhole, and yelled, "Run! I'm right behind you!" and shoved him into a gallop. He stumbled and then moved forward on his own accord.

My rifle in one hand, I fought the concertina wire with the other but only managed to get my sleeve caught. I tried to break free by heaving my entire body away; the hoops of wire simply followed. I began to panic and tried to fight free, becoming further tangled; then I told myself to stop. I looked at the claws of wire forked through the stiff cotton of my cammies and the canvas of my gear. I released my weapon and let it dangle from my vest, breathed deeply, and exhaled slowly. Carefully, I gripped and steadied the wire with my free hand, then yanked my arm away, tearing the fabric.

My arm was free.

The roar of the firefight continued.

I repeated the technique on my trouser legs and vest, carefully ripping them away from the wire until I was uncaught.

Sprinting for the building, I looked to my left and saw an object slowly arc over the courtyard wall towards me and wondered to myself, *Why would someone throw rocks at me with all this going on?*

The object hit the deck nearby. I ran past—never breaking stride, even as the explosion shook the ground and propelled me forward.

Top Bruce was waiting inside the door. "Sir! You okay?"

"I'm okay…I don't feel anything, but—"

"Turn around, sir. Let me get a look at you. *But* what?" He patted me down. "You're bleeding, sir—you're hit—it looks like you'll need stitches in your arm."

"I'm not hit—that's from the concertina wire. My hands too." I held up a bloody palm.

"You sure?"

"Yeah, but my grenade—"

"You still got it, sir. Right there," he laughed, tapping the grenade safely in its pouch and hanging from my vest.

"I know. I could have thrown it back at whoever threw theirs at me. I—I forgot, Top."

⌘

Mujeed returned not long after the fight at the Health Compound. We met and spoke about operations, logistics, the Ministry of Defense failing to pay his soldiers on time, and the Old Testament, a not-too-rare subject for us. Mujeed's version of Abraham at Mount Moriah identified Ishmael, not Isaac, as the designated sacrificial lamb. I knew better but didn't argue, leaving well enough alone.

He didn't mention the rape.

One morning Sergeant Ski shook me awake, whispering, "Sir, get up, quick. A convoy from Kilo Company just got hit up by Racetrack. A Humvee got blown up."

I sat up in my rack. The small, windowless room reeked of stale booze breath and Leo's sour feet. I checked my watch:

0430. Quietly, I collected my trousers, T-shirt, and boots, slipped out, and walked to the radio room. "What are they doing out there at zero-four-thirty in Humvees"

"No idea, sir. Maybe coming back from an ambush?"

Sitting down, I pulled on my boots, sans socks. "You couldn't convince me to go up Racetrack in anything less than a tank at this hour. How many?"

"Four KIA, perhaps more. They're still missing somebody."

"How many is that for Three-Eight?"

"Fourteen or fifteen, this'll make nearly twenty," replied Sergeant Ski.

"Sounds about right. No telling how many wounded—five or six times that."

"I saw a casualty report yesterday. We broke a hundred KIA in country this month, and the month ain't even over."

"Nearly half those are here in Ramadi. The National Guard's been hit pretty badly, and the Hundred-'n'-First has taken its fair share."

"What are they going to do with this place, sir?" asked Sergeant Ski.

It was the obvious question that nobody seemed to have an answer to. To the people responsible for making the decision, it may have seemed abstract and not time-sensitive, especially since they were likely in Baghdad or D.C. To us, it was photorealism at its best, without novel perspective or romantic lighting—and urgent. As far as I could tell, it was a stalemate—tit for tat on a daily, weekly, and monthly basis. No moving forward, no moving backward, only shuffling the pieces around and removing them from the board, one life at a time.

I bent over to lace and tie my boots. "I don't know, Ski. Leo—Captain Essex and I've heard talk about clearing it out, block-by-block. That's what I would do, but I ain't the boss of nobody but us."

"Why not? We did it in Fallujah."

"Each time someone decides to do it, someone else says there's a political solution. The argument is that clearing it with a kinetic fight will make the situation worse."

"Worse, sir?"

"I know. It's about as bad as it gets."

Ski picked up a manila folder with "Intel Reports" written in bold letters across the front and waved it at me. "Sir, I read a few days ago the folks in town who are housing the Mooj have put up no-vacancy notices."

"Really?"

"Yes, sir. Mooj are coming in from other counties—Yemen, Egypt, Chechnya, Syria, wherever. Now the Ramadiites have run out of space to keep them." He pulled out two pages. "Know what else?"

"What?"

"The Mooj are using midgets."

"Little people?"

"Yeah—to emplace IEDs."

I huffed. "Did you read that on the shitter wall?"

He handed me the pages. "I'm just the messenger, sir."

I made a jar of tea while we listened to the radio traffic. It took nearly an hour, but they found the missing Marine, blown a hundred meters from the vehicle. Dead.

Once the radio chatter subsided, we went outside to smoke. A pinch of morning sun broke over Ramadi.

I lit a cigar while Sergeant Ski puffed a cigarette.

"Sir, that day at the Health Compound—"

"What about it?" I sipped from the jar, gazing at the sunrise.

"Sir, if you hadn't—"

"That's not so. Don't say that again—to anybody. Understand?"

"Roger, sir."

⌘

Near Camp Phoenix there was a garbage dump where the U.S Army pitched their throwaway stuff. I say their "throwaway stuff" and not *garbage*, because the Army threw away a lot of things that the *jundi* found useful—pads of paper, pens, old uniforms, old boots, office furniture, and the like. Much of the stuff they tossed was, in fact, brand new, a sin in the perennially cashed-strapped Marine Corps.

One evening Leo and I were smashing up ammo boxes, making kindling, when we saw a pack of *jundi* pushing two makeshift wheelbarrows piled high with an assortment of loot.

"What did you tell that Army major the last time he came down and demanded you stop them from digging in the garbage?" asked Leo.

I stomped a crate apart with my boot. "Same thing as the time before. I'll do my best to stop them." I waved at the *jundi*; they waved back. "But that would be like asking my kinfolk back home to quit poaching deer and spearing pike. It's not going to happen."

"I'll get us a drink, sir." Leo walked off.

By the time he returned, I'd piled kindling and we sat for a while, not saying much. I re- read letters—Kate's, my mom's, and John's—Leo did the same.

When it was nearly dark, I lit a fire and Leo poured our drinks. After telling me one of his kids was showing great potential as a baseball player, he asked what I'd heard from home.

"Kate's fine. She's got beautiful handwriting, like my mother. My ma's starting garden plants inside the house." I took a drink and thought of D.C.

John Dunne wrote that his show in Brussels sold out. He was now trying to line up a one- man show for me at the Hutchinson Collection. Though I was glad for him, it all seemed a long way off, and small.

The dry wood of the ammo boxes burned brightly, crackling loudly as it threw off sparks. Leo folded his letters. "Sir?"

"What's that, Leo?"

"Nick told me something a bit unnerving about Mujeed."

"Hmm?"

"He said when Mujeed got hit leaving Taji, his protective vest was stuffed with bills—American bills."

"You mean Benjamins and Grants?"

"Indeed, sir. Those kind."

"Really? No SAPI plates?"

"Apparently not."

I took a drink, drew my lips back, and exhaled. "I'll not be asking him about that. There's something I *am* going to ask him about, though."

"Sir?"

"The ghost *jundi*. What we call corruption is their way of life. We've got our own. I know, I've done business in Washington, D.C.—but Mujeed's got way too many ghost *jundi*."

"How many do you think he's got?"

"Can't be sure, but there are supposed to be about three hundred and eighty *jundi* in his battalion. One third are always on leave, and a platoon stays at OP Hyrea. Still, I've never seen more than one hundred twenty together. So I figure there are around one hundred fifty unaccounted for. Dead, wounded, deserters, whatever."

Leo picked up a stone, cocked his arm, and threw it at the Port-a-John standing fifteen meters away. It hit the plastic door with a hollow sharp wallop. He brushed his hands off. "And they're still on the pay roster."

"Good shot." I picked up a rock and was about to do the same when I heard the spring holding the door shut groan.

The door slammed and Doc's voice rang out. "What the hell, gentlemen!" He cinched his belt. "A man can't even take a peaceful shit around here," he laughed.

"Sorry, Doc—it was Captain Essex."

Doc laughed again and walked away.

I tossed the rock straight up, caught it in the palm of my hand. "I assume everybody's getting their cut of those bags of money the officers haul back from the Ministry of Defense in Baghdad each month. Best guess, a third of it goes unclaimed, and Mujeed and his officers split that. I'm not on a crusade, but I've got to warn Mujeed it will bite him in the ass eventually."

"Are you going to speak to him about the rape?"

I rolled the rock between my fingers. "When the time's right. Learn anything new about that?"

"It's about the same with a couple of caveats."

"And those are?"

"The two *jundi* that raped the kid have done it before."

I tossed the rock up and caught it again.

"That's what Major Thalmer says. He didn't say it was common, but he says it happens."

"I wonder if Mujeed knows that I know."

"No telling," replied Leo. "I'm surprised he hasn't spoken to you about it already." Leo stared at the fire, fingering his lower lip. "Thalmer told me two older *jundi* caught the young one alone in the barracks while everyone else was at chow. The Iraqi lieutenant on duty just happened to be walking by and heard the kid crying. Apparently, he drew his pistol and brought it to a halt, but the sons of bitches were already underway, hammering the kid in the ass. Damage done."

"Damn. Right in the heat of day and all. That's rough." I shook my head. "We infidels may keep dogs, watch Hollywood movies, and think Jesus is the Son of God, but we don't pin down young troops and peg them in the ass on a Thursday afternoon." I closed my fist over the rock. "You know, Leo, I like Mujeed, Ayrab or not. He's personable, and he holds this battalion together. I read there was a graduation from boot camp in Taji last week. Afterwards, they lined the new troops up in formation, praised them as great and fearless warriors, and then told them they were headed for Anbar Province."

I stood and wound up as if I were at a pitcher's mound. "Then, right there, I mean *right there* in formation, they took their gear off, threw it on the ground." I hurled the rock at the shitter—and missed. "Just quit."

"Wow."

I sat back down. "Sergeant Ski got the report from somewhere." Leo looked away. "We can't take him out again, sir."

"I know," I sighed. "He's been broken since the fight at the Health Compound."

"What do we do with him?"

"Leave him be. I'll find some place to let him get his mojo back." I thought of the Marines on my team. "Staff Sergeant Craig."

"What about him, sir?"

"He's been on every mission we've been on—patrols, ambushes, and searches—whatever. Still shakes like a leaf, but I don't really notice it anymore. I'm worried that DUI may prevent him from ever making gunnery sergeant."

"You think?"

"Likely. But he's the bravest we've got, never loses his head. I'll say that in his fitness report, and Headquarters Marine Corps can decide after that. He's what we need out here, DUI or not."

CHAPTER 23

Outside, only the mornings and evenings were enjoyable. With the temperature hovering over a hundred degrees each day, the midday heat was stifling.

The mud caused by rains earlier in the year baked into a crust of cracked clay that covered the ground. Alexander marched over this ground; the Romans fought near here. Eastward lay Baghdad—the Mongols sacked it, the Turks conquered it, and the British occupied the land after that. Now my own war was here, right in the middle of Satan's front yard where so many had endured or been consumed.

The heat had an impact on the fighting; the Mooj restricted their movements to late afternoon hours, when the shadows stretched long. The heaviest work, laying IEDs, they did at night. Route Michigan, the main road into and through Ramadi, went from perilous to treacherous with improvised explosives of varying sizes and designs tearing apart armored Humvees as if they were made of plywood. One week, the Army lost two M1 Abram tanks to massive IEDs. Marines from Three-Eight caught it the worst simply because they operated from vehicles so often. There were rumors of better bomb-resistant armored vehicles arriving in theater—a modification of the V-bottomed South African model. My

Marines and Mujeed's *jundi* moved on foot and only took moderate losses—seven dead and eighteen wounded.

I knew one of the *jundi* who got killed rather well. In fact, we traveled on patrol together on several occasions, and he'd taken to bumming cigars off me when no Iraqi officers were around. He died an agonizing death on patrol when he unwittingly squatted on a concealed gallon can of nails, screws, metal scraps, and a brew of explosives, and it detonated. Ten yards away when the bomb blew, I saw him soar into the air, descend, and land with a thump. We carried him back to the Government Center and transported him to Charlie Med aboard Camp Ramadi. He died in surgery three hours later. X-rays showed hundreds of perforations to his anus, large intestine, and abdominal area, his testicles severed from his crotch.

I took Mujeed to see the man's body. The lance corporal working at the cooler walked us inside and unzipped the black bag to reveal the corpse. Mujeed prayed over it, and we left.

Rumors flourished of a block-by-block takedown of Ramadi—à la Fallujah. In the meantime, we kept patrolling, conducting operations, and training the *jundi*.

Around this time, I noticed Lieutenant Lott quit going to chow with the other Marines. I asked Leo about it.

"Sir, he's taken to eating with some Army females."

Standing under a shaded porch area of the command post and staring at the shimmering horizon, I turned my head to Leo. "You're kidding me." Like me, Leo was stripped to his undershirt and sweating.

He removed his cover and wiped sweat from his brow. "No, sir."

"What do the others think about it?"

Leo shook his head. "The lieutenants keep clear of him. Craig and Sergeant Ski have been busting his balls about it."

"Right. There's always one in the crowd willing to—"

Sergeant Ski stepped outside and cut me off. "Sir. Lieutenant Colonel Dean is on the hook for you."

I snapped my fingers, pointed at Leo, and grinned. "Somebody is always willing to venture to the dark side, Leo." Walking away, I added, "Keep an eye on it."

I hadn't heard from Dean since our run-in at Camp Taji. Once again, I had the nagging feeling I knew the guy.

I picked up the radio handset. "Drifter-Six here. Over."

I listened as Dean told me that he, the Iraqi division advisor, Colonel Marr, and his team planned to come and visit us.

"Roger. I'll pick you up at Camp Ramadi LZ tomorrow. Over."

"Roger. Out," Dean transmitted.

When I got back outside, Leo was smoking a cigar. "Colonel Marr's coming tomorrow," I said and leaned again on the brick wall. Shaded, it still retained some of the night-time cool. "Dean's coming with him."

"Why, sir?"

"Sounds like a routine visit."

Leo dragged on his cigar. "Routine, sir? We haven't seen anybody in our chain of command since Taji."

"Let's keep it that way. I'll brief the colonel on our overall plan. You stick with Dean. He strikes me as the nosy type."

"Anything special we need to discuss with them?"

"No. Don't share our problems with Kilo Company."

"Wouldn't matter anyway. When I spoke to Captain DeMarco…."

The plywood door of the command post creaked open. "Sir." Sergeant Ski was back.

"Dean again?" I asked, pushing myself away from the wall. "Leo, hold that thought."

Inside I picked up the hook. Dean explained to me he needed a convoy escort from East Fallujah Expeditionary Camp to Camp Phoenix.

"Sir, I thought you were flying in. When you said Ramadi, I thought you meant Camp Ramadi, at the LZ where I am, not Ramadi where the Hundred-'n'-First is. That's seven klicks away and on a black route that's been black since last year—it's blacker than black. Every time anyone goes out there, someone gets smoked."

"We don't have time to drive the northern route," Dean shot back.

"Sir, if daylight is the issue, you can stay here overnight and drive back the next day. I'll pick you up at the back gate. No one's been hit there for a while. I strongly recommend you take Colonel Marr that way."

I couldn't convince him. He got angry and stopped using my name, referring to me only as *Major.*

"Sir, okay, come as you wish. I'll call the Hundred-'n'-First. They have tanks and can guide you. I'm not taking my men out there in Humvees. I'll call you back once we've coordinated the tanks. Out." I ended the transmission, even though he had initiated it.

⌘

The visit with Colonel Marr went well. I briefed him on the progress of the battalion and showed him our plan to improve Mujeed's unit. It helped that we had already accomplished two- thirds of our training goals. He could see we were on the right track and had a solid plan.

I explained why Leo coordinated the tank escort for him and how we stayed off the roads in Humvees unless absolutely necessary. Colonel Marr knew that most of the casualties occurred while traveling in vehicles and told me it was a good call.

Colonel Marr met Mujeed; we all smoked and drank tea.

Before they left, Dean walked past me and remarked, "Nothing happened. We didn't even see anything on the road."

"You got lucky, sir," I said.

I shook Colonel Marr's hand when he left. Leo and I stood in the shade of the porch and watched them drive away.

"Son of a bitch," I said to Leo.

"Still can't remember where you know him from, sir?"

I lit a cigar. "No. It must have been when I was a lieutenant—when everything was a blur. My recollection vault will open, though, and I'll remember. Don't worry. By the way, the colonel didn't care who escorted him here. It was Dean."

"It was?"

"Colonel Marr's a first-rate officer; he knows the deal. Read any consolidated casualty report, and it shows folks get killed driving around in Humvees. It's a pattern."

"Why was he so insistent about us guiding him in?"

"Who knows? Probably just wanted me to jump when he said jump. Or maybe he simply didn't want to flex once he had the plan set."

"Lieutenant Colonel Dean mentioned us moving to Fallujah."

"So did the colonel. Ignore it. As I said, one day Colonel Steeples will call me and say, 'Pack your shit and move to Fallujah,' and that will be it. Until then, it's all talk, like the tale that there's a political solution to Ramadi."

⌘

A few days later, Leo brought a Navy lieutenant—a SEAL—to see me. I was aware of the operations they were executing with the U.S Army and Marines.

Leo recommended I hear the man out. We invited him to our fire and shared our booze and cigars with him.

The young man explained his situation. "Sir, we can't operate in town without Iraqis. Partnering is a requirement. Until we get some Iraqis to work with, all we can do is support the Army and Marine battalions."

I could sense his frustration and sympathized with him.

"It doesn't matter to me," I said. "Mujeed probably won't go for it, though."

"Why not, sir?"

"Long story, but the *jundi* have a superstition about SEALs, and they refuse to train with them."

I described the situations with the boot sole, the burned-up vehicle, the fate of the roasted cadavers, and the tie-in with the SEALs. It caused the young man some consternation, but I told him I'd take it up with Mujeed and to come back the next day.

After he left, Leo asked, "You really going to speak to Mujeed about this, sir?"

"Sure. If we worked with the SEALs, we'd have an excuse to dump DeMarco and Kilo Company. Which would you choose, SEALs or those buffoons? Trick-or-treat request or not, that guy's on our side."

"Trick or treat?"

I explained it the way it was told to me.

Leo blew cigar smoke. "Sir, when I spoke to DeMarco, it was as if he wanted us there just so they can say they're conducting operations with the Iraqis. You're right, they aren't much interested in developing them."

"Well, I can understand on one hand. This is combat, not the ideal training environment—we're trying to do both at once. But that's our mission. I've tried to explain this to Captain DeMarco. It doesn't help."

I spoke to Mujeed about the SEALs' desire to train with the *jundi*. I was given an emphatic *no*. He wouldn't even consider it, saying it would cause a mutiny. I didn't press him too much and left mystified.

When the SEAL came back, I explained to him Mujeed's intransigence. Undeterred, he asked to speak to Mujeed. I suspected he was having problems working with Three-Eight. They owned the battle space, not the SEALs; he needed leverage to get into the fight on his own terms.

I took him to Mujeed's office.

Mujeed and the sailor spent an hour discussing the training the SEALs gave his men.

They both characterized it as outstanding. Mujeed was cordial but remained firm that his men's perception of past events prohibited further partnering. He rejected every workaround the young officer offered. Worn down, the SEAL finally quit trying to change Mujeed's mind, and we left.

"I've got to tell you, I am sorry, Lieutenant. I've never seen Mujeed dig in quite like this," I said.

"Sir, we were not the people who did it," he said bitterly.

"We all look the same to them. You wear the Trident, and to them, that's the path to a bad death and a questionable burial. Irrational, I know, but that's the deal."

He left disappointed. I never saw the man again.

⌘

Leo planned a patrol using two Iraqi companies but without the Marines from Kilo coming along; he wanted to see what the Iraqis could do by themselves. I gave it the thumbs up, and we worked out the details with Mujeed and Major Thalmer, keeping the objective simple—check out a pair of blasted-out buildings across the street from Observation Post Hyrea. Duty at Hyrea was intended to be a rest period, so the platoons didn't patrol from it. The problem was, real rest was sporadic because every couple of nights Mooj slipped into the buildings across the street and exchanged fire with the Marines and *jundi* in OP Hyrea.

Marines staying at Hyrea said they knew when they killed someone in the buildings because dogs came in packs afterwards and, they claimed, feasted on the corpses. Although we assumed this was rumor, we were curious.

The Iraqi solo operation didn't go well from the start.

It was an overcast morning. While we waited in the courtyard doing final prep, an F-18 Hornet screamed along Route Michigan, buzzed the Government Center, making a roar that echoed like a giant, inch thick, piece of paper being ripped in half. I only caught a glimpse of it as it tore by. For some reason it dropped flares. They burned like tiny white suns against the slate-gray sky.

The unexpected attention was unsettling.

Just before stepping off, we got word that someone across the street was observing the Government Center with binoculars. Shortly after, three M16 shots rang out.

I tuned my radio to the Kilo Company local security channel and listened to the aftermath. Two men were shot and lay in the rubble right outside the gate. From inside the courtyard, we heard them moaning and crying in agony.

Chatter on the radio went back and forth between the post security sergeant and the Kilo Company HQ element. The issue was whether or not to go get the men.

Our mission was postponed while Kilo Company worked to resolve the issue.

Meanwhile, we milled about—waiting and trying to ignore the men's suffering. There were nearly forty *jundi* in the courtyard with nothing to do but listen to the shot men groan. The pitch of the *jundi* voices increased.

Sergeant Muhammed approached me. "Sir, I'm going to get the men."

"Let Kilo go get them. They did it," I said.

"Sir, it's not that—the *jundi* want to help them."

Looking at the unsettled Iraqis, I knew it would be worse to wait. "Go get them, and hurry."

Muhammed and six or seven *jundi* left the compound. They returned five minutes later, four of them hauling a man by his limbs. He was dead. They dropped him beside a Texas barrier protecting an entrance to the Government Center. Another two *jundi* came in close behind, helping an injured man, his white man-dress drenched in blood.

A corpsman from Kilo Company began treating the wounded man. Sergeant Muhammed translated as the man sobbed, shook his head, and spoke his language. I was about to address the issue of the dead body lying in the dirt when the traffic on the radio increased. The Marines at the guard post reported seeing more civilians moving in the rubble, near the place where the two men had been shot. I turned my back to the corpse, bent my head to my radio to listen. After a few seconds, Leo stepped in front of me.

I cocked my head towards the wounded man behind me. "What's he saying?"

"Sir, he says that the dead man is his father, or uncle, Sergeant Muhammed can't tell which. The man claims they weren't observing the compound, said they didn't have binoculars."

"Ahhh, shit. Did Sergeant Muhammed find any binos?"

"He didn't know to look. We'll check when we leave."

"What a mess." I turned towards the growing commotion of the *jundi*, now pointing in the direction of the wounded man and the heap of flesh and bloody man-dress lying at the base of the barrier. Muhammed and my Marines were amongst them, trying to calm them down.

"Sergeant Muhammed!" I barked, motioning him over.

"Get that dead man out of here," I ordered the Kurd. "Haul the body back behind that building." I pointed to one of the outlying shacks. "Cover him up with a blanket. We're about to step off on patrol, and the *jundi*, they're losing any mind for business. Get it out of here."

"Roger, sir." He hustled off.

"Leo, go tell the corpsman to move the man inside—now."

"Roger, sir, will do."

"Staff Sergeant Craig, Lieutenant O'Shannihan—Randolph!" I yelled, walking towards them. "We're going out the other gate. Get the *jundi* back into patrol formation. Five mikes," I said, holding up my hand and stretching my fingers apart.

"Aye, aye, sir," replied O'Shannihan. "Sir, they're pissed. They think we—the Marines on post—killed the man for nothing."

"I don't know why they killed him, but we need to move before this gets bad. Get them out of here."

"Roger, sir. Five mikes. We'll be ready to roll," said Randolph. He and O'Shannihan turned away. Staff Sergeant

Craig was already herding the *jundi* into two parallel files, signaling with his hands and speaking broken Arabic.

Captain DeMarco never came out of the Government Center to get eyes on the point of friction. Likely, it was better that way.

According to our plan, Leo's element was to check out the objective. Mine was to search a nearby gas station that was reported to be suspiciously busy. It was a questionable reason for a search since I never knew a place in Ramadi that didn't seem suspicious in some way. I had no desire to patrol a place where dogs ate the dead, so I left that to Leo. He hadn't concealed his curiosity.

Leo's element split off when we got to the gas station. O'Shannihan stayed with me. By this point I was in a hurry, having decided the whole mission was a boondoggle.

A minute after Leo left, I pressed the go-button on my radio. "Drifter-Five, make it quick."

"Roger, Drifter-Six," Leo replied.

We were only at the gas station five minutes when the whole area went quiet—no vehicle traffic, no kids running about, no shop business—nothing. Then somebody started howling over the loudspeaker of a nearby mosque. I assumed it was their afternoon prayer and checked my watch. Something was out of place.

I looked around for Nick. "What's he saying?"

"Suh, hold on." Nick leaned his head in the direction of the loudspeaker, listening for a minute before replying, "Suh…he's saying something about a funeral."

"You mean for the dead guy back at the compound?"

Nick continued to listen. After a minute he said, "No, suh, not him. I can't tell. It *is* something about a funeral, but I think he means…I think he means a funeral for you, suh."

I searched for a place to sit. I spotted a phone booth with a chair's skeleton inside, an array of angry-looking wires reaching out from where a phone had once hung. Near it lay a cinderblock. I nudged the cinder block with my boot—no wires connected. I sat down on it and waited for Leo.

Twenty minutes and a nervous cigar later, he arrived back, winded. "Nothing there. We hurried."

"I can see that. Don't stop the patrol. We'll fall in behind you."

"Roger."

"Didn't find *anything?*"

"Nothing, sir. The place is a shambles, a good hiding place to shoot at OP Hyrea from. That's about it."

"Okay, nothing here either. It's been quiet." I looked around for a minaret. "I don't know why they don't bulldoze this whole place down—everything."

Leo and I stuck together on the way back. As we crossed an empty street, a single shot fired from the south just missed Leo, taking out a fist-sized piece of masonry above his head. From across the few meters that separated us he glanced my way, then disappeared around the nearest corner. I darted for cover in another direction.

Immediately, the *jundi* began firing their rifles at a four-story building to my left, 300 meters away, where the road we were crossing ended. I didn't relish getting pinned down; we still had most of the patrol that needed to cross the street. It was an easy fix. I pulled the smoke grenade from my protective vest, yanked the pin out, and tossed it 25 meters towards the building between us and whoever had shot at Leo. I caught O'Shannihan's eye and motioned for him to do the same. Top Bruce, still on the other side of the street, followed his lead. Somebody threw another for good measure. It took thirty seconds for the smoke to billow and another thirty for the *jundi* to stop firing. Then we were on the move again.

I called to where I saw Leo go, "Leo!" No answer. "Leo!" Still none. "Leo, you okay?"

"Sir, I'm fine. I'm just thinking," he said from a few yards away. He fell in behind me as I passed the pile of rubble he'd been crouched behind. "Son of a bitch."

The sun came out.

We hurried through the smoke and silence of the ragged, bullet-ridden, trash-strewn maze that had once been a thriving city. As we approached the Government Center, I looked across the street and saw the Muscle Man sign I'd noticed while out on patrol the very first time. An ordnance blast had obliterated the upper half of the figure's torso. Only his head, arms, and lower body below his navel remained.

When I got back to Camp Phoenix, I sat down in the radio room next to Sergeant Ski and wrote my daily report to Lieutenant Colonel Steeples.

SUBJECT: 3-2-1 MiTT DAILY REPORT
Conducted routine search mission. NSTR.

Finished, I handed it to Sergeant Ski. "Send this to the Brigade MiTT."

He took the slip of paper, read it, and laughed. "Okay, sir, NSTR, but have you seen the women of Ramadi? You might want to send it instead."

"You mean Arab chicks?" I turned to leave the room. "No thanks."

"No, sir. I mean the female soldiers and Marines aboard base." Ski held a thumb drive up to me. "You've got to see the photos, sir."

"I've got to look at those filthy creatures every time I go to the chow hall or the PX," I said. Ski stuck in the thumb drive. "You can't buy a decent cigar over there, but they've got a hundred different varieties of feminine napkins and all colors of mascara. Ever wonder why that is?"

"No, sir," he said, fingering the keys on the computer.

"The females are the only ones that fill out the complaint cards. No self-respecting man would lower himself."

"That's true, but someone left it on a recreational computer on base. It's actually titled, *The Women of Ramadi*. Those nasty bitches have taken hundreds of photos of themselves—tits, muff shots, costumes, you name it. You'll even recognize some of them."

"No, I won't. I never look at them long enough to recognize them again."

Ski turned the computer so I could see the screen. "Oh, c'mon, sir, just look a second. This'll make you sick." A photo of a nude woman—reclined on a cot in a plywood-sided room, digital cammie blouse pulled back, breasts revealed, and wearing red lace underwear—smiled at us. A rose was tramp-stamped below her navel. "Told you, sir," he laughed.

Ski's enthusiasm was infectious. I sat with him looking at tawdry photos for five or ten minutes while he laughed and provided commentary.

"Sir, it's ugly, but you got to have 'em. Prostitution's illegal, we got rid of the baggage train a hundred years ago, and we kicked the strippers out of the clubs on base. But we couldn't live without 'em, so we recruited them."

Just then, Leo stuck his head into the radio room and rescued me. "Ready, sir?"

I stood up.

"Okay, sir, but you're giving up all this for a drink with Captain Essex. Go ahead, go ahead," said Ski.

I looked at the sergeant and winked.

"Sir, you don't think I know?"

I came to attention. "Marine, drinking in Iraq is a violation of General Order Number One. *Thou shalt not have a drink due to the sensitivity of Arabs to alcohol and their exemplary attitude towards women when sober. Furthermore, while risking life and limb for your fellow countrymen getting drunk and watching football on television back home, alcohol is inappropriate. Signed George*—whatever his middle initial is—*Casey.* An officer and a gentleman such as me and Captain Essex would never partake under these circumstances."

CHAPTER 24

Near the command post I found a three-foot tree limb, an inch round at one end and tapered to a point. Nearly straight, it was crooked enough in a few places to be interesting, a curiosity since there weren't any trees near Camp Phoenix. I kept it.

Late one afternoon, I was standing in front of the command post playing with the stick when a U.S. Army sergeant first class drove up to Camp Phoenix in a Humvee and approached me.

"What does it look like?" I gazed down and scratched circles with the stick in the baked earth.

"It's a white Ford Ranger," the soldier replied.

"Why are you looking for it?"

"We need it."

"What was it doing in the garbage dump?"

He scanned the area. "We're going to blow it up for demolition practice."

"Haven't seen it." I scribbled out the circle I'd etched. "I'll let you know if I do."

The soldier stared at me; I stared back.

When he'd had enough, he walked to his vehicle and left. After he was out of sight, I went to the back of the command post where the white Ford Ranger was parked. Hussein and a handful of *jundi* were nearby, cooking carp in a fire pit.

Hussein flashed his grin. "Hello, Major. *Feesh?*"

"Hello, Hussein. No thanks. Where's Mujeed?"

"Mujeed?"

"Yeah, that guy. I need to talk to him right now." I pointed at the ground with my stick.

Hussein stood up, still grinning.

I changed tactics, pointing to my chest. "Me. Mujeed. Talk. Now."

His smile vanished, and he mumbled, "Hello," before shuffling as fast as he could towards the command post.

I waited.

After a minute, Mujeed strode out of the building, followed by Hussein and Sergeant Achmed. His hair was tousled, his boots untied; he'd been taking a nap. Concern wrinkled his forehead as he walked towards me.

Hussein glanced my way and moved smartly back to the cook pit. Sergeant Achmed remained at Mujeed's side, his arms folded, weapon slung over his shoulder.

Shielding his eyes from the setting sun, Mujeed looked at me and said, "Major, something wrong?"

"*Na'am, Sati.*" I pointed at the Ford. "That vehicle." The hood was raised, and two *jundi* worked beneath it, tools strewn around. "Get it out of here."

Mujeed opened his mouth to speak; I cut him off. "*Sati,* the Army is looking for that vehicle. Get rid of it—move it away from here."

"But...we find it...in...garbage. Engine...no good."

I tucked my stick under my arm. "I understand, *Sati,* but the Army wants it back—for practice. Army blow it up.

Boom!" I said, throwing my hands in the air. "If you want to keep it, move it now. Understand?"

He looked at his watch. "*Na'am,* Major. Okay, gone." He barked something at the men working underneath the vehicle. When Mujeed finished, Sergeant Achmed walked towards the mechanics, clapping his hands and echoing whatever it was Mujeed said.

At dusk, I walked to the back of the command post; the vehicle was gone. Not satisfied, I went inside, dug into my seabag, and pulled out a pair of Steiners I'd never used hunting Mooj. I went back outside, scaled the ladder to the roof of the command post, and lifted the binos.

My vision magnified eight times, I focused in on the garbage dump about 900 meters away. No white Ford.

I scanned the horizon in every direction—no vehicle.

Still not satisfied, I climbed down the ladder and walked 200 meters towards the *jundi* barracks. No vehicle. I saw Sergeant Muhammed seated on an ammo crate next to a fire, two other *jundi* sitting near him.

When he saw me, Muhammed stood and shouted, "Major, you need something?"

I placed my hand over my heart. "Evening, Sergeant Muhammed."

"How are you, sir?" He greeted me with a handshake. "Hungry?"

I took in the bean gruel, rice, and flatbread. "Looks good, but no thanks."

He glanced at the binoculars hanging around my neck. "Are you looking for something?" I tucked my stick under my arm and plunged my hands into my pockets. "Sergeant Muhammed, have you seen the white Ford that's been out back of the command post the past few days?"

Muhammed put his hands on his hips and shook his head. "Ahhh, Major. I heard about it. But I think it's gone now."

I leveled my gaze at Sergeant Muhammed. "How gone?"

He laughed. "Well, sir, I'm pretty sure no one around here will ever find it." I nodded. "Thanks, Sergeant Muhammed."

"Ahhh, sir. Can I ask you why the Army was going to blow it up?"

"That's what you heard?"

He adjusted the U.S.-issue tanker holster that held a .45 caliber M1911 Springfield. "I think someone said that."

"Well, I don't know who told you that, but the Army asked me to help them find it. Maybe they wanted to practice on it."

"I heard it was a perfectly good truck, sir. Good tires, nice interior, nice body, not too many miles. They say the only problem was the base steel of the engine."

"The engine block?"

"Yes. It was broken. A small, uh…" He made a jagged up-and-down motion with his first finger.

"Cracked, the engine block was *cracked*."

"Yes, sir, that's the word—*cracked*. Fix that and it is a perfectly good vehicle."

"Thanks, Sergeant Muhammed. I'll quit looking. If the Army comes back and they're not convinced, I'll leave it to them to have a look around."

"Okay, sir." He smiled and rubbed his black mustache, following the whiskers with his thumb and forefinger from under his nose, around the corners of his mouth and down to the base of his jaw. "But it won't be anywhere near here."

⌘

Kilo Company planned a cordon and search mission targeting an area south of the Government Center. Once again, the *jundi* built a terrain model, this time of a twenty-block section of the city.

I met Captain DeMarco when he and his men arrived at Camp Phoenix for the brief. His finger was bandaged. The battalion operations officer, Major Miller, was with him.

The mission was to be conducted jointly, but unlike other missions, Kilo Company was to lead it, with the Iraqis providing supporting manpower. All three Iraqi companies were needed, a battalion-sized operation—a first for Mujeed's men. The Marines planned to bring two platoons, dog teams, and sniper teams for overwatch. In addition, we requested an Army tank platoon. The Army sergeant leading the designated tank platoon attended the brief.

Captain DeMarco briefed his plan while Nick translated. I sat next to Mujeed, tapping my boot with my stick. Five minutes into the brief, I stopped DeMarco because he was passing classified information with the Iraqis present. I glanced at Major Miller. Seated with his hand on his chin, he shut his eyes and shook his head. It was a minor interruption.

While DeMarco spoke, Mujeed stood, politely waiting for a chance to speak. I raised my hand to DeMarco. He stopped talking, and I said to the group, "Colonel Mujeed's got something to say."

Mujeed talked and Nick translated. "Suh, Colonel Mujeed says that we should search the area from east to west, not north to south, because the streets are shorter that way and won't allow anyone to fire at us from long distances."

"Shorter axis of advance, you mean?" I said, looking at Mujeed and then to DeMarco. "Sounds reasonable."

DeMarco began defending his plan. He droned on for ten minutes about how it wouldn't matter which way we attacked. Listening to him pontificate was tiring and reminded me of suffering through a Saturday-evening variety show broadcasted by National Public Radio. It was already planned, he explained, and it was too late to change it.

Mujeed remained opposed.

We went back and forth for a half hour with various officers on both sides weighing in. In the end, we decided to stick with the original plan.

Mujeed wasn't pleased.

When the brief was over, I realized the tank platoon sergeant hadn't briefed his role. I pulled him and DeMarco aside to discuss the omission.

I thought the soldier may have been unfamiliar with how Marines did business and assumed his part was simply too obvious to be briefed. I learned otherwise.

"Sir," DeMarco began, "I decided we didn't need the—"

"We don't need the tanks?" I cut in.

As I spoke, Major Miller joined us.

"Sir. No. They're just going to be—"

"We need the tanks," I interrupted again. "If nothing else, they're intimidating; we'll set them on the corners of the cordon," I pointed at the terrain model with my stick, "there, there, there, and there. They'll have clear fields of fire to cover the box created by our cordon. If the Mooj try to cross into our operating area and disrupt us while we're doing our business, the tanks have heavy machine guns and can mow them down." I turned to the tank platoon leader. "Right, Sergeant?"

"Sir, that's what I thought we planned, yes."

I glanced at Miller. He raised his eyebrows.

"Well, I was just thinking—" DeMarco started. Major Miller cut him off. "You need the tanks."

DeMarco raised his hands, palms facing me. "Okay, gentlemen, have it your way."

I reached out and shook his hand. "Thanks. I'll see you about zero-six at the Government Center."

⌘

I waited outside under the moonlight, eating a chili con carne MRE with MRE cheese squeezed over it. It was 0500. I'd been awake for two hours.

I heard footsteps behind me, and Mujeed appeared in full combat gear. "*Sati, salam alekum,*" I greeted.

"*Alekum salam.* Thank you, Major," he replied.

"First battalion-sized operation, *Sati.*"

"*Na'am,* Major. Very good. Thank you."

"In the old army, you did many battalion operations?"

"Yes, Major, but then…it was different. These *jundi* are new, and my officers…they most not in old army."

"*Na'am,* I understand."

Mujeed lit a cigarette.

I spooned out chili and cheese, took a bite.

"Major, I still think the…how do you say…*akksees…*?"

"Yes, axis of advance, as we term it anyways."

"Yes, uhhh, still not so good for this operation."

"*Na'am, Sati,*" I said, holding breakfast in one hand and waving with the other. "I agree with you, but Kilo planned the operation. We'll be there to provide the search element. Nothing we can do now."

"I say nothing more, Major."

"Thank you, sir. Sorry."

Leo knew how I felt about the Kilo Company commander. Telling a fellow Marine officer you're disappointed
in another Marine officer is one thing, but telling an Iraqi is
different. I looked at Mujeed smoking his cigarette, dressed
in his battle gear, waiting on men who relied on him, and
spat, "That guy's a fucking jackass."

Mujeed studied me for a moment and nodded.

I headed towards the command post to check for updates
from the radio watch, Sergeant Ski. As I passed our vehicles,
I saw three of my Marines silhouetted against the building,
gathered in a tight cluster. I walked closer. Their heads were
bowed. It was Randolph, Craig, and O'Shannihan. I heard
Randolph's voice; he was leading them in prayer. A few paces
away, I stopped and bowed my head. My mother prayed for
me every day, I knew; likely three or four times a day. I hadn't
bothered—she was still toting my load with the Lord for me,
just as she always had.

"...with us today, Lord, as we set out for another day
in the presence of our enemies. In Jesus's name we pray,"
Randolph said. In unison, they all followed with, "Amen."

My thoughts remained on my mother a moment. When
I looked up, all three men were staring at me. Nobody spoke.
Craig nodded at me, and I moved on.

⌘

The cordon was set by 0800. We stepped off for the
search with each Iraqi company assigned a sector and partnered with a section of Marines from the Kilo Company.

We moved slowly.

By 1000, the search element to my left uncovered a large
cache of explosives and small arms. Top Bruce and I moved

with the element advancing along the middle axis. Just after noon, we came under heavy machine-gun fire. We kicked open the door of a two-story townhouse and spread out. Top went to the second floor with four *jundi* and Marines from Kilo Company, searching for a vantage point to engage the enemy. I stayed on the first floor with two *jundi* and sat on a sofa, talking on the radio and coordinating our fire and movement with the elements moving to our left and right. The clanging of metal hitting metal somewhere near the rear of the house interrupted my concentration.

I signaled for the two *jundi* to watch the front door and stood up.

Turning off both my radios, I carefully moved into the next room, my weapon at the ready.

The room was furnished with a low table surrounded by ornate pillows and carpeted with plush Persian rugs. Nothing. At the other end of that room was the entrance to another. In it, I saw cooking utensils hanging from hooks and pots strewn across the floor. I approached cautiously, my thumb rested on the safety of my weapon.

As I crept forward, I recalled a friend who I drank with years earlier—a grizzled sergeant major who'd served with Fifth Marines in Vietnam. There he sat, on a stool and leaned over the bar of a Kinville karaoke joint outside the back gate of Camp Hansen, Okinawa, a dozen years retired, beat down and broken by booze, telling me, "Don't ever run to your death."

The memory flashed in and out of my thoughts in a matter of seconds. Focusing and stepping heel first in my rubber-soled combat boots, I inched towards the entrance of the room.

A burst of machine-gun fire in the distance startled me. I froze.

The Marines on the second floor began firing.

Once the gunfire slowed, I edged forward again. I held my breath so I could hear above my heart pounding against my front SAPI plate. Two feet from the entrance, I began easing my weapon off safe, then stopped, afraid to make a sound.

From where I stood, it appeared the room was a long rectangle, eight feet deep from the door to the wall, width unknown. I inhaled deeply and lunged towards the opposite side of the kitchen, sending a pan clanging across the ceramic tiled floor. I landed with my back against the opposite wall and my weapon trained along the expanse of the room, my finger on the trigger, safety off.

Over the front sight post of my weapon was a woman in a black burka hunched over three small children, pulling them close to her bosom. She was wearing a pink frilled garment under the burka and black high heels with silver trim. The kids were barefoot.

I sank to the floor. I'd come a cunt hair away from shooting women and children.

Trembling, I clicked my weapon on safe and rotated the muzzle to the ceiling. I held out my other hand, palm forward and open, gazing at the woman and the kids. She began sobbing and babbling her language, pulling the children closer. I shook my head, steadying my shaking knee with one hand, trying to push myself to my feet with the other; I couldn't. I leaned against the wall and breathed deeply. She never looked my way. I waited. When the shaking ebbed, I stood and braced my palms on my knees. "I'm sorry."

When I stepped back through the entrance to the adjacent room, I puked chili with cheese on the rugs.

After the gunfire abated, we continued the search. Along the way, Top and I fell in with a Marine and his German shepherd. Every ten minutes or so, the handler refreshed the dog by giving it water from a plastic bottle.

The dogs we used relished doing their business. Despite knowing Arab's views on canines, we took them into the houses we searched.

Our dog team joined three other Marines and entered a house, while Top and I waited outside.

Ten minutes later, the Marines exited with four blindfolded men, their hands zip-tied behind their backs. The handler emerged a few seconds later, struggling to keep a hold on his animal as it growled and lunged at the men being escorted away.

"What's going on?" Top asked.

"The fuckers started arguing with us when we told them we were taking them in, and Jeb nearly ate the sons-a-bitches. They quit bitching and let us tie them up after that. He hates Mooj and gets excited whenever we bag a few," said the Marine, hugging the animal's neck and quenching its thirst with the water bottle. "Jeb's getting old and cranky too."

We uncovered two or three other stashes of weapons and ammunition, along with multiple U.S.-issue maps with mortar positions and the corresponding elevation and deflection necessary to shell the Government Center drawn on them.

As we continued, there was more firing. One of the sniper teams shot and killed a man fleeing the cordon on the back of a motorcycle; somehow the driver sped away, apparently unscathed. He didn't get far. A soldier manning the .50

caliber machine gun mounted on one of the tanks cut him in half with a burst of fire.

About 1500, a single shot rang out somewhere in the distance.

Immediately, Leo's voice broke on the radio, *"Drifter-Six, this is Drifter-Five. Over."*

I pushed the go-button. "Go, Drifter-Five."

"We've got a man down, gut shot. Sniper."

I stared at my radio. Young Webb was with him. "Who is it?" I held my breath.

"The Iraqi captain with us."

I exhaled. "Roger. How bad?"

"Can't tell. He's not bleeding much. We're calling a medevac."

"Keep me apprised, Drifter-Five."

"Roger, Drifter-Six. Out."

I listened while Leo coordinated the medevac with Kilo Company headquarters. It took a minute before I realized Captain DeMarco was running the operation from the Government Center.

We didn't finish the mission until after 1800. As we neared the Government Center, we joined the Iraqi platoon and the Marines Leo was with; Leo and I walked together. We passed Muscle Man—he still had his head and both legs, but his crotch was shot out and his right arm was gone from mid biceps up to where his hand gripped the barbell.

Inside the Government Center complex, we found a place in the shade to take off our helmets, sit, and rest.

I pulled two cigars from my pocket.

We lay back. With Marines and Mujeed's *jundi* grouped around me, some already dropping off for a quick nap, I gazed up at the palm fronds, motionless against the blue sky, and enjoyed the cool of the shade, smoking and letting the strain of the day fade away.

After a while I asked Leo, "What happened when he got hit?"

Leo sat up, blinked.

"He was walking down the middle of the road, just like we've trained them *not* to do, and he went down. Nick and I dragged him off the street and into a courtyard. I thought there would be more blood—went right through his gut and out his back."

"We'll go see him when we get back to Camp Ramadi. Mujeed was right about attacking along the short axis."

"It's hard to say. It may have happened regardless. Can't second-guess it now."

I dragged on the cigar and blew a perfect smoke ring. "Mujeed won't say anything."

"You don't think so?" asked Leo, eyes fixed on the dissipating hoop.

I repeated the trick. "Nope. He told me he wouldn't mention it again. He won't." I thought about the mission. "We've come a long way in the past four months, from doing platoon-sized patrols to this—a battalion-sized operation—all in combat."

"Indeed, we have. Did you see the four men that got rolled up?"

"I was there," I said.

"I heard the radio traffic up to battalion. Apparently one of them is an Associated Press reporter."

"A reporter?"

"Yeah, the Marines recognized him from a wanted poster inside the Government Center."

"Get it in the logbook."

"Roger, sir."

I pulled on the cigar and looked around at the Marines and soldiers, reclined, their weapons cradled in their arms or resting against an outstretched limb; the sign came to mind. "Hey, Leo, you ever notice that sign right out the front gate, the muscle man one?"

Leo nodded. "The guy with the barbell, all shot up?"

"I want it. 'Course, I'm not going out there to get it."

"What would you do with it?"

"Keep it and splash some paint on it. Hang it in my house in Wilmington and tell people it's art. Some sort of collage that would make Robert Rauschenberg cry." I pulled on the cigar and readied the smoke for another ring.

"Rauschenberg? The collage guy from the fifties?"

I laughed, blowing the smoke forcefully, obliterating the potential ring. "Yes, that one. Damn, Leo, you're good."

⌘

Back at Camp Phoenix, Leo and I jumped in one of the Russian jeeps and drove to Charlie Med aboard Camp Ramadi. A medic took us into the workspace where we met the Army doctor, a captain about thirty years old, who'd operated on the Iraqi officer.

"You're telling me the bullet didn't even touch his guts?" I asked in disbelief.

"That's correct, sir. It entered here," he pointed to a spot on his own abdomen about four inches lateral from his bellybutton, "and came out here," he slid his finger around towards the middle part of his back. "It nicked his spine, shearing off a tiny piece, but it didn't touch the intestine."

I poked my thumb into my gut. "How does that happen?"

"One in a million, maybe. We did more damage stringing his intestine out looking for perforations than the bullet did."

We shook hands with the doctor and left.

"Huh. What's the chance of that, sir?" Leo asked as we drove away.

We approached a line of Humvees pulled over on the side of the road. Marines stood in full combat gear around the vehicles. From fifty meters away, the posture and hand motions of one of the Marines caught my eye. "Like the doctor said, slim to none—pull over."

Leo glanced at the Marines and yanked the steering wheel, skidding the jeep to a halt. I leaned my head out the window, took my cover off, and waved it. The marine I noticed was Lieutenant Willington; he walked towards me.

I smiled as I got out of the vehicle. "Lieutenant Willington. What the hell? How did you get out here so fast?"

We shook hands.

"Sir, I got out of the infantry course in January, went straight to Lejeune, and got a rifle platoon in India Company."

I pointed towards the group he'd just left. "What's going on there?"

"I'm briefing the boss. We got in a fight this morning—up by Racetrack."

"I know it. I'm working with the Iraqis, in charge of the MiTT. We operate with Kilo Company."

"Oh, you poor bastard, sir."

"I like working with the Iraqis."

"Not that." He lowered his voice and raised his eyebrows. "It's Captain DeMarco. He's fucked up."

"We'll talk about that later. What happened today?"

"We got ambushed from a newspaper stand. One of my Marines got hit. We're not supposed to destroy property, but

I cleared all the locals out and threw in a piece of C-4. The place—" he cocked his head back and spread his hands "—went up in flames. *Pwwwoofff!* It was great."

"Wish I'd been there."

"Sir, you would have been proud. I didn't hesitate. But I've got to go. The battalion commander is waiting." He laughed again.

"Come see me. I'm living at Camp Phoenix outside Camp Ramadi—next to the shit-pond."

"Okay, sir. I'll get over there to see you for sure." When we pulled away, Leo asked, "Who was that, sir?"

"Second Lieutenant Birmingham J. Willington." I paused and lined up my facts. "Nick name: Brim; Born: Easton, Maryland, 1979; enlisted in the Marine Corps: 1998; served four years before being awarded a four-year NROTC scholarship at The George Washington University; major: International Relations; GPA: 3.6; hobbies: fishing, drinking, and chasing pussy; personality traits: joke cracker, forthrightness, and curiosity. We commissioned him last spring."

CHAPTER 25

The day after the cordon and search operation, Leo came to me, concerned about an incident involving a *jundi* and Marines from Kilo Company. During mission planning, Captain DeMarco requested that *jundi* be posted with the Kilo Marines on the edges of the cordon to coordinate with the locals.

The Iraqis complied, but when we collapsed the cordon at the end of the operation, the Marines simply jumped into their vehicles and left behind one of the *jundi,* or so Major Thalmer told Leo. Alone, he was vulnerable—had the Mooj caught the soldier, they would have likely tortured and executed him, possibly sawing off his head and videotaping it for all the world to see.

I was livid, and it was the only time I ever saw Leo angry.

The next day, Mujeed mentioned the incident. I assured him I'd address the issue with Captain DeMarco.

After that, using Nick to translate, he told me about the rape and asked me what he should do. I recommended punishment, but since there was no judicial system in the new Iraqi army, *jundi* could desert, steal, run away in combat, and apparently rape one another—without consequence. That

293

left us few options; we agreed the best Mujeed could do was send the men home.

I used the opportunity to ask about the ghost *jundi*.

"*Na'am*, Major. If we go to Fallujah, no problem. Not so many dead and wounded *jundi*. Then we will see," he said as if he'd considered it already.

Mujeed never actually admitted that the ghost *jundi* existed. I had a hunch he used part of the money to send to the families of the dead or wounded, as a sort of ad-hoc life insurance or disability payoff. Such a measure likely garnered Mujeed great *wasta* from his men. Because of that, I asked him to reduce the number, not to eliminate them. I'm sure Mujeed was far less selfish with the embezzled funds than Meyerstone was with my money.

A few days later, we did a routine patrol out of the Government Center. The city was quiet again—NSTR. I took that opportunity to speak to Captain DeMarco about the claim that the *jundi* got left behind.

I found him inside his can at the Government Center taking a nap. I woke him up.

He sat up on the edge of a cot, barefooted, wearing boxer shorts and a green T-shirt.

Printed in red on the T-shirt was the image of a Marine straddling a descending two-thousand- pound bomb; emblazoned in yellow underneath were the words "Give War a Chance."

"All I'm asking you to do is check it out and see if something like that happened," I said. "I'm not accusing anyone."

He shook his head. "Sir, my Marines wouldn't do that. I'm not going to entertain it."

"Don't take this personally. You and I both know Marines don't always do the right thing. Do me a favor and ask. It'll mean a lot to Colonel Mujeed and his men."

"Sir, you people—"

"Hey! It's not *you people*. See this?" I pointed to the Velcro name tag embroidered with my blood type and rank beside the Eagle, Globe, and Anchor attached to my protective vest. "I'm training them and fighting alongside them—what the Marine Corps told me to do. Now, are you going to ask? Remember, *we're* on the same team."

He shook his head, bottom lip protruding. "No, sir."

Lieutenant Webb was waiting for me with the *jundi* in the back of the 7-Tons, ready to return to Camp Phoenix. He looked down from the truck. "You look pissed, sir."

"Good eye," I replied. "We're going to make a quick stop on the way home. I need to speak to the three-eight commanding officer. I've got a problem with the Kilo commander."

"Him again?"

I climbed in the cab of the truck and explained the detour to the driver. He nodded and motioned for the gate to be opened, and we pulled out of the Government Center. The battalion command post was less than a kilometer away and along the route back to Camp Phoenix. Inside, I asked a master sergeant if he'd seen the commanding officer.

"Sir, he's out with the Headquarters Company, and the XO is out with Lima Company. Major Miller's in."

I walked down the hallway into the operations room—a dozen Marines manning radios, watching live drone video feed of Ramadi, and updating map overlays. I found the battalion operations officer in an adjacent office, bent over a table studying a map of Ramadi.

"Major Steerforth." He grinned when he saw me. "How's the fight?"

"The Mooj is still out there, but that's not why I'm here."
I reached out to shake his hand. "I can see your hands are
full. But I can't find the CO or XO."

He straightened up, dropped the grin, and feigned seriousness by folding his arms and furrowing his brow. "How
can I help you?" His smile returned immediately.

I chuckled. "It's not that bad."

I gave him the rundown of the allegation and Captain
DeMarco's response.

"That's not good." He shook his head and pinched his
lips from the sides with his thumb and forefinger. "Look, I'll
talk to him. I'm not surprised, though. That's just *him*." He
cocked his head sideways and peered down the passageway.

"He's immature," Miller said in a low tone. "But the battalion commander, he's got a soft spot for that buffoon—
they were both instructors at The Basic School."

I released my M4 from my grip, let it swing from the
sling, slid my hands in my pockets, and sighed.

"Sorry," he said.

"Not much I can do then. You talk to him. Tell him I was
looking for the CO or XO."

"The XO's on our side," said Miller.

"DeMarco's useless."

"That's the general consensus. That's what I was doing at
the brief, keeping an eye on him." He held up his index finger, rotating it before his gaze. "He caught a small fragment
from an RPG one morning up on Racetrack. He quit the
fight, stuck his finger at his first sergeant, and said, 'Look,
I'm wounded!' He got a Purple Heart for it."

"Too bad." I looked around the office. A humidor sat on
top of a lone filing cabinet.

"Hold on," said Miller and walked out of the room. A minute later he returned with a map in his hand. "This came out of the stuff you all captured the other day. Intel is done with it. Take it."

"Thanks much," I said.

He shook my hand, said "Anytime," and walked back to his spot. He was bent back over his map when I left.

After my exchange with Captain DeMarco, the tension between us increased, morphing into a silent undercurrent that wore steadily at the heels of our daily operations. Knowing I wasn't the only field-grade officer who knew DeMarco was an idiot eased my frustration.

At night, Leo and I chatted by the fire and nipped at our booze. Leo was of the opinion we should simply stop operating with Kilo Company. Both of us knew, however, that was unlikely to happen because Mujeed didn't own any ground. It was symbiosis at its worst—we needed Kilo Company to allow us into the battle space, and they needed us to fit the guidance to partner. Time passed with little to show for it.

The good thing was Ramadi remained quiet.

One day, Gunny nearly soiled himself when the soldiers at Camp Ramadi's fuel farm filled the Iraqis' two-thousand-gallon diesel tank with regular gasoline.

"We can't use it?" I asked Gunny.

"No, sir. And they won't take it back. It's contaminated with diesel fuel."

"Pump it on the shit pond—I'll light it. Hopefully, we'll get relief from that smell for a day."

"Damn, sir. I know, but that's a lot of fuel to waste."

"I come from people who save old milk cartons and can vegetables from the garden. You're black and from the country—you know the type. A few days ago, I read in *Foreign*

Affairs that U.S.-government types in Baghdad lost track of a three-ton shipment of one-hundred-dollar bills. Two-thousand gallons of fuel ain't even a drop in the bucket. Burn it."

We all agreed it was the biggest fireball we'd ever seen. An hour later, the shit pond still smelled like shit.

⌘

My sketchbook was nearly full. I hadn't heard from John Dunne in six weeks. I wondered if anything had changed with the spring exhibit schedule at the Hutchison Collection. I decided no news was good news.

One evening, Sergeant Ski called me in from the fire to speak to Lieutenant Colonel Steeples on the radio. I went inside, picked up the hook, and listened to him. When he finished, I tossed the handset onto the desk. It hit the radio, ricocheted off, and dangled, bobbing from the end of its pigtail cord.

Sergeant Ski was sitting on the couch, reading an intelligence report and waiting for explanation.

"Pack your gear, Marine," I said. "We're leaving."

"Sir?"

"We've got ten days to get Mujeed and his battalion to Fallujah." I walked outside. Leo joined me. He had already heard the news.

We stood for a long minute, hands in our pockets, staring at the flames. "I'm going to miss this." I reached into my breast pocket and pulled out two Muniemaker Breva 100s.

"Indeed. This is the best part, sir," said Leo, taking the cigar and patting for his cargo pocket.

"I'm surprised none of our crew is dead or wounded." Leo lit his cigar. "We've been lucky."

"Yeah. Luck—just when I start thinking it's something we did right, I remind myself that a lot of Marines and soldiers out there thought they were doing the right thing until it simply ended."

"What did Colonel Steeples say?"

I mimed a phone with my hand and raised it to my ear. "'Drifter-Six, Steelcage-Six here. Move Three-Two-One and your MiTT to Fallujah by twenty May. Ensure the Iraqi battalion leaves all air conditioners and refrigerators in place. Over.'"

"That's it?" he chuckled.

"Yep."

"How the hell are we going to get the Iraqis to leave the air conditioners and fridges?"

"I'll tell Mujeed to leave them."

He looked at me as if I had a dick growing out of my forehead. "Just like that?"

"Just like that. We paid for them. Someone's moving in here—they'll need them. I want them counted in the morning. If Mujeed already knows they're not to be moved, there won't be anything to count, anyway."

We stood, lost in thought, smoking. After a while Leo said, "That first patrol seems like forever ago."

I kicked dirt at the fire. "When we killed that guy in the Benz?"

"That wasn't the first, but close enough."

"I still think about him—none of the others, though," I said, recalling the heap of man-dress and flesh lying in the road next to the Mercedes, a pool of blood drained from his head.

"I think about the time when we went inside that building across from OP Hyrea."

"Me too, and it's one of two things, Leo: either Marines kill everybody inside or the thing about the dogs eating the corpses isn't true—the Mooj don't leave anyone behind."

"Yeah, and you'd think that if the casualties were that bad there, they wouldn't keep coming back."

"Maybe it happened once and the legend grew. What makes you think about it?" I asked.

Leo pulled his Listerine bottle out of his cargo pocket. Without a canteen cup on hand, he sipped from the bottle and then held it out to me. "I just had to see it. I'm a bit ashamed. We didn't *have* to go there."

"No reason to be ashamed." I drank. "Had we gone to another place, our good luck may have run out."

"Maybe."

"Curiosity. It's human nature. The macabre has its allure, thus the likes of Edgar Allan Poe, Stephen King, and the late drawings of Goya."

"The Spaniard?"

I handed the bottle back to Leo. "Damn, Grasshopper. That's three you knew—Bacon, Rauschenberg, and now Goya! You art history guru, master of the obscure."

"Luck," he said, taking a drink.

I wondered out loud how fate had collided us. "Leo, how did you draw this mission?"

"I came from the Headquarters Battalion. I volunteered."

"I know that, but your parents are both professors. You went to Berkley. How does the son of left-wingers end up in the Marine Corps?"

"I don't know, sir," he said and stuck his chest out. "My mom gave up on me when I was still in diapers. She never let me watch war things on TV, no violence whatsoever. One day, sitting in my high chair, I molded my Wonder Bread into a pistol and started shooting." He mimicked making a pistol shape with his thumb and forefinger and pointed at the fire. "*Bang! Bang!* After that, she quit trying to steer me right."

"I've got one for you. When I was a kid, the Apollo landings were still going on. At the dollar store, my older brother showed me a six-inch white plastic figure, an astronaut in full gear holding an American flag. He asked me if I wanted the twenty-five-cent toy. I asked him where the man's gun was." I drank from the bottle. "He told me astronauts didn't need guns, that there wasn't anyone to fight on the moon. I gave him back the toy. I offered Leo the booze. "I haven't taken an interest in NASA since."

"Here's to high adventure, sir!" Leo took a swig and handed the bottle to me. I snorted. "We still have Fallujah."

"Indeed we do, sir."

"The same rules apply—train the Iraqis, stay out of the Humvees, and sneak a drink." I laughed.

"Sir," Leo hesitated, "you know we were pissed when you made us come up with training objectives. The lieutenants said it was like being back at The Basic School. But, little by little—once in a while by leaps and bounds—we've completed our objectives for training the Iraqis. The final one was the cordon and search, a battalion-sized operation. What's next?"

"In Fallujah, Mujeed will have his own battle space, so whatever's next will be easier," I said. "I expect the Iraqi brigade will be more involved, but we won't have to deal with that moron DeMarco."

"I bet he'll be sporting that Purple Heart on his field uniform like an Iron Cross."

In the far distance, an explosion sounded. Leo and I swung our heads towards Ramadi and the sound. The glow of a fire lit the sky near the middle of the city. Not speaking, only passing the bottle back and forth, we watched black smoke billow and then fade into the darkness of the night.

"That's where the monster lives," Leo said.

I held the whiskey in my hand and pulled on my cigar. "The monster?"

"Ever wonder how to explain this to folks who haven't been here?"

"I won't bother," I said.

"One of my boys is afraid of the dark. Just imagine if I stuck my head into his room one night, put my finger on the light switch, and said, 'Son, you know those monsters you think are hiding under the bed. Well, they're real and they've got hatchets—they're going to try to kill you tonight. Good luck. And, *click*."

The next morning, I woke up early enough to watch the sun rise over Ramadi, a finger of smoke from the previous night's fire rising above the buildings. When I finished a jug of tea, I got my shaving gear and went back outside to shave.

Sergeant Ski approached me as I worked in front of the Humvee driver-side mirror. "Sir, Lieutenant Colonel Steeples is on the hook again."

"Any idea what he wants?"

He puffed his cigarette. "I didn't ask. I'm a sergeant; he's a colonel."

"Hold on a second. Let me finish." I glanced from my reflection in the mirror to Sergeant Ski. "Are those Miamis you're smoking?"

"Yes, sir."

"Where'd you get them?"

"Hussein bought four cartons for me the last time he went on leave. They're a quarter of the price of Marlboros."

"You speak to him?" I wiped my face with the towel and slung it around my neck.

"Who do you think tells him that you like his fish so much? The fish that's turning your balls Kadrak Orange or whatever you called it."

"It's Cadmium Orange," I laughed and walked away.

Inside the radio room, I picked up the handset and transmitted, "Steelcage-Six, this is Drifter-Six. Over."

"Steelcage-Six here, Drifter-Six. Submit all awards that you intend to push up the chain when you get to Fallujah."

"Roger, copy."

"Steelcage-Six. Out."

"Leo!" I barked.

After a minute, Leo stuck his head into the radio room. "Sir?"

"Find Randolph. Give him the logbook and get ready to write awards."

Sequestered in the radio room for three days solid, Randolph and I wrote combat awards for my Marines.

Leo worked with the team, preparing our departure. Lieutenant Webb and Staff Sergeant Craig counted the air conditioners and refrigerators at Camp Phoenix; miraculously, they hadn't disappeared. Lieutenant O'Shannihan and Gunny worked to get the Iraqis licensed to operate Humvees. Lieutenant Lott and Sergeant Ski crafted certificates of completion, conferring on the training an official sheen. The *jundi* that qualified were overjoyed with the Intel Marines' handiwork. Top Bruce and Doc secured two gunner's cupolas for our vehicles from the National Guard. They were the old, bulletproof-glass types, rather than the newer steel ones, but they provided a modicum of protection for the gunner sticking out the top of the Humvee.

The *jundi* were incapable of doing collective calisthenics, not using any exercise techniques I knew. When we tried, the uncoordinated effort was so bizarre, each soldier doing a different version of a jumping jack or knee bend, none of us could keep from laughing long enough to lead the routine and make it worthwhile. However, they loved soccer. No team we put together ever beat them. As I watched Randolph, Webb, O'Shannihan, and Craig get pounded by three *jundi* and a soccer ball one evening, I heard vehicles approaching and saw Humvees kicking up clouds of pinkish dust. I walked from the soccer field in back of the command post towards the road and stood, waiting. A convoy of four vehicles pulled up; Lieutenant Willington climbed out from the second Humvee and waved.

I waved back. "What the hell, Marine!"

He walked towards me. Unshaven and filthy, a smattering of Copenhagen juice crusted on the front of his protective vest, he reached out to take my hand. "So this is where you live?"

"For a few more days. We're moving."

"I heard. I took the opportunity to have my vehicles worked on. We're racking at the Camp Ramadi motor pool tonight."

"Can you stay a while?"

"Yes, sir. How long?"

"As long as you want."

He glanced at the convoy. "Can you give me a ride back to the motor pool?"

"Sure."

He waved his men off. The Marine on the driver side of the first Humvee stuck his arm out the window, pointed his thumb skyward, and pulled away.

I put my hand on his shoulder, realizing for the first time that Brim was three inches taller than my own six feet. "When was the last time you had a drink, Marine?"

He laughed.

I took him inside the command post, showed him our digs, introduced him to my team, and toured him around the compound. The *jundi* were eating supper.

Walking towards the fire pit, he asked, "What's that they were eating?"

"Bean gruel and flatbread."

"Looks nasty."

"It's not bad actually, but it gives one the *shee-ites*."

Brim dropped his gear while I built a fire. He told me how he'd finished his training, never taking leave, calculating to get into a unit deploying to the war.

Leo joined us.

"Old habits die hard, sir," Brim said, declining a cigar. Instead, he drew a can of Copenhagen from his left breast pocket and thumped it, Staff-Sergeant-Craig style.

"Captain Essex?"

"They do, sir." Leo reached in his cargo pocket and pulled out our bottle.

"Get your canteen cup, Brim," I said.

Brim told us the man captured in the cordon and search was named Bilal Hussein, a Pulitzer-Prize-winning journalist made famous while living with insurgents and photographing them during the November 2004 takedown of Fallujah.

"We think he was videotaping the attacks on the Government Center. The attacks never succeeded, but it makes great propaganda when this Bilal guy sends the footage to Arab news outlets, promoting the good fight against the infidel."

"Makes sense," I said.

"Our man got scooped up by U.S. plainclothes types lickety-split. Three fat guys and an ugly chick with short blonde hair—State Department maybe."

"I wonder where he is?" Leo pondered out loud.

"Hopefully dead, but probably in jail," said Brim. "You should have seen DeMarco taking the credit for it, like he was the guy who caught him—singlehandedly."

"The best I remember, it was four Marines and a dog named Jeb," I said. "What do you know about that jackass?"

"I know he got a Purple Heart for a scratch on his finger, and his first sergeant despises him. Plus, he complained about his mission, constantly crying that his operating area was too big. He now only holds the Government Center and OP Hyrea. We got stuck with the rest."

"How's your platoon, Brim?"

"Great, sir. My squad leaders know their business. We've gotten into so many fights now, when I hear the first shots, I just think, *Time for a dip*. I take out my Copenhagen, get a pinch, tuck it in, and begin passing word on the radio."

"Has it slowed any?"

Brim looked up from the fire and thought a moment. "Sir, you know, I think it has."

"Perhaps this Bilal Hussein character was some type of enemy center of gravity—the go-between for the Mooj and the Arab media."

"Could be, sir. But they could always find another."

"One with his contacts and credibility?" I said.

⌘

"Be careful, Brim."

I sat in the passenger side of the vehicle, Leo at the wheel. We had reached the motor pool. Brim stood outside the jeep, peeing in the road.

Buttoning his trousers, he turned towards me. "I'll do what I can, sir." He stuck his hand through the open window. I gripped it tightly.

"Don't breathe on anyone," I said.

"Got it, sir. I'm good."

"Famous last words."

"See you back at Lejeune, sir, or maybe at the D.C. waterfront. We'll chase some tail—two Bluetick hounds right out of the truck, sniffing the dirt."

"I'm in love, by the way."

"What's that, sir?" He crammed his hands in his pockets and leaned in close to me, eyes wide.

"No shit, Marine."

"Who? The hottie you brought to the commissioning?"

"That would be her."

He leaned back and cocked his head towards the starry sky, booming laughter. He raised his arm in the air and smacked his outsized palm on the jeep's hood with a bang. He walked away and into the darkness and shouted, "That's hilarious, sir. The world has truly come to a fucking end!"

"See you, Brim," I said softly.

⌘

Two days before leaving, the Iraqis exploded into a packing fury. It took some convincing, but Mujeed left the air conditioners and refrigerators. On the morning we were scheduled to leave, the *jundi* with their blankets, mattresses, combat gear, cooking equipment, a few goats, and a handful of chickens, piled haphazardly into twenty or so trucks. Three of them failed to start, so they hooked them with ropes to the operational trucks. Finally, the whole battalion drove away with hurrahs and a barrage of rifle fire splintering the air.

Any USMC roadmaster would have keeled over at the malfunctionous spectacle. We simply stood and watched.

ANOTHER WAR

ANOTHER WAY

CHAPTER 26

When we moved to Fallujah, Mujeed assumed responsibility for patrolling and maintaining a presence of force in the southern half of the city. He owned it. Two other battalions from the brigade shared the northern half.

Because the tactical situation dictated it, I split my crew. Lieutenant Webb and Staff Sergeant Craig went with one of Mujeed's companies to an outpost at the Euphrates River. Lieutenant Randolph went to a company outpost on the opposite edge of town with a Marine from Lieutenant Colonel Steeples's team. The rest of us lived and operated out of an abandoned industrial complex known as the Soap Factory. Located on an entire city block in the center of the city and surrounded by a ten-foot cinderblock wall topped with concertina wire, it consisted of a single four-story building the size of a high-school auditorium and thirty smaller buildings, ranging from tin sheds to barracks that could sleep twenty men. There was space for all our vehicles and even a lot designated for physical training. A metal gate, the size of four standard garage doors and controlled manually by two *jundi,* restricted access to the facility. I searched, but I never found any evidence that soap had ever been made at the Soap Factory.

In Fallujah, I took to sleeping until after 0700.

Mujeed claimed his own living quarters in a walled-off subsection of the complex. His men took up residence by squads and platoons in buildings Zuhair assigned to them. My men bunked by twos in air-conditioned, dormitory-sized rooms that had once been offices. A kitchen, a head with a shower, and an outside dining area was set aside for us. There were no toilets, so we defecated in bags suspended from a makeshift toilet and then burned them in a corner of the compound. The smell of burning feces and urine was fouler than the shit pond at Ramadi.

Fallujah is a town with more than a hundred mosques, and Arabs pray five times a day. When they pray, a *muezzin*—a preacher of sorts—turns on a loudspeaker wired to a minaret and begins howling. Immediately, another *muezzin* at another mosque chimes in; soon there are a few dozen voices all singing the same, slightly out of sync, tune. I've heard some folks say it's an enchanting sound; to me it sounds like death. I've never decided which was worse: the killing in Ramadi, or the preaching in Fallujah.

Mujeed received twelve armored U.S. Humvees when we got to Fallujah. His boss, Brigadier General Azizi, attempted to withhold them on the grounds that the *jundi* didn't know how to operate the vehicles. After Mujeed showed Azizi the Humvee operator certificates that Sergeant Ski made, and with intervention from Lieutenant Colonel Steeples, Mujeed's men drove away in the vehicles as if they were escorting the prime minister. Lieutenant O'Shannihan and Gunny beamed.

We kept our Humvees lined up near the gate and ready in case our outposts needed reinforcement or medical assistance.

A week after we arrived at the Soap Factory, Lieutenant Colonel Steeples convoyed with his crew, travelling five miles from Camp Fallujah to visit us. I walked him around our position and briefed him on the progress of the battalion. On Mujeed's five-by-nine-foot operations map posted on the wall in the Iraqi operations room, I pointed out our positions in the city.

Studying the map, Colonel Steeples asked, "What's Mujeed like?"

"Well, Mujeed's...he's an Arab, but he's a professional soldier. His men are loyal to him; he's able to maintain a low desertion rate, despite paltry food, lack of pay, death, and..." I considered mentioning the rape. "Well, his men go out on patrol every day."

"Ghost *jundi?*"

"Right, sir. Seventy-five. It used to be one-fifty."

"What does he do with the money?"

"Best guess, he keeps twenty-five percent, gives his officers twenty-five percent, and uses the other fifty as a slush fund to send home with the dead and the wounded."

"What about his executive officer?"

"Zuhair. I don't know him well. Mujeed hands out the goodies, Zuhair lays down the law. He doesn't talk much."

Colonel Steeples glanced around the operations room. Two *jundi* on watch sat next to the radio sets. He motioned me towards the exit and walked outside. "Mujeed and his men have some reputation," he said. "As you said, the desertion rate is low, and they fight. It's drawing attention."

"Drawing attention?"

"Azizi has his own agenda. I think Mujeed's on his shit list."

"No kidding?" I was genuinely surprised.

"There's seven or eight officers, Azizi's cronies, who hang around headquarters, waiting for a job and a bigger cut of whatever pot they're stealing money from. Azizi's likely eyeing Mujeed's battalion for one of them." Steeples hesitated a second then asked, "Is Mujeed Sunni?"

"Never thought to ask."

"Hmm…Azizi's Shia."

"You think he'll move Mujeed?"

"He'd need approval from the Ministry of Defense. That's a mystery too—the MOD's a black hole."

"That's bad," I said. "Mujeed holds the battalion together. Whatever he does, it works."

"I agree. My concern is the stability of the city. If Mujeed is in fact that good, we need him."

I looked around the compound, removed my cover, and scratched my head. "Sir, I like Mujeed."

"Of course you do," he said. "You've fought with his unit for the past four months. Let's hope for the best. Later, if we have to, we'll plan for the worst." He smiled. "By the way, a reporter from *U.S. Gazette* is coming to do a story about the development of Iraqi forces. They want to embed with a MiTT team, and, *tag*—you're it."

I placed my cover back on. "Sir, are you sure?"

"I'm sure. You've got the largest part of the city, you just came from the worst place in theater, and you've got Mujeed."

"Right. Aye, aye, sir. When?"

"Next week. My Marines will pass the details."

"Okay. I'll tell Leo."

"Leo?"

"Captain Essex. He handles details for me."

"What about the detail of your combat award?"

I pulled the bill of my cover down, hiding eyes. "*My* award?"

"Yeah, I forwarded the ten you gave me up the chain."

"Sir, I didn't—"

"Get on it, Marine. Make yours match the others, and I'll tweak it."

"If you say so."

He slapped me on the shoulder. "I say so."

The colonel stayed three hours. We ate MREs and talked about Ramadi. I told him we'd be using our Humvees more in Fallujah than we had been, and we still needed two gunner's cupolas; he recommended I check the motor pool aboard Camp Fallujah and call him if I needed reinforcing fires. When he was ready to leave, I walked him to his vehicle, shook his hand, and waved as he and his men departed.

⌘

Leo and I sat in our air-conditioned sleeping quarters, smoking cigars, and sharing a drink.

"So he thinks Mujeed's days are numbered?" asked Leo.

"Seems like it."

"Why?"

"Who knows? He said General Azizi has his favorites—cronies, he called them. Just like any other organization. Suggested it may be religious, the Sunni-Shia thing."

"You know, sir, I've heard a lot of criticism of the Iraqis for doing the same things we do," he said. "They just do it more crudely."

"Do you mean pettiness and envy?"

"Yes, sir."

"Capitol Hill-style greed, graft, and corruption?"

"Now you're talking, sir." Leo raised his canteen cup in toast.

"I reckon the seven deadly sins bridge the Christian-Muslim divide."

"I suppose so."

"Leo, the awards. You write the last one."

"The last one?"

"...Me."

"You left that out?"

"Did you think I was going to write my own award? You do it. Hand it off to Colonel Steeples's guys, and they'll give it to him. Look at the logbook; just do like I did with the others. Leave the drinking part out, though, and don't mention I sleep late."

"Okay, sir," he laughed. "I'll get on it in the morning."

"Sorry, Leo. This is the dirty business of war."

A week later we convoyed to Camp Fallujah to get the reporter and search out two cupolas for our Humvees. I elected Sergeant Ski to stay behind and square away a sleeping space for the journalist.

We drove to Lieutenant Colonel Steeples's office and confirmed the reporter was still joining us and then drove to the base motor pool. Lieutenant O'Shannihan and Gunny went inside to see if cupolas were available while the rest of us waited. They returned a few minutes later.

"Sir, there's a kid in there who says he knows you, a Lance Corporal Graves," said Gunny.

"In the motor pool?"

"Yes, sir. When we asked for cupolas, the sergeant hem-hawed. Then Lieutenant O'Shannihan said, 'Major Steerforth's going to be pissed,' and that lance corporal asked if he meant Major Steerforth from Headquarters Battery. We said yes, and he told the sergeant he knew you, so the sergeant said we could have them. It'll take an hour to get one on; he said he'd put the other aside until we bring back the other Humvee."

"Let me go say hello to Graves," I said. I climbed out of the vehicle, walked inside the motor pool and found him inside. His back was to me. "What the hell, Marine?"

Lance Corporal Graves turned around, his mouth stretched into a grin, gold tooth glistening. "Sir, how the hell are you?"

"I'm doing fine, Marine. Is it all you imagined it would be?"

"Living the dream, sir…. Living the dream, one nightmare at a time."

"What've they got you doing?"

"Bolting on a cupola for my old boss right now. Other days, running convoys and fixing engines worn out from too much sand and dust."

"So you get off base?"

"Every other day we escort someone through IEDs, ambushes…whatever."

"What about Corporal Harder?"

"He got pushed out to Ramadi two weeks ago. So many vehicles getting blown up out there, they needed more recovery operators. He'll be back next week when we rotate out. Didn't you hear?"

"Hear what?"

"A month or so after we got here, he went to retrieve a Humvee out by the river and got ambushed. The staff sergeant with them got hit. Corporal Harder took over, killed four shitheads, and came back with *all* the vehicles. I don't know how he did it, but damn sure he'll be getting a medal— one of them kind with a '*V*.'"

"I expected that from Marines like you two. Glad to hear it. You'll save the other cupola for us?"

"It's yours. I won't let anyone else have it."

"Thanks, Marine." I shook his hand.

After Graves bolted on the cupola, we drove to the Public Affairs office. The reporter turned out to be a woman.

After introductions, we drove her to the Soap Factory. "Sir, what the hell?" asked Sergeant Ski after we arrived.

"I didn't pick her," I said. "She was just there waiting for us when we got to the Public Affairs office. I couldn't tell her no."

He stared at me and puffed his cigarette.

"How're the Miamis treating you?" I asked. "Hussein still coming through?"

"They're not bad. Anyways, they're cheap."

"Maybe she smokes?"

"I doubt it." He scanned the area. "Where's she going to sleep?"

"I told her you were taking care of that."

"I did, but the female part changes things," he said. He shrugged and crossed his arms. "She can stay in the extra rack I set up in my can. I'll move into the radio room. Doc can bunk with Lieutenant Lott and O'Shannihan. I'll tell Doc to work Lieutenant Lott over with a psychiatric review. I gave up."

I put my hands on my hips and leaned towards Ski. "It took you this long, Marine?"

"Ha! When did you give up, sir?"

"When he printed out the photos of The Women of Ramadi and started hanging around the chow hall trying to match a set of bad tits and a pimply ass with an ugly face. He even ate with them. Anyway, treat her like a human being. She says her dad was career Army, a full colonel."

Just then, one of the cats that lived at our compound slunk by. I'd never seen anything like these cats—extra-long torsos and walnut-sized gonads swinging between their legs. "Those cats have some big balls."

"What's she want, sir?" said Ski, ignoring me.

"She wants to hang out, see what we do, and write a story. If she needs to talk to somebody, get O'Shannihan. Keep her away from that pervert Lott." I snapped my fingers and pointed at the cat. "And run that cat off. She'll think that we're *all* weirdos. Is the shower clean?"

"Sir, it's filthy. There's man scum everywhere. You're the only one who's brave enough to go in there without shower shoes."

"Put that in the logbook."

Sergeant Ski blew smoke sideways and shook his head.

"You never know—our faces may end up on the cover of *Rolling Stone*," I said.

"I thought you said she writes for *U.S. Gazette*?"

I bent my head towards him and smirked.

"Aye, aye, sir. Got it."

I cleaned the shower while Leo dug a dozen hamburgers out of our freezer and cooked them on a grill that Gunny rigged from a piece of chain-linked fence.

Her name was Abby; she was the first woman I'd spoken to face to face in five months.

Leo and I talked to her about books and about her home base—Washington, D.C. She was graceful and well mannered, yet I sensed she wasn't to be underestimated. She wanted to go on patrol and meet Mujeed. I told her that we'd start with a tour of the compound and address the rest as opportunity arose.

I went to my can, found my binoculars, and rejoined her in the dining area. "Don't be shocked by the way the Iraqi soldiers live," I said. "They're filthy. They fight, though, and that's what we want."

I took her to where the *jundi* were billeted. They gawked as we passed through their quarters. They cooked, ate, cleaned chickens, slept, urinated, and stunk, all inside of a fifty-foot radius. It was the heat of the day, and they lay lounging on dirty mattresses, drinking tea, and smoking hookah pipes inside the shade of their billeting. Abby was likely the first Western woman they had ever seen.

"I could let you check out the area alone," I said as we walked around, "but they'll molest you like a twelve-year-old boy at the King of Pop's birthday party."

She scowled at me.

As we passed our Humvees parked near the front gate of the compound, I said, "We've got a mission tomorrow night down by the river. Some shitheads threw grenades at one of our patrols, and we know where they live. My staff sergeant, Lieutenant Webb, and the Iraqis will go get them after midnight. You can't go on that mission, but you can go on patrol with the *jundi* that live here."

She looked at me, now worried.

"Lieutenant O'Shannihan and Doc will go along with you. If anything happens they can't handle, we'll come help. My Marines and a handful of *jundi* are always on standby."

We climbed a flight of stairs to the second floor of a three-story building. It was littered with *jundi* feces and discarded water bottles; we stepped lightly. "It never *doesn't* stink," I told her.

We climbed to the third floor and scaled a ladder towards the rooftop. When I stuck my head through the square opening in the ceiling, a hot gust of wind swept across the flat concrete surface and kicked sand into my mouth and eyes.

I rubbed my eyes with the back of my hand and told Abby, "Cover up. I just got a face full of sand."

Two *jundi* sat behind tiers of sandbags and a screen of bulletproof glass. We joined them. I shelled out cigars and handed Abby my Steiners. With her red-and-white checked scarf blowing in the wind, she raised them to her eyes. I pointed out the features of the city. To the west, the flow of the Euphrates shimmered in the relentless heat. Near it and above a series of buildings waved Iraqi and USMC flags— our river outpost. I pointed north towards the railroad tracks and explained it was from there that the U.S. forces launched their attack on the city in 2004. Eastward, across flat desert, lay Camp Fallujah. To the south, a ten-foot-high berm, built by U.S. Army engineers, rimmed the city against the open desert. Beyond it, the wind drove waves of dust, rising and falling as they swept from east to west, obscuring our view of the single blacktopped road that ran that way. In every direction lay a maze of city blocks full of mud-brick buildings, blowing dust and trash, and the spikes of minarets.

⌘

Leo and I stayed up after midnight talking to Abby about our time in Ramadi. She took notes and asked questions, never straying from her journalistic endeavor. Her hair was reddish; her skin pink. When she smiled, she pulled her shoulders back and cocked her head to one side.

Leo gave her a cigar, and she smoked it.

The next day, Abby went on patrol. O'Shannihan told me she stuck by Nick, asked the locals questions, and handed out candy she kept squirreled away in her protective vest. Despite the heat and the thirty pounds of gear she wore, she never complained.

I took her to meet Mujeed. When she asked him about his battalion, Mujeed spoke with pride about his mission in Ramadi and his new one in Fallujah. Hussein served us tea, and Mujeed invited Abby to stay while he hosted visiting sheiks. She sat with him, scribbling away in her notebook as he addressed the tribal leaders' concerns about garbage collection and being paid for land and buildings leased by their people to the U.S. government.

Even Sergeant Ski warmed up to her and showed her photos he'd taken in Ramadi.

⌘

"Sir, they're in the cage," said Staff Sergeant Craig.

A twelve-gauge shotgun and his trophy AK-47 dangled from their slings. His eyes were streaked red. "We quit about zero-three, took them from the post, and brought them here."

"How many?"

"Six. One of them is young, maybe fifteen. We can't keep him—have to throw him back."

In the distance, a single howling voice opened the first morning prayer.

Craig spat Copenhagen onto the ground, pulled a pack of cigarettes from his trouser pocket, and lit one.

"Where's Webb?" I asked.

"In the radio room, getting some rack time."

"Anything?"

"Normal stuff—bomb-making material, AKs, and a few hand grenades. Hand-drawn maps of our positions. They're the shitheads."

From every direction, mosque noise flowed in.

Craig spat again and puffed on the cigarette. "They admitted it."

"Okay," I said. "I'll take Abby to the pen. She'll want to see."

"Who's Abby?"

"We've got a reporter staying with us—a female." Craig adjusted his rifle. "Is she hot?"

"She's attractive and charming," I said. "But she's a reporter."

"Do you really want her to see them? They kicked the fuck out of them, sir."

"The *jundi*?"

"Yes, sir. These shitheads will be in jail for three weeks and then back here to throw more grenades and shoot at us. The *jundi* encouraged them not to come back."

I touched my temple with my thumb and scratched my eyebrow with my middle finger. "How bad?"

"Nowhere that shows."

"Good job," I said. "Catching them, I mean."

"Sir, we didn't beat them, the *jundi* did. There's two of us and nearly fifty of them. We can't watch them twenty-four-seven. They're like kindergarteners on steroids...with guns."

The holy cacophony trailed off. Craig tossed his cigarette butt to the ground and crushed it with the heel of his boot. "Thank God that's over."

Waiting in the kitchen area for Abby, I drank tea and had a smoke. When she came out of her quarters she was carrying a powder-blue shower bag. I explained to her we had detainees she may want to see and gave her the rundown of the previous night's mission.

While she took a shower, I sat nearby and watched the door so that no one accidentally entered. When she came out, she smelled like lilac flowers.

We walked through the alleys in the compound to a small brick building with windows caged off by chicken wire. The six men, each clothed in dirty man-dresses and wearing plastic sandals—one beardless, the rest full-grown scrawny men—sat with their arms folded around their knees or hunched down, heels touching their buttocks; they never looked at us, interaction limited to our voyeurism and their pungent odor.

She studied the men. "That's them?"

"They're out of their element and without weapons. What did you expect?"

"Well…" She reached into her cargo pocket.

"You didn't think people that look like that would want to kill you?" I ventured.

"I guess. Back in D.C., I spend my Saturday mornings buying flowers at Eastern Market, but I don't go there at night." She pulled out her notebook and a yellow number-two from her pocket. As she touched the pencil to paper, she drew it back and looked at the tip—only splintered wood. I dug into my cargo pocket and pulled out my jackknife. Pressing my thumb against the blade, I snapped it open and held my hand out for the pencil.

"Trying to figure out who wants to kill you out here," I said as I shaved the soft wood away from the lead to make a fine point, "is like trying to figure out which one of your buddies wants to roger your girlfriend—simply hard to tell." I handed the pencil back. "While they look pathetic, they'd kill you if they could. But you're a woman and—"

"I know that part of the culture," she said, putting the newly sharpened pencil to her notebook.

I watched as she wrote. Her fingers were slender and her nails were painted Cerulean Blue. She gripped the pencil firmly and wrote in cursive script.

"Seen enough?" I asked after she quit writing.

"I have."

"We'll go with them when they take them to the detention facility."

"When's that?"

"In about an hour," I said. "Don't worry, I won't leave you behind."

We returned to our billet area, and I fixed more tea. I rummaged through the boxes in the kitchen for something special and found Girl Scout cookies, the ones with chocolate and coconut; I served them to her along with the tea. She ate the cookies while I smoked a cigar. When she finished, she pulled out her notebook. "Was Ramadi worse than Fallujah?"

Watching her sharpen her pencil with her own jackknife, I said, "I never thought about that. I don't know what Fallujah was like back in '04."

With the pencil sharpened to a point and poised to record my thoughts, she looked up, made direct eye contact and said, "That's what I'm wondering."

"I can't be sure. The assault of Fallujah was a quick fight—what Marines like to do. Ramadi is a slow grind."

"You and your men, you fight alongside the Iraqis—I just realized that means you're alone with them in combat. What's that like?"

I thought back to the patrols and firefights in Ramadi; it took a minute of smoking before the answer came. "I trust them as much as I can, but they aren't Marines. Marines are trained to fight and kill anything that needs to be fought and killed. We know what to expect from each other. When you're with the Iraqis and the shit hits the fan, they scream on the radio. That's the worst part. You don't get used to that."

She eyed her pencil briefly before making more notes.

I heard footsteps behind me. "Sir, we're ready to roll." It was Leo.

I grabbed my weapon and gear and helped Abby into hers. We walked to where our Humvees were parked, engines running. It was easily over a hundred degrees Fahrenheit.

"Lieutenant Webb, where are they?"

"In the Humvee, sir."

I peered through the Humvee window but didn't see anyone other than Doc at the wheel, a burning cigarette between his fingers. He winked.

Craig pointed towards the trunk. "Sir, *there.*"

"Open it up," I commanded.

Inside, five men lay, head to feet, on their backs, their hands and legs bound with zip-ties; they were blindfolded. With their sweat-soaked man-dresses hiked up, the beatings showed.

"What the fuck?" I asked.

"Sir," said Leo, "it's that or the Toyotas. If we get hit in the Toyotas, they're dead or, worse, wounded, and then we have a real problem on our hands. It's only ten minutes to the train station."

"Let's move," I said.

It took fifteen minutes to get to the train station. Three Marine military police came out to meet us. We opened the trunk and pulled the men out.

"Damn, sir. That's how you keep them?" asked a gunnery sergeant.

"Better than having them blown up in a Toyota," I said.

He shook his head. "We'll take them from here."

Abby stayed three more days. On her last night, we stayed up drinking tea after the others retired. She told me she was writing a novel about a female reporter on detail in a war zone.

"Autobiographical?" I asked.

She crossed her arms, tucked her chin, and looked up at me. "It's my first novel. Aren't they always?"

"Let's keep in touch, maybe I can read the draft. I've read more than one novel."

"You don't look like the type who reads women authors."

I grinned. "I've read Erica Jong."

"Really?"

"College."

"That doesn't count."

"Yeah, you may be right," I sighed. "Plus it was twenty years ago."

She uncrossed her arms, leaned an elbow on the table, and rested her hand in her chin. "I've been meaning to ask you, what gives?"

I glanced at her.

"You're a forty-year-old bachelor. What's the deal? You're obviously not gay, and I'm sure you've melted more than one heart with those blue eyes, that crooked grin, and that practiced Southern drawl. There's likely more than one woman who's tried to reconstruct that wannabe rebel in you." She leaned back and crossed her arms again. "You play the country bumpkin, but I looked you up on the Internet; besides being a Marine, you're an artist, and you show your paintings at galleries in D.C. Playboy?"

"Hmm, reporter, author, private investigator, and personality analyst all in one?"

"They go together." She smiled and nudged my chair with her combat boot, goading me for an answer.

I was at a loss for words. Behind a dangling lock of Abby's hair, dampness glistened on her forehead. I reached out and brushed the hair back, my hand trembling. Finally, I managed to reply, "It's been a long time in the making. Does it matter right now?"

"No," she answered.

The next morning, Gunny traded the *jundi* a half-gallon can of mixed nuts for two dozen eggs, and I cooked breakfast. Abby was still taking notes when we loaded her gear into a Humvee. I let her ride in my seat, the passenger side of the second Humvee in the convoy, on the way back to Camp Fallujah.

Standing under a tree in front of the Public Affairs office where we'd first met, I handed her backpack to her.

"You've got a nice group of guys," she said. "Thanks for everything, Major Steerforth."

"It's been great having you aboard, Abby. I enjoyed talking about books. Normally it's just Leo and me." I looked at the convoy, parked and waiting for me. Leo, his arm resting on the opening of his Humvee window, stole a look at us and then turned away. I looked back at Abby. "I'm looking forward to seeing what you write—and reading your book."

"It'll be a few weeks for the article, a lot longer for the book," she said. "Get home safe."

"See you around D.C." I reached out to shake her hand.

She took mine, pulled herself in close, and kissed me on the cheek.

CHAPTER 27

T he Marine staying with Randolph was due to take R&R. Lieutenant Colonel Steeples's team planned to send a replacement but not for two weeks. I couldn't leave Randolph there alone. Sergeant Ski hadn't been on any missions since he turned to stone at the Health Compound.

"Why not someone else, sir?" Leo asked.

I clasped the lid shut on the ammo can filled with water, hand soap, my salt-stained T-shirts, and dirty underwear. "Send Sergeant Ski." I hoisted the ammo can and shook it violently.

"Sir?

"Send Ski."

We visited the posts every ten days and then drove aboard Camp Fallujah to resupply and pick up mail. One week, I received three letters and a card from Kate. With the same delivery, I got a box from my mom—in it, six or seven bags of candy and a note telling me to give it to the Iraqi kids. A package from John contained a book, *Modigliani: Nudes*, and a Listerine bottle full of whiskey.

Waiting for Leo to finish coordinating the supply pickup with Colonel Steeples's Marines, I rested in my Humvee and read Kate's card:

> *Dear Clay,*
>
> *I'm doing well, and I miss you. Just a short note to let you know that I saw Andy yesterday. The Hattery is closed. I saw him on Prospect Street in Georgetown selling his hats from a push cart. He didn't say why he closed his store. Even though he didn't always pay me on time, he was my friend, and I loved selling hats. I am very sad it is shutted down.*
>
> > *I love you,*
> > *Kate*

I dug in the box John sent me, pulled out the book of Modigliani nudes, and closed the flaps back over the whiskey. Inside the book was a note:

> *Modi did his best work sober, but I guess you could use this right now. Saw Babs at the Corcoran.*
> *She ignored me when I mentioned your name. Arranged a one man show for you late next spring at Hutchinson's.*
>
> > *Congrats and Best, John*

On the way back to the Soap Factory, we passed through a residential area. Top Bruce and Lieutenant O'Shannihan manned the machine guns and tossed candy to children. Watching the kids scramble for the treats, I called Leo on the hook. "Pull over. I don't want to run anybody down."

We stopped on the side of the road and handed out the candy. One barefoot little girl in a filthy green-and-orange flowered dress got pushed down by the boys as she ran for a butterscotch. She jumped up from the dusty road, and, to no avail, tried again. Beckoning her to me with one hand and shooing the boys away with my boot, I held out a handful of starred peppermints. Just when she got within reach of the candy—her arms, hands, and fingers stretched out as big as the joy on her face—a fat pre-teen of a bastard three times her size bum- rushed me and lunged for the candy, knocking the girl in the dirt again. I jerked the goodies from his reach, placed the sole of my boot on his belly, shoved him back, and laughed. "Trick or treat, turd."

She got her candy, but the pleasure was likely short-lived. I'm sure the boys rolled her and took what they wanted after we drove away.

While Sergeant Ski stayed with Lieutenant Randolph, the Iraqi interpreter on post got shot in the middle of the back on patrol. Since he was wearing U.S.-issued body armor, the bullet only knocked him down. He landed tits down but walked away with nothing more than a ruined SAPI plate, a grapefruit-size bruise below his shoulder blades, and a scraped face.

Sergeant Ski was with the patrol when the man got hit. When I questioned Randolph about Ski's conduct under fire, he said the Marine had performed well, and that the team had guessed why the sergeant hadn't been on any missions since long before we left Ramadi.

When he returned to the Soap Factory, Ski walked with renewed swagger.

While Leo and I discussed business over tea one morning, Ski walked out of the kitchen area with six bottles of Aunt

Jemima syrup hooked under his fingers. An unlit Miami dangled from his lips.

"Hey, Marine," I called out. "Where are you going with those?"

He held up the bottles. "We got two cases when we first arrived here. No pancake mix, though." He put the bottles on the ground and fished into his pocket for his lighter.

"And?"

He lit the cigarette. "You know when we capture the shitheads and impound their vehicles?"

"Yeah."

"Well, we catch them and they stay in jail for a week or two. Then they come back, laughing at us, demanding their vehicles back.

"And?"

"It pisses me off." He drew on the cigarette. "Now I won't feel so defeated when I hand the keys over. I'm sure they won't get far with one or two of these poured into the crank case."

"Carry on, Marine." I turned back to Leo. "Go ahead."

"Sir, Lieutenant Colonel Dean wants to go on a mission with us."

I spat on ground, kicking up a bit of fine dust. "He does?"

"He called earlier. I told him you were visiting Mujeed."

"What else?"

"Nothing. I gave him a rundown of the upcoming missions. He asked us to let him know which one was best."

"He's had plenty of chances to go on missions. Probably wants to get a close look at how we operate. Maybe get a combat action ribbon."

I hoped never to see Dean again. In his position on Colonel Marr's staff, he could cause me trouble—meddle in my business. I needed top cover.

"I wonder if Colonel Steeples knows?" I thought out loud. Leo waited.

I thought for a second more; we were due to make another supply run. "I'll let Colonel Steeples know tomorrow. Leo?"

"Sir?"

"What do you think Abby thought about those shitheads we stacked in the trunk?" I asked.

"Hard to say."

I shook my head. "If she bungles it, it could get bad." Leo rubbed his chin. "For us, you mean?"

"No, for me. I'm the one who gave it the *hominous dominous.*"

"We'll have to wait and see. I wouldn't worry about it."

"She said it would be about six weeks before the article is published. We'll be nearly outbound by then. I'd sure hate to get put on legal hold, or cause trouble for Lieutenant Colonel Steeples."

Leo looked off at the compound, still rubbing his chin with his hand, likely thinking of his boys.

"Leo?"

"Sir?"

"Don't worry. If anyone has to answer for it and has to stay behind, it will be me. I'll roger up to any allegations of abuse."

"I wasn't—"

"Don't sweat it. We have other problems—real ones."

"Like what?"

"I'm out of smokes."

Leo laughed. "Give me a minute, sir. I have two boxes."

⌘

The next day we drove to Camp Fallujah.

I found Lieutenant Colonel Steeples and spoke to him about Dean's request. He told me that Dean likely wanted to get away from the head-shed.

I left it at that. We loaded up our supplies and mail and drove to the chow hall.

Waiting in line, I spotted a Marine I knew, a fellow major from the Judge Advocate's office at Camp Lejeune.

When we got our food, I led Leo and Sergeant Ski towards him. "Long time no see, Marine," I said.

The major stood up and shook my hand. "Steerforth, right? Headquarters Battery—Artillery."

"Alena?" I asked.

"Good memory," he said.

As we stripped off our gear, the major commented, "You look busy."

"Wait until you smell us, sir," Sergeant Ski cracked.

I sat down. "Living out in town with the Iraqis."

"How long have you been here?"

"Five months plus—six or seven weeks left. Came from Ramadi."

"Ramadi?"

"Yeah, it's all you heard it is."

"That's not good."

I laughed. "Nope."

We ate and made small talk about courts-martial he'd handled for me back home.

When Leo and Sergeant Ski finished eating, they excused themselves and left to sort the mail.

I went for a cup of tea and a cup of coffee for Alena. When I returned, I asked, "Anything interesting going on?"

"Interesting, no. Petty shit? All the time."

"Petty?"

"People getting busted for drinking—"

"Drinking?"

"Yeah, there's been a crackdown on a lot of stuff, and booze in theater didn't have any legs to begin with." He tested his coffee with a quick sip. "A lieutenant colonel got sent home last month when someone smelled liquor on him."

"During work hours?"

"All hours are working hours, and everyone knows the rules, funny man. I've seen eight cases since February."

I combed my fingers through my hair and thought about my booze stashed under my rack in a box and covered with unfolded underwear. I didn't know where Leo kept his. "Well, not much of that where I'm at."

"If there is, keep it low. It's a draconian atmosphere."

"That bad?"

"Maybe not in Ramadi, but here it is. You've seen the MPs, right?"

Starting to laugh, I sucked in liquid and choked. I blew tea through my nose and onto the table but managed to say, "Yeah, pulling folks over for speeding on base."

"It's funny, but that's just the tip of it." He sipped his coffee. "Depending on which side you're on, it can be tragic."

I ran my fingers through my hair again, thinking of the shitheads stacked in the trunk of the Humvee.

"Had a captain from First Tanks—one of you MiTT guys—a major-select. He made it through the initial fight in '03 and again in '04 right here. Was awarded for valor twice. He'd been going over to Regimental Headquarters regularly, screwing a female captain and talking about it on the Internet."

"He was on a MiTT and had Internet?"

Alena shrugged. "His own Marines, lieutenants found out about the on-duty fucking and turned him in. The lieutenant colonel in charge of the team is a Bible thumper, and the female getting fucked was married."

"That's never good."

"Married, but separated. Her husband's in country, out with one of the infantry battalions. He couldn't care less."

"What happened to the captain?"

Alena drained his coffee cup. "Office hours with the general. He's done. Sending him home."

I shuddered. "What about her?"

"She'll finish the tour, unless she comes up pregnant." He paused, sipped his coffee. "She's good-looking. You know the deal."

I held the teacup to my lips with both hands and nodded. "I've seen it before."

We both sat for a few seconds. My tea was empty. Again, I thought about the detainees. "Hey, I need to ask you something...lawyer-like. You mind?"

"No, shoot."

"Coffee?"

"Half."

"I'll make it quick." I took his cup and left.

I returned, sat down again, and looked to my left and right. "That bad?" he asked.

"It's not about liquor or women, so that's a start, but this female reporter came to my position—"

"I thought you said it's not about a woman? Was she married?" he chuckled.

"No, it's nothing like that," I said.

I laid out the events that led to the detainees getting loaded into the trunk, sardine-like and beat up, and transported to the train station.

He listened. "Anyone say anything?"

"None of my Marines would, I don't think. The Marines at the detention facility raised an eyebrow."

"You got any enemies around here?"

"None I can think of. My boss is a great guy. Lieutenant Colonel Steeples—"

"I know him. Hornet pilot."

"Right. His boss, Colonel Marr, he's solid. He'd understand."

"You haven't mentioned it to them?"

"No. I don't think it's a big deal, but I came from Ramadi where folks did whatever was necessary to accomplish the mission."

"You could mention it to your boss, that's up to you. That leaves the reporter, and you don't know what she'll write."

"'Xactly."

Alena pushed his coffee cup away. "If she's neutral, no big deal. If the article's a scorcher, somebody's nuts will likely get…" He raised his fist, grabbing and turning an imaginary lever, "…viced."

"They'll be my nuts, getting pounded flat with a hammer. I gave the good-to-go."

"All you can do is wait."

"Thanks. Last thing, while I have the chance."

"Shoot."

"It's sort of odd, but the fight in Ramadi? Working with the Iraqis while they scream over the radio and shit any place they can, and me thinking of every angle I can to complete the mission while keeping my men alive; we never dodged a mission."

Alena looked around the chow hall, packed with soldiers, Marines, contractors, sailors, and Air Force folk. "A lot of guys do."

"I refused to escort somebody through death's alley once. Otherwise, we embraced every chance to do our mission. The thought of being disgraced because I stuffed some shit-heads in the back of a vehicle disturbs me."

"That's how the captain felt."

"Oh, so you spoke to him?"

"I was his defense."

I stood up and began pulling my gear on. When I finished, Alena and I walked outside together.

Leo and Sergeant Ski were waiting by the Humvee, sifting through mail spread over the hood.

I reached out to take Alena's hand and thanked him. "Hopefully we won't see each other out here again."

"Don't worry," he said and buddy-punched me on the shoulder. "If it *does* get you, it'll likely come down from above after the article hits—way beyond my pay grade."

I walked to the vehicle.

Leo looked up at me. "Something wrong, sir?"

"No, no, I was just giving the major a rundown of Ramadi. I used your line about the monster under the bed. He got the picture. Did I get any mail?"

"Sorry, sir."

"Okay. Maybe next week."

"Don't worry, sir." Leo held up a box and shook it. "From Wife. Looks like two more boxes. That should hold us."

⌘

Mujeed was gone again.

My sketchbook was full, so I started another, but the drawings were lackluster compared to those I'd turned out in Ramadi.

I recommended to Lieutenant Colonel Dean that he join my men at the river post for a routine cordon and search operation.

Three days before the mission, Craig called Leo and informed him that some type of sores were spreading on Lieutenant Webb's face. He needed medical attention. We took Doc to the river post. He examined Webb and recommended we take him to Charlie Med aboard Camp Fallujah to be treated. Lieutenant Lott stayed behind with Staff Sergeant Craig.

Webb, my youngest Marine, had been at the river post for six weeks, living on MREs and *jundi* porridge. Besides the scabs on his face, he told me he'd had the shits for over a month. His eyes were sunken and his uniform hung like a sack from his shoulders; he'd lost twenty pounds. On top of it all, he needed a haircut.

I stayed in the Humvee while Leo walked with Webb towards Charlie Med. They stopped halfway and stood, exchanging words. The young man kept looking away and shaking his head.

I watched Leo laugh and slap Webb on the back before turning towards the Humvee, leaving the lieutenant to continue by himself. Leo was still chuckling when he climbed in the driver's seat.

"What's so funny?"

"He says Staff Sergeant Craig is driving him crazy, fretting over the fate of his Marine Corps career because of his DUI."

"Really? Craig's tough, shakes or not."

"Webb says he sits on the edge of his rack and repeats over and over, 'Thirteen years, eight deployments, all for nothing.'"

"Eight deployments?" I said, "I only have five, and *that's* a lot."

I thought about how it would have been, the emaciated young lieutenant stuck by himself with Craig for hours on end as the veteran staff sergeant tortured himself with regret. "I'm surprised he survived as long as he has," I said.

Leo lowered his head. "When we resupplied them, Webb didn't look that bad."

I regretted not taking the time out and spending a few days at the river post. I put my boot on the dash of the Humvee and smacked my hand over my knee. "Let's keep Webb with us at the Soap Factory for a few days. We'll drop him back at the river next week and bring Lott back."

"What about the mission with Lieutenant Colonel Dean?"

I shook my head. "Webb looks like a scarecrow. Get him a haircut. Craig and Lott can handle it. Lott's a weirdo. I swear he was conceived by a hand job, but he'll do fine with Craig there."

It turned out that Webb had contracted impetigo. The doctors gave him antibiotics and intravenous glucose and told him to use only bottled water to bathe and brush his teeth. A female nurse reprimanded him for eating *jundi* food. He said he wouldn't do it again.

On the day before the mission, Lieutenant Colonel Dean and his convoy stopped by the Soap Factory to confirm Craig and Lott were expecting him. He planned to stay at the river two days and have the Marines who dropped him return and pick him up. I didn't think all the driving was prudent, but, this time, I kept it to myself. I met him as he pulled in and gave him the thumbs up; he left without getting out of his vehicle.

The cordon and search kicked off at 0800. I stayed in Mujeed's map room, tracking the mission on the radios. Zuhair was there, smoking cigarettes backwards, doing the same.

By 1500 the operation was over. NSTR.

Leo and I left Mujeed's map room and enjoyed a late lunch of MREs and cigars. As we smoked, Sergeant Ski stuck his head around the corner. "Sir, Staff Sergeant Craig is on the hook, in the U.S.-only room."

"Roger." I stood up. Leo followed me.

I picked up the handset. "Drifter-Six here."

"Roger, Drifter-Six. We think the shitheads are crossing the river south of here at night, moving weapons by boat. Request permission to check it out."

Leo listened on the squawk box. I glanced at him. "Drifter-Three, where did the information come from?"

"Somebody the Iraqis talked to during the mission today."

"How reliable?"

"Hard to tell. We can see a klick down the river from here and haven't seen anything. All we're going to do is check it out."

"Stand by, Drifter-Three." Placing my finger on the map posted on the wall over the radio, I traced a line from the location of the river post; a thousand meters south, the river narrowed there. "What do you think?" I asked Leo.

"Never know, sir."

Thinking out loud, I said, "Dean's with them. He's a big boy, but I don't like doing things on the fly."

"I wonder if they've run this by Zuhair?" asked Leo.

"Good question." I pressed the go-button on the handset. "Drifter-Three, is this cleared through the Iraqi chain?"

"Roger. The Iraqi battalion XO gave it the good-to-go ten minutes ago."

"Okay, Drifter-Three…." I couldn't recall Lott's call sign. "Keep an eye on Lott. Is the visitor going?"

"Roger."

"You're cleared hot. Once you get the kick-off time and the details, pass them on this net."

"Roger. Copy. Drifter-Three. Out."

⌘

Leo and I stood together in Mujeed's map room listening to the sparse radio traffic.

Zuhair and Major Thalmer were there, sitting with a few Iraqi radiomen. I looked at my watch; it was 0100.

About 0200, from the Iraqi radio, I heard yelling.

Zuhair picked up the hook and spoke, his voice rising as he talked.

After a minute, Staff Sergeant Craig's voice—calm and even—came on my radio.

"Drifter-Six, this is Drifter-Three. Over."

I pushed the go-button on the handset. "Go, Drifter-Three."

"We've got heavy contact from fifty meters south. Iraqi company commander down. Gunshot wound to the chest and left shoulder. We've got a pressure bandage on his chest. I poured QuikClot in the shoulder wound. We need Doc's help."

"We'll be there in ten mikes. Drifter-Six, out." I dropped the receiver and turned to follow Leo out.

"I go with you, Major. I help my men. Please." Zuhair stood holding his cigarette in his three-fingered hand. It was the most English I'd ever heard him utter. He exhaled smoke through his nose and snuffed out the cigarette on the table-top where the radios sat.

I nodded at him; he tossed the crumpled butt into the corner and followed me outside.

In less than five minutes, my Marines and Iraqis pulled on our gear, mounted machine guns onto four Humvees, and pulled out of the Soap Factory—into the dead of night.

CHAPTER 28

The fireball lit the surrounding area for an instant and flashed out. The shockwave and thunderous *boom!* rocked my vehicle. A heavy object landed on me, pinning me against the Humvee door. It was Sergeant Ski, dropped out of the gunner's hatch. Debris continued peppering the vehicle.

"Sergeant Ski?" I said and gently pushed him away from me. He didn't answer.

Leo commanded the first Humvee and O'Shannihan had the tail-end Charlie. Zuhair's Humvee was third—it took the hit.

Doc backed the vehicle up and stopped. We stretched Ski out on the console of the Humvee. While Doc pulled his flashlight from his vest and bent over Ski, I picked up the handset. "Steelcage-Six, this is Drifter-Six. We've been hit. Stand by for SITREP."

Doc pried Ski's eyes open with his thumb and index finger and searched with his flashlight.

"How bad, Doc?" I asked.

"He's bleeding from his ears and nose. Severe concussion. Vital signs, affirmative. Non- responsive. He's in shock."

The Marines and the *jundi* debarked the Humvees and set up a cordon. Leo found me and told me what he'd gathered in the five minutes since the explosion. Doc left to assess the other casualties.

"Steelcage-Six, this is Drifter-Six. Over," I transmitted.

"Go, Drifter-Six."

"Sir, bomb buried under the tarmac. No small arms fire at this time. We're a klick west of the Soap Factory on Route Michigan. Will remain in place. First report: One KIA, three WIAs so far. We've got one missing. One vehicle destroyed. Need MEDEVAC and assistance."

"I'm on my way, Clay. Steelcage-Six, out."

I wiped the blood from Ski's face and made a pillow for him with the Humvee seat cushion. I left him stretched out and went to help my men.

Zuhair's vehicle was flipped over, doors and wheels blown off. We pulled his driver out. He was dead. The gunner, although alive, was bleeding badly from his mouth, nose, and anus.

O'Shannihan's gunner, a *jundi*, took debris to the face. Because he was wearing the safety glasses O'Shannihan gave him, his eyes weren't damaged, but his face was lacerated in numerous places.

After searching for fifteen minutes, the *jundi* and Lieutenant O'Shannihan found Zuhair on the other side of the highway divide, blown thirty meters from his vehicle.

It was likely the concussion from the blast killed him.

They hauled Zuhair's corpse into the cordon, carried by all four limbs, head hanging down, wobbling at the neck. One of the *jundi* carried his protective vest.

The Iraqi commander hit in the shoulder and chest bled out. His men hauled him back to the river post on an ornate iron door ripped from someone's courtyard wall. We drove our casualties to Charlie Med at Camp Fallujah where Zuhair's gunner died.

Because Sergeant Ski's brain swelled, the Army doctors decided to fly him to the hospital in Baghdad. Just after dawn, Leo and I followed the ambulance to the airfield and watched the medevac fly away with our sergeant.

⌘

Major Thalmer called Mujeed and told him Zuhair was dead. Mujeed came back the next night. Before he arrived, one of General Azizi's cronies, a major wearing parachute wings, showed up at the Soap Factory to take Zuhair's position as the battalion executive officer.

We were all worried about Ski. Lieutenant Colonel Steeples's men contacted the Marine liaison in Baghdad; she knew little. Lieutenant Webb was distraught over the company commander getting killed. They had worked together since we arrived in Ramadi. I went to the river post, passing Dean going the other way on Route Michigan, to be with Staff Sergeant Craig and Lieutenant Lott. We talked about the captain's death, played chess, and swam in the Euphrates. I made them wash the blood off the door they carried the captain in on and take it back. Leo relieved me after two days. He gave us the news that Sergeant Ski was stable and talking but would soon be on his way to Germany and then CONUS.

We were three weeks from flying out when we got word that the Ministry of Defense wanted to visit the battalion—and meet Mujeed.

⌘

"Is the MOD coming to visit your battalion a good thing, *Sati?*"

I was visiting Mujeed's office. Nick wasn't there. Mujeed sat at his desk dressed only in U.S. Woodland trousers, a T-shirt, and leather sandals. Behind him on the wall hung a scarlet two-by-three-foot flag with *3-2-1 MiTT* stitched on it in thick gold-thread embroidery, a gift from our team. A television in the room blared a man preaching Islam.

Mujeed fiddled with his cell phone and offered me sweets—dates garnished with crushed walnuts and confectioners' sugar. They were delicious.

He shook his head. "The…the brigade commander…I don't know."

Hussein came into the room with a broom and swept. When we finished our tea, he brought more.

In the corner of his office, Mujeed kept his equipment on a gear tree, a cross-shaped structure about three feet high, built with two-by-fours. His helmet sat on top the vertical post, while his body armor fit through the horizontal arms of the cross bar. Another set of body armor lay neatly beside it.

"Zuhair's gear?" I asked.

Mujeed nodded.

I finished my cigar and a fourth cup of tea. When I couldn't stand the noise on the television any longer, I stood up to excuse myself.

Mujeed rose from behind his desk, extended his hand, and shook mine. With his brow furrowed and without smiling, he placed his hand in the middle of his chest. "Major, thank you for working with the battalion. I have enjoyed our friendship."

Both his seriousness and sentimentality set me back. It took a second before I returned the Arabic gesture. "*Afwan, Sati*. My pleasure. See you tomorrow."

⌘

The next morning, I learned from Lieutenant Colonel Steeples's crew that General Casey was accompanying the Minister of Defense to the Soap Factory. Two days before they arrived, I got a visit from the commanding officer of the Marine regiment assigned to the Anbar Province, Colonel Frank. Having been wounded badly a year before, he returned to duty in record time and was a growing legend in the USMC. Colonel Marr and Colonel Steeples accompanied him. I walked them around the Soap Factory, gave them a rundown of the tactical situation, and explained what happened when Zuhair and the others got killed.

Colonel Frank asked, "Major Steerforth, what's Colonel Mujeed doing right?"

"It's hard to say, sir. He cares about his troops, and he relies on his officers. Plus, he stays engaged."

"How many ghost *jundi* does he have?"

I glanced at Lieutenant Colonel Steeples. He winked at me.

"Probably seventy-five. That's seventy-five out of the three-hundred men in the battalion, give or take," I said.

"Less than a quarter?"

"Yes, sir. He cut it in half before we came here." The colonel didn't respond. "I've crusaded about as much as I can, sir. Mujeed may in fact be keeping some of the money, but if he is, part of it's going to the *jundi*."

"That's prudent on your part," said Colonel Frank. "As distasteful to us as it is, it's just their way of doing business.

They have to make it work. Keep doing what you're doing, Major." He looked at me for a second then said, "Ramadi?"

"Yes, sir."

"Damn. That place is a hell hole. Three-Eight just lost three more yesterday, a platoon commander and two of his Marines."

Concerned, I waited for Colonel Frank to speak more about the three Marines he'd just mentioned; he didn't.

I walked the colonels back to their Humvees. As they geared up to depart, a captain from their convoy approached me. "Sir, I'm the admin officer for the Division MiTT."

I recognized him. "Sure, I remember you from Taji."

"Right, sir. You leave in the next few weeks, correct?"

"We do."

"Colonel Marr signed all of your awards, and I forwarded them to First Division."

"Thanks for the word."

"Some of them will get approved here in-country, but some will have to go all the way to Tampa for General Mattis's signature."

"Mattis, eh?"

"Yes, sir."

I nodded. "Never met him, but I understand he's a hard dick." The captain nodded back. "Sir, I need two witness statements."

I furrowed my brow and raised my chin to him.

"For a mission Lieutenant Colonel Dean went on with your men. I believe a Lieutenant Lott and a Staff Sergeant Craig," he said.

"Yeah, that's them." I considered what Dean may have done that needed my men's official confirmation. "I'll pass the word, and the next time they're back at Camp Fallujah, they'll address it."

As he turned to get into the Humvee, I asked, "Captain, do you see the casualty reports from Ramadi?"

"I have access to them, yes. Why?"

"I know Marines in Three-Eight. Colonel Frank mentioned a platoon commander got killed out there. Any idea what his name was?"

"No, sir, but I can find out for you."

"I'll come see you when I bring my Marines to write the statements."

"Roger. See you then."

A few days later, Lieutenant Webb, his face clearing up and ten pounds heavier, returned to the river. Leo and Lieutenant Lott came back to the Soap Factory.

During a resupply, Leo bought a plastic footlocker at the PX to send gifts and extra gear home. Half full, it sat in our room next to our racks, doubling as a coffee table and a bar. Leo poured whiskey into my canteen cup. It was good to have him back.

We hadn't turned the air-conditioning unit off since we moved in nearly two months earlier.

"While you were gone, I remembered..." I began enigmatically. He drank and raised his eyebrows.

"...where I know Dean from."

He chuckled.

"What's so funny?"

Leo reached under his rack and pulled out a box of cigars. "He asked a lot about you when he came to Ramadi."

"He did?" I set my cup down, stood up, and lifted the window, letting in hot air and the drone of generators. "Why didn't you say anything to me?"

"We never really talked about him again, and by the time we got here, Ramadi seemed forever ago."

"Camp Fuji, 1993," I said, leaning my palms on the windowsill and staring at the Humvees parked next to the compound gate. Recalling the majestic views from the slopes of the volcanic mountain I asked, "Ever been to Fuji?"

"No."

"It's beautiful and peaceful, not like here." I sucked in hot desert air. "We were shooting those old WWII-model 05s. The breeches had 1944 stamped on them."

Leo held out the cigar box. "Shooting 05s is before my time."

"Nearly before mine—I was a second lieutenant." I stuck a cigar between my teeth and pulled my matches from my pocket. "Only smoked one a day back then." I struck a match and lit the cigar. "I was at the observation post on the slope of the mountain, camped out with two lance corporals."

"No other lieutenants?"

"Nope, just me. I woke up one foggy morning at zero-five-thirty, shaved, and got ready for the check round." I drew on the cigar and licked my lips, relishing the taste nearly as much as I enjoyed recalling my time on the mountain. "I studied the impact area with my binos and didn't see anything. So I called Range Control and got the thumbs up to shoot. At zero-six on the dot, I gave the go-ahead to the battery."

"And Dean was in the impact area..." He couldn't finish because he was laughing.

"No, I'll get to that. The battery called over the radio, 'Shot, over,' and I said, 'Shot, out.' I heard the bark of the gun seven or eight klicks behind me and waited to see the impact of the round." I moved my arm in an arc from left to right, the cigar between my fingers, trailing smoke as I traced a trajectory to a spot in the center of the room. "It landed right in the middle of the impact area, where it was supposed to be—that's when I saw a white range-control vehicle come barreling out of one of the deep draws, fleeing. I grabbed the hook: 'Check firing, check firing, vehicle in the impact area.'"

Leo laughed again, this time so hard he choked on the liquor.

"Easy boy. I was ordered to Range Control. But by the time I got there, the issue had been resolved, or was in the process of being resolved, and a certain *Captain* Dean was the range-control officer."

"That's it?"

I laughed. "He'd lost track of his people. It was range-control Marines I'd nearly hit. He was at half attention and a full-bird colonel, who looked as old as dirt to me, was leaned into the side of Dean's face, spitting a fierce cussing. At full attention, I announced, 'Second Lieutenant Clarence J. Steerforth, Battery L, Forward Observer, reporting as ordered, sir!'"

"The old man turned from Dean and, calm as a Sunday morning, asked me, 'Son, you're the battery forward observer?'"

"'Yes, sir, that's me,' I said. I was ready for the gallows."

"'You didn't do anything wrong, Lieutenant. Get back on the hill. Keep shooting,' he said and turned around and recommenced chastising Dean. My mistake was that I looked at Dean before I left—right smack in the face."

"So what's his beef?"

"Well, Dean was the range-control officer—that by itself is nearly a career killer. He was likely struggling to stay on active duty. That incident may have sealed his fate, and off to reserves he went—and here I am today, been on active duty for fifteen years."

"That's it?"

"That's enough. He's known all along. All I had was a face to recall—two minutes of time in fifteen years. He had a face, a name, and a voice that's probably rung in his ears ever since. Pour another drink, and I'll tell you the kicker."

Leo obliged.

"Somebody put him in for a medal. Likely a Bronze Star—for valor."

"For what?"

"For the Bronze Star? Well, the same thing the rest of us have done: our job in combat. For the *V* part? I don't know. That's where we come in—Lott and Craig."

Leo put the pieces together. "He needs witnesses."

"Exactly, and I don't care what Lott and Craig say."

"Do you want to see them about this?" Leo asked.

"Hell, no. Get them back to the rear to make the statements."

⌘

General Casey and the Minister of Defense arrived. With them were six American and Iraqi generals of different varieties and an entourage of nearly fifty people, military and civilians. I sat next to General Casey while Mujeed briefed them on his unit's progress.

When it came time for photos, I snuck off for a smoke. If Abby's article drew attention, I didn't want General Casey to end up somewhere on the front page of the paper or on TV beside me, accused of abusing detainees.

I showed back up when the crowd was loading into their vehicles and shook Casey's hand when he left.

⌘

General Azizi's crony was young and energetic. He didn't go on leave but did spend a lot of time in the rear with Iraqi headquarters. I never saw him and Mujeed together.

353

Leo and I drove Staff Sergeant Craig and Lieutenant Lott back to Camp Fallujah to make witness statements. I went inside the Division MiTT's headquarters with them. The admin officer wasn't in, so I left Craig and Lott to wait.

With a bit of time on our hands, Leo and I decided to go to the PX. When we tried to enter the gate, two blood-shot-eyed Ugandan guards stopped us, asking to see our military IDs. I exchanged a glance with Leo.

There we stood, in full gear with eight months of dust and sweat on our uniforms, armed to the teeth, stinking, and as American-looking as a pop star prancing around on stage—three- quarters naked, painted with stars and stripes, and an eagle feather poking out his rear end.

Chagrinned, we showed our credentials.

"You'd think that they'd at least find some Germans or Italians—people who won't fight but can recognize a bona-fide U.S. Marine to guard the gate to the PX," I said as we passed by.

"Sir, I think the Germans and Italians have quit the war, and the Ugandans are probably cheap," he said. "They're just doing their jobs. Two weeks left, sir. Two weeks."

I searched the PX magazine rack for a *U.S. Gazette*. I found one, but there was no story by Abby. I gave it to Leo for a second check. Nothing. I was beginning to hope the piece never appeared. I purchased the magazine anyway.

I received two boxes of cigars in the mail that day and three letters from Kate.

Driving to the Division MiTT office, I opened an envelope from Kate. "Those are fancy letters, sir," Leo teased, referring to the red-wax seal Kate embossed on the back of each one.

I held out the letter. He leaned over, sniffed, and nodded. "Smells good, doesn't it?"

We pulled into the dirt lot. I was still reading when Leo said, "Here they come."

Staff Sergeant Craig, Lieutenant Lott, and the admin officer from the Division MiTT were walking towards us, the captain in the lead. I wiped the ever-present sweat from my forehead with my sleeve and waited.

The captain reached the vehicle first, then stepped aside to let Staff Sergeant Craig by.

Craig stopped in front of me, his lips parted, but he didn't speak. "It was Lieutenant Willington," I said.

Craig nodded.

After a moment, the captain stepped closer to the vehicle. "Sorry, sir. Staff Sergeant says you knew him well."

I sat staring in the rearview mirror of the Humvee. With my forefinger, I reached out and touched the smooth reflection of the sun-bleached plywood buildings to my rear, their shabbiness suddenly apparent to me. I'd thought of Brim frequently since leaving Ramadi, imagining us back home and drinking beer in the bar at the riverfront in Wilmington, telling war stories and laughing. Now, the pieces didn't fit together. Brim was dead—we'd never speak again.

I sat that way for a full minute before realizing the Marines were waiting for me to respond. "Thanks, Captain," I said. "It's better than learning it in passing. Any details I need to know?"

"Gunshot wound."

"Instant?"

"I don't know. I'll ask around."

"No. Leave it be. Thanks again, though." I reached out and shook his hand. "See you around." I looked at Craig and Lott. "Time to go home, Marines."

When we got back to the Soap Factory, I sat in the Humvee for a long time thinking about the day in Rosslyn when Willington and the others got commissioned. I recalled the night we met the girls from Alabama. I imagined Brim's men admiring him for disregarding the rules of engagement and burning down the newspaper stand. I remembered him laughing and banging on the Russian jeep when I told him I was in love.

It was dark when I heard the scuffle of Leo's combat boots on gravel. "You okay, sir?" He was carrying my stick.

"Yeah, I'm okay. What are you doing with my stick, Grasshopper?" He held it out to me. "I know you like it."

"Thanks." I took it, letting my arm hang down outside the Humvee window.

"You two laughed nearly the entire time the evening he came by and had drinks with us," said Leo.

I tapped the stick against the Humvee. "I'll go see his people when I get back. I was the duck the midshipmen learned to follow." I tapped again. "Some of them, like Willington, I served with for three years, a long time in Marine-Corps time. Think about us, we only met nine months ago, and it seems like forever. But you know what, Leo?"

Leo reached into his cargo pocket and pulled out the Listerine bottle.

"Willington knew the deal," I said and struck side of the Humvee so hard that Leo flinched.

Leo swigged from the bottle and offered it to me. "Indeed, sir. We all do."

I took it and got out of the vehicle.

As I drank, Leo said, "Staff Sergeant Craig's got something to say."

I handed the bottle back. "About Willington?"

"No, sir."

⌘

The three of us sat together in our can, canteen cups sitting in front of us on the plastic footlocker. Leo poured us drinks.

"Sir, I hate to bother you about this right now," said Craig. I shook my head. "You're not bothering me."

Craig waved his hand. "I ain't making a statement. Sir, I got it that the Bronze Star is, well…." Craig hesitated.

Leo handed me my canteen cup, and I took a drink. "Say what's on your mind, Marine."

"It's kind of standard for you field-grade officers."

"Captain Essex is a company-grade officer, and I put him in for one. You say *you* like we're strangers."

"I don't mean you and Captain Essex, sir." Craig thumped his Copenhagen can and slipped in a dip. "We spent four and a half months in that shithole, Ramadi. We liked it and did what we were sent here to do."

"We did. It seems fun in retrospect, at least until days like today and the night we got hit."

"Yes, sir. Sorry about your friend." Staff Sergeant Craig raised his canteen cup. "And here's to Ski." We all drank. "I don't care about the medal. It's the valor device that's bullshit."

"Staff Sergeant, you don't have to write the statement. I don't know why you're so pissed off."

Leo cut in. "What pissed you off so bad?"

"Sir, the citation makes it sound like Lieutenant Colonel Dean took over when the Iraqi captain got shot. All he did was fire back, and any Marine fires back. The *jundi* took care of the captain. They stripped him down, *wham-bam*," Craig said, slapping the knuckles of one hand into the palm of the other, in step with the cadence of his words, "just like Doc taught them. Lieutenant Lott and I took over after that. Lott did a damn good job, by the way."

"So don't make a statement. It takes two to make it legit," I said.

"Nobody's going to force me?"

"Hell no. If somebody says anything, I'll tell them to stick it in their ass. Quit worrying." I picked up the bottle and poured another shot into the canteen cups. "And forget about the DUI. I'll take care of you on your fitness report. I can't make the DUI go away, but I can make it seem insignificant compared to what you did out here."

"Okay, sir, if you say so." Craig sipped his whiskey.

"I say so, Marine." I swirled around the whiskey in my cup and thought about the scene at the river. "The captain got shot in the chest. I assumed the round went in from the side, under his body armor."

"I'm not sure, said Craig. "There was blood everywhere, but the wound was mid-chest, I know that." He shook his head. "We kept pressure on it until he died."

"You did a good job, Staff Sergeant. You always do. You're the best man we have," I said.

"Thank you, sir."

"I've got one more question and then we'll quit talking about it." Leo looked at me, curious.

"What happened to the captain's gear—his protective vest?"

Craig gently massaged his receding hairline with his fingers. "I don't know, sir. The *jundi* probably took it. They don't throw anything away."

CHAPTER 29

Our outbound flight was locked on—six days and a wake-up away. The crew replacing us had been on deck for four days, in from the Third Marine division in Okinawa.

I hadn't seen Mujeed since the Ministry of Defense and General Casey visited. General Azizi's crony was running the battalion.

I followed Leo's lead and bought a footlocker to send gear home. The shipping was free, and I would only have to lug my rucksack aboard each bus, helicopter, and plane during the ten-day ordeal of getting back to Camp Lejeune.

I placed in the bottom of the box my cold-weather gear, a never-worn pair of desert boots issued to me at Camp Pendleton, and a dozen M4 magazines. The books John sent to me went next. I sat for a while thumbing through *Modigliani: Nudes* and resolved to return to painting figures when I returned home. Before packing the book, I tucked inside the back cover the captured map of Ramadi Major Miller gave to me. Three packets of Kate's wax-sealed letters went on top of the books. Next my mom's letters and then cards from John.

When I picked up the postcards featuring Motherwell's paintings, I lit a cigar and shuffled through them, studying each one, reading titles and dates. *Elegy to the Spanish Republic, No 57*, 1959–1960; *Elegy to the Spanish Republic, No 133*, 1975; *Elegy to the Spanish Republic, No 78*, 1962. Most of them were painted in black and white only; *Elegy to the Spanish Republic, No 34*, 1953, included patches of the three primary colors: red, yellow, and blue. There were other paintings in the series from 1961, 1965, 1967, 1973, 1969, and even 1978. I scratched my head. More than twenty years on one series of paintings, all featuring a simple motif. Whatever it was about the Spanish Civil War that fascinated Motherwell, I had found nothing so stimulating in Ramadi or in Fallujah. Perhaps seeing the paintings in the flesh in New York, as I planned, would reveal the secret to me.

I picked up my own sketchbooks and paged through them—one complete, one barely started. Most drawings are better in retrospect; such was the case with these. They were the last things I packed before I closed the trunk and lay down for a nap.

A half hour later, Leo woke me and told me that Dean was in the compound, waiting to speak to me. I strapped on my shoulder holster and pistol, put on my cover, and glanced at my watch. It was 1200. Walking into the dusty compound, I found Dean near the front gate, leaned against the hood of his Humvee, his arms folded across his chest.

I stopped four paces in front of him. "Sir, how can I help you?"

Dean shifted his weight from one leg to another and eyeballed me. "Major, when were you going to tell Lieutenant Colonel Steeples about the men you stacked in the trunk of that Humvee?"

I shrugged. "I didn't think it was a big deal. It was safer that way."

"Five men, beat to shit, tied up and blindfolded, stuffed in a trunk in 120-degree heat? That's your definition of *safe?*"

I shrugged again. "Safe as it gets out here."

Dean started to smile, then concealed the pleasure of watching me defend myself by massaging the corners of his mouth with his index finger and thumb.

Resisting the urge to point at him I said, "Are you implying that I abused those detainees?"

"I'm *telling* you that you were careless with human lives."

I sucked in the heat and slowly exhaled it through my nose. I felt a bead of sweat crawl down across my temple but kept my hands in place. "I gave them the best and safest transportation I had on hand."

"Keep telling yourself that, Steerforth," he said. "Have you ever imagined you may have to answer for that?"

"Not really, sir, I haven't thought much about it." I felt the sweat drip down my neck. It was all I could do to keep from wiping it away with my hand. "The reporter was standing there. She would have said something if it had been a big deal."

Dean turned the palm of his right hand inward, preening his middle fingernail with his thumb. "So you rely on civilians to determine right and wrong for you? That's the kind of officer you are?"

A surge of adrenaline caused me to stuff my hands in my pockets and curl them into fists. Feeling a strong urge to knock the man out with a palm-heel strike to the chin and then smash his skull with boot-heel stomps, I plunged them deeper into place and gripped the pocket lining.

I waited until he looked up from the field-expedient manicure. "No, I rely on civilians to overreact to trivial shit, like a handful of detainees loaded into the trunk of a vehicle on a fifteen-minute ride to jail."

Folding his arms back in place, he cocked his head back and sniffed. "Maybe that's what they thought at Abu Ghraib."

I glared at Dean's fleshy face, disdaining his softness, and thought about the man in the blue sedan we killed in Ramadi. The pool of crimson blood drained from his head, the mess of flesh and bone on the black tarmac. I could do nearly the same to Dean and almost as quickly, with nothing more than the Marine Corps Martial Arts training I'd received a year earlier.

I gripped the pocket lining tighter, fingering the stitching in the corner.

Law had not constrained us on that day in Ramadi; for me, on this day, it did.

"If you're equating what my Marines and I did to protect a handful of shitheads who threw grenades at our partners to a bunch of college wannabes playing horseshit kiddy games, you're wrong. Plain fucking wrong."

Dean relented to pleasure and smiled. "That's your opinion of what is generally considered a war crime?"

"I wasn't the judge in that case. Run this up the chain of command and brief it as you wish. But you'll have a hard time finding evidence I acted with ill intent."

Satisfied he had raised my ire, Dean unfolded his arms, walked to the passenger side of his vehicle, and glanced back. "It's called *negligence*, Major. You better hope that reporter makes you shine like a diamond in a goat's ass. If she tells it like it is, you'll never wear silver oak leaves."

I found Leo in the dining area, packing his footlocker.

"Leo, who told Lieutenant Colonel Dean about the shitheads we loaded in the trunk?" He carefully placed a folded prayer rug in the locker and looked at me. "Sir?"

"Somebody told Dean about the detainees we transported in the Humvee trunk. He just gave me a grilling."

"Is it a big deal?"

"If someone makes a big deal about it, it will turn into one. Think what a fiasco Abu Ghraib turned into. I'm sure that's what Dean has in mind—visions of Nuremberg." I reached into my breast pocket for a cigar. "Abu Ghraib—a bunch of dumbasses with a camera who joined the Army Reserve for college money and found themselves in a theater of war, led by a female dingbat of a general. Then some ignoramus reporter hunting to be the next Woodburn and Goldstein blows it out of proportion, and the next thing you know, everybody in uniform gets painted with a broad brush of ineptness."

Leo stroked his crew cut with his palm. "You think this is that bad?"

"I don't know," I sighed. "But people are getting sent home for drinking, screwing, and anything else that doesn't fall in line with the letter of the law."

"It must have been Lott…" said Leo. "When Dean stayed with them at the river."

I nodded. "Yeah."

"Either way, we'll just have to wait. If we don't know anything before we leave, it may be easier to be back in the rear if it turns out bad."

"I'd rather be here if it does." I bit a small piece of tobacco from the end of a cigar and spat it on the ground. "Imaginations will run wild back at Lejeune. They're probably still arguing whether or not to award Lieutenant Mahone for valor—a kid who got blown up and mangled for life when he volunteered to run building supplies over the most dangerous fifty miles in Iraq."

Leo turned back to the locker and pulled the lid down into place. "It's shitty," he said. "By the way, have you seen Mujeed?"

"No."

"Nick thinks he's gone. All the gear in his office is gone— the flag we gave him, his television, and his air conditioner. Hussein and Sergeant Achmed are gone too."

That night I spoke to Nick, and he confirmed what Leo said about Mujeed leaving. When I was finished, he asked me if he could speak to me about a personal matter. "Suh, I want to study in America."

"Yeah. I remember. You want to be a dentist, right?"

"Yes, suh. I only want to go for a year, study some basics, then I'll return to Iraq."

"What can I do?"

"Can you ask the new major if he would help me? If we start now, I may know something by the time he leaves."

"What do your parents think about this?"

"My father was a general in the old army. He was not a Baathist."

"Did I say that, Nick?"

"Everybody asks, suh. He had a lot of money then."

"I'll pass the word to the new team. I'll emphasize that you're not a Baathist." I laughed. The young man stared at me.

"Nick you're supposed to laugh," I said.

"I don't get American humor, suh."

⌘

Our flight was due out in three days. I'd heard nothing more of the shitheads we stacked in the trunk. We drove to Camp Fallujah to coordinate our final departure. I went directly to see Lieutenant Colonel Steeples. I found him in the gym on the side of his headquarters, a fifty-by- fifty-foot area with weights, a bench, and a pull-up bar, all shaded by camouflage netting hung from ten-foot poles and net spanners. He was doing pull-ups. He dropped from the bar when I walked in. First off, I told him about Mujeed.

"I think the brigade commander has his own man for the job and Mujeed made it easy for him."

"Sir, he didn't even say goodbye," I said. "Mujeed and I were pretty tight."

"It's Iraq, Clay. We'll never really get them."

"Huh. Yes, sir. We never will."

Colonel Steeples gazed out of the shaded area and across the parking lot that separated his offices from the Iraqis'. "We tried to put Major Thalmer in Zuhair's place, but Azizi insisted his man take it."

I took my cover off and combed my hair back with my fingers. Although above my ears it was shorn to the skin, it was six inches long in front. I concealed the length by greasing it straight back.

"Have you seen the article in *U.S. Gazette?*" Colonel Steeples asked me.

"No, sir."

"Hold on." He walked out from under the netting and disappeared around the corner. I heard a spring creak and then the slam of the plywood door; thirty seconds later he came back with a magazine in his hand. "I got it in the PX two days ago."

I held it in one hand and put my cover back on. "Anything bad, sir?

"No. I liked the part about Jesus. Were you expecting something?"

"One never knows, sir."

"Take it with you," he said. "Check your departure time with my guys. I'll come and get you the evening of. We'll smoke a cigar and take you to the LZ."

"Thanks, sir—we'll be ready."

I reached out to shake his hand, but he seized my forearm instead of my palm. I grasped the thick muscles below his elbow and shifted my weight to my rear foot to avoid being overpowered. With little effort, he pulled me halfway to him. A smile broke out under his large black mustache. "I told Dean to kiss our ass, by the way."

I felt my face flush. "Thanks, sir."

"What the hell did you do to that guy? He is *not* a fan of Major Clarence J. Steerforth."

"That's a story for another day, sir." Our hands remained locked in place. "You've been a great boss. Thanks for everything."

"That's my job, Marine. I'm a Hornet pilot—pride of the Marine Corps!"

We laughed and let each other go.

"You and your men have done real well, Clay."

Leo and my crew were waiting outside for me. I jumped inside my vehicle, grabbed the handset off the radio, and pushed the go-button. "Leo, let's roll."

"Roger, Drifter-Six. We're Oscar-Mike."

"Roger, out," I ended the transmission. As we pulled away, I opened the magazine.

Advising the Iraqi Army

U.S. forces prep Iraqi army to take over the fight against the insurgency

Fallujah, Iraq—Eleven U.S. Marines, camped at an old soap factory in the industrial section of the city, make up one of two-hundred military transition teams (MiTTs) operating in Iraq. This particular MiTT is responsible for partnering with the 3rd Battalion of the new 1st Iraqi Division, with the goal of training the Iraqi battalion to take over when the Coalition Forces withdraw. Partnering the Iraqi army with American MiTT teams, according to Lt. Gen. Peter Chiarelli, the commanding general of Multinational Corps-Iraq, is the key to rebuilding the nation.

I'd never heard of Lt. Gen. Peter Chiarelli. I skimmed the rest of the introduction, landing on my name.

Major Clay Steerforth is the officer mentoring the Iraqi commander of the 3rd battalion in Fallujah. "We figure if Iraqis don't run, don't shoot their buddy, and don't create a blossom of death by firing at everything that moves, we're doing all right," he says of their mission. After five months of firefights, snipers, and ambushes in Ramadi, Steerforth's team moved with the battalion when it was reposted in Fallujah last month.

The Iraqi soldiers, called jundi, are predominantly Shiite, operating in a mostly Sunni town. But it's not only the insurgency and local suspicion that challenge the jundi. Critical shortages of equipment, ammunition, supplies, and even water and fuel interfere with their progress. The jundi are often left waiting on uniforms and wages.

The article described the patrols Abby had been on and Mujeed's meeting with the sheiks.

Finally she described the shitheads we'd captured:

> *One of the five suspected insurgents is underage and will be released later. A nineteen-year-old admits to being paid two hundred dollars to throw the grenade that injured two Iraqi soldiers. Along with three others, he will be taken to a nearby detention facility by convoy. When it's time to depart, Steerforth asks where the prisoners are. "Are you kidding me?" he says, when a Marine points him to the trunk of a Humvee. Captain Essex suggests that the men are safer in the protection of the trunk for the eight-minute ride than in the uncovered flatbed Toyotas.*
>
> *Later that day, after the detainees are delivered to the detention center, the MiTT team learns that a generator will arrive at their command post to provide air-conditioning for the Iraqi soldiers and relief from the 117-degree average temperature. Steerforth says, "It's not Jesus turning water into wine, but it's something."*

I laughed out loud, stuck the magazine over the sun visor, and pulled out a smoke.

⌘

Sitting on our gear in the dark, we waited at the Fallujah LZ. A Marine CH-53 helicopter landed. In single file, I led the ten of us towards the waiting bird. When we were all buckled in, the crew chief gave the thumbs up, the engines whined, the rotors churned the hot air, and we lifted off.

I craned my neck to the porthole behind me and watched the lights of Anbar Province recede. Then I turned away and peered at my Marines, bathed in the dim red glow of the bird's interior lights, their backs against the steel hull of the rattling machine. If any of them had ever complained about the mission we'd been assigned, I'd never heard them. Through willpower and training, they'd defied or overcome the natural fear of death and forged ahead instead.

As we flew, I looked at each of them and remembered some incident when they'd avoided the pitfalls of cowardice and rashness and embraced, rather, that dignifying intangible known as *courage*. I recognized in them dignity—that kernel of grandeur and romance that germinates on the steaming dung-heap that is war—and I realized what Motherwell had captured in his paintings. By intent or accident, he hit the mark.

Luck had been on our side.

AFTERMATH

CHAPTER 30

The married Marines' families met us at Second Reconnaissance Battalion HQ when we arrived back at Camp Lejeune. It was zero-two-thirty Eastern Standard Time—the middle of the day on the Iraqi clock. Just as we finished turning in our weapons, Sergeant Ski arrived, his wife pushing him in a wheelchair. Laughing, he puffed a cigarette, pulled his Purple Heart from his left breast pocket and showed it to me.

Leo's wife was there with his two boys. Since they lived halfway between Camp Lejeune and Wilmington they drove me home. My car was where I left it—in the yard next to my house. We jump-started it.

"I need to get the boys to bed, sir," said Leo.

With the car door open, I sat tapping the gas pedal and watching the tachometer needle oscillate in the orange illumination of the instrument panel. Leo patiently waited. Finally, I looked up at my companion. "Okay, Leo. Thanks for everything."

"Best time of our lives, sir."

"Indeed," I said, reaching out to shake his hand. I only let go when his wife honked the horn of his SUV.

He butted his boots together and flashed a quick salute. "See you later, sir." Then he trotted away.

I drove across the drawbridge spanning the Cape Fear River to the Leland Walmart and left the car running while I went inside and bought a cell phone. Afterward, I cruised through downtown Wilmington, gazing at the unbroken glass of the shop windows. A group of mannequins behind one large pane startled me. Still wide awake, I drove to the port where I watched longshoremen arriving for the morning shift. Finally, I drove to Hardees and bought a sausage, egg, and cheese biscuit.

When I got home, I put on a pot of water for tea, sat on my porch, and lit a cigar. From every direction I heard birds singing their morning song. I stared around at the foliage and breathed in the dampness. The whistle of the teapot brought me to my feet. I reached for my weapon, panicking for an instant when all I gripped was uniform and pectoral muscle.

When the sky lightened above the dark wall of water oaks and towering pine trees, I called my mom.

"Clare, is that you?"

"It's me, Ma. I'm at my house in Wilmington."

"Oh! Wilmington. I've been wondering about you. I haven't heard from you since you called…was that last April? It was before I planted the garden."

"I think it was, Ma. I got back a few hours ago. You're the first person I called."

"It's so good to hear your voice, Clare. I'm not going to bother you and ask you how it was."

"Not much happened," I said. "I stayed on base most of the time."

"That's not what it sounded like in the article I read," she said with lightness in her voice.

"You read that?" I asked.

"One of the girls from class saw it and brought it over to the house."

"Hmm," was all I could muster.

"What about the girl you met, the one in your letter?"

"Kate?"

"Yes, the one you said goes to church."

"I'll bring her home for Christmas."

CHAPTER 31

Mujeed lay awake in his bed, his wife beside him, her breath becoming even and steady as she fell deeper into sleep. Gently he pushed himself to the edge of the bed, sat up, and slid his feet into a pair of sandals. Reaching up, he pulled his night *dishdasha* from the hook where it hung, stood up, pulled the garment over him, and walked across the room to the short flight of stairs leading to the rooftop of his house.

Hafa moved in the bed. "Abdul, where are you going?" she asked.

"I can't sleep. I won't be long."

The night air felt good on his face. He walked across the rooftop to where he could see the street below. From his pocket, he pulled a pack of cigarettes. He lit one and thought of Farah and the children. Staying with his brother while he honeymooned with Hafa, they were due to return the next day. He breathed in deeply and coughed. Holding the Marlboro up, he wondered if it was time to quit smoking. Hafa was likely to give him children, and he needed his health if he intended to see them grow up. Impulsively, he threw the cigarette from the roof and watched red ashes scatter when it hit the street below. He grinned. The sight made him think of Major Steerforth, laughing with his men, taking a last drag from the nub of a cigar, and with the fierce flick of his finger, launching it into a long arc.

⌘

"So," I said to Sam, "the catalogs will be ready this Tuesday?"

We sat across from each other, leaned back in our chairs, and looked out over the Potomac from the Georgetown waterfront, enjoying the last holiday of summer. Nine or ten yachts tied to the pier bobbed in the water while folks enjoyed drinks and music on their top decks. Below deck, the party was visible through the boats' portholes. A sea of umbrellas shaded people sitting at tables and eating dinner. The two outdoor bars were jammed, two or three deep—the singles bunch, eager to get the next drink. I spotted a few Marines, likely from Eighth and Eye. A small mountain of splintered empty crab shells and wooden mallets sat on the red checkered tablecloth in front of us. A din of talk and laughter, waves beating against the river wall, and music filled the air.

Next to me, Kate cracked one last claw.

"I'll drop the catalogs off as soon as I get them. The show's on Thursday, right?" said Sam.

"It is."

"Need any help getting the stuff on the walls?"

"It's done," I said. "John helped me hang everything yesterday. He's definitely not a master carpenter, but we got the job done."

"Any press?"

"A young guy from *The Georgetowner* is going to cover it," I said. "He's a new columnist, but he knows his craft—no fluff."

I'd been back from Iraq for a year. I spent all of my free time painting; the red was working these days, you could say. I'd managed to make it back to D.C. a few times, but this was the first occasion I had to meet with Sam. Kate was still in school, studying nursing now. And she had a new job, selling cars off a lot on Lee Highway just outside Rosslyn. She was good at it and she got paid on time.

When Kate tossed the claw into the pile with the rest, Sam and I lit cigars and ordered more beer.

I looked around the crowd for Nick.

Sam asked if I knew of a SEAL—a lieutenant—killed in Ramadi a year earlier and posthumously nominated for the Medal of Honor. I glanced towards Lee's old estate—Arlington Cemetery—and shook my head. "I never met him."

"Do you mind if I ask what happened to Lieutenant Willington?"

I put the events together in my mind's eye. "Brim...yeah."

"He was a popular guy at George Washington," said Sam.

I raised my beer bottle. "I saw him last in Ramadi, we had a drink together. I wasn't sure what happened until I saw McCook." I took a drink. "He came to my place in Wilmington, we hung out on the riverfront and had a drink, and he told me the details that he got from Brim's Marines at Lejeune." I put the bottle to my lips, then lowered it without drinking. "Brim got killed one night moving with a squad of his men to reinforce the rest of his platoon."

Kate stared, wide-eyed. I'd only told her the funny parts about Iraq.

"Apparently, he entered a building right before some Mooj came in from another way—they got between him and his crew. It was one of those things—wrong time and wrong place—chance, really. When the shooting was over, Brim was down, shot in the neck, his jugular severed. He bled out there on the floor in the dark, his men trying to save him.

I looked to my left, at the cemetery again. "I went to see his family. They're good people. They had his picture on the mantel over their fireplace along with his medals." I emptied my beer. "Let's have another drink."

"I'll get it." Sam got up and walked towards the bar, towering over all other patrons.

I scanned the crowd and said to Kate, "Nick's just a kid. You'll like him."

"Who's Brim?" she asked.

"A friend of mine—a Marine." I stood up to stretch my legs and searched the crowd again. I spotted Nick, shouted his name, and waved. When he saw me, he made his way through the packed patio.

He reached his hand out. "Suh, great to see you." I introduced him to Kate.

"Very nice to meet you, Mick," she said.

"It's Nick, sweetheart."

"Nick, Mick, Rick, I get them all." He laughed. "Just don't call me Nicky."

"At least you've learned to laugh, Nick."

"I learned that here in America."

Nick ordered a whole fish, bone-in, which he picked clean with the knowledge of a fishmonger. I introduced him to Sam, and we chatted about veterans' programs in America. Nick took great interest in our conversation, comparing Sam's work to the lack of organized assistance for Iraqi soldiers returning from the battlefield. We discussed Nick's travel to the States and his studies. He was enrolled at George Mason University, just down the road in Virginia. I asked about our battalion.

"After you left, we got into some bad gun fights in Fallujah," he told me. "One of the Marines that replaced you got killed. One day we fought so long, I was down to using my pistol when help finally arrived."

"What happened to Sergeant Muhammad?"

"He quit the army and became an interpreter. Ten times the money."

"And Hussein?" I queried.

"Don't know, suh."

With no small amount of anticipation, I asked, "Mujeed?"

"Suh, I saw the colonel when I went through his district in Baghdad on my way home to tell my parents goodbye."

"How is he?"

He smiled. "He has two wives now."

I looked towards the Key Bridge in the distance, drew on my cigar, and smiled with Nick.

"I think the new wife is my age, suh."

"Just like he wanted," I laughed. "Is he still in the army?"

"He's at home."

"For work?"

"I think nothing. Maybe engineer work, but I don't think so."

"He must have some money if he's supporting two wives?"

Nick laughed again. "And he has that white truck you gave him."

"I didn't give it to him. He found it."

"Yes, suh, that's right."

"He must have some money stashed away? Did he get it from Zuhair?"

"Uh-huh." Nick grinned, showing his perfect teeth. "I think so."

I crossed my arms, stared at Nick, and nodded slowly.

"Zuhair got it from the people in Taji, the American dollars, anyway. He knew people there—family, I think. The Americans paid his family to buy food for the *jundi* training at Taji. Zuhair was the one who got the contract from the Americans, so he got a cut of the leftover money. There was a lot of it."

I nodded for Nick to go on.

"Mujeed got his cut because he and Zuhair worked together for so long. That's what I heard, anyway."

I rubbed my chin. "The American dollars. They removed the Kevlar plates from their protective vests and stuffed cash in them because they knew no American would ever suspect it."

"Probably," said Nick. "I know Mujeed kept some of it there, I saw it."

"Mujeed had Zuhair's vest in his office just before he left," I said and Nick smiled. "That's when I understood why Zuhair wanted to go with me the night he got killed—the company commander's vest."

Nick rubbed the top of his head with both hands. "I think so. But maybe Zuhair just wanted to go with you. All the captain had was Iraqi money—dinars." He paused for a moment, as if suddenly aware of the intrigue he had lived through. "Mujeed and Zuhair got the dollars from the Taji people, suh. Thousands. The Americans paid something like twenty dollars a day for each *jundi's* rations, but it cost almost nothing to feed them."

"Yeah. I ate it now and then."

Now understanding he was helping me piece things together, Nick cut to the quick. "But that's not why Mujeed had to leave. Nobody else but Mujeed and Zuhair knew about the American money, I don't think."

"Right. Mujeed left on his own accord because the Iraqi money was small potatoes. The brigade commander didn't know about the American money; he simply wanted a cut of the ghost *jundi* money, so he put his crony in Zuhair's place."

I waited for Nick's confirmation.

Sam and Kate sat in silence, listening intently.

"Yes. Once Zuhair was dead, the American dollars from Taji were finished. But the bags of money the officers got for the *jundi* from the Ministry of Defense were still there to take."

I leaned forward and rested my arms on the table. "So Zuhair got American money through a food contracting racket at Taji. He took his cut and split it with Mujeed, because they were essentially brothers, and that still left the Iraqi money." Nick nodded. "Since Zuhair and Mujeed didn't need it, they gave it to their officers who shared it with the men, and that's why those *jundi* stayed around and kept fighting for him."

"Something like that. I mean, suh, that's…" Nick couldn't find the words.

"That's Iraq—right, Nick, right." I looked around at the teeming crowd gathered at Tony and Joe's Riverside Café. Thinking out loud, I said, "Really, though, that's the whole damn world."

Nick nodded knowingly.

"I'm assuming Mujeed took care of Zuhair's wife and children?"

"I'm sure he did. Like you said, they were brothers. They were…how do you say it? Two peas in a bean."

I laughed. "Two peas in a *pod*."

"Yes, suh. That's it. They were two peas in a pod. They were brothers—brothers from the old army."

ABOUT THE AUTHOR

David Richardson is from Waterford, Michigan. From an early age, he was taught to draw and paint by his mother, an artist and art teacher. Richardson served as a combat arms officer and martial arts instructor for twenty-two years in the USMC, later retiring to paint and write. He served three tours in the wars in Iraq, Afghanistan, and Africa. Richardson was awarded for valor by General James Mattis. *War Story* is his first novel.

KING ARTHUR AND THE KNIGHTS OF THE ROUND TABLE HAVE BEEN REBORN TO SAVE THE WORLD FROM THE CLUTCHES OF MORGANA WHILE SHE PROPELS OUR MODERN WORLD INTO THE MIDDLE AGES.

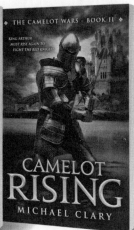

EAN 9781618685018 $15.99   **EAN** 9781682611562 $15.99

Morgana's first attack came in a red fog that wiped out all modern technology. The entire planet was pushed back into the middle ages. The world descended into chaos.

But hope is not yet lost— King Arthur, Merlin, and the Knights of the Round Table have been reborn.

PERMUTED PRESS

THE MORNINGSTAR STRAIN HAS BEEN LET LOOSE—IS THERE ANY WAY TO STOP IT?

An industrial accident unleashes some of the Morningstar Strain. The

EAN 9781618686497 $16.00

doctor who discovered the strain and her assistant will have to fight their way through Sprinters and Shamblers to save themselves, the vaccine, and the base. Then they discover that it wasn't an accident at all—somebody inside the facility did it on purpose. The war with the RSA and the infected is far from over.

This is the fourth book in Z.A. Recht's The Morningstar Strain series, written by Brad Munson.

GATHERED TOGETHER AT LAST, THREE TALES OF FANTASY CENTERING AROUND THE MYSTERIOUS CITY OF SHADOWS...ALSO KNOWN AS CHICAGO.

EAN 9781682612286 $9.99   **EAN** 9781618684639 $5.99   **EAN** 9781618684899 $5.99

From *The New York Times* and *USA Today* bestselling author Richard A. Knaak comes three tales from Chicago, the City of Shadows. Enter the world of the Grey—the creatures that live at the edge of our imagination and seek to be real. Follow the quest of a wizard seeking escape from the centuries-long haunting of a gargoyle. Behold the coming of the end of the world as the Dutchman arrives.

Enter the City of Shadows.

PERMUTED
PRESS

WE CAN'T GUARANTEE
THIS GUIDE WILL SAVE
YOUR LIFE. BUT WE CAN
GUARANTEE IT WILL
KEEP YOU SMILING
WHILE THE LIVING
DEAD ARE CHOWING
DOWN ON YOU.

ZOMBIE APOCALYPSE PREPARATION
HOW TO SURVIVE IN AN UNDEAD WORLD
AND HAVE FUN DOING IT!
DAVID HOUCHINS & SCOT THOMAS

EAN 9781618686695 $9.99

This is the only tool you
need to survive the zombie apocalypse.

OK, that's not really true. But when the SHTF, you're
going to want a survival guide that's not just geared
toward day-to-day survival. You'll need one that
addresses the essential skills for true nourishment of
the human spirit. Living through the end of the
world isn't worth a damn unless you can enjoy
yourself in any way you want. (Except, of course, for
anything having to do with abuse. We could never
condone such things. At least the publisher's
lawyers say we can't.)

PERMUTED
PRESS